About the Authors

Helen Lacey grew up on a steady diet of *Anne of Green Gables* and *Little House on the Prairie* reruns. These childhood classics inspired her to write her own stories when she was seven years old, usually about a girl and her horse. She continued to write with the dream of one day being a published author and writing for Mills & Boon is the realisation of that dream. She loves creating stories about cowboys and horses and heroines who get their happily ever after.

Margaret Way was born in the City of Brisbane. A Conservatorium trained pianist, teacher, accompanist and vocal coach, her musical career came to an unexpected end when she took up writing, initially as a fun thing to do. She currently lives in a harbourside apartment at beautiful Raby Bay, where she loves dining all fresco on her plant-filled balcony, that overlooks the marina. No one and nothing is a rush so she finds the laid-back Village atmosphere very conducive to her writing.

Kandy Shepherd swapped a fast-paced career as a magazine editor for a life writing romance. She lives on a small farm in the Blue Mountains near Sydney, Australia, with her husband, daughter, and a menagerie of animal friends. Kandy believes in love at first sight and real-life romance – they worked for her! Kandy loves to hear from her readers. Visit her website at: www.kandyshepherd.com

Australian Nights

HIS-AND-HERS FAMILY

HELEN LACEY

For my dad, William Lacey

1926 – 1994

Who taught me to love books and who
I still miss everyday

Chapter One

It was the third time she had seen him in two days. And because she had a vivid imagination, Fiona Walsh had created all kinds of possible scenarios as to why the most gorgeous man she'd ever clapped her eyes upon appeared to be following her every move.

Who was he? An admirer? Lottery official? *Stalker?*

Yesterday morning she'd spotted him across the road outside her house, leaning on the hood of his car and speaking into his cell phone. She'd gone to collect her morning paper from the footpath and hung around by the gate for a few minutes, feigning interest in her wilted herb garden. Then he appeared by the foreshore that same afternoon while she ran her dog along the beach. Same car. Same kind of well-cut clothes. Same dark hair and superbly chiseled features.

Now he was at the riding school where she stabled her horse.

Fiona eased Titan, her Thoroughbred gelding, to a halt in

the center of the sand arena and lifted the rim of her helmet. The man remained by his car, leaning against the door as he watched her. There was nothing threatening in his demeanor. He appeared more mildly curious than anything else. With the idea he wasn't about to attack her and toss her in the trunk of his car firmly out of her head, Fiona experienced a strange warmth across her skin. Handsome, nice car, the kind of clothes that oozed confidence—she couldn't help but be intrigued.

He was on his cell again, talking as he watched her. Fiona collected the reins and clicked Titan forward. The big gelding obeyed instantly, and she maneuvered him toward the entrance gate. No more guessing games. She'd find out who the man was and just what he wanted. Right now.

She dismounted and tethered Titan to the hitching rail. Once he was secured, she pulled off her riding hat and wasted a few seconds adjusting her hair. As she left the arena and walked purposefully across the yard, Fiona watched him end his call, slip the cell phone into a pocket and straighten to his full, broad-shouldered height.

Ten feet away she stopped and clipped her booted heels together. He was ridiculously good-looking and appeared to be in his early thirties. Even though sunglasses shielded his eyes, Fiona knew he was staring at her. She suddenly had a silly thought about her appearance and wished she'd worn something other than her grass-stained riding breeches and century-old T-shirt.

Silence stretched like elastic. Finally, she summoned the nerve and drew in a deep breath. "I guess you're not here to tell me I've won the lottery?"

He cracked a half smile and flipped the sunglasses off. "No."

She clamped her hands on her hips and tried to ignore the

way her belly rolled over when she met his perfectly brilliant blue eyes. "Then why are you following me?"

"I'm not," he said and took a step toward her.

Fiona widened her gaze. "Three times in two days?" She clicked her fingers. "That's quite a coincidence."

"It's not a coincidence at all," he replied. "I've simply been waiting for the appropriate time to speak with you."

Fiona raised her chin as annoyance wove up her spine. He had a little too much self-assurance for her liking. "With me? What on earth for? I don't know you, and I—"

"Are you Fiona Lorelle Walsh?" he asked quietly, cutting her off.

She stilled and her breath grabbed at her throat. "What do you want?" she asked as suspicion crept along her skin.

He took another step. "To talk to you."

Fiona stared at him. He knew her full name? Who was he?

She had the urge to retreat. Get away. Put distance between herself and his lovely eyes. "I'm sorry, but I'm busy at the moment. I have to get back to my horse," she said and pivoted on her heels.

"Miss Walsh?" he called after her. "Fiona?"

She stopped midstride and took another breath, deeper, longer. Titan moved restlessly from his spot by the gate as though he sensed her unease. She spotted Callie Preston, owner of the riding school and her closest friend, walking across the arena toward the two remaining riders. If she needed her friend, Callie would be at her side in a moment. But she kept her wits. Whoever this stranger was, she wasn't afraid of him. Fiona turned around and faced the man behind her.

Her heart continued to thump madly. In the sunlight his hair appeared almost black and shimmered in a way she'd usually find attractive. But a voice told her not to think about him like that. "Who are you?"

"My name is Wyatt Harper."

She didn't recognize it. "What do you want?"

"To talk."

"What about?"

He stepped closer. "Perhaps we could go somewhere a little more private."

Fiona bristled. "This is plenty private."

He glanced toward the other riders and then back to her. After a moment he drew in a breath. "Okay. Firstly, let me assure you that I'm not any kind of threat to you."

Fiona didn't feel threatened. But her curiosity was at an all-time high. Sensing she needed every advantage she could get, she didn't quite let him off the hook. "I guess I'll know that when you tell me what you want." He smiled, and Fiona's insides gave a silly leap. "So, start talking."

He nodded. "Like I said, my name is Wyatt Harper." He pulled a small card from his shirt pocket and held it toward her.

She knew he stood still deliberately, allowing her the chance to move forward so he wouldn't appear intimidating. Smooth, she thought. And clever. She took a couple of steps, snatched the card and read it as she moved backward again. Sure enough, it said Wyatt Harper in bold print, with the title of managing director of Harper Engineering underneath it.

So, he had an impressive-looking job. It didn't explain what he wanted with her. "And?"

He met her gaze directly and took his time replying. "I'm here on behalf of Cecily Todd."

Cecily Todd? Fiona shook her head. "I don't know who that—"

"Cecily is my niece," he said quietly, interrupting her, "and the child you gave up for adoption fourteen years ago."

Her world quickly tilted on some invisible axis.

No. I don't believe it.

Oh, my God...is this happening?

She'd thought about this moment for years. Imagined it. Dreamed it and dreaded it. And her knees, usually rock-solid and strong, weakened like a bowl of jelly. Fiona bowed over fractionally as the air tried to squeeze into her lungs.

Breathe...just breathe...

He stepped forward but she raised a hand to warn him off. "Take deep breaths."

He was clearly concerned but Fiona wasn't in any mood to be grateful. "Yeah," she huffed and cast him a sharp look. "No problem."

"Perhaps you should sit down," he suggested and looked around. "There are steps by the house. You could—"

"No," she said raggedly and gulped in air. "Please...just... stop."

He placed a hand on her shoulder. "I can't do that."

She grabbed her knees for support, took a deep breath and then straightened. He dropped his hand and stepped back. She drew in another steadying breath, trying to rally her strength.

"I'd like to talk with you about my niece," he said.

"Your niece?" she echoed vaguely, suddenly light-headed. Fiona put a hand to her temple. It was surreal. Dreamlike. As if it was happening to someone else, in some kind of alternate reality. "I feel a little woozy," she admitted.

He grasped her arm and this time she didn't ward him off. "Come on, you need to sit down."

She let him lead her toward the house. There were three steps, and he urged her to sit on the bottom rung. Fiona dropped her head between her knees. "I'm not normally like this."

"I surprised you," he said evenly. "I'm sorry."

"Surprised?" Fiona craned her neck to look at him. "You just shocked the hell out of me."

"What's going on here?"

She looked up. Callie stood twenty feet away. Her friend looked suspicious and regarded them seriously.

"It's all right, Callie," Fiona said. "I felt a little dizzy for a moment. I'm okay now."

"Who's this?" the other woman asked.

Fiona glanced at the man standing near her and saw his masked irritation at being spoken about in the third person. "Wyatt Harper," he said.

Fiona pulled her head up before her friend had a chance to respond. "Thanks for coming over, Callie, but I'm fine now."

She didn't look convinced. "If you're sure…"

"I'm sure," Fiona said quickly.

She lingered for a moment, nodded and then walked off in the direction of the stables.

"Friend of yours?" he asked once she was out of earshot.

"Yes," Fiona replied. "She owns this place."

He nodded vaguely. "Are you really feeling okay?"

"I'm fine, thank you."

He nodded. "About Cecily, I wanted to—"

"Are you sure?" she asked, cutting him off. "I mean, are you sure she's…or that I'm her…"

"Her birth mother?"

She swallowed the heavy emotion in her throat. "Yes."

"If you're Fiona Walsh, then yes, I'm sure. I have documentation to support that you gave birth to Cecily."

She took a deep breath, drawing strength. "And you're her uncle?"

"That's right. My sister and her husband adopted Cecily."

A lovely couple. That's what she'd been told by the adoption agency. People who would be able to give her daughter everything she couldn't. Stability. Safety. A perfect home. She'd had fourteen years to imagine what they were like. Fourteen years where she hadn't known her child's name.

Fourteen years to dream about reconnecting with the baby she'd given up.

But not like this. Not when she was totally unprepared and caught off guard. Whoever he was, and whatever he wanted, Fiona had no intention of falling apart in front of him. She didn't do vulnerable. Ever.

She stood and crossed her arms. The only words she could form came out. "Why now?"

He waited to respond, taking stretched-out seconds as he looked her over. "Because Cecily wants to meet you."

She shook her head instinctively. No one was going to turn her world upside down. Not ever again. She wasn't fifteen and gullible. She was nearly thirty and called the shots in her own life. If Wyatt Harper thought rocking up unannounced was going to give him an advantage, he could think again. *If* she had this conversation, she'd do it when *she* was ready, and not before.

"I can't do this here," she said and tilted her chin, defiant and with way more strength than she felt. "I won't. I need time to think. Goodbye, Mr. Harper."

"Fiona, you need to—"

"Goodbye," she said again and turned on her boots. She walked in a straight line back to the dressage arena and felt the sear of his gaze right up until she was out of view.

Minutes later she heard the sound of gravel crunching beneath tires. He was gone.

Fiona spent the following hour in a daze. She attended to Titan, got him untacked, fed and rugged, and headed home before Callie had a chance to question her about Wyatt Harper. She wasn't in the mood for an interrogation, not even from her closest friend.

Once she opened the door of her small house, dropped her

keys on the hall stand and made her way to the living room, she let out an emotional shudder.

My daughter.

She sank down into the sofa.

My daughter's name is Cecily. Fiona had wondered so often what they'd called her. She hadn't had the strength to name her baby. It was better that way…that was what she'd been told.

The only way.

But how she'd despaired over her decision. Even knowing that at fifteen she hadn't been in a position to care for a baby and giving her up had been her only option.

The hardest decision I'd ever make.

That's what the nurses at the small country hospital where she'd given birth had said.

Your baby will be better off.

And then her great-uncle's voice, reminding her about her own mother.

The apple doesn't fall far from the tree.

Back then she'd believed him. Memories of her mother, Shayne, were etched into her mind. Unreliable, self-absorbed, an irresponsible flake, more interested in staying out late and getting high than being a parent. A woman who'd forfeited her chance for an education at seventeen to raise a child she never really wanted, and who'd married a man she'd never loved. A marriage that had lasted two years. Tired of her life in the small town where she'd been raised and the rules she was forced to follow living in her uncle's house, Shayne packed up a then five-year-old Fiona and began following the rodeo circuit. She chased one cowboy after another, dragging Fiona through countless motel rooms and a string of transient jobs.

When she was fifteen, Fiona had been shipped back to her great-uncle…alone and scared and pregnant. Fiona had few illusions about Shayne. Her mother's reaction to her pregnancy was borne out of anger and resentment. Three weeks after Fiona was left at her uncle's farm, Shayne and her much younger rodeo-rider boyfriend were killed in a railway-crossing accident. She didn't grieve, didn't *feel*. There was too much hurt, too much betrayal, too much pain.

Six months later Fiona had given up her baby after only fifteen minutes of holding her. She'd said goodbye to her precious daughter and handed her over to strangers, hoping with all her heart that her baby would be treasured by her new family, knowing that because she'd agreed to a closed adoption she could never look for her, and lived on the hope that one day her daughter would seek her out. But she'd never really believed it. Never let hope linger for too long.

Until Wyatt Harper dropped into her world.

Her daughter's uncle. An envoy. Clearly here to check her out. Although, since he knew her full name, he'd probably done a fair amount of checking already. Fiona gripped her hands together. How much did he know? The paper trail was meager at best. With Shayne dead there was nothing linking Fiona to her mother's lover. Or what had happened on that terrible night.

Nothing except Cecily.

No one knew the truth. No one ever would. Fiona had held on to her secret for over fourteen years. There was no mention of him anywhere. She hadn't talked about it since the day she was dumped on her uncle's doorstep. Her daughter's birth certificate stated father unknown. He was dead. What good would rehashing it do now?

Only…Wyatt Harper had turned up and she knew he'd have questions. *Questions I can't answer.* There would be no nice way to admit the truth about her daughter's conception.

So what did he really want? Did her daughter actually want to meet her? And if so, where were her adoptive parents? Why had Wyatt Harper been sent on this digging mission?

If she wanted answers, she had to pull herself together.

First, a shower and a change of clothes. And then a strategy. She liked strategies and lists and being organized. She didn't like being in the dark. She didn't like Wyatt Harper knowing things about her when she knew nothing of him.

She fingered the business card he'd given her. Seconds later she was at her computer and typed *Harper Engineering* into the search engine. It wasn't long before she had a dozen or so hits. He was from the third generation of Harpers to run the steel-fabrication business. With well over one hundred employees at the huge factory on the outskirts of Sydney, he appeared to be doing everything right. There was a nice picture of him, too, with his father and grandfather. It was clearly a *family* business in the truest sense of the word.

Fiona flicked off the computer and headed for the kitchen. Muffin, her energetic Tenterfield Terrier, jumped up at the back door, and she quickly let the dog inside and fed her. The card in her hand burned her fingertips. There was only one way to find out what he wanted.

He'd failed. When he'd promised Cecily he wouldn't. Fiona Walsh obviously wasn't prepared to talk, and Wyatt felt as if the door had been well and truly slammed. She'd said she needed time—but time for what? She'd looked horrified when he'd faced her with the news. Her pretty face had turned ghost-pale, emphasizing the brightness of her lips and sparkling blue-gray eyes.

He shouldn't have confronted her out in the open. Yesterday would have been better. But the moment he'd spotted her walking from her little house in her cute pajamas, he'd forgotten why he was there. Forgotten that he had a job to do and forgotten that Cecily was relying on him to *not* screw it up. But by the time he'd shaken the image of Fiona Walsh's bouncing hair and pretty face out of his head, she had disappeared inside.

Now, back in his hotel room, Wyatt had time to think about the way he'd ruined his chances. Cecily would be bitterly disappointed, and the last thing his niece needed was more of that. He checked emails and called his personal assistant. Glynis had been with him for ten years; she'd been with his father for twenty before that. The sixty-year-old widow was his right arm, sometimes his conscience and often his sounding board.

"Your flight is booked for tomorrow morning," she told him. "You *are* still coming back tomorrow, aren't you?"

"I'm not sure."

She made a disagreeable sound. "And Miss Walsh?"

"I've made contact. We'll see what happens." He wasn't about to admit he might have screwed up.

"Just be careful," she warned. "Sleeping dogs sleep for a good reason. Sometimes the past is best left where it is."

"It's what Cecily wants," he said and ended the call, feeling the weight of his promise to Cecily press between his shoulder blades.

When his niece had asked him to find her birth mother, Wyatt hadn't been surprised and he had understood her motives. Cecily wanted answers. Now that he'd met Fiona Walsh, Wyatt was intrigued and wanted some answers, too. He knew she was a teacher and had lived in Crystal Point for five years. Before that there had been a series of jobs at various schools, none lasting more than six months. She appeared to go from one small town to the next, never settling until now. What made Crystal Point different? Did she have roots in the small community? From the investigation he'd undertaken, Wyatt knew there were no relatives, only a great-uncle who'd passed away twelve months earlier and left her a modest inheritance after the sale of his property out west. There were no parents. No siblings. Not even a distant cousin she could claim as family.

Fiona Walsh seemed to be as alone as a person could possibly get.

She wasn't married…but maybe she had a boyfriend? She was as pretty as hell, after all. Her hair was an amazing color, not red, not blond but an unusual mix of both. In more normal circumstances, Wyatt would probably have been attracted to her.

Whoa…where did that come from?

He was here on Cecily's behalf. The kid had been through enough over the past eighteen months. Now she wanted to find her birth mother, and it was Wyatt's job to help her. He wasn't about to get caught up in Fiona's lovely blue-gray eyes. He wasn't about to rush into getting caught up with anyone, not after the disastrous end to his engagement eighteen months earlier. Yvette's betrayal had left a bitter taste in his mouth.

He knew he had to see Fiona again. He had to make her listen.

His cell rang and he picked up on the third ring. "Wyatt Harper."

"I'll meet you in half an hour."

Her husky voice was unmistakable. She'd called. Maybe he hadn't screwed up after all? "Great. Shall I come to you?"

"No," she said quickly. "I'll come to you."

Wyatt gave her the name of the hotel.

"Okay," she said. "I'll meet you in the foyer at five o'clock." Then she hung up.

Fiona's drive into Bellandale took twenty minutes. The town was four hours north of Brisbane and had a population of sixty thousand. The streets were typically quiet for a Sunday afternoon, and she scored a parking spot outside the hotel. With her nerves severely stretched, she walked through the front doors and into the lobby.

There was no sign of him. She checked her watch. Three minutes to five.

Fiona ignored the concierge and headed for the lounge area in the centre of the lobby. There was a bar close by, and a waiter immediately approached to take her order. She declined and sank into one of the leather sofas. The foyer was eerily quiet, except for the faint sound of piped music and the occasion click of heels over the polished floor.

"Hello, Fiona."

She snapped her neck around. Wyatt Harper had approached and stood only feet away. Fiona did her best to overlook the way her traitorous belly flipped over. Okay... so he was good-looking and possessed the kind of body that was hard to ignore in his dark chinos and a white polo shirt. And he had great hair and glittering blue eyes. *Big deal.* The world was full of gorgeous men. And because this one had just dropped a bombshell into her organized little life, Fiona had every intention of ignoring the way her blood heated when he was within a six-foot radius.

"Hello."

He looked at her oddly and the heat intensified. Fiona pushed her hair back with shaking fingers, suddenly nervous of his scrutiny. Something flashed in his eyes. Approval? *Disapproval?* Did she look as if she was trying too hard with her sensible denim skirt, modest print blouse and even more sensible sandals? Maybe she should have put her hair up instead of letting it curl madly around her head? She bit at her lower lip to get rid of the lipstick she'd dabbed on.

"Thank you for coming," he said.

Fiona noticed the narrow black folder he carried. "I don't see the point in hiding from the truth."

He nodded, sat down opposite her and placed the folder

on the low table between them. "So you acknowledge that you're Cecily's birth mother?"

Fiona inhaled. "I admit that I had a child fourteen years ago." She pointed to the folder. "You seem to have all the evidence that she's the baby I gave up for adoption."

"I do have proof," he said quietly. "Although one look at Cecily would be enough to convince you." He pushed himself back in the lounge. "She looks just like you. Same hair. Same chin. Same..." He looked at her mouth for a moment and Fiona's skin warmed. "Same color eyes."

She managed a brittle smile and twirled a lock of hair between her fingertips. "Poor kid got stuck with this color."

He watched her actions with blistering intensity. "She's very pretty."

Fiona's heart began to beat a little faster. She drew in a breath and asked the question that burned on the end of her tongue. "What does she know about me?"

Wyatt Harper's eyes darkened fractionally. "She knows you were young when you had her. Cecily has always known she was adopted. My sister Karen and her husband, Jim, were open with her from an early age and supported her decision to find her birth mother when she was ready."

"And she's ready now—is that what you're saying?"

He nodded. "She began talking about finding you nearly two years ago. Karen and Jim planned to start searching but..." He stopped and took a moment. When he spoke again, Fiona heard rawness in his voice. "They were killed eighteen months ago."

Emotion she didn't understand clutched her throat. "I'm sorry," she whispered. "How did it happen?"

"They were rock fishing," he replied. "They got swept off a rock shelf. It was a crazy accident. They were mad for a dangerous sport and paid the price. When they died, that left Cecily—"

"Alone," Fiona said quickly and covered her mouth when she realized how it sounded.

"No, not alone," Wyatt told her pointedly. "She has her family. I was going to say that it left her with a lot to deal with. She handled it pretty well, considering. A few months ago, she announced she was ready to find you."

"She really wants to meet me?"

He nodded. "Yes, she does."

Her breath caught again. *My daughter wants to meet me.* Fiona got goose bumps. This was what she wanted…right? To know the child she'd given up. She had everything to gain from such a meeting. *Everything. Then why does the thought of it make me want to run?*

"When?" she asked and pulled herself forward.

"It's not that simple," he said quietly.

Fiona twisted her hands in her lap. "What do you mean?"

"I mean that Cecily has been through a lot, and as her legal guardian, I am going to make sure she is protected."

"From me?" she whispered and fought the rising annoyance. His responses were vague at best, and it irritated her no end. Fiona pulled her fractured nerves together. "I would never hurt her."

"Perhaps not intentionally. But I have to be sure about you. I need to be certain you won't do anything to jeopardize Cecily's emotional state."

Dumbstruck, Fiona glared at him with a mixture of disbelief and slowly gathering rage. His inference was insulting. But she quickly bit back her infamous redheaded temper. Getting mad with him wouldn't serve her. He held all the cards. And he knew it. "So what do I have to say to prove that I wouldn't do anything to upset her?"

He leaned forward and rested his elbows on his knees. "How about you start by telling me why you gave your baby away?"

Chapter Two

Wyatt knew he was out of line. She looked as if she wanted to slap his face. But he had to know what kind of person Fiona Walsh was before he'd let her into Cecily's life, no matter how much his niece wanted to know her.

It didn't help that she was so incredibly pretty his mind kept wandering.

"Isn't it in the file?" Her eyes darkened as she pointed to the folder between them. "I'm assuming that's some sort of report about me, about my life? If you've done your homework, you'd know that I was fifteen when I had Cecily and not in a position to care for a child."

"And your parents?"

"My mother's dead," she supplied. "But I guess you already knew that."

"Yes," he said. "I know your mother was killed in a train-crossing accident with her boyfriend."

"And you know the man she claimed was my father died when I was three years old."

"Claimed?" he asked.

She shrugged. "She married Eddie Walsh and I was born six months later. They only lived together for two years. I was told he disappeared and then died in a rodeo accident, although I'm not actually sure that's true. He could have skipped to avoid paying child support for all I know. What else do you want to know?"

There was enough bristle in her tone to make it clear she had a temper but was doing her best to keep it under wraps. "You're being very candid."

She raised a brow. "Isn't that what you want? Answers… and an opportunity to see if I'm respectable and responsible enough to meet Cecily?"

"I don't—"

"And once you figure that out, Mr. Harper," she said, cutting him off without batting a lash, "you can answer *my* questions."

There's that temper.

Wyatt might have liked her to simply back down and agree to everything he said but he didn't really expect it. And he respected her spirit. "Wyatt."

"What?"

"My name," he replied. "It's Wyatt."

"Okay…*Wyatt*…so ask me another question. Ask me as many questions as you like."

He went for the most important. "Cecily's father? There's no record of him on the birth certificate."

"No record." Visible shutters quickly came up and it waved like a red flag. "That's right. It's what I wanted."

Wyatt pressed on. "Is there any chance he might make an appearance in her life?"

"No chance," she replied hollowly. "He's dead."

Dead? He hadn't expected that. "Who was he?"

"No one."

He immediately wondered if she knew *who* Cecily's biological father was, but didn't like how the question sounded rolling around in his head. "Does he have a name?"

"Since he's dead it really doesn't make any difference."

"Unless his family tries to have some claim on Cecily in the future."

"They won't," she said stiffly. "No one knows about him. My mother made sure of it."

Wyatt's interest grew. "She didn't approve?"

"What mother would approve of her fifteen-year-old daughter being pregnant?"

He nodded slowly. "You said you weren't in a position to care for a child? Did you mean because of your age or something else?"

"I lived with my elderly great-uncle," she said stiffly. "My mother was dead. I was two years away from finishing high school. I had no income and no way of supporting myself or my baby."

It sounded like an impossible situation for a teenage girl. "If it's any consolation to you, Karen and Jim loved Cecily very much. They'd been trying to have a baby for a long time. Cecily brought them a great deal of happiness."

She smiled and the sparks in her eyes faded. "They didn't have any other children?"

Wyatt begrudgingly admired how she'd seamlessly moved the questions onto him. "Just Cecily."

"And you're her guardian now?"

"That's right," he replied. "Karen was the daughter from my father's first marriage and she was twelve years older than me."

She nodded fractionally. "So, you and your wife care for her?"

"I'm not married," he said but was pretty sure she knew that already from the look on her face.

Her expression narrowed. "Does Cecily live with you?"

"She spends most of her time at Waradoon, our family property in the Hunter Valley, which is just over an hour's drive from Harper Engineering. My parents are retired and my youngest sister still lives at home. Cecily goes to the local high school and is well settled. I have a place in the city but go to Waradoon most weekends. If not, Cecily visits me in the city."

"Why did they grant guardianship to you?"

He'd wondered it himself in the beginning. Neither Karen nor Jim had discussed what would happen to their daughter upon their deaths. Finding out he was named sole custodian of their precious child had come as a shock.

"Jim had no siblings and his parents are both in poor health," he explained. "My mother spends as much time with Cecily as she can. But my father is over seventy with a heart condition, my sister Ellen has a four-year-old and two-year-old twins, and my youngest sister, Rae, is twenty-five and in her third year of studying veterinary medicine."

"So you don't actually spend a lot of time with her?"

It was a pretty mild dig, but it annoyed him anyway. "I have a business to run and I get home when I can, which is usually most weekends. Cecily understands that. She also likes living at Waradoon. She has her horse there and her friends are close—"

"She has a horse?"

"Yes," he replied. "Something you have in common."

Wyatt stared at her, intrigued by the way her eyes changed color. He liked the coppery shine of her hair and the way it bounced around her face. He liked it a lot. And her perfectly shaped mouth was amazing. Something uncurled low in his abdomen, a kind of slow-burning awareness. He'd met pretty girls before. Prettier even. But he couldn't remember the last time a woman had attracted him so much and so quickly.

"So," she said after a moment. "What now?"

Wyatt forced his focus back to the issue. "That's up to Cecily."

He watched as her bottom lip disappeared between her teeth for a moment. "It looks like it's up to you."

"I'm not about to rush into this." In fact, Wyatt had no intention of rushing into anything ever again. If he'd shown that same sense less than two years ago, Yvette might not have had the opportunity to wreak havoc on his life and his family. "Although I understand how difficult that must be for you to hear."

"Do you?" she asked quietly.

Wyatt didn't miss the rawness in her voice. "There are a lot of people who risk getting hurt, and my primary job is to protect my niece." *And you.* He didn't say it, but the notion lodged firmly behind his ribs. He had what might be considered old-fashioned values…about some things. Maybe it came from having an older father. Whatever the reason, Wyatt wasn't about to start making decisions that had the potential to turn lives upside down, without thinking them through long and hard.

"Can I see that?" she asked and reached across to finger the edges of the folder on the table.

"Of course."

She slid it across her lap and opened the folder. Wyatt remained silent as she examined the contents. Her expression changed several times as she flicked through the pages, shifting from annoyance to sadness and then a kind of strained indignation.

"You've done your homework." She pushed the folder toward him. "You've got everything from a copy of Cecily's birth certificate to my sixth-grade report card. I hope you paid your investigator well for all the hard work."

Wyatt's spine straightened. "I needed to know who you were. Investigating your background was simply part of that process. I'm sure you can appreciate that."

"That's not who I am," she said as she grabbed her small handbag and stood. "That's a pile of paper."

Wyatt quickly got to his feet. "Then tell me who you are."

She glanced at the folder again. "I think you've already made up your mind. I think you know all about my childhood, you know my father ran off and that my mother was a junkie who couldn't hold down a job and never had any money in her pocket. I think you've read about how I've moved nine times in as many years. And I think you're wondering if I'm not just a bit too much like my mother and can't quite be trusted to meet Cecily and that I might taint her in some way."

She was close to the mark and he didn't bother denying it. "I have to consider what's best for Cecily."

"Yes," she agreed. "You do. But *you* came to *me*. You came to me because Cecily has questions about where she came from. I understand that. I know what it is to have an empty space inside. When I was fifteen, I was manipulated into agreeing to a closed adoption—forfeiting any hope I ever had of finding my daughter. I wasn't allowed to know anything about the people who had her. And then you show up with your nice smile and ultrapolite conversation and throw a few crumbs in my direction about the possibility of meeting my child." She took a shuddering breath. "Whatever your opinion of me, Mr. Harper, I won't be manipulated again or walked over. Now, if you'll excuse me, I need some time to consider what *I* want."

Without another word, she turned and strode away from him and out through the door. Wyatt stared after her through the glass windows, watching the way her hair bounced as she walked, suddenly mesmerized by the stiffness in her shoulders and the gentle sway of her hips.

He only let out a breath once she got into her car and drove off. Wyatt grabbed the folder and closed it. Nothing in the report had prepared him for that exchange. He'd expected... what? That she'd be so grateful to reconnect with Cecily she wouldn't put up any kind of resistance? That she'd be compliant and agreeable to everything he suggested or wanted? Right now he didn't know what to think. Had he scared her off? Did she actually want to meet Cecily? Fiona Walsh had gumption and he liked that about her. She wasn't a pushover. She was strong. He'd give her some time to settle into the idea, and then he knew he had to ask her straight out if she wanted to meet Cecily. Wyatt pulled his cell from his pocket. Glynis picked up on the third ring.

"Change of plans," he said.

"Which means?" his assistant asked.

"Cancel my flight for tomorrow."

There was a moment's silence. "I see. Do I rebook?"

"I'll let you know."

Glynis tutted. "How long are you staying?"

Until I fix this. "I'm not sure," he said and ended the call.

Fiona couldn't drag herself to work the following morning and called in sick. Which wasn't exactly a lie. She did feel genuinely unwell. Her head ached. Her heart ached. She never took time off. She kept herself in good health and loved her teaching job.

I just can't face all those happy little faces today.

She blamed Wyatt Harper for it, of course. Since he'd entered her life, she'd become an emotional mess. Crying...for Pete's sake, she never cried. When she opened the front door to Callie that afternoon, it took all her strength to not collapse in a heap at the other woman's feet.

"I was worried when the kids said you weren't at school today," she explained as she crossed through the door. "With good reason by the look of things."

Fiona sniffed and pushed up the sleeves of her dressing gown. "I'm sick."

Callie's perfect brows rose sharply. "Try again. And this time include what it has to do with that tall drink of water you were talking with yesterday."

Fiona hesitated for a microsecond. But this was Callie, her best friend and one of the few people she trusted, and the only person she'd told about her teenage pregnancy. "Remember how I told you I had baby when I was fifteen?"

Callie's eyes popped wide. "Absolutely."

Fiona quickly explained how she'd agreed to a closed adoption and who Wyatt Harper was.

"Are you sure he's telling the truth?" Callie asked once they were settled on the sofa, each with a coffee cup between their hands.

"Yes. He has Cecily's birth certificate and he says she looks just like me."

Callie looked at her over the rim of her cup. "Did you ask to see a picture?"

Fiona shook her head. "No...I wasn't sure I could bear seeing her photograph. In case I never get to see her for real. Does that make sense?"

Her friend nodded gently. "So what are you going to do about it?"

Fiona shrugged. "I'm not sure. That's to say, I'm not sure what *he's* going to do about it."

"You have rights," Callie said. "She's your child."

"A child I gave away. Wyatt Harper is the one with all the rights. He's her legal guardian. He's who her parents entrusted to care for her."

"But you said she doesn't live with him?"

"She lives mostly with her grandparents. But from what he said, I'm guessing they're a close-knit bunch. He runs the family business, and his parents are retired, so they'd have more time to look after her. His younger sister lives there also."

"Must be a big house."

"It's a hundred-acre property," she explained. "His father runs a small herd of Wagyu cattle—his mother dabbles in showing orchids. They're squeaky-clean and look like the perfect family."

"And he's what, thirtysomething and single and now a part-time parent to a teenage girl?" Callie rolled her big eyes. "Nothing is that perfect."

"He seems like one of those annoyingly self-sufficient men who can handle *everything*. I'm sure one little teenager wouldn't bring him down."

Callie smiled. "He is very nice-looking. Not that you'd ever be swayed by a handsome face."

"Er…no."

"Maybe you should see a lawyer?" Callie suggested. "I mean, he hasn't contacted you since yesterday—for all you know he's gone back to Sydney."

"I don't think so. He wanted something and he didn't get it. I don't think he's the kind of man who retreats easily, and I didn't exactly leave him on friendly terms." She smiled when she saw her friend's look. "Yeah, I lost my temper."

Callie's expression softened. "So, how do you feel about it? I mean, how do you feel about reconnecting with your daughter after so long?"

Fiona sucked in some air. "Confused and shocked. I always had hope but I tried not to get swept away with the idea of meeting her one day. It was too painful. But now it's a reality…and I'm scared. Because I'm still the person who gave her away." She expelled a heavy breath. "What must she think of me?"

Callie made a reassuring sound. "You were young—not much older than she is now. She'll understand once you explain. She's come looking for you, Fiona. That's a positive sign."

Fiona hoped so. But she had doubts. Reservations. What if Cecily didn't understand? What if all their reconnecting did was to upset her daughter? She didn't want that. Cecily had lost her parents, and Fiona didn't want to do anything that might add to her pain.

When her friend left about ten minutes later, Fiona, tired of looking like a washed-out rag, took a long shower. Once done, she finger-combed her hair, changed into comfy sweats and fed the dog. She had some assignments to grade and curled up on the sofa with her work and a fresh mug of coffee. She was about halfway through her pile of papers when Muffin started growling and rushed toward the front door after the bell rang.

When she pulled the door back, she found Wyatt Harper standing on the other side of the screen.

"Hello," he said casually, belying the sudden awareness that swirled between them.

She stepped back on her heels and ignored the way her heart seemed to be beating a little faster than usual. "What do you want?"

He held up a bag. "Dinner."

"I don't think—"

"For three," he said, cutting her off. "In case you have company."

"I'm alone," she said as her suspicions soared. "And I'm not hungry."

He raised both brows. "Are you sure?"

Fiona fought the impulse to close the door. She didn't want

to be nice to him. But she wanted to know more about her daughter, and he was the key.

"You can come in." She stood to the side and allowed him to cross the threshold.

He wore beige cargoes and a black golf shirt, and she couldn't stop herself from checking him out. Okay, so the man had a nice body. She wasn't a rock. She was a perfectly normal woman reacting to a good-looking man. She wasn't about to beat herself up about it.

"Thank you," he said and walked past her. "Where do you want this?" he asked as he motioned to the bag in his hand. "Chinese. A bit of everything because I wasn't sure what you liked."

"The kitchen," she replied as she shut the door and then frowned as Muffin, the traitor, jumped up and down excitedly by Wyatt's feet, demanding attention. "This way."

He patted the dog for a moment before following her. When they reached the kitchen, Fiona stood on one side of the small square table and waited for him to take his place on the other side. She needed something between them.

She watched as he unloaded half a dozen small containers from the bag, then pulled out two sets of cutlery and a couple of serving spoons and grabbed two beers from the fridge. "Only light beer, I'm afraid."

"No problem."

Fiona placed everything on the table and scraped a chair across the tiled floor. "How did you know I'd be home tonight?"

He shrugged. "I didn't. I took a chance. It's a school night... and I figured you'd stay in."

Fiona pushed both beers toward him and he disposed of the caps quickly. "Actually, I didn't work today." When he didn't respond, she explained. "I wasn't much good for anything after our conversation yesterday."

He pushed a beer back toward her. "That's honest."

"One of my many flaws," she said and took a small sip. "I have plenty. I often blurt things out before I think about what I'm saying. And I have a bad temper."

His blue eyes shone brilliantly. "Really?"

Fiona started opening the tops of the cartons and when she was done scooped a dumpling out of one of them with her fork. "Big surprise, huh?"

He grabbed a carton of noodles. "So, is there a boyfriend or significant other in the picture?"

She looked at him and colored beneath his penetrating stare. "Just me."

"Good," he said and piled food onto his fork. "More noodles for us."

Fiona was tempted to smile. There was a casual, easygoing way about his mood and she liked it. Too much. She didn't want to think about him *that* way. He was her ticket to her daughter, and she had to keep her head on straight. Imagining anything else was nonsensical.

"Wyatt…" She lingered over his name and discovered she liked the sound of it rolling around on her tongue. "What are you really doing here? I know it's not to share Chinese food or inquire about my love life."

He placed the fork on the small cardboard container. "I was concerned about you."

Fiona's skin tingled. "There's no need to be," she assured him. "I'm fine. I'm always fine."

"So you're fine?"

He was smiling at her, and Fiona experienced a strange dip low in her belly. Really low. She marshaled her wits. "So what have you decided to do about Cecily?"

He looked at her. "After our conversation yesterday, I thought it was more about what *you* wanted to do?"

I want to see her.

"I don't really know," she said instead. "I thought I did. I thought I knew how I'd react if this moment ever came. Instead I'm completely unprepared. In my mind, when I played this moment over and over, Cecily was an adult and came to find me on her own. Then I could have faced her as an adult. But she's a child and I know I have to be the strong one... like I should know exactly how to respond and react. But I don't," she admitted. "Part of me is overjoyed. The other part..." She paused, waited and couldn't believe she was exposing her most vulnerable thoughts. "The other part almost wishes you'd never come here."

The air crackled as she waited for him to respond. "You are strong, Fiona. Anyone can see that. But I don't want you to have any illusions," he said directly. "Cecily wants this reunion—but she's a kid and at the moment is caught up in the excitement of the prospect of reconnecting with her birth mother. Once the dust settles and the novelty passes, the questions will start. And perhaps the blame. Are you ready for that?"

No, I'm not. She knew what questions would come. But she wasn't about to admit that to the man in front of her. "Are you saying I *can* see her? That you approve of me?"

Wyatt wasn't sure what he was feeling. He'd read the investigator's report and could easily come to the conclusion that Fiona Walsh was a good person. She was a schoolteacher and had friends in the small community. Was it enough? She *seemed* suitable to connect with Cecily. But he'd been wrong before. And he couldn't be sure what Fiona intended, either, despite what she said. He knew what Cecily wanted, and that didn't make the decision any easier. She was as headstrong as they came, particularly on this issue. But there was bound to be fallout—and he didn't want his niece, his family *or* Fiona paying a heavy emotional price.

"I think...I think you'll do what's right for Cecily."

"I will," she said solemnly. "You have my word. My promise." She stalled for a second and then spoke again. "What's she like?"

"She's terrific. Cecily's a nice kid, but she doesn't hold back. She says what she thinks, blurts out whatever is on her mind and has a temper to match her red hair." His mouth flattened in a half smile. "Sound familiar?"

She nodded, and Wyatt saw her eyes shining just a little bit more than usual. "Do you have a picture?"

"Of Cecily? Yes," he said and took out his smartphone. He pressed a couple of buttons and passed it to her.

Silence stretched between them. Food and beer were forgotten. She blinked a few times and drew in a deep breath as she stared at the picture on the small screen. The resemblance between them was unmistakable, and Wyatt knew that seeing her daughter's image for the first time was difficult for her.

"Thank you," she said and pushed the phone across the table. "Can you send me a copy of that?"

"Sure." Wyatt popped it back into his pocket. "Have you any questions?"

"Hundreds."

He grinned and reclaimed his fork. "Fire away."

"Does she like school?"

"Yes. She's a good student."

"She has friends?"

"More than I could count."

She nodded. "Is she happy?"

"Most of the time. She struggled after Karen and Jim died. But with a lot of love and support, she pulled through. She's strong, gutsy." Wyatt watched Fiona's eyes shadow with a hazy kind of sadness. It twisted something inside his chest. Made him want to offer...*what?* Comfort? *Get a grip.* "She's a lot like you."

Fiona laughed. Brittle. Uncertain. "I'm not gutsy."

"I've read the file, remember?" he said and then wondered if mentioning it was wise. She didn't react and he decided to push deeper. "Why have you moved around so much?"

"Habit."

Wyatt's brows shot up. "That's not it. Tell me why."

She speared another dumpling and slid the carton across the table. "Looking for roots, I guess."

"Did you find them?"

She ate the dumpling, and when she licked her lips, his heart smashed in his chest. *I definitely have to stop looking at her mouth.*

"I found Callie and Evie, my two best friends," she explained. "And I like this town. I enjoy my job and my little house." She glanced around the room. "Plus I can have Titan nearby."

"So, no boyfriend?"

Her lips curled up. "Didn't we cover that already? I'm single."

"Happily?"

She stopped tossing her fork through a carton of spicy chicken. "Who's happy about being alone?"

She had a point. Although since he'd broken up with Yvette, Wyatt hadn't wanted to pursue anything serious with anyone. He'd dated one woman since then, and that had faded before it had really begun. He wasn't in any kind of hurry to lay his heart on the line again. He doubted he ever would be. "Better to be unhappy alone than miserable with someone else."

"Spoken from experience?" she asked.

He shrugged the question off. "Old news."

She swapped cartons. "You know things about me. It's only fair for you to share a little, don't you think?"

Wyatt grabbed the spicy chicken, took a bite and then

washed it down with the beer. "I was engaged. It didn't work out."

"Do you miss it?" she asked. "Being with someone, I mean? Just belonging, having somebody to talk with, having someone who *gets* you?"

"My relationship with my ex-fiancée wasn't that romantic."

She frowned. "But you loved her?"

Nothing he said was going to get him away from Fiona's inquisitive gaze. "I guess."

He knew it didn't sound all that convincing. But he wasn't convinced he actually had loved Yvette. There'd been attraction and a certain compatibility, sure...but love? It was a nice idea, but did it really exist?

"Did a number on you, did she?"

Pretty, smart and intuitive. "You could say that."

"At least you've had the courage to try," she said in between a mouthful of noodles.

"Have you ever been close?"

She shook her head. "Nope. I'm always the best friend."

"What?"

She smiled. "You know, the best friend. There's the girl who always gets the guy...and then there's the ever-faithful best friend standing on the sidelines. That's me."

The best friend. Who was she kidding? She made herself sound about as exciting as an old shoe. Ridiculous. When he could feel the vibration of her through to his blood. Her skin was as clear as a camellia flower, and that hair... He suddenly had a startling image of it trailing across his chest.

Wyatt cleared his throat and drank some beer. "I suppose we should talk about Cecily."

She looked up. "That is why you're here, isn't it?"

"Of course," he replied, choosing his words. "Before I agree to anything, I need to know if you *really* want to connect with her. Or if you feel ambivalent or like you have no other choice because it's what Cecily wants. If that's the case, believe me, I'll leave tomorrow and you'll never hear from me again until you're ready to make the next move."

Panic quickly filled her eyes. "No...don't do that."

Wyatt didn't respond. He waited. She had to make a decision. There were no acceptable half measures. Fiona Walsh was either in or out.

"I want..." She stopped, paused, took a long breath. He waited some more for her to speak again. "I do want this," she said finally, and Wyatt didn't miss the way her eyes glistened. "I want a chance to explain why I gave her up."

"And the hard questions?" he shot back. "Because she's going to ask them and you need to be ready."

"I will be."

Wyatt wasn't sure. Something was amiss; he felt it through to his bones. There was something she wasn't telling him. He pushed the food aside. "Fiona, about Cecily's father—I think there are things you're not saying."

She shook her head quickly. Too quickly. "There's nothing. He's dead. He can never hurt her."

Wyatt immediately picked up on her words. "Did he hurt *you?*"

Fiona's eyes fluttered. "I didn't mean that. I meant...I meant he's dead and won't ever be a part of her life."

"And that's all?"

She nodded. "That's all."

Caution rattled around in his head, but he stopped the interrogation. "Okay, I'll talk with Cecily when I get home. We'll work something out. Cecily's welfare is my priority, so you understand that any initial contact will be supervised?"

She nodded. "Of course. I'd like to write her a letter, if that's okay with you. There are some things I'd like to say to her, and I think a letter might be a good way to start. I'll understand if you need to read it before she does."

Her lips glistened and looked delicious, and Wyatt's libido took serious notice. "Sure. I'll text you my address." He pushed the beer aside. "I should probably be going. I have an early flight in the morning."

She stood up, and he lingered for a moment before he got to his feet. Suddenly, leaving didn't seem like such a great idea. Stunned to realize how much he enjoyed her company and wanted more of it, Wyatt remained by the table and stared at her. The air between them grew thicker, hotter, as though some kind of seductive force had blown into the room.

She was closer now, barely a couple feet away. Close enough to touch if he reached for her. His fingertips tingled at the thought.

"Are you all right?" she asked a little breathlessly.

"I'm just…" He stopped. *I'm just thinking about kissing you.* "Nothing." He pulled the car keys from his pocket and rattled them. "Thanks for the beer."

"Thank you for dinner."

"No problem. I'll be in touch."

She smiled. "Well, good night."

"Good night, Fiona," Wyatt said and got out of there as quickly as he could before he forgot all the reasons why he shouldn't be attracted to her and did something really stupid.

Chapter Three

"So, what's she like?"

Wyatt had barely walked into the main house at Waradoon late the following afternoon when his mother corralled him with the question. He dropped his keys on the hall stand. "She's nice."

"Nice?" Janet Harper's silvery brows rose swiftly. "That's all?"

In no mood for the third degree, Wyatt uncharacteristically ignored his mother and headed for the big kitchen at the rear of the house. He grabbed a bottle of water from the refrigerator and tossed the lid in the trash.

"Yeah…nice," he said when he spotted his mother ten feet behind him, with her hands firmly on her hips.

"Have you agreed for her to meet Cecily?"

It hadn't been a difficult decision. He instinctively knew Fiona was a good person. Despite also knowing she was holding something back, his concerns were minimal. It was unrealistic to think she'd simply lay her life open because he wanted answers. He could wait. In time he'd know everything about her. He'd make sure of it. "Eventually. Once I've talked with Cecily about it."

"She'll be home from her riding lesson soon. And full of questions. She's almost jumping out of her skin over this." Janet's voice dropped an octave. "I hope this woman doesn't—"

"She has a name," he said quietly. "And don't stress—you'll like Fiona."

Wyatt wished he didn't like her as much as he did. He'd spent the past twenty-four hours thinking of little else.

And the fact I wanted to kiss her last night.

"Fiona," his mother echoed, and he quickly got his thoughts back on track. "Yes. And she's nice. So you keep saying."

Wyatt frowned. His mother had way too much intuition for his liking. "Stop smiling."

"I trust your judgment," she said and sat at the long table. "If you say she's nice, I'm sure she's exactly that. You'll do what's right for Cecily and the family. You always do."

Did he? He certainly hadn't when he'd jumped into his relationship with Yvette. He'd invited her into his family and paid the price. But Wyatt understood the meaning of his mother's words. He had every intention of ensuring Cecily's wellbeing. And he wanted to protect Fiona, too. As for the family, they were all curious about Cecily's birth mother, especially his sisters. He certainly wasn't about to unleash them on an unsuspecting Fiona.

"Uncle Wyatt! You're here!"

Cecily stood in the doorway dressed in her riding garb, and he was amazed how much she looked like her mother. *Not her mother. That was Karen. Her birth mother.*

She raced across the room and landed against him with a resounding thud.

He hugged her tightly. "Hey, kid, good to see you."

"You, too," she said on a rushed breath. "So, tell me everything. Did you see her, did you talk to her, does she want to meet me?"

"Yes, yes and yes."

Cecily's eyes filled with moisture. "Really? I can meet her. I can talk to her?"

Wyatt nodded. He knew Cecily was eager, but he also knew he needed to show caution and get her to take things slowly. "She's going to write to you. Once she's done that, you can make up your mind about what you want to do."

Cecily pulled back and straightened her shoulders. "I already know what I want, Uncle Wyatt. I want to meet her. And soon."

She gave a determined sniff and left the room to change and attend to her homework.

"I told you she was keen."

Cecily wanted to meet her birth mother. Fiona wanted to reconnect with the child she'd given up. If it worked out, everyone would be happy. But if not, Wyatt could see the potential for disaster.

"You know," his mother said in that way that meant he was supposed to listen, "you could take some time off and take Cecily to see *her*. It might be easier for Cecily to meet her birth mother away from Waradoon. I'm sure Miss Walsh would feel overwhelmed to come here with all of us hanging around, if that's what you were planning."

He wasn't planning anything. The logistics had been on the back burner. But bring her to Waradoon? Wyatt's focus had been on getting to know Fiona before he made any decisions.

And now that I know her, I can't get her out of my mind....

He paid his mother attention again. "You mean take Cecily to Crystal Point?"

"Why not? How long has it been since you've taken a vacation? And you know how Cecily loves the beach." Janet raised her brows. "It might do you some good, too."

He didn't miss the dig. "I don't need a vacation."

She clearly didn't agree and pulled no punches in telling him so. "Your father had his first heart attack when he was forty-two because he worked too hard. I don't want to see that happen to you. There's more to life than Harper Engineering."

Wyatt knew what was coming. He needed a life. He needed a wife. But that wasn't going to happen.

"The business will be—"

"Fine," she assured him. "Alessio will be there," she said of his brother-in-law and right-hand man. "Take a few weeks and—"

"A few weeks?" Wyatt stared at his mother. "I can't do that."

"Sure you can," she said and smiled. "School breaks up soon for two weeks. I don't think pulling Cecily out of classes for an extra week would hurt her."

A few weeks in Crystal Point? Cecily would jump at the opportunity, he was sure. And Fiona…would she agreed to whatever he suggested if it meant having the chance to reconnect with her daughter?

I'm just not sure I should be spending three weeks around Fiona Walsh.

But other than sending Cecily to Crystal Point alone, which he would never do, or invite Fiona to Waradoon, which he wasn't sure she'd agree to, what option did he have?

"So it's all arranged?" Fiona asked her friend Evie Dunn.

"Yep," Evie replied. "They're booked to arrive on Saturday and are staying for nearly three weeks." Evie's black brows rose sharply. "You know, I've told you this at least four times already."

She knew that. But she wanted to hear it again. And again.

Her daughter was coming to meet her. *My daughter is coming here.*

The reality was both exciting and terrifying.

Cecily had read the letter Fiona had sent via her uncle and had quickly replied with an email, including photographs, and Fiona had choked back tears as she'd read her daughter's words. They'd been heartfelt and full of courage.

Fiona found herself holding her breath. "I know…just checking."

"Good thing we had that cancellation," Evie said.

Evie's bed-and-breakfast, Dunn Inn, was a popular retreat in the small town and usually had full occupancy. The cancellation of guests meant that two rooms were available, and Fiona couldn't have been happier.

"You're gonna be loco by the time they get here," Callie said and passed Fiona a drink. It was Friday night and the art class in Evie's studio was over. Two other participants had bailed ten minutes earlier, and it left Fiona sharing a drink with Callie, Evie and Evie's younger sister, Mary-Jayne Preston. They liked to think of it as Friday night cocktails, but with Evie only three months away from having a baby, they made do with peach iced tea instead of alcohol. Only Mary-Jayne, or M.J. as she was called, complained. Fiona was happy to keep her mind buzzing.

"So, he's hot? The uncle?" M.J. asked in her usual boots-and-all manner.

"Yep. Hotter than Hades." It was Callie, who was married to Evie and M.J.'s older brother, Noah, who replied. "The original tall, dark and handsome."

Fiona sipped her tea. She wasn't going to think about Wyatt. Definitely not.

"And single?" M.J.'s eyes popped wide. "From a wealthy family and running a successful business? Interesting."

Fiona pushed aside the niggling resentment forming in her blood. It shouldn't matter to her that another woman might find Wyatt attractive…but it did. If she dared summon the courage, she would admit the truth—that she was nervous about seeing him again.

He'd emailed her with details of their upcoming visit, and Fiona knew she'd read, and then reread, each of his messages more times than was sensible. But Wyatt was hard to ignore, even through something as bland as an email or text message. Of course, there was nothing even remotely personal in his messages. They were only about Cecily. Which was what she wanted, right?

His indifference gave her the opportunity to focus on her daughter. She learned about Cecily's school, her friends, her beloved horse, Banjo, and the family who clearly adored her. Talking with her daughter seemed so natural and not awkward, like she had imagined for so many years.

Awkward she saved for Wyatt. And the stretched nerves she took with herself everywhere she went—she saved them for him, too. And the fluttering in her belly whenever she thought about his blue eyes and perfectly sexy smile.

"Earth to Fiona?"

She snapped her thoughts back to the moment and discovered her three friends staring at her with raised brows and widened eyes. "I was thinking about Cecily," she said and took a drink.

"You sighed," M.J. told her. "Loudly."

"I cleared my throat," she said in defense. "So, who's up for more iced tea?"

Callie checked her watch. "Count me out. I have to get going. I promised Noah I'd be home early."

Fiona didn't miss the dreamy look on her friend's face. Callie adored her husband and four stepchildren. And with a pregnant Evie soon to marry Callie's younger brother, Scott, the two families were now intimately linked. Sometimes, when she watched them interact and observed the friendly rivalry and obvious affection the siblings felt for one another, Fiona experienced a sharp pain in her chest.

She'd never known family. Her great-uncle Leonard had done his best to provide her with a safe home after her mother dumped her on his doorstep, but he'd been a dyed-in-the-wool bachelor with old-fashioned morals and hadn't known how to handle a pregnant and emotionally fraught fifteen-year-old girl. He kept her fed and clothed and gave her a place to live—in his mind that was enough.

There had been no question about her keeping the baby.

The deal was done before she'd gone into labor. A married couple was taking her baby—that was all Fiona was told. The adoption would be closed. She could never contact her child.

But now I have my daughter back….

Well, she had a *chance* at least.

But she knew there were going to be challenging times ahead. Cecily would have questions, and she still wasn't sure how she would answer them. *And Wyatt?* She knew he'd be watching her every move and trying to discover her secrets. But even knowing that, Fiona held a seed of optimism in her heart. And when she returned to her empty little house a short while later, Fiona didn't feel half the loneliness that normally weighed down her shoulders when she opened the front door. She felt…hope.

Purple. Or as the woman behind him said in a chirpy tone, lavender. Wyatt had never been in a room that was so *pretty*. As he dumped his bag by the foot of the bed, the hostess told him the room was usually used by honeymooners and couples. Cecily was happily entrenched in the smaller room next door, a much more appealing space decorated in beige and white. This was too much.

The big bed was strewn with more pillows than he'd ever seen. He couldn't sleep in here, surrounded by flowers and purple cushions. And what the hell was the scent hitting his nose like a boxing glove every time he moved...*potpourri?*

"So, I'll let you settle in," Evie Dunn said cheerfully.

Wyatt didn't have a chance to object. The woman walked out of the room, and seconds later Cecily bounded through the door.

She wrinkled her nose. "Uncle Wyatt, it smells like a perfume shop in here."

That did it. "Let's switch rooms."

"My allergies," she protested. "And I've already unpacked."

Yeah, her three cases. One for every week they were staying in Crystal Point.

"Right, allergies." He forgot about the sickly sweet room for a moment. "Are you ready to go?"

Cecily nodded. "Yep. I don't know why we couldn't meet here?"

"The hotel is better," he said quietly. *Neutral.* It was what Fiona wanted.

"But Evie said we could use the front living room, and I—"

"You know the deal. Let's go," he said, gently cutting her off. Sometimes Cecily's exuberance was exhausting.

"Do you think she'll like me? Do you think she'll be disappointed?" Cecily popped out questions at a million miles per hour. "What if she—"

"Cecily—relax. She'll like you," he assured his niece. "I promise. And where's all this sudden anxiety coming from anyway? You've been talking on the phone and by email for two weeks now."

"But this is face-to-face," she said in a rush of breath. "And that's way different."

Yeah...way different. The tension knocking inside his chest was inexplicable. He didn't ever get like this. But thinking about Fiona Walsh stirred his blood. And considering the circumstances, Wyatt knew it was out of the question to be attracted to her. He couldn't afford to be sidetracked by Fiona's pretty face and lovely curves. He'd been swept away by physical attraction before. He wasn't about to make that same mistake again.

He only had to look at Cecily to know he had to keep his head on straight.

"You're going to be a hit. Trust me."

"I do, Uncle Wyatt," she said and hugged him. "I want it all to work out so much. I want Fiona to like me, and I want to like her back, too."

"I'm sure you will," he assured her. "She's nice."

Cecily shrugged. "Well, she *seems* nice. But you never really know what someone is like at first."

Wyatt heard the waver in his niece's voice. "Cecily, are you having doubts about this?"

She quickly shook her head. "No…just nerves, I guess."

He didn't doubt Fiona would be feeling the same apprehension. "We can go home anytime you want. Just say the word."

"I don't want to go home," she replied. "Not yet. I want to try and see if we can be…I dunno…friends maybe."

Wyatt admired Cecily's maturity. But he'd make sure he was on hand if the pressure became too much for her young shoulders. "Okay. Then let's go."

He herded her out of the bedroom and down the hall. The drive into town took fifteen minutes, and by the time he parked the rental car and took the lift from the basement car park, they were only a few minutes away from their meeting time.

He settled Cecily in the foyer, on the same leather sofa where he'd met with Fiona a couple of weeks earlier. The place was quiet, and he was glad they'd have privacy and not be crowded out by the familiar faces of Fiona's friends, like at the B and B.

"Uncle Wyatt?"

He shifted his attention back to the moment. "Yeah, kid?"

Cecily's voice dripped with anticipation. "Is that her?"

He turned, and sure enough, Fiona was walking through the hotel doors. He hadn't forgotten how pretty she was, and seeing her again only confirmed that the sensation rumbling through his chest was attraction. She wore a green dress and her strawberry blond hair flowed loose around her shoulders. *Lovely.*

When she came toward them, his blood seemed to stop pumping in his veins. She stood before them, all eyes and expectation as she looked at Cecily, then him, then Cecily again.

"Hi," she said softly.

Wyatt answered quietly. "Hello, Fiona."

This is one of those moments, he thought, *when worlds collide.* Fiona's world, his world, now forever joined by the young girl who stood by his side, stepping back and forth nervously on her heels.

"Hello, Cecily."

His niece took a moment, as though unsure about speaking to the woman who had given her life. Wyatt knew she wasn't really scared. Cecily wanted this. And Fiona...he made out caution and uncertainty and plain old happiness in her blue-gray eyes. It was uncanny how alike they were. Same hair, same complexion, same spirited temper.

"Um...hi," Cecily said quietly. "Thanks for coming."

Fiona stepped a little closer, and Wyatt wished he could harness all his strength for a second and give it to her, so this moment could pass easily between them.

"I'm really glad you wanted to meet me...and...found me," Fiona said a little uncomfortably.

"Well, it was Uncle Wyatt who actually found you," Cecily replied with a small smile.

Fiona looked at him, and the tightness in his chest expanded. "I know he did," she said, then faltered a little before she spoke again. "So, how was your trip?"

"Good," Cecily replied. "Uncle Wyatt let me have the window seat."

Fiona laughed softly, and the sound vibrated through him. She looked nervous, and he discreetly touched Cecily's arm, urging her forward. It was awkward for a moment, until Fiona smiled again and opened her arms slightly. Cecily stepped forward, and within seconds mother and daughter were together, hugging close, clearly emotional. Wyatt watched their exchange and swallowed the lump tightening his throat.

Fiona looked at him over Cecily's shoulder and smiled. Tears hung on her lashes and her eyes grew huge. Seeing her so vulnerable, so raw with joy and glowing with a kind of radiant happiness, made his insides hurt. Cecily was crying, too. There was no sadness, no regret. Just new feelings, new dreams, new hope.

And he knew instinctively he'd made the right decision in coming to Crystal Point. It was right for Cecily to meet her birth mother. All he had to do was get a handle on the growing attraction he had for Fiona.

Easy...yeah...right.

Fiona experienced such acute and all-consuming love as she held her daughter in her arms for only the second time in her life. Images of the baby cruelly snatched away within minutes of her birth, which up until this moment were the only memories she had, suddenly faded.

She looks like me....

Wyatt was right.

Wyatt...

Her heart rolled over as she looked at him. So tall and strong and handsome. It seemed right having him near. It gave her strength knowing he was only steps away. His closeness gave her courage to hold on to Cecily and let all her pent-up feelings rise to the surface.

"Let's sit down," she suggested and linked her arm through her daughter's.

"Why don't I leave you two alone for a while?" Wyatt said once they reached the sofa.

Fiona watched as Cecily stepped toward him. "No...don't go."

He sent his niece a peculiar look and then glanced toward Fiona. Something shimmered between them, and Fiona suddenly longed for his reassurance. And Cecily clearly wanted him on hand. "Cecily's right," she said and tried not to be wounded by the fact her daughter was unsure about being alone with her. "I'd like you to stay for a while, too." She looked at Cecily. "Okay?"

Cecily nodded. "Yes. Uncle Wyatt's cool."

Fiona didn't miss the affection in Cecily's words. She was undoubtedly attached to her uncle, who had taken over the role of parent. "I'm sure he is."

He grinned fractionally and sat down on the other sofa. Fiona relaxed and turned all her attention to the girl sitting beside her. Cecily was remarkable, and pride, pure and simple, surged through her blood and across her skin.

This is my daughter...my child... I made this exquisite creature.

Whatever happened from this moment, Fiona knew she would treasure the memory of Cecily's small hand clasped within hers. Regret and shame tapped at the back of her mind, but she wasn't about to let those kinds of thoughts invade the precious moment she was sharing with her daughter.

They talked for an hour, about everyday things. Cecily asked when she could see where Fiona lived and when she could visit Titan. They talked about their dogs and Cecily's friends.

"Nan and Pop are great," she said excitedly. "I can't wait for you to meet them. Auntie Rae knows everything about horses, and Auntie Ellen is so good with kids. She's got twins and they're really cute. She lets me help with them when I stay with her and Uncle Alessio. He's Italian. And his family is superrich. Not that she married him for his money... He's really good-looking, too."

Fiona waited for Cecily to take a breath and stole a glance at Wyatt. He was smiling, silent and intense as he regarded them.

"If it's okay with your uncle, maybe we could go see Titan this afternoon?"

"Can we, please?" Cecily begged Wyatt as she got to her feet.

He nodded. "If you like."

"I'll go get my boots," her daughter said eagerly. "They're in the car. I'll be back in a minute," she said once Wyatt handed over the car keys.

She left the foyer like a whirlwind and headed for the elevators.

Once she was out of sight, Fiona looked at Wyatt. "She's incredible."

"She certainly is," he agreed. "A pocket dynamo. But adorable."

"She loves her family a lot," Fiona said without envy and ridiculously conscious of his powerful stare. "And you especially."

"It's mutual," he replied. "She's a great kid."

She looked toward her feet. "I guess she'll have a lot of questions?"

"Yes," he assured her. "But she probably won't ask them straightaway. She doesn't want to scare you off."

Her gaze darted upward. "I don't scare easily."

"Are you sure?"

His mouth twisted in such a sexy way Fiona's breath rushed out. "Positive," she replied and wondered if they were still talking about Cecily. The air seemed uncommonly warm.

"Cecily is smart and mature for her age. She's had to be," he said quietly, and Fiona picked up on the strain in his voice. "She wants you in her life—although in what capacity I'm not sure. I don't think she quite knows herself. Meeting you is the first step. From here it's up to you both to work out what kind of relationship you'll have."

"With you standing on point to make sure I don't mess it up?"

He shrugged. "My job is to protect her. Karen trusted me with that responsibility, and I'll do it as best I can."

Fiona wrapped her arms around her waist and sat forward. "I won't screw this up. And I'll be whatever she needs me to be. There's no question about me trying to replace her mother. But I can be her friend."

"Yes, you can."

She let out a breath and experienced a heady warmth deep in her belly. There was something in his expression that heightened her awareness of him on every level. It was futile to deny it—Fiona got a look from his glittering blue eyes that said he was as aware of her as she was of him.

She pushed some words out. "So, I guess considering you're her legal guardian, *we* should be friends, too."

Another look…longer, hotter. Hot enough to raise her temperature a degree or two.

"Logically. But I get the sense that whatever's going on here," he said, flicking a hand in the air, "hasn't got anything to do with friendship."

"I don't think—"

"And everything to do with sex."

Chapter Four

Not one usually lost for words, Fiona stared at him. Of course, it was the truth. But put out there, it sounded dangerous. Dangerous because she wanted to focus every ounce of her attention on her child.

Falling in lust, or anything else, was absolutely out of the question.

"Cecily is…"

"Our priority," he said, finishing her sentence. "Exactly. The last thing we should do is complicate that."

"I agree."

"So, whatever this is, we'll ignore it?"

She could do that. For Cecily's sake. For her own. "Absolutely."

He stood up abruptly and Fiona's pulse raced. In jeans and a navy shirt, he looked so good it was sinful. His broad shoulders, solid chest and well-cut arms were undeniably worth a long look. Everything about him screamed *sexy*. Everything.

And Fiona's libido raced up to smack her around the head, yelling, *I'm here and what are you gonna do about it?*

Nothing…a mutually decided nothing.

Besides, she had a disastrous track record when it came to men.

She'd had a few lovers. And no one since Russ Daniels had bailed on her over two years earlier. Of course, Fiona had expected him to walk. *I always expect them to walk.*

And they never disappointed.

If they weren't walking out the door, they wanted to be just friends. She wasn't sexy. She wasn't beautiful. Pretty at best. Cute. Perky. Friendly and funny and exactly the kind of woman who made a great *gal pal*.

And Wyatt Harper would figure that out soon enough.

"I'm back!" Cecily announced as she bounded across the foyer, riding boots dangling from one hand.

"Great," Fiona said as she got to her feet. "Let's get going." She looked at Wyatt. "You are coming with us?"

He looked as though gears were grinding around in his head and he was quickly calculating his next move. "No."

Fiona bit back her surprise. *He trusts me.* "Oh, I thought—"

"You can drop her back to the B and B when you're done, okay?"

Of course it was okay. "I'll make sure she's returned by five o'clock."

He nodded slowly. "See you then."

"We could all have dinner together?" Cecily suggested, clearly forgetting her earlier reluctance about being alone with her. "So we can celebrate. What about here?"

Wyatt spoke. "I'll see what I can do."

Cecily hugged him before they left, and Fiona fought the sudden urge to do the same. She had an inkling those arms would feel wonderful wrapped around her.

Instead, she smiled, said goodbye and turned on her heels.

* * *

The few hours she spent alone with Cecily were some of
the most precious in her life, and Fiona knew she would treasure them always. As expected, her horse-crazy daughter fell
in love with Titan. The big chestnut Thoroughbred gelding
was primed and in show condition and looked magnificent
beneath the glow of the warm winter sun.

"Banjo has a problem with his pedal bone," Cecily explained with a frown. "So he's not suitable for dressage. But
soon," she said as she buried her face in Titan's neck and inhaled the beloved horsey scent. "Uncle Wyatt says he'll buy
me a new horse. Of course, I'll keep Banjo as a com-
panion pony." She rubbed her small hands down the gelding's shoulder. "My aunt Rae will help me find the right
horse. Or…" She lingered over her words for a moment. "Or
maybe you could?"

Fiona's heart contracted. "I'd like that."

Cecily looked at her. "It's funny, don't you think, that we
both have a horse? Like a sign or something. Do you believe
in signs?"

"I do. Very much so."

"Uncle Wyatt says it's just coincidence."

He would. "Well, he seems like a practical type of person.
It's good to have different points of view."

Cecily smiled. "That's what he says, too."

Uh-oh. She didn't want to keep finding commonality with
him. That was more dangerous than thinking he was the most
gorgeous thing on two legs. "We're both right, then. So, do
you want to go to my house and meet Muffin?"

Cecily checked her watch and it made Fiona smile. Excited,
passionate about life and incredibly sensible. She loved that
about her daughter.

"I guess…for a while. But we have to be back by five
o'clock."

"I remember," Fiona said and linked her elbow through Cecily's.

Twenty minutes later, Muffin was a big hit. Cecily was in the kitchen of her little house, scratching the dog behind the ears. "She's cute. I like your house."

Fiona smiled. "It's small compared to what you're used to."

Cecily shrugged. "I guess. Waradoon is huge. My real house was sort of midsize."

"Your real house?"

Cecily met her gaze. "Where I lived with my parents." She went quiet for a moment. "They were good parents, in case you were wondering. I mean, I was happy most of the time."

"Most?"

Cecily immediately looked as if she wished she hadn't said the word. "I meant I was happy, that's all. I loved my parents a lot. My mother was always there for me…." She stopped and glanced down to her feet. "My dad was funny and told really bad jokes."

There was a sting in her daughter's words. But Fiona didn't press her. Wyatt had warned her to expect some resistance. As much as it hurt, she had to allow Cecily her feelings. "I'm glad. And it's okay living at Waradoon with your grandparents now? Your uncle told me he gets back every weekend?"

"That's right," Cecily replied quietly. "Uncle Wyatt is good at looking after me."

"I figured that."

"And he's not all serious and worried about me as though I'm going to fall apart or something like Nan and Pop. Not all the time anyway. Pop's been really sad since my mother died."

Fiona's throat tightened. "He lost his daughter. It will take time for him to stop being so sad."

"I guess." Cecily stroked the dog some more and stared toward the floor. "Did it…did it take you a long time…I mean, when you lost me?"

But I didn't just lose you. I gave you up. I abandoned you. Her heart contracted in a viselike grip. "Forever," she admitted and was relieved when Cecily looked at her.

"I guess you didn't have much choice, you know, when you decided about the adoption thing?" she asked, then immediately looked as if she wished she hadn't. "That's what Uncle Wyatt said."

Fiona remembered what Wyatt had said about Cecily not wanting to scare her off with too many hard questions too soon, and she swiftly tried to put her at ease. "It was a difficult time. And I'm really happy that you have a nice family who love you."

"I do," Cecily assured her, and then a little firmer, "They really love me. And Uncle Wyatt is the best."

Fiona nodded. She was starting to realize that herself.

Wyatt hadn't any idea how he was supposed to fill his time while Cecily and Fiona became acquainted. After making dinner reservations at the hotel, he drove back to the B and B but refused to hang out in the ridiculous purple room. Instead he grabbed his laptop and headed for the kitchen. Evie Dunn was in residence, baking something that smelled so good his stomach growled.

"Coffee?" she asked when he entered the room.

"Sure. Thank you."

She passed him a mug. "There's milk in the refrigerator."

Wyatt declined. "This is fine," he said, then asked politely, "When's your baby due?"

She patted her expanded belly. "In three months."

"Congratulations," he said and drank some coffee. He remembered Fiona telling him Evie was getting married soon.

Evie smiled. "Thank you. You know, it's good of you to allow Fiona this time with your niece."

"It's what Cecily wants."

"And Fiona."

What *did* Fiona want? He immediately wondered and his thoughts had nothing to do with Cecily. He knew it was foolish thinking about her in any way other than Cecily's birth mother. Cecily was the priority. The kid had been through the emotional wringer, and he wasn't about to do anything that might upset her. Specifically, acting on his attraction for Fiona.

He'd get over it.

"She's a good person."

Wyatt looked at Evie. "I know."

Evie's dramatically arched brows rose. "She's more fragile than she likes to make out."

He wasn't about to disagree. He also wasn't about to get into a discussion with this woman, who was obviously a close friend of Fiona's. Wyatt was struck by a sudden surge of loyalty toward Fiona. "I know. So, is there someplace I can get internet access?"

She gave him a look, a half smile and then let him off the hook. "The study is the second room off the front hall—help yourself."

Wyatt grabbed the coffee and laptop and left the room.

As promised, Fiona returned Cecily at five o'clock. Wyatt had spent a couple of hours in the office, made a call to Alessio to discuss a new contract acquisition and sent a few emails. His niece took no time in telling him what a great afternoon she'd had and how Fiona owned the most beautiful horse on the planet. He switched off the computer and swiveled in the high-backed leather chair.

Fiona stood in the doorway. She smiled at him and Wyatt's insides crunched. He cleared his throat. "Dinner's all set. I'll pick you up at six-thirty." Cecily nudged his shoulder. "*We'll* pick you up."

"Sure. Thanks. I'll see you later, Cecily."

Wyatt remained seated and watched as his niece hugged Fiona.

Once she had left, Cecily perched herself by the desk. "Well?" he asked.

She nodded. "I like her."

"And?" he prompted.

Sometimes mature beyond her age, Cecily looked every one of her fourteen years as she bit her bottom lip. "And nothing. I like her. She's nice, just like you said. Do you think I could ask her about my father?"

Wyatt wasn't sure. Fiona had been vague at best about the man. He had told Cecily her biological father had passed away, and his niece had accepted the news with quiet acceptance. But she had questions only Fiona could answer, and he wasn't convinced Fiona would tell the truth. He sensed she was hiding something from him—something that wasn't in the investigator's file. And knew he had to find out what it was and decide if it was something he wanted Cecily to know about.

"Maybe you should take some time getting to know her first?" he said. "Relationships take time."

Good advice. Pity he didn't take it when he'd jumped into his engagement to Yvette.

She shrugged. "I suppose. But I really want to know about my father. And my grandparents and any other relatives I had. Do you think she regrets giving me up?"

Wyatt chose his words carefully. "I imagine she'd have some regrets."

His niece drew in a deep breath. "She did say she was glad I had a nice family. I didn't know what to call her, though," she admitted, and Wyatt immediately reached out and grabbed Cecily's hand, squeezing it tightly. "The idea of calling her Fiona feels weird...but it's not like she's really my mother or anything."

"Maybe you could ask Fiona what she thinks about that?" he suggested gently. "You could come up with a name together—like a nickname?"

Cecily's eyes widened dramatically. "That's a good idea." She nodded, smiled and hugged him quickly. "Thanks, Uncle Wyatt. I'm going to get changed."

After lingering at the desk for another five minutes, he shut the computer down and headed back to the purple room. He showered in the en suite bathroom and changed into fresh clothes. Cecily tapped on his door at six-twenty as he was clipping his watch onto his wrist.

"How do I look?" she asked as she flounced into the room and twirled, showing off wide-legged jeans covered in sparkly diamanté. "Too much?"

When it came to Cecily's fashion sense, she had her own style. "You look great. Come on, let's go."

She laughed and bounded ahead as Wyatt grabbed the keys to the rental car.

The drive to Fiona's house took only minutes, and the sun was setting as he pulled into the driveway. He saw her silhouette pass by the window. The outline of her curvy body was unmistakable as she moved, and the way his insides rolled over simply thinking about her forced Wyatt to sit in his seat for a long moment after he'd switched off the engine.

"Uncle Wyatt?"

Cecily's voice turned his thoughts around. "Yeah?"

"Are you okay?"

"Sure," he said and sucked in a breath and opened the door. "Jump in the backseat and I'll be just a minute."

By the time he reached her front door, Wyatt felt as if he was sixteen years old and picking a girl up for a date.

But this is not a date.

Fiona pulled the door wide as he tapped on the frame. "Hi," she said. "I'm ready."

Stupid, he thought, to imagine she would be as uncomfortable as he was. Except something about her demeanor got his attention, and he knew, without a doubt, she was experiencing the same spike in awareness. The little black dress she wore, which fell over her hips and showed off all her lovely attributes, didn't help. "Cecily's waiting."

She smiled, flicked off the light from inside the doorjamb and shut the door. "Like I said—I'm ready."

Wyatt was ready, too…ready to take her in his arms and kiss her beautiful mouth.

He stood aside and let her pass. Once inside the car, Wyatt did his best to ignore the flowery scent of her perfume, which hit him with lightning force every time she moved. The drive into town was only made bearable by Cecily's endless chatter.

He parked the car and they headed up and within minutes they were being seated in the restaurant.

"Champagne," his niece insisted to the hovering waitress once they sat down.

Wyatt shot her a *no chance* look. "Wine," he said and picked a bottle from the list. "And one raspberry lemonade," he added to the smiling attendant before she walked away.

Cecily heaved a dramatic sigh. "Uncle Wyatt," she complained. "This is a celebration. How can I celebrate with soda?"

"Easily," he replied. "I'm sure Fiona understands." He looked at her for the first time since they'd been seated. He wasn't sure why, but he wanted her to think him responsible and a good fill-in parent for Cecily.

She nodded and he appreciated the unity. "Soda will work just as well," she said and touched Cecily's hand. "So let's order because I'm starving."

Their drinks arrived, and once they ordered food, Cecily insisted on toasting to being reunited with her birth mother.

"To new beginnings," Fiona said quietly, and as they clinked glasses, Wyatt didn't miss the glitter of moisture in her eyes.

"To family," Cecily said and grinned.

The tears Fiona had valiantly tried to suppress tipped over. But they were happy tears. She *was* happy. Being with Cecily filled her heart in places that been empty for so long. The years of being afraid her daughter would reject her had faded because Cecily had accepted her into her life. Fiona admired her daughter so much.

Her gaze flicked to Wyatt. *This, on the other hand, is where it gets complicated.* In all her life she couldn't remember any man having such a potent effect on her. But with Cecily bouncing in her seat beside her, Fiona knew having feelings for Wyatt...any feelings...was completely out of the question. She remembered what he'd said about logic and sex. Logical was out. It was illogical to want him. Not when she had such a disastrous history in relationships and not when Cecily was bound to be caught in the middle when she failed to hold his attention for longer than a moment. As for sex? She didn't do casual. She didn't have sex with men she hardly knew.

Only, on some level, she felt as if she did know Wyatt and that he knew her. Looking at him, sharing molecules of space with him, she was inexplicably drawn toward the awareness thrumming through her entire body.

I really want him....

And worse.

I really like him....

They chatted about ordinary things, and once dinner was served, Cecily stopped talking and ate with gusto. She had a healthy appetite and it made Fiona smile, counting all the ways she and her daughter were alike.

"More wine?" Wyatt asked as Fiona speared the stuffed chicken breast on her plate.

She nodded, afraid to speak because her mouth was dry and cottony.

"Can we go shopping sometime this week?" Cecily asked her uncle between mouthfuls of fettuccine.

"Sure," Wyatt said as he poured. "For anything in particular?"

Cecily gave him a big grin. "Well, I was thinking about Christmas in July."

He frowned. "What?"

"You know—a Christmas celebration in July. Auntie Ellen was telling me about it. Apparently lots of people do it."

He didn't look convinced. "What people?"

Cecily made a face and looked at Fiona. "Christmas is always a big deal at Waradoon," she explained and played with her fork. "I thought it would be nice to celebrate it now, since we've missed out on so many real Christmases together. What do you say, Uncle Wyatt?"

The holidays had never been a particularly cheerful time for Fiona growing up. Shayne had rarely remembered to celebrate the event and her uncle had been too busy running the farm to be bothered with a tree or gifts. Since she'd settled in Crystal Point, Fiona usually spent the day with Callie or Evie and her family. Things had changed now Callie was married. And since Evie's wedding to Callie's younger brother, Scott Jones, was only a couple of months away and their baby was due a month after that, Fiona wasn't sure she would fit within the Preston fold anymore. She'd be the outsider, like she had been so many times before. But she would do anything to see happiness radiating on her daughter's face.

"I think it's a great idea," she said and smiled at her daughter. "I'll put up a tree."

Cecily laughed. "That would be cool. We can get gifts and put them under the tree." She turned to her uncle. "Now you *have* to take me shopping so I can exactly the right gift for Fiona."

"Okay," he said.

"And we should go, too," she suggested to Cecily, and her heart flipped over when she saw her daughter's infectious smile in between another mouthful of pasta. "I'm sure you want to get something for your uncle."

Cecily giggled. "Ha—he's already got everything he wants."

Fiona looked at Wyatt and burned hot and dizzy beneath his stare as the awareness between them sizzled.

"Not everything," he said evenly.

She took a long drink and focused her attention on her meal. Was she imagining how highly suggestive his words sounded? She didn't dare look at him. Didn't dare let herself get caught up in his brilliant blue eyes.

Fiona inhaled deeply and started a conversation about horses, clearly Cecily's favorite thing. "We could go riding together," she suggested. "Callie will have a horse you can borrow while you're here. Of course, as long as your uncle says it's okay."

"I'm sure you'll keep her safe," he said as he looked at her over the rim of his glass.

As she met his gaze, Fiona was struck by how handsome he was. She'd never been one to be swept away by good looks. But he had his own brand of magnetism, which was quickly becoming impossible to ignore.

"Of course."

Cecily nodded happily and excused herself to use the bathroom. Once she was out of sight, Fiona picked up her glass and pretended to drink her wine, acutely conscious of the heat between them.

He pushed the plate forward. "Would you like to spend tomorrow morning with Cecily?"

"I'd like that," she said and smiled. "I appreciate that you trust me with her."

"I wouldn't be here if I didn't. But you should know that Cecily has questions for you," he explained. "You were expecting questions, right? She wants to know about her father, her grandparents...your family."

I don't have a family. Only Cecily...

Panic set in behind her ribs. Of course she knew questions would come. "I'll tell her——"

"What?" he asked. "I'd like to know exactly what you plan to tell her. I'd like to know what wasn't in the investigator's file."

He knew everything about her life—at least, he thought he did. No one knew about the man who'd taken her innocence. Not the nights she'd been left alone in motel rooms while Shayne chased one cowboy after another. Or the hunger from entire days without food. No one needed to know that. Especially not Cecily. But the questions about her father weren't going to be avoided easily. Especially when Wyatt had made it clear he wanted to know, too.

"He was...a friend," she said, thinking it wasn't exactly a lie. Jamie Corbett had been her mother's lover and someone Fiona had trusted...until the night Shayne had left them alone together in their shabby hotel room.

"A friend?"

"Yes. And like I said, he's dead. Talking about him won't change that."

He shifted in his seat and looked at her. "Is there something you're not telling me?"

Panic wound up her spine. Okay, so he could see right

through her. It wasn't really surprising. She was vulnerable around Wyatt. Her attraction to him had been steadily building, like a rising tide. Spending time with him increased those feelings. If she were to keep her secret safe, Fiona knew she had to avoid being alone with him and concentrate on Cecily.

"I've told you everything I—"

"I'm back!"

Cecily's announcement silenced Fiona immediately. "Good. We were just about to tuck into the rest of your fettuccine."

The smiles all around belied the tension now ingrained in her bones. She feigned interest in her dinner and concentrated on not looking at Wyatt for the rest of the evening.

They left about an hour later, and by the time he pulled the car up outside her house, Fiona was a bundle of nervous energy. Cecily was dozing in the backseat and muttered a weary-sounding goodbye as she listened to her iPod. Before Fiona could protest, Wyatt was out of the car and had opened her door. Chivalrous, too, she thought with an inward groan. And handsome and so sexy she could hardly breathe as she stood beside him and walked toward the front door. The tiny porch seemed even smaller with his six-foot-something frame now standing by the door.

She fumbled with her keys and felt his closeness like a cloak. The dim glow of the overhead light created a heady intimacy. The white shirt he wore amplified the broadness of his shoulders and narrow waist. Warmth crept along her skin, followed by a lightning bolt of lust. But Cecily was in the car barely meters away, and Fiona knew she shouldn't be having such thoughts.

"Would you like me to do that?" he asked. "You look like you're having trouble."

Fiona pushed the key in the lock. "No, it's fine. Well, good night. Thank you for dinner."

He watched her with burning intensity. "I'll drop Cecily off tomorrow so you can spend the day together."

"Okay. I appreciate your—"

"Good night, Fiona," he said and dipped his head to kiss her cheek.

She shouldn't have sucked in a sharp breath. She shouldn't have felt as though her knees were going to give way. *It's just a kiss on the cheek, for heaven's sake.* But she did. And worse, a sound, half moan, half groan, rattled low in her throat. She knew he heard it because he smiled against her skin.

When he pulled back, he was still smiling. *Like he knows I want him.*

"Good night, Wyatt."

He headed down the three steps and took a few strides. Before Fiona had a chance to push the front door on its hinges, he turned. "Hey," he said quietly to get her attention.

Fiona drew in a breath. "Yes?"

He gave her such a sexy smile and she was quickly intoxicated. "You know, you look really good in a dress."

As he drove off, Fiona slumped against the door.

I will not like him.

Too late.

Chapter Five

"Tell me about the kid."

Fiona turned from her spot in Evie's kitchen. It was day three. The past forty-eight hours had been wonderful. Even better, she hadn't been in a position to spend any time alone with Wyatt. There had been no more questions, no more inquisitions. Cecily had asked about her father and for the moment had accepted Fiona's brief acknowledgment of the young man who'd been a rodeo cowboy and had been killed in an accident. She didn't mention the part about him being her mother's much younger lover. Or how he'd forced sex without her consent. There was an ugly word for what happened, but Fiona didn't like how it sounded on the edge of her tongue. Cecily didn't need to know the violent details of her conception.

Fiona had arrived at Evie's bed-and-breakfast at eleven o'clock and found Cecily and Evie's son Trevor shooting hoops near the studio at the side of the house. Evie was in the main part of the house with her other guests, and Fiona had taken over making sandwiches in the kitchen.

And now Wyatt stood framed in the doorway, dressed in jeans and a T-shirt, glaring at her.

"The kid?" She raised her brows, took her hands off the kettle and tried not to think about how her knees turned weak. She grabbed a tea towel and covered the plate of wrap-style sandwiches she'd made. "Trevor? He's Evie's son."

He nodded. "He's been monopolizing Cecily all morning. You know, I didn't bring her here so she could get mixed up with some—"

"Relax," Fiona insisted when she realized where the conversation was heading and that Wyatt looked ready to punch someone in the nose. "Trevor's a nice boy. Sensible and trustworthy."

"Like all teenage boys, right?"

She stiffened and gripped the countertop. "Like he's been raised to be by his mother, who is my friend." Fiona grabbed a mug and poured coffee into it. "Here, drink this and calm down."

"I don't want to calm down," he said as he strode into the room. "I want to know that my niece is—"

"She's perfectly fine," Fiona said, taking no interest in his scowl or the fact he clearly didn't like being interrupted or pacified with caffeine. "She's shooting hoops, not smoking a crack pipe. And she's having fun with someone her own age."

"It's the kind of fun that concerns me."

Fiona suppressed a smile. "What, they don't have teenage boys where you're from?"

He didn't like sarcasm, either. "You're not helping."

"What exactly do you think she's going to get up to?" she asked and pointed to the coffee again. "She's a sensible girl. She won't do anything foolish."

"Even sensible girls can get into trouble."

She didn't miss the meaning of his words. So there it was, out between them. And to his credit, Wyatt immediately looked as though he wished he hadn't said it. But out was out. And Fiona had no intention of pretending otherwise.

Besides, being annoyed with him helped her stop imagining him naked. Which she'd done with alarming regularity over the past few days.

"She's not me. And I've never claimed to be sensible."

"I shouldn't have—"

"Don't," she insisted. It didn't matter what he thought. She wouldn't let it. One silly kiss on the cheek didn't make them... *anything.* "I'd expect you to have an opinion. You've read the file. You know everything, right? The hopeless mother, the father who didn't want me, the countless schools. I wasn't exactly the poster child for a normal life." Fiona crossed her arms and drew air deep into her lungs. "But when I look at Cecily, when I see what an incredible girl she has become, I could never regret any of it. If I did that would be like saying I wished she'd never been born...and imagining a world without Cecily in it would be impossible to bear."

As speeches went, this was right up there. Right up there with making him feel like a complete jerk. Wyatt huffed out a breath and sat down. "I apologize. I'm not usually so clumsy."

She actually laughed. "I'd bet you've never had a clumsy moment in your life."

Except around you. He didn't say it. And didn't want to start thinking about why she affected him as she did. "I'm not about to start judging you, Fiona. If I'm acting like an overprotective parent, it's because I have no idea what I'm doing."

She came around the bench and settled her hips against the counter.

Wyatt tried to not think about how good her legs looked

stretched out from the short skirt she wore. He had a hell of a time thinking about anything else when she was so close.

One brow came up. "You were surprised they granted you guardianship?"

"Yes," he replied and wondered how she seemed to know what he was thinking. "My sister three years younger is married with her own children so I assumed Karen would believe that Ellen and Alessio would have been the better option."

"I think they made the right choice," she said quietly. "Cecily thinks you've hung the moon, so you're off to a good start."

"I don't want to screw it up for her sake. She's been through enough."

"You won't," she assured him. "It's been eighteen months since her parents passed away and she's happy and healthy."

Wyatt bit back a laugh. "I'm not sure if that has anything to do with me."

"You'd be surprised. In my experience, as a teacher," she qualified, "I see children from different backgrounds and situations, single parents, foster parents, grandparents, two-parent families, and they're all doing the best they can. The thing is, Wyatt, no one gets it right every time."

He knew she was right, and her words offered the kind of comfort he'd somehow forgotten existed. "Do you mean like thinking every teenage boy who so much as looks at her is after something?" Spoken out loud, it sounded ridiculously paranoid.

She nodded. "Exactly. I wouldn't encourage her to be friends with Trevor if I thought he couldn't be trusted. You didn't expect Cecily to spend every minute of her holiday with either of us, did you?"

"I'm not sure what I expected," he said candidly, suddenly wanting to kiss her so much his whole body was on high alert. "I didn't expect…"

She stilled. "What?"

"I didn't expect I'd be this…" Wyatt stopped, pausing to consider if admitting anything was wise at this point—when they both knew it couldn't go anywhere. But for the past few days, he'd been going quietly out of his mind thinking about her. "I didn't expect I'd be this attracted to you."

Fiona sucked in a breath. *Okay…what now?* "Me, either." Not the most sensible response. Not even close.

"Inconvenient, then?"

She nodded. "Very."

"Is avoiding me helping any?"

Fiona rubbed her hands down her thighs and didn't miss the way his eyes followed her every move. "Not so far."

Something hot and seductive swept into the room. It toyed with them for a moment, tracing the edges of the building awareness, and she experienced a surge of longing so deep, so intense, her knees threatened to give way.

"Fiona…"

How he came to be in front of her she wasn't sure. She vaguely heard the chair being scraped back. There were no other sounds. Only her heart beating madly. Only some far-away voice telling her to stop whatever was about to happen.

"Wyatt…we can't… It's not…"

"I know we can't," he said softly.

Fiona said his name again. Anything more wouldn't come. When his arms moved to either side of her, trapping her against the counter, it merely intensified the desire scorching her skin, her blood and her very bones. She tilted her head back to look at him and recognized the raw hunger in his blue eyes.

She drew in a soft breath, waiting, feeling the heat between them rise like a coiled serpent. Her lips parted, anticipating his kiss. And wanting it. When he touched his mouth to hers, every ounce of lingering resistance disappeared. There was nothing else. Only feeling. Only his kiss. Only Wyatt.

She reached up and laid her hands on his shoulders. He was solid, strong, just as she'd expected. She'd been kissed before, had experienced desire before. But never like this. He leaned into her and continued to kiss her mouth, slanting his lips over hers with gentle provocation.

Whoosh...

She'd heard about it, read about it, secretly dreamed of one day finding someone who would make her feel so alive.

It's only lust.

Powerful, heady and electrifying. Exactly what it should be. But the warning voice in her head prevailed.

It's only sex.

And sex wasn't enough to sustain anything other than a brief, forgettable relationship. She knew that. But as his tongue gently wound around hers, for one crazy moment it felt enough. The fact he wasn't touching her in any way other than the kiss was incredibly erotic to her senses. Nothing rushed. No quick hands. No hasty gratification. No demands. This was slow and seductive and captivating, and he coaxed a response she gave willingly.

When the kiss was over and he lifted his head, Fiona kept her hands where they were. She looked up, met his gaze and knew her lips quivered, knew he'd see every scrap of desire brimming in her eyes.

"Not a good idea?"

She swallowed hard. "No."

He pulled back and straightened. "You're right. It won't happen again."

It seemed like a monumental promise. Too big. Too much. Something neither could hold to. He wanted her. She wanted him. But wasn't enough. Cecily was too important. "You're right…it won't."

"I should back off."

"Yes, you should."

He stepped aside and put space between them. Luckily, because just then Cecily and Trevor bounced through the back door, laughing loudly as they bundled into the room.

The kiss was forgotten, and Fiona caught Wyatt's sudden disapproving look when he saw Trevor and she frowned at him. He got the message and immediately switched to a smile so fake she almost laughed out loud. When the kids said they wanted to go to the beach, his pasted-on smile looked frozen onto his handsome face.

"Lily's going to be there," Cecily announced.

Lily was Callie's stepdaughter and Trevor's cousin. Fiona had introduced them the day before, and the girls, almost the same age, had hit it off immediately. The fact it was winter didn't seem to put the kids off going swimming. The weather was mild and she knew the water would be bearable. "As long as your uncle says it's okay."

He didn't waste any time saying, "We'll go with you."

Fiona didn't miss the inclusive *we,* and Cecily's startled expression stood out like a beacon. "You hate the beach."

"We'll all go," he said, firmer this time, and Cecily clearly knew not to argue the point. Once the kids left to change into their swimsuits, Fiona turned to Wyatt. "Don't like the beach, huh?"

"In the middle of winter? Not particularly."

Fiona grinned. "City boy," she teased. "So why are *we* going?"

"I like teenage boys even less."

Fiona sighed heavily. The man was as stubborn as they came. "Trevor's a good kid. Didn't we already go over this stuff?"

He shrugged. "Humor me anyway."

"Doesn't look like I have a choice." She moved around

the bench and flicked the kettle switch. "I just have to get brunch into the front dining room for the guests and then I'm all yours."

Probably not the best way to put it. The words smacked of innuendo. Wyatt raised a brow and got rid of the fake smile. "Can I help?"

"Are you good in the kitchen?"

He smiled in a sexy way. "I know my way around."

She didn't doubt it. If he was good in the kitchen, she didn't dare imagine his skill in the bedroom. "I've got it," she said and grabbed the sandwiches. "I'll meet you outside in fifteen minutes."

He nodded and left the room.

Fiona's fifteen minutes turned into twenty-five. By the time she headed outside, Wyatt was pacing the front driveway.

"Sorry," she said breathlessly. "Just had to let Evie know we're heading off." She looked around. "Where are the kids?"

"Five minutes ahead of us."

He let them go unsupervised? "I'm impressed."

"I'm trusting your judgment."

"Smartest move you've made today." She took a few steps and then turned back to face him. "Well, let's go. Don't want that five to turn into ten."

She crossed the road and headed across the grassy stretch toward the pathway that led to the beach.

Wyatt caught up with her in mere seconds. "It's what, a ten-minute walk?"

"About that," she replied as he came beside her. "This path leads down toward the patrolled beach in front of the tourist park. You remember the beach, don't you? You followed me down there once."

"That first day—I remember."

She grinned and forgot that she should be jumping out of her skin to avoid enjoying his company. "Stalker."

Wyatt laughed and the sound vibrated through her. He was so easy to be with. Easy to like. The sound of waves crashing along the shoreline and the scent of wild jasmine in the air created a relaxed mood between them. That kiss would usually have put her on high alert. Strange that it didn't. Strange that all she wanted to do was keep talking with him. And kiss him again. *And kiss only him for the rest of my life.*

"Why aren't you married?"

His question quickly shoved her back into the moment. "I told you already."

"Because you're always the best friend. Yeah, right. What's the real reason?"

She shrugged. What could she say? Men weren't exactly lining up for her. The ones that had always found her lacking in some way. Of course, Fiona knew why. She had too many secrets. Too much baggage. Things she couldn't tell.

"I've never been in love," she said and felt the truth of her own words through to her bones. "So what about you?" she asked, determined to shake him off the subject of her loveless love life. "How come your engagement didn't work out?"

He didn't falter a step, although Fiona sensed his reticence. "We were incompatible."

"That's a good shot at avoiding the question without giving a real answer."

He flicked sunglasses on. "I worked long hours. She didn't like it."

"Being committed to your job isn't exactly a deal breaker. What's the real reason?"

The woman was relentless, Wyatt thought and tried to not think about how much he longed to take her hand in his. He couldn't recall the last time he'd wanted to do that. Maybe never. He felt ridiculous even thinking it. Stupid and foolish, he knew it was inappropriate. But as he walked with her beneath the late-morning sun and remembered how sweetly she'd kissed him, Wyatt experienced an odd tightening in his chest. Because it felt as if they were…what?

Courting.

He almost laughed out loud.

People didn't do that anymore. He didn't do that ever. Sappy, romantic notions had never been his thing. He was practical and pragmatic. He worked hard, played fair and believed a man was measured by his integrity and how he treated others. Pretty girls with nice smiles didn't turn his head and make him forget he had a job to do. Reuniting Cecily successfully with her birth mother was his job, and he'd promised his niece he'd do everything he could to ensure it worked out. Karen and Jim were gone and he'd played his part in that. *He'd* suggested they take a break and work on their marriage. Little did he know that advice would send them to their deaths. He owed Cecily a chance to have a mother again, and he wasn't about to screw it up for her.

"Wyatt?"

He glanced at Fiona and the truth tumbled out. "She slept with someone else."

The pathway rounded a corner, and she stopped at a narrow bridge crossing just before the tourist park. "I'm sorry."

He shrugged. "It happens."

"I guess. Doesn't make it hurt less, though."

Was he hurt? Wounded, maybe. And angry. And disappointed that he'd been so blind about Yvette. Wyatt was also man enough to take some responsibility for what had happened between them. He'd jumped into their relationship quickly, and he wasn't about to make that mistake again. Wyatt liked Fiona. And desired her. But Yvette's betrayal made him wary and suspicious. He barely knew Fiona and couldn't be sure her attraction to him was genuine. It seemed real. It felt real when she'd kissed him. But his ex-fiancée had pretended to care for six months before he'd found her out. How could he be sure Fiona wasn't using the attraction between them to get closer to Cecily? He couldn't.

But still, she was smart and pretty and sexy. The whole package. Exactly the kind of woman Wyatt imagined he'd want. There was no outward pretense with Fiona Walsh. There was a deep earthiness in her manner, a kind of sweet honesty. Sometimes blunt, always sincere…just…*lovely.*

"I'm sure you will."

She looked at him oddly. "You're sure I will what?"

"Fall in love."

She half smiled and the air between them crackled. "I'm not holding my breath. Although Cecily has already hit me up for a little brother or sister one day."

"Really?" Wyatt wasn't really surprised, though. He knew his niece didn't relish being an only child. "Karen and Jim wanted to give her everything," he explained as she began walking again. The rise to the beach was ahead, and when she trudged up the sandbank, Wyatt followed.

She moved back and grabbed his arm. "I wasn't criticizing them."

Wyatt placed his hand over hers and rubbed his thumb over her fingertips. "I know that. Cecily was the only child in the family for a long time so I guess we all indulged her."

"Your sister and her husband didn't try to adopt again?"

"No. They'd tried to have a baby for a long time before Cecily came into their lives. Jim had been working up north for several years when they started adoption proceedings. Actually, they were only three weeks away from returning to the Hunter Valley when Cecily became available."

She stiffened and tried to pull her hand away. He held on. "That didn't come out right."

"It's the truth," she said on a heavy sigh. "I gave her up. I let her go. She was *available.* I didn't get a say in which family she went to. My uncle and your sister insisted on a closed adoption, and I was so upset I agreed without really considering what it would mean—for me or my baby."

Her pain struck him hard between the ribs. "Karen should have—"

"I don't blame her," Fiona said quickly. "In her shoes, I might have done the same thing. I was told what I needed to hear—that my baby had gone to the perfect couple."

Perfect? Wyatt fought the urge to set her straight. Instead, he remained loyal to his sister. He owed Karen as much. "They loved Cecily dearly."

"Then I guess I was right to let her go."

"Fiona, I want—"

"Hey!" Cecily's voice, loud and excited, crashed through the moment.

Wyatt dropped Fiona's hand and watched his niece climb up the small sand hill. She had a towel wrapped around her waist and water dripped over her bare feet. "Enjoy your swim?"

"Yeah." She laughed. "The water's cold, and Lily and I dunked Trevor. So…" She raised her eyebrows and looked at them both, grinning broadly. "Wanna explain why you guys were holding hands just now?"

"We weren't really—"

"No," he replied the same time Fiona started to protest. Wyatt knew better than to give in to Cecily's curiosity. The kid had all the tenacity of a terrier.

She laughed again. "Hah—you're so busted."

Fiona moved forward, clearly mortified. "Well, I'm going over to the surf club to check my roster. I volunteer for beach patrol," she explained and looked quickly toward Cecily. "Have fun in the water—if it's too cold, don't stay in for too long. And swim between the flags."

She walked down the sand and headed back onto the path

and into a nearby building. Once she was out of earshot, Wyatt turned back to his niece. "Was that necessary?"

Cecily gave a cat-who-got-the-cream grin. "You're the one caught making out, not me."

He frowned. "We were not making out," he said and got a powerful flashback of kissing Fiona in Evie's kitchen. "I was helping her up the sand bank."

They both knew it sounded like the lamest excuse they'd ever heard.

And Cecily had no compunction in telling him so. "You know, I'm not a little kid. I'm okay with it if you like her. I like her, too."

"The reason we're here is so *you* can get to know Fiona. That's all."

"I get that," she replied and pulled her hair from its band. "All I'm saying is that if you want to take her out sometime, I wouldn't mind." Her eyes widened. "You could take her back to that restaurant we went to and get one of those tables in the corner where it's quiet and I dunno…romantic."

I am not standing here getting dating advice from a fourteen-year-old.

"And you can ditch whatever silly ideas you've got going on in your head and get back to your friends."

Cecily rolled her eyes. "Chill out, Uncle Wyatt. You are old enough to date, you know."

She skipped off back down the embankment, and Wyatt remained where he was until he saw her regroup with Trevor and Lily. Once assured she was safe, he stepped down the bank and headed for the building where he knew Fiona was hiding out.

"What's this?" Fiona asked Cameron Jakowski as she looked over the beach-patrol duty roster. "No Saturday shifts for the next three weeks?"

Cameron, full-time local police officer and part-time life-guard, smiled and shook his head. "That's right."

Fiona settled herself on the other side of the counter. The surf club had two levels, and she was on the bottom floor where the lifeguards hung out when they weren't patrolling the beach. "Are you sure?"

"Positive. Enjoy the time with your daughter."

Of course he knew about Cecily. Cameron was Noah Preston's best friend, just as Callie was her best friend. Callie was married to Noah; it was natural Callie had told her husband about Cecily. And Fiona liked Cameron. They'd been friends since she'd first settled in Crystal Point. They'd even dated a few times. But there was no chemistry between them and their relationship was completely platonic.

"Thank you. You're a gem."

He grabbed her shoulders and squeezed. "I know. So, is Cecily going to Lily's sleepover this Saturday?"

"Absolutely. Now that Cecily and Lily are firm friends, I haven't a chance of keeping them apart."

Cameron laughed and hugged her tighter. At precisely the same time Wyatt rounded the doorway. He stopped, stared and didn't look happy about what he saw. Not one bit.

Chapter Six

There was suddenly enough raw testosterone in the room to make up a football team. Fiona extracted herself from Cameron's brotherly hug and introduced the two men. They shook hands, although Wyatt looked as if he'd rather arm wrestle.

Is he jealous?

Jealously suggested he had deeper feelings. And although she figured he was attracted to her, to imagine it was anything more than that would be foolish.

Once Cameron left to start his rotation on the beach, Wyatt leaned against the counter and crossed his arms. "Old boyfriend?"

Fiona folded her roster into her pocket. "Old friend," she said and offered to show Wyatt around. "The whole top floor is being refurbished after a fire a few months ago," she explained as she motioned for them to head from the office and into one of the three larger rooms out front. "The local residents' committee worked hard to get the funding and the project will take about eight months to finish. The space upstairs is used for courses in self-defense and martial-arts classes. And downstairs for things like first-aid skills training."

"Fiona?"

She walked toward the stairway. "Of course, it's wonderful to have a newly refurbished building for people to come and—"

"Fiona, stop."

She stilled as her foot hit the bottom stair.

"I want to talk to you about what Cecily said."

Fiona didn't feel like dealing with that particular issue. She'd talk with her daughter privately about how they were *not* holding hands. Without Wyatt around to distract her. "I'd rather not."

He didn't let up. "She's just being *Cecily*."

"She thought we were holding hands," Fiona said as awkwardness crept along her skin.

"Actually, we *were* holding hands. But that's not the point. You don't have to worry. She's fine with it."

"I don't want her to be fine with it," she replied sharply. "Or her to think I'm…that I'm…"

"That you're what?"

"Easy," she breathed out.

Wyatt took a step toward her. "Easy?" he echoed. "Because I was holding your hand?"

Fiona dropped her shoulders. "Because I was… Because we were…" She stopped and filled her lungs with air. "Maybe it doesn't make sense to you, but I don't want her to think I would do anything to act on…" She waved a hand between them. "*This.* We kissed and that complicates things."

"If we let it."

"Sure, if we let it. Only, I'm not the kind of person who

gets involved casually. I want Cecily to know I'm someone who makes good choices. Let's face it, I'm at a disadvantage. I've got a lot of ground to make up."

Fiona meant every word. It was important she behaved like a woman her daughter could respect. Lusting after Wyatt didn't put her in that category.

"Cecily is a good judge of character," he said and took a couple of steps upward. "She'll make up her mind about you because of what she knows about you now and not because of something you did when you were fifteen years old. The only person who believes you are defined by that moment, Fiona, is you." He kept walking and reached the landing.

"But the investigator's report—"

"Was a stupid idea," he said and cut her off. "And you were right—it was a piece of paper. It didn't tell me who you were. It didn't tell me that you were honest and kind and clearly a good person. I know you'll do what's right for Cecily."

Fiona's breath caught in her throat. "Thank you," she said and knew she sounded wobbly. "That means a lot."

He nodded. "So, let's get on with this tour you promised me."

She got her attention back on track and climbed the stairs. There was a class in progress on one side of room, which was sectioned off from the remaining space with trestles and painting gear left from the workers who'd been in the building the day before. A small group of elderly women were doing tai chi, and they watched the participants through the glass door.

"This will be a great facility when it's complete. The funding was a lifeline for the building."

"You're frowning," he observed.

"Am I?" She shrugged lightly. "I was thinking how I wished we could get the same windfall for the school where I work."

"You want a place where the kids can practice tai chi?"

She smiled as his lame joke. "We need a new canteen."

"Something wrong with the old one?" he asked and followed as she headed back down the stairs.

"Everything," she replied. "We've applied for funding every year for the last…" She paused and did a mental calculation. "Well, the five years I've been teaching there and another two years before that."

"I gather it's not a high priority."

"Not exactly," she said unhappily. "It has a roof and four walls—apparently that's all the kids need. Mostly it needs renovating—you know, new walls inside, some painting, that sort of thing."

"Have you tried fundraising?"

"For sure," she said as they walked through the front door and back onto the pathway, avoiding a pair of wobbly cyclists. "And we've had some success. But people's purses only stretch so far, and in between saving the foreshore, the seabirds, the mangroves and the local turtle population, there's not a lot left over for one tiny school and its need for a new canteen."

"Kids should have a place to buy food, though." He stopped walking. "Show me."

"Show you? Why?"

"I'm curious. Can you access school grounds on the weekend?"

Fiona nodded. "Of course. It's school break so it won't make any difference. But I don't understand why—"

"Like I said, I'm curious."

She didn't understand his motives but didn't see the harm. "Okay. How about tomorrow? I'll clear it with the principal to make sure. About nine o'clock."

"It's a date," Wyatt said easily and headed for the sand hills and disappeared over the embankment.

* * *

Wyatt picked her up the following morning at three minutes to nine o'clock. Alone. Fiona hopped into his rental car and tried not the think about how her heart was doing a kind of silly fluttering thing as she gave quick directions to the school.

"Where's Cecily?" she asked as she put on her seat belt.

Wyatt slanted her a sideways look. "With Trevor. I'm learning to trust. Impressed?"

"I don't imagine it's something you do easily."

"Trust?" He steered the car around. "Probably not."

She dropped her small tote at her feet. "I suppose it's natural to be wary after you've been, you know…"

"Cheated on?"

Fiona nodded. "Did you suspect it? I mean, before—"

"Before I caught her in bed with someone else? No."

She didn't bother to hide her distaste. Perhaps it was a leftover hang-up from all the years she spent on the road with Shayne, watching her mother fall into the arms of one cowboy after another, many of them married men with families. It was a behavior she'd vowed to never emulate. And then Jamie Corbett came along and took what she wasn't prepared to give.

"We're not all like that," she said and quickly realized how intimate it sounded.

"I know," he replied lightly. "It takes two people to cheat."

"Monogamy doesn't seem like much of a price if you really love someone."

He looked at her. "*If* you love someone? Exactly. I'll probably thank Yvette one day."

Yvette? It was a fancy-sounding name. Fiona would bet her frayed sneakers that his ex-fiancée was beautiful. She suddenly wished she'd done something stupidly female like slap on a little makeup that morning. Or at least deck herself out in new jeans instead of the old favorites that fit like a glove but were older than Methuselah.

"Do you still see her?"

Sheesh...isn't that the dumbest, most painfully obvious question ever uttered?

Thankfully they pulled up in front of the school before Fiona had to decide if he was grinning. She opened the door as swiftly as she could and grabbed her bag.

"The gate is over—"

Wyatt looked at her over the top of the vehicle. "I don't see Yvette," he said. "I'm not seeing anyone. Just so you know."

"I do know," she said quickly and shut the door. "Cecily told me. I mean, I'm sure there are many women who would want to go out with you." Fiona stopped and cringed as heat crept over her skin and up her neck. "I only meant that if you were seeing someone you wouldn't have...you know..."

"Kissed you?" He was grinning.

She ignored his words and waved an arm toward the school. "We're here."

"Let's take a look."

Fifteen minutes later, Wyatt stepped back from the doorway leading into the canteen area and looked up toward the roof.

"Well, it needs rebuilding, that's for sure."

Fiona's hopes sank. "Really? Which means thousands of dollars, right?"

"Tens of thousands."

Her eyes popped wide. "But it looks almost structurally sound."

"Termites," he explained. "Which have compromised the building's structural integrity. It needs to be pulled down. No decent builder would attempt renovation."

Fiona sank onto one of the low lunch seats underneath a

shelter. Designed for the first graders, the position forced her knees up almost to her chin. "Well, that's that, then."

Wyatt swiveled on his heels. "Not necessarily."

She looked up. "Without funding, we couldn't possibly afford to rebuild."

He stepped back and shrugged in a way that made her stare at his shoulders and think how well he pulled off the whole jeans-and-white-T-shirt thing. "You could with some help."

"Yeah, but as I said yesterday, there are so many different causes and our school—"

"I'll help you," he said, cutting her off.

Fiona jumped to her feet. "Why would you want to do that?"

He looked toward the building for a moment. "Because you... Because the school needs a new building. And because I'd like to."

"Wyatt, I couldn't possibly let you—"

"You talk with whoever you need to and I'll get plans drawn up. Harper's has a charity fund, and helping places like your school is exactly what the fund is for. My company will supply all the materials, and from this end you can work your magic and organize the contract labor."

"My magic?" she echoed, feeling more than a little spun out by his suggestion.

"Yeah," he said and smiled. "I'm sure you'll be able to coax a few volunteers."

Fiona planted her hands on her hips. "Why are you doing this?"

"Because the kids need a canteen," he replied. "And I need something to do for the next two weeks."

Was he so bored? It miffed her a bit. This was her home. Did he find the place so lacking? *Does he find me lacking?* Of course he did. She'd never been able to hold any man's attention. Why would Wyatt be any different? *Not that I actually want his attention.*

"Sure," she replied, not one to pass up such an offer. The school did need a new building. Refusing help would be foolish. "I'll have to speak with Annette Brewer, the principal. But I'm certain she'll be only too happy to accept your generosity."

"Good. Once we get started with plans and submit for council approval, I reckon it will be about four months and you'll have a new canteen for your kids."

Fiona drew in some air. "Thank you, Wyatt. We should get going," she suggested, pushing back her budding irritation because he might be bored with her, and her growing attraction for him. "By the way, I promised Cecily I'd take her shopping tomorrow for our Christmas-in-July celebration."

They walked past the administration block in step with one another.

"No socks."

She snapped her head sideways. "Socks?"

"From Cecily," he replied. "No socks, ties or, heaven forbid, handkerchiefs."

Fiona laughed and it urged her a little away from her bad mood. "The perfect gift for the man who has everything."

"Not everything," he corrected.

They were at the car and she allowed him to open her door. "Is there anything you'd like?" she asked and felt the heat rise up between them the moment the words left her mouth.

Wyatt moved closer, and Fiona pushed back against the door. "Anything?"

"Yes. To ease your boredom maybe?"

"My what?"

"Isn't that why you want to help out here?" she asked. "Because you're bored?"

He reached across and looped a lock of her hair between

his fingers. "Ah, Fiona, you know, you're killing me," he said softly and touched her cheek. "I'm not bored...I'm frustrated as hell."

"Sorry." Fiona shuddered out a breath. His fingertips, warm against her skin, curved over her jaw and cupped her chin.

"Me, too." His thumb traced her bottom lip. "Sorry, I can't stop thinking about kissing you again. Or stop imagining what it would be like to—"

A car passed and beeped loudly. Fiona recognized Cameron's police patrol vehicle immediately and ducked sideways. "Please," she said as the car traveled up the road. "Someone could see and I..." She stopped and straightened. "Please, take me back."

He pulled back instantly. "Of course."

When they were both in the car, Fiona summoned the gumption to say what was on her mind. There was no point in putting it off. It had to be said. "Wyatt, I can't be alone with you like this," she admitted and felt her heart tighten. It *was* right to say. But it hurt. It hurt so much. "I'm not going to get involved with you any more than I already am. It's blurring... the reason you're here—and Cecily. I have to stay focused. I won't make this situation about myself. I have a chance to get back something I thought I'd lost, and I don't want to risk that. Not for anything."

Not even for you.

He took a moment, then spoke. "It won't happen again."

"That's what we said yesterday," she said on a sigh. "You know, I've been alone most of my life. Even when I lived with my uncle, I was alone. He tried, but most days I felt as though I lived in this singular vacuum, apart from everyone and everything. And now..." She paused, eyes down, head bent. "Now, for the first time in a long time, I don't feel alone. And I'm not sure if it's because of Cecily...or because of you."

"Fiona, I—"

"Let me finish, please," she protested and raised her hands before dropping them back into her lap. "There's no point in whitewashing this. The truth is, I don't want to find that at the end of these few weeks I have a whole lot of…feelings. I don't want to fall for you. I don't want to fall for anyone. I just want a chance to be what Cecily needs me to be. I love my daughter," she said. "And she's all I have space inside myself for."

She noticed he gripped the steering wheel. "I'll take you back."

As he started the ignition and eased the car onto the road, she knew she'd made her point. In two and a half weeks, he'd be gone. After that, she figured Cecily would commute during holidays to visit. He wouldn't have to return to Crystal Point again.

The realization didn't settle the discontent in her heart. Or the knowledge she was in deep. Way deep.

"So, he's building the school canteen himself?"

Fiona sat lotus-style on her sofa and nodded to her friend. Callie dipped a spoon into a tub of vanilla ice cream topped with chocolate sauce and Oreo cookies and looked at her after she'd asked the question.

"His company is supplying the funds for plans and materials," Fiona replied. "We're organizing the labor from this end."

"And he's doing this because…?" M.J. asked as she grabbed a spoon and dug into her own tub of chocolate-mint.

Fiona shrugged and ignored the way her stomach rolled. Thinking about Wyatt had been off her agenda for two days. She wasn't about to put him back on it. "To help the school."

"Or to get into your good books?" Callie suggested with raised brows.

"Or your pants?" M.J. offered with a delightful squeal.

Callie tossed a cushion at her sister-in-law. "Behave," she admonished playfully.

Fiona did her best impression of a poker face. "He wants something to do, that's all. I suspect he's bored since Cecily and I are together most days."

"I like the whole panty concept better," M.J. said and scooped a mouthful of ice cream. "Much more exciting."

"Will you let up?" Evie scolded her sister and dipped an Oreo into ice-cold milk.

M.J. smiled and raised her provocative brows. "Although, if you are going to toss your panties, who better than that gorgeous man to catch them?"

It was Friday night and her friends had abandoned their pottery class at Evie's studio for an evening at Fiona's. Cecily, Lily and another friend were in the guest bedroom playing Wii karaoke and shoving down copious amount of soda, potato chips and cold pizza.

"I think it's admirable that he wants to help. So, instead of questioning his motives, accept it as an act of goodwill," Evie said. She appeared to be the only one not romanticizing the whole situation. And Fiona needed an ally tonight.

"Exactly," Fiona managed to squeak out, still reeling from the whole tossed-panties idea.

"He's taken over my office," Evie said as she dipped another cookie. "Not that I mind, of course, if it means the school will benefit. But he doesn't talk much. Seems like a man with a lot on his mind."

Fiona offered a smile, which didn't quite cut the mark, and Callie pushed herself off the sofa. "Let's go and make some more tea," her friend suggested.

She nodded and followed her friend down the hallway. Once they reached the kitchen, Callie turned. "Do you like him?" she asked.

Fiona stepped back. "Like him? If you mean—"

"You know exactly who I mean. And what I mean."

She didn't bother to deny it. "Sure. I like him."

"And he likes you, right?"

"I guess."

Callie's blue eyes widened. "But you're avoiding him?"

She shrugged. "We're keeping it real."

"What does that mean?"

"The situation," Fiona replied. "Why he's here. Why Cecily's here. I want to have a relationship with my daughter."

"Who says you can't have both?"

"I say." She grabbed hold of the counter. "I never get the guy, Callie. I always get the let's-be-friends speech at the end of it. And when it's done and dusted, I never speak with them again because I'm so humiliated. I don't want that to happen here. I won't let it. Do I like him? Yes. Do I want him? Yes. But I won't get wrapped up in some romantic notion…not when there's so much at stake."

"Cecily?"

She nodded. "Loving a child…it's life-altering."

"Yes," Callie said and watched her. "But so is loving a man."

She didn't know that. Her few and brief relationships had been infatuations, nothing more. And when over they'd left her what? Not heartbroken. Not anything really. It kept her safe, whole. Becoming unhinged, being *all* feelings. She thought she wanted it, but now, when looking directly into the face of those kinds of feelings, Fiona was terrified.

She drew in a breath, grappling for a strength she didn't quite feel. "I am not going to fall in love with Wyatt Harper."

I'm not…

On Saturday morning, Wyatt opened his emails and took a call from Glynis, who worked through his request to incorporate the Crystal Point School as a recipient of the Harper charity fund. He also emailed his sister Ellen, who was on the board, and asked her to push the request through quickly. Once the correct paperwork was filed and the board in agreement, he could take steps to submit the building plans through council. He'd forgotten how much he liked creating plans. Since being drafted into Harper's only two years after graduating from college, he hadn't had much use for his architecture degree. His father's second heart attack had changed Wyatt's plan to work outside of the family business for a few years before taking over the reins of the company.

But drawing up the plans for the small school building was satisfying and it shifted his mind off other things.

Fiona...

He hadn't seen her for three days, although he got daily updates from Cecily about their activities—from shopping to horse riding to a girls' night in with a group of friends. His niece was happier than she'd been for a long time. Maybe ever.

It was strange how that realization didn't bring up a whole lot of loyalty issues. He was usually fiercely protective of his family. But his loyalties were conflicted. He liked Fiona. And his attraction for her had grown from a slow-burning awareness to a fierce need.

And she wasn't giving him the time of day.

It stung. Even though he understood her motives. She was right. Getting involved was out of the question. But logic, once a strong ally in his organized life, had deserted him. He didn't feel the least bit logical when it came to Fiona. Because his desire for her, which a week ago, he was convinced, had been about physical attraction and sex, had somehow morphed into something else. Something deeper.

He liked her. And he...missed her.

Idiot.

She was messing with his head. He *never* got this way.

Not even Yvette had distracted him so much. Why was that? Why did someone he'd known mere weeks twist his insides like a pretzel? And why the hell was she ignoring him? Okay, so she didn't want to get involved. He didn't, either, did he?

Except all he could think about was seeing her again.

Chapter Seven

"So, how come you don't have a boyfriend?"

Fiona was in the kitchen making lasagna for her daughter's sleepover at Lily's house when Cecily popped her head into the room with Muffin in her arms and asked the question.

"What?"

"A boyfriend?" her daughter asked, moving into the room. "It's just that you're really pretty and a nice person—you *should* have a boyfriend."

Fiona placed the cheese grater on the countertop. Talks about boyfriends were part of being a parent but she wasn't exactly prepared for them. Plus, she'd imagined the talk would be about her daughter's dating life, not her own. "It's not that simple. I haven't met anyone I liked for a while."

Cecily looked at her and smiled. "Do you like Uncle Wyatt?"

The million-dollar question. And one she should have expected. "Well, I—"

"I mean, I know you like him," Cecily said, cutting her off as she placed Muffin on the floor. "But do you *like* him?"

Fiona sucked in a breath, fought back her embarrassment and faced her daughter. "Where's this all coming from?"

Cecily shrugged again, less enthusiastic this time, and pulled out a chair. When she slumped into it, Fiona knew her daughter had something big on her mind. In the brief time she'd known Cecily, Fiona had been in awe of her happy-go-lucky personality and constant smiles. But in the past couple of days, as their relationship had developed, she'd observed something else. A mother's instinct perhaps. She wasn't sure. But there was something going on with her.

"I don't know," she said after a moment. She rested her elbows on the table and propped her chin in her palm. "I only thought it would be sort of nice if you guys liked each other in that way."

That way? The problem was Fiona did like Wyatt in *that* way. Very much. But anything happening between them was out of the question. She'd made her resolve very clear.

"We've become friends," she said carefully. "And we both agree that you are what's important at the moment."

Cecily's eyes widened and she gave a little smile. "So, if it's all about me, I should get what I want, right?"

Fiona stilled. "Er—that depends on what it is."

"I want what I used to have," she said and looked as though she were doing her best to sound cheerful. "Look, don't get me wrong, Nan and Pop are great and I love them a lot. But they're my *grandparents* and they're old. I know they are pretty cool for their age, but Pop's already had a couple of heart attacks and what if…what if they…die soon?"

Fiona's heart surged. "Is that what you're afraid will happen?"

"I guess." She nodded and let out a heavy sigh. "I know Uncle Wyatt is my legal guardian, and he tries to spend time with me when he can. But he's busy and has to run the company and can only get to Waradoon on the weekends. I just thought that if he got, you know, married or something, then it would be like it was when my parents were alive. Like a proper family."

Her words cut through Fiona like a blade. A proper family? How often had she longed for that when she was a child? Even now, in her deepest heart, the longing remained. And her daughter, who had endured so much loss in her short life, was now echoing her own secret wish.

"There are all kinds of families and each one is unique." She took the seat next to Cecily and grasped her hand. "Your grandparents love you. As does your uncle, and I'm sure your aunts feel the same. And I love you."

Cecily's bright blue-gray eyes glittered. "I know. I'm grateful for everyone caring about me, really I am. But having a mother and father and being together all the time…that's how it should be. Even when I knew my parents weren't happy together sometimes, at least we were together. Being together is what's important."

Fiona caught the tremor in Cecily's voice. It wasn't the first time her daughter had intimated that Jim and Karen Todd's relationship had been anything other than perfect. But all marriages went through challenging times, didn't they?

"They fought," Cecily said quietly, as though unsure if she should be saying anything about it. "Not always. I wasn't supposed to know. But I heard them sometimes. I'd hear my mother crying and Dad kept saying he was sorry all the time. And then it sort of got better. Except then they died."

Fiona squeezed her hand. "It's normal to want things that make you feel safe."

"I guess. I just don't want Uncle Wyatt to marry someone I don't like," she said, sounding every one of her fourteen years. "Like what's-her-name."

Fiona was pretty sure Cecily knew exactly what the other woman's name was, and smiled to herself. "Well, unfortunately, I don't think you get a say in who he marries."

Neither do I.

"But if he married you, we'd be a real family."

Marry Wyatt? Sweet heaven. Despite the crazy fluttering in her belly, Fiona knew she had to put a halt to Cecily's active imagination. "We're not getting married. We're not in love. And that's the only reason why two people should get married."

It sounded good. It sounded as if she meant every word. But in her head it sounded too good. *I'm trying too hard here.*

"So, let's get the lasagna cooked for this sleepover and I'll drop you at Lily's."

Cecily smiled. "Sure. And thanks, Fiona—thanks for listening."

"Anytime," she said and hugged her as they stood.

Maybe I'll get this mothering thing right after all.

Wyatt pulled the car outside Fiona's at precisely three minutes to seven. He'd had five hours to figure out what he was doing and came up with zilch.

I shouldn't be here.

Too late to back out now, he thought as he walked up the driveway. He heard her little dog bark. The door opened before he made it to the bottom step.

She looked beautiful.

So lovely he could hardly draw breath, which seemed to have become an all-too-frequent reaction when he was within six feet of her. She wore a long white skirt and soft green sweater scooped out wide over her shoulders. The awareness quickly turned into an all-out surge of raw hunger so fierce he could barely swallow.

Great start.

"Wyatt?"

"Hi," he said and took the steps. "Did Cecily get to her party okay?"

"Yes. What's that?"

He held up the wine bottle in his hand. "From a local winery a short stretch from Waradoon."

She looked at him and frowned. "What are you doing here?"

"I thought…I thought we could talk."

"Talk?"

She looked about as convinced of that as he did. "Yeah. I haven't seen you for a while and figured we needed to touch base about Cecily."

Her eyes widened. "Is something wrong? Have I done something to—"

"Nothing's wrong," he assured her. "I just wanted to talk."

Her expression went from concern to suspicion. "At night, alone and with a bottle of wine?" One brow came up. "Do you really think that's a good idea?"

"Probably not." He let out a heavy breath. She didn't want him on her doorstep. He should have had more sense. "You're right. I'll go."

"It's okay," she said quickly and moved back through the door. "You're here now, so you may as well come inside."

"Are you sure?"

She nodded and Wyatt followed her through the door. He was immediately drawn into the unique warmth of her little house. The textured shabby-chic furniture, paisley throws and craftwork dotted around the living room were far removed from the contemporary lines of his city apartment or the country charm of Waradoon. But something about the place had an unusual calming effect.

The dog shuffled around his feet for a moment and then scurried into her wicker basket in the corner of the room.

"I'll get glasses."

She disappeared down the hall and Wyatt let out a breath. *Keep your head.* He cruised around the room for a moment and lingered by a cabinet along one wall. There were photographs in frames—of her horse and her friends. He searched for anyone who looked like family. It made him think of the big staircase at Waradoon and the gallery of photographs lining the walls that displayed generations of Harpers.

"I'd like to get one of Cecily."

She was behind him, holding glasses and a corkscrew. "Of course," he said and took the items from her. "I can take some of you together if you like?"

"Yes, I would like that."

"Is that your mother?" he asked when he spotted a faded picture stuck into the corner of a larger frame.

She stepped closer. "Yes. That's Shayne."

"Shayne?"

"She liked me to call her by her first name. It made it easier for her."

"Easier to what?" he asked and opened the wine.

Fiona stared at the photograph for a moment. "To pick up," she said as she turned away and sat on an overstuffed love seat in the corner. "Didn't you get that about her from your investigation?" she asked and held out the glasses.

"I was more interested in you." *And still am.*

After a moment, Fiona spoke. "She was a buckle bunny."

Wyatt stilled. "A what?"

She said it again. "A woman who follows the rodeo circuit," she explained. "Not a pretty story."

Wyatt half filled their glasses and sat on the sofa. Miles away from her. Although he felt the vibration coming off her skin. "And a hard one to tell?"

She shrugged. "I guess, like all sad childhood stories.

Shayne was kind of lost. Unfortunately she dragged me through her lost world for many years."

"Before you went to live with your uncle?"

"When I was expecting Cecily."

"And your mother died a few weeks later."

"Yes, in a railway-crossing accident. She was an addict anyway…which probably would have killed her if the train hadn't."

Wyatt didn't bother to hide his surprise.

"Does that sound harsh?" she asked and sipped her wine. "Maybe it does. She was my mother, but I was rarely *mothered,* if that makes sense. She drank a lot, used drugs when she could get her hands on them, drifted from one place to the next looking for someone…some man to hold on to. I felt alone most of the time."

He stretched back into the seat and rested the wineglass on the arm. "And Cecily's father?"

Shutters came up. "I don't want to talk about that."

"You'll have to at some point."

"Why?" she queried. "It's in the past. You said I wasn't defined by my past."

"I know what I said. I meant because Cecily will want to know."

She drew in a heavy breath. "I just don't want to dredge up a whole lot of painful stuff that really—"

"Painful?" he echoed quietly and looked directly into her eyes. "What happened to you, Fiona? You're trying so hard to not talk about it."

Her eyes were bright. "What I'm *trying* to do is look to the future and not dwell on the past. I want to concentrate on this short amount of time I have with Cecily. But if you're concerned about the way I'm handling things with her, I would—"

"Actually, for someone who had an emotionally absent

mother, you're quite remarkable with Cecily." Wyatt propped his glass on a side table. "In fact, I've never seen her happier. I'm not about to pull her out from under you, Fiona. So relax."

"Relax? Around you?" She gave a brittle laugh. "You can't be serious. I've never been less relaxed in my life."

Wyatt shrugged. "If it's any consolation, I feel the same way."

"Then why are you here?" she asked.

"Because I wanted to see you. Without Cecily. Without Evie. Without any one of your numerous friends standing guard."

Wyatt got to his feet and stared out the window. She wished she knew what he was thinking. His broad shoulders looked tense and she fought the urge to go to him. It was better this way. Better to stay strong.

"We agreed we wouldn't do anything."

He turned back toward her. "I know that. Which doesn't mean I have to like it."

Fiona swallowed hard. She didn't like it, either. But wasn't about to admit that. She needed to stay grounded and keep her head. Her relationship with Cecily depended on it.

"You know, we've been thrown together because of the situation with Cecily. I'm not so naive that I'd think for one minute you'd be interested in me in other circumstances."

Annoyance sharpened his expression. "You think I'm attracted to you because it's convenient?"

"Well, I—"

"Believe me, Fiona, for the past few days it has felt damned inconvenient."

Fiona shot up from her seat and wobbled on her heels. "Well, it hasn't exactly been a picnic for me, either!"

The room filled with heat, swirling around, catching her skin, her blood and her quaking bones. It took about three seconds to register Wyatt's expression as it changed from irritation to raw desire. There was no denying it. And Fiona couldn't deny it, either. She wanted him. It was clear he wanted her, too.

"Cecily wants you to get married," she said, trying to grasp on to some sense, some way of holding off the feelings running riot through her body, and hoping it would have the effect of a bucket of cold water over the rising desire whirling between them.

He raised a brow. "To whom?"

"To someone she likes. She wants parents again—a mother and a father."

"I suppose that's to be expected." He moved across the room. "She had that before. It makes sense she'd want it again."

Fiona stepped back and her legs collided with the love seat. "She said...she said something today. She said your sister and her husband weren't completely happy."

He looked at her sharply for a second and then shrugged. "They had some problems."

"What kind of problems?"

Wyatt moved around the coffee table and grabbed her hand. "What does it matter?"

"Cecily said—"

"It was nothing," he said and threaded their fingers. "Enough about them."

He pulled her toward him and she went without protest. Some faraway voice told her to resist, but the echo quickly faded as he drew her against him. "Wyatt, I—"

"And enough talk," he said gently. "I'd rather kiss you."

"We said we wouldn't."

"Yeah...but that promise isn't working out so well for me. Is it for you?"

Fiona shook her head. "Not so far."

"If you want me to go, I'll go. If you want me to stop, I'll stop."

She moved against him and curved an arm up to his shoulder. "I don't want you to go," she breathed. "And I don't want you to stop."

He smiled, dipped his head and captured her lips. Fiona opened her mouth and gave herself up to his possession. Heat fueled her blood, and she grasped his shoulders to steady her weakening limbs. Wyatt's kiss was soft and seductive, and as he slanted his mouth over hers, she leaned into his embrace. Every ounce of longing in her heart rose up, and she knew, without a doubt, that what she was feeling was more than just desire. All her plans not to fall for Wyatt deserted her the moment he groaned against her lips and whispered how much he wanted her.

They didn't make it to her bedroom. She urged him backward to the sofa, still kissing, still feeling and wanting like she'd never wanted before. The tiny voice in the back of her mind telling her to stop before things went too far became a distant echo. Recriminations could come later. The moment was now. And for once, she longed to live in the moment.

He laid her gently on the big sofa, knelt beside her and kissed her again. When he trailed his mouth from her lips to the incredibly sensitive spot below her ear, Fiona shuddered. She grasped his shoulders and felt the heat of his mouth against her collarbone and moaned when his tongue trailed across her skin. He pushed the sweater off her shoulder and kissed her there, and then down toward the rise of her breast. His hand splayed over her rib cage and beneath the sweater, and he drew tiny circles with his fingertips. Fiona sighed with pleasure and moved her hands over his shoulders and down his arms. His biceps were solid, strong, and suddenly it occurred to her that everything about Wyatt was strong. His character, his integrity, his very self. *That's why I'm falling.*

It wasn't only that his touch made her come alive. Without knowing how, Fiona's feelings surged from physical desire to a raw emotional need.

She tugged at his shirt and he quickly chucked it over his head. His chest was so well cut Fiona swallowed hard before she traced her hands over the defined muscles. He trembled when she touched him, and her growing feelings rose to the surface. She might have blurted it out had he not possessed her lips in a searing, drugging kiss.

His hands were suddenly impatient and he pushed her sweater up. The filmy bra she wore did little to hide her pebbled nipples, and when his mouth closed over one, she arched her back. Pleasure arrowed downward in a rush and she gripped his hips, looping her fingers around the band of his jeans. She was all impatience, all need, all want. Wyatt smiled as he kissed her. It didn't take long for him to ease her sweater off and flick the two hooks holding her bra. Topless, Fiona fought the urge to cover herself. But there was no need for coyness. Wyatt clearly liked what he saw and touched her breasts again, caressing her with skillful seduction. Her nipples ached for him and he gently flicked one tight bud with his tongue while he pushed her skirt over her hips. Within seconds the garment was on the floor. Her briefs quickly followed.

Naked beneath his penetrating gaze, Fiona forgot her usual insecurities. A man didn't fake that kind of desire. The freckles felt like sun kisses; the faded stretch marks on her belly from when her teenage body had carried a child didn't fill her with the usual modesty. Wyatt knew her story. He knew her.

"You're so lovely," he said as he stood and kicked off his shoes. Jeans and boxer briefs followed.

Mesmerized by the sheer magnitude of his beauty and arousal, Fiona pressed back against the sofa and raised her arms in clear invitation. He took a second to extract something from his jeans, and she squashed a frown back when he placed a condom on the table. The idea that he'd prepared for this and that he might have expected it created a little resentment, a little uncertainty. But then she remembered how much she wanted him, despite her feeble denials over the previous week, and all her doubts were forgotten.

He lay beside her, and Fiona was eternally grateful she had a big couch. She'd never sit on it again without remembering how it felt to have Wyatt pressed intimately against her. He kissed her hotly and she returned each kiss, savoring the taste of him and the feel of his tongue wrapped around hers. Fiona couldn't get enough of him. His skin, like silk stretched over hot steel, was divine beneath her fingertips. He touched her breasts, her hips, her belly and lower to where she screamed to be touched. His fingers worked magic, sending her wild and quickly to the brink. When she could take no more, when she felt herself falling, Fiona found her voice.

"Wyatt…now…please."

He didn't stop. "Not yet," he whispered against her mouth. "I want you to come apart."

"But you—"

He silenced her with a kiss and touched her with gentle intimacy, touched her like no other man ever had. As if he knew, somehow, what she longed for, what she needed. The pressure built, taking her higher, making her fly. When her body exploded in a burst of incandescent pleasure, he held her through it, kissing her, stroking her over and over as the pulsing waves receded and she returned to earth.

When she could breathe again, Fiona looked into his eyes and with a tiny smile reached out a hand and grabbed the condom. She'd never been the seductive type. Her lingering hang-ups about what happened when she was fifteen whirled around her head for a moment. She'd taken sex back a long time ago, refusing to allow one person's brutality to hold her hostage for the rest of her life. But being with Wyatt made her realize she had been holding back. Waiting for this. Waiting for him. As she ripped the foil packet with her teeth and watched his expression darken with desire, Fiona felt sexier than she ever had in her life.

He grinned and took the condom. Seconds later he moved over her. Fiona gripped his shoulders and didn't waver from his gaze as he entered her slowly. There was nothing hasty about Wyatt. He took his time, watching her as she shifted her body to accommodate him inside her in the most intimate way possible. It felt right. It felt real. When he moved, stars exploded behind her eyes and she held on tight, feeling more a part of him than she ever had of anyone.

"Wyatt...I..."

"I know," he said against her lips as they moved together. "I know."

It was like another world, a world she'd only ever dreamed of. A world where she was desired so completely, so profoundly, nothing but wanting and pleasure and raw hunger existed. And she was in that world, driven by longing, by the relentless need to feel him everywhere and in every way imaginable. His skin, his kiss, his breath...everything reached her, everything made her want him more.

The tension built, the rhythm became a mutual ride as they moved together, as one, joined by more than bodies. Fiona experienced pleasure so incredibly acute she shook with emotion as she climaxed. When he followed moments later, she held on, giving, taking and holding him with all that lay in her heart as he shuddered against her.

When their breathing returned to something resembling normal, and still taking all his weight on his elbows, Wyatt looked down into her face.

"Are you all right?"

She managed to nod and whispered, "Yes."

"Regrets?"

"Right now?" She smiled and touched his face. "No. Later...probably."

He drew in a heavy breath. "Well, that's honest at least. I think you're probably the most sincere woman I've ever met."

It was a lovely compliment, and because her emotions were jumping all over the place, she couldn't help the tears that filled her eyes. "Thank you."

He smiled gently and drew away from her. "Let's go to bed."

"Bed?" She shifted on the sofa, suddenly conscious of her nakedness and Wyatt's unmistakably semi-aroused state. "Oh, I thought..."

He stood up, reached for her hand and urged her to her feet. "You thought what? That we were done?" He gave a sexy laugh and pulled her close. "Oh, no, we're not done."

Fiona smiled and her heart rolled over. And she knew, at that moment, that she was completely and irrevocably in love with Wyatt Harper.

Chapter Eight

Morning-afters were never easy. And Fiona wasn't looking forward to this one.

She'd left Wyatt asleep in her bed. They'd made love again at dawn, and he'd wrung every ounce of pleasure from her. Physically spent, she'd dozed for an hour and woke when Muffin jumped up on her side of the bed. Wyatt hadn't stirred. She'd slipped out of bed, pushed her arms through a soft oversize T-shirt and lingered in the doorway for a moment. He slept on his stomach, one arm outstretched, and his dark hair was a stark contrast against the white pillow. She was tempted to crawl back into bed and trace her fingers up and down his smooth skin.

Instead she took a quick shower and then padded down the hall into the kitchen, fed the dog and cranked up the coffee machine.

Well, I've gone and done it now.

She pressed her hips against the countertop and let out a

heavy breath. Okay, so they'd had sex. And she'd realized she was in love with him. But in the cold light of morning, clarity returned. Loving him was one thing…but imagining he loved her in return was something else altogether. Love hadn't rated a mention during the past twelve hours. She certainly wasn't about to announce her newly realized feelings.

Fiona poured herself a cup of coffee, took a long drink and waited for the caffeine to kick in.

It didn't help much. With Wyatt asleep down the hall, her body aching in places she'd forgotten could ache and her mind reeling with the knowledge she had fallen in love with a man she hardly knew, Fiona needed more than a double espresso to calm her nerves.

She pushed the coffee aside and sat down.

So, think. Think hard. And think quickly. Because he's not going to stay asleep forever. And I'll have to talk to him.

But think what? That it was a onetime thing? A quick roll in the hay? Physical attraction gone wild. A one-night stand?

Ouch.

Fiona didn't do one-nighters. Ever. She'd seen firsthand the damage indiscriminate sex could cause. Shayne's example was burned into her memory bank. Her head felt as if it would explode when she considered the enormity of what she'd done. *Some good example I am for my daughter.*

She didn't want Cecily to think she was…what? A flake like Shayne? She'd told Wyatt she didn't want her daughter to think she was easy. But it was more than that. She'd missed out on fourteen years. Years where Cecily had managed quite effectively without her. Years where she'd had near-perfect parents. And a perfect mother.

She couldn't compete with that. She didn't want to be Karen Todd. She could only be herself. More importantly, a version of herself whom Cecily could respect. Fiona had to show her daughter she was reliable, dependable…worthy.

And a one-night stand with Wyatt didn't make her fit into that category.

Despite Cecily's eagerness to get them together, Fiona knew it was a fantasy. He'd be gone in two weeks and Cecily would be gone with him. Of course, she'd still see her daughter during school breaks. But for Wyatt…it would be a holiday fling at best. Casual, noncommitted sex between two people attracted to one another. In other circumstances she might have been okay with that. She might have accepted whatever she could have of Wyatt even if only for a short time. But not with Cecily stuck in the middle.

When she heard the shower hiss a few moments later, she got to her feet, pulled out the makings of breakfast from the refrigerator and grabbed a fresh mug. Ten minutes later Wyatt walked into the kitchen. Jeans unbuttoned at the fly, bare chest, bare feet, hair damp and a towel tossed over one shoulder—he looked so good her knees wobbled.

"Coffee?" she asked as she grabbed a skillet from its hanging spot above the stove top.

"Sure," he said as he came to the other side of the bench. He rubbed a hand over his chin. "I need to shave."

Fiona barely dared to look at him. The faint stubble across his jaw was too sexy for words. And she remembered how the gentle abrasion had felt across her skin as he'd trailed kisses over every inch of her body. Too good.

"Are you hungry?" she asked as she pushed a mug across the bench.

He looked her over and grinned. "I guess we did forget to eat last night."

"I'll make breakfast now," she said so cheerfully her ears hurt.

Wyatt took the coffee. "I swiped a towel. Hope you don't mind."

She smiled and wondered if her jaw would stick in that position. "Fine. How do you like your eggs?"

"Fried, scrambled." He shrugged. "Whatever."

Scrambled like my brain. "Omelet it is," she said and began cracking eggs into a bowl.

"Can I help?" he asked.

She pointed to the cutlery draw. "You can set the table."

"Sure." He got the job done quickly and came back around to the counter. "You like to cook?"

"I guess," she replied. "I like to make cakes. Sometimes I make them and take them over to Callie's. The kids always go crazy for my fudge brownies."

"I'm sure they do."

Oh, Lord, it sounded so sickly sweet, and if they were any more excruciatingly polite, Fiona's teeth would fall out. "Actually, my baking's not the best, but the kids don't seem to care."

Fiona could feel the heat of his gaze on her. The thin cotton T-shirt seemed way more provocative in the cold light of day—especially considering she wore nothing underneath. She remembered her discarded bra and briefs still on the floor in the living room and wished she'd shown the sense to snatch them up. Staring at his bare chest wasn't helping, either.

"Do you need help with anything else?"

She shook her head. "I'm good," she said and began whisking eggs.

He put his mug aside and braced his hands on the counter. "So, are we going to have the postmortem now or after we eat?"

Fiona stopped whisking. "After," she said quietly and returned to the task. "Or not at all."

"We'll probably have to at some point."

She shrugged. "It is what it is."

"And what's that?"

Fiona felt his stare through to her bones. "You tell me… You're the one who came here with a condom in your pocket."

Wyatt rocked back on his heels. She sounded mad. Her cheeks were pink, her eyes as sharp as daggers. Okay, so she *was* mad. "Let me get this straight—you're angry because I brought protection?"

She dropped the utensil in her hand. "I'm not angry."

"No? So you just *look* like you want to whack me over the head with a frying pan?"

She glared at him, but he was relieved when he caught a little smile crinkling her lovely mouth. Of course, thinking about her mouth quickly crammed his head with memories of exactly what she'd done with it the night before. His libido spiked and wasn't helped one bit when she moved across the kitchen and the thin T-shirt, which only just reached her thighs, shimmied over her delightfully curvy bottom.

He cleared his throat and tried not to think about how much he wanted her again. They had to talk first. "Fiona?"

"I'm not angry," she said again. "I'm not anything. Honestly, I'm not exactly sure what I'm feeling at this point."

Wyatt appreciated her truth. "Look, I didn't come here last night just for…" He stopped himself from calling it *sex*. Because being with Fiona had felt way different from any sex he'd ever had before. "Let me try that again. I wanted to see you. Did I want to make love to you? Yes. Was that the only reason I was here? No. I like you, Fiona. That's why I'm here."

It sounded lukewarm at best, and Wyatt wasn't surprised that she looked as if she wished a great big hole would open up beneath his feet and swallow him.

But he wasn't about to admit to anything else. Or even consider anything else. He'd jumped quickly into his last relationship and it had ended in disaster. He'd met and proposed to Yvette within months. He wasn't about to do that again anytime soon. Whatever happened with Fiona, Wyatt knew now wasn't the time for any kind of declaration about feelings.

"What I'm trying to say is—"

"It's okay," she said, cutting him off as she banged the skillet. "I get it."

She looked so lovely with her hair curling around her face and her cheeks ablaze with color. Wyatt moved behind her. "Fiona, please turn around."

She stilled, dropped the skillet and turned. "Yes?"

Wyatt propped an arm on either side of her. "I'm not entirely sure what's going on in that beautiful head of yours."

She looked up and he noticed a pinkish mark on her neck. Not exactly a love bite, but close enough. The scent of her shampoo assailed his senses and kicked warmth through his blood. No one had ever had such a strong effect on his libido. She noticed the shifting mood and her blue-gray eyes shadowed with a sexy haze. Wyatt wrapped his arms around her and urged her close, then ran his hands down her hips and over her lovely behind. The moment he got a handful of bare skin and realized she was naked beneath the thin T-shirt, his building desire leaped forward like a racehorse at the starting gate.

When she dropped her forehead against his chest, he experienced a sharp and uncharacteristic pain behind his ribs. He kissed the top of her head, and she quickly shifted position and offered her lips to him. Wyatt took her mouth with such possessiveness he startled himself for a second. When he moved to pull back, Fiona pushed forward. She returned the kiss in the kind of hot, heady way he was becoming used to. She tugged at his fly and shoved his jeans down his hips, and he smiled at her eagerness. Need suddenly overshadowed finesse. He lifted her up and propped her on the edge of the bench.

"Fiona," he muttered against her lips. "Protection…we have to get—"

"Let's improvise," she suggested huskily and wrapped her legs around his waist.

Improvise? He could do that. Wyatt grabbed the towel dangling around his neck and tossed it on the counter behind her. "Okay," he breathed raggedly. He lifted her T-shirt and pushed it upward as he encouraged her to lie back. "Let's improvise."

She sighed as he ran his palm between her breasts and rib cage and lower, across her belly and lower still. She moaned her pleasure when he cupped her gently and parted the soft red hair covering her. She was divine. A goddess. *My woman*, he thought with an unusual pang of male possession. And he wanted to brand her with his kiss, his body, his very soul.

He kissed her belly, her hips, anointing every part of her with his mouth. And for the next hour they went beyond pleasure, beyond reason, beyond any feeling he'd experienced before.

Much later, once the passion had receded and they'd tumbled back into reality, they got dressed and then Wyatt finished cooking breakfast while Fiona fed the dog. They ate in silence, and he was painfully aware of the altering mood between them. Doubt and regret were suddenly filtering through the air, and by the time the meal was over, she seemed so wound up she looked as if she wanted to scream.

"I think…I think you should go."

Breakfast was over and the dishes done, and he stood by the countertop, watching her intently. Her request wasn't a great surprise. "If that's what you want."

She nodded and moved around the table. "It is."

"Can I see you tonight?"

"No."

"Fiona, if we—"

"I don't want to see you," she said quickly and then added, "unless Cecily is with us."

He pushed down the stab of annoyance. "It's a bit late for a chaperone, don't you think?"

She sucked in a breath. "I told you I wanted to concentrate on Cecily, and despite what happened last night…and well, just before…despite all that, I still feel the same way. Cecily is what's important. This…" She waved a hand. "This is a complication neither of us need."

Wyatt looked deep into her eyes. She was right. He knew that. He'd brought Cecily to Crystal Point to meet her mother…not so he could get Fiona into bed. They'd crossed the line. Big-time.

When he spoke again, there was quiet, deliberate control in his voice. "Then I'll see you Saturday…with Cecily. Goodbye, Fiona."

Fiona pulled the Christmas tree from its box and glanced at the impossible-to-comprehend instructions that came with it. She felt a little ridiculous putting up a tree in the middle of the year, but it was what Cecily wanted, and she was inclined to do whatever made her daughter happy. She really wasn't in any kind of mood to be assembling trees, but considering she'd promised Cecily, Fiona tried to develop some enthusiasm.

The fact her life was a mess had nothing to do with the fake tree and its incomprehensible instructions. She hadn't seen Wyatt for two days. Not since the morning where she'd completely lost her mind and did a whole lot of things with him that she'd never done with anyone ever before in her entire life.

Wild and erotic things. Things that made her cheeks burn with the memory. And her body burn with a shameless longing for more.

"I told you it was a cool tree," Cecily remarked five minutes later once Fiona had plumped out the branches and plugged the transformer into the wall socket.

"I'm not so sure," she said and watched the tree change color from green to red and then a brilliant blue. A real pine would have been more suitable, but she hadn't the heart to dampen Cecily's enthusiasm for the modern optical version. Finding a tree at a store in the middle of the year had been a feat in itself.

"Wait until we stack the presents around it," her daughter said. "Then it will look real."

Fiona smiled. "Shall we do that now?" she asked, thinking of the stash of gifts in her spare room, all wrapped in assorted paper. Even Wyatt had given his niece some to put beneath her tree.

"Yes," Cecily said excitedly. "But you mustn't try and guess what I got for you. I tried to wrap it so it didn't look obvious."

Fiona crossed her fingers over her chest. "Cross my heart."

"Or Uncle Wyatt's to you," she said, and Fiona stilled at the mention of him. "I told him to wrap it different, but he's too sensible for all that."

"Mmm. So let's get these gifts."

Fifteen minutes later, all the gifts were around the tree. The gift Wyatt had bought her was obviously professionally wrapped. The flat, two-foot-square object was intriguing, and she did her best not to grope the shiny bronze paper.

"Um…Fiona," Cecily said once the tree was sorted and they were in the backyard, playing with Muffin and drinking sodas. "Have you and Uncle Wyatt had a fight?"

Fiona stalled midsip but quickly gathered her wits. "Of course not. Why?"

Cecily tossed Muffin her toy. "I don't know…he just seems really cranky."

Yeah, cranky because she wouldn't talk to him. And probably cranky because she wouldn't sleep with him, either. After her shocking behavior in the kitchen, she could barely look at him. Loving him was one thing; acting so outrageously needy just because he said she was beautiful and looked at her as if she was the only woman on earth, well, that was another thing altogether.

But she was right to send him away. Fiona loved him—but she loved Cecily, too, and was determined to do what was best for her daughter. Falling in love with Wyatt wasn't sensible, and she would inevitably end up nursing a broken heart. And right now she didn't want to think about how he was feeling. It was simply too hard.

"I'm sure he's fine."

Cecily tossed the toy again. "I'm not so sure. If you guys have had a fight, couldn't you just make up or something?"

Guilt hit Fiona between the shoulders. "I promise I'll—"

"Everyone was angry that last Christmas at Waradoon," Cecily said quietly and dumped the toy because Muffin lost interest. "You know, the one before my parents died. I wasn't supposed to know, of course. But like I wouldn't know they were hardly talking to one another. And Uncle Wyatt was mad about something, too. He didn't even come to our house that year on Christmas Eve like he always did. My mother didn't kiss my dad under the plastic mistletoe. My dad sat in the corner and didn't say a word. And the worst thing about it was everyone kept telling me everything was fine. Well, *fine* just doesn't cut it anymore. So if it's not fine, I'd rather you told me the truth."

There was so much pain in her daughter's voice, and Fiona wanted nothing more than to soothe her. Cecily had lost so much. She wasn't about to let her own lack of control and foolishness impact her child in any way.

"I promise you that we really are fine. He's coming here

tomorrow night for our Christmas-in-July thing, right? So, if we were fighting then he wouldn't be. We just needed some time apart this week. It's not a big deal," she added when Cecily raised both her brows. "Don't read too much into it. The fact is all I want to do is spend as much time as I can with you while you're here."

Cecily considered her words and nodded slowly. "I want that, too. But I want you guys to like each other."

"We do. I promise." And it wasn't a lie. She did like Wyatt. The problem was she also loved him, and that seemed a whole lot more complicated than she could handle. "Adult relationships can be complex."

Cecily stared at her. "Because of sex?"

Fiona almost swallowed her tongue. "Er—yes…and because when two people like one another in that way, things get complicated."

"So you like Uncle Wyatt in that way?"

As things plummeted fantastically downhill, Fiona wanted to cover her ears. A mother-daughter sex talk she hadn't prepared for. "Well, the point I was trying to make is that sex isn't something to rush into with someone."

Cecily grinned. "Is this the part where you tell me I'm too young to think about it and should steer clear of all boys until I'm twenty-one?" She laughed and scooped the dog into her arms. "Uncle Wyatt has already given me that talk. His ears were red when he was saying it, which was pretty funny. Anyway, I think he was happy when I told him I wasn't interested in all that stuff yet. I know he said it because he doesn't want me to get into trouble and wreck my life."

Fiona's throat tightened. Cecily's words hit with the precision of an arrow. And they both knew it.

"Um—sorry," she said quickly. "I didn't mean that you'd wrecked your life or anything."

"It's okay," Fiona said assuredly. "I've never, not for one minute, regretted having you."

Cecily tried to smile. "Did you love him? I mean, my father?"

Fiona's heart thundered. *I'm not ready for this.* But Cecily deserved an answer.

"I didn't know him very well." That wasn't a lie. Jamie Corbett had been Shayne's lover for less than a month before the night they'd been left alone together. Shayne should have known better. And Fiona, starved of attention for so long, hadn't realized her harmless flirting was not harmless at all. Jamie Corbett mistook her clumsy attempt to get his attention, and it wasn't long before she endured the worst hour of her life. Afterward, sore and bruised and ashamed, Fiona vowed she'd never tell anyone what had happened. When Shayne discovered Fiona was pregnant, it didn't occur to her mother that her own lover was the father. Not until Fiona told her mother the truth. A truth Shayne didn't believe—instead she'd called Fiona every kind of tramp and accused her of trying to steal her boyfriend. Twenty-four hours later, Fiona was dumped at her uncle's farm, and she never saw Shayne or Jamie Corbett again.

She looked at Cecily and managed a smile. Her precious daughter wouldn't be tainted by the brutality and shame of her conception. Fiona would see to that with ever fiber of her being. "I was young and didn't have a lot of support at home. But if I hadn't met him, you wouldn't be here...and I wouldn't change that for the world."

Cecily's eyes glistened and she hugged the dog close. "I'm going to miss Muffin when I have to leave. Pop's got working dogs for the cattle and they're too big to pick up."

"I'm sure she'll miss you, too." *Like I will.* Fiona didn't dare let herself think about the day she would have to let her daughter go.

"You could come visit us at Waradoon."

She nodded, but in her heart she knew it wasn't likely. Her life was in Crystal Point. Cecily's life was at Waradoon. She would have to make do with school-vacation time to see her daughter. It would have to be enough.

Wyatt flipped his cell phone into his top pocket once he finished a call to his office. He and Cecily were due at Fiona's in an hour. He tried to ignore the anxiety filling his chest. He hadn't seen Fiona all week—at her request. He respected her wishes and didn't push the issue. Her impassioned words that morning were imprinted in his mind. She didn't want recriminations. She didn't want to discuss it. End of story.

But tonight was their Christmas-in-July celebration, and he didn't want to disappoint Cecily. Wyatt pushed past his battered ego and agreed they would spend the evening together.

It was near half past six when he stopped the rental car in her driveway behind her zippy Mazda. The porch light flickered and she opened the door as Cecily jumped out of the passenger seat. His niece was across the yard and up the three steps within seconds, and he watched as they embraced and Fiona dropped her head back as she laughed. His stomach rolled over. *Great start.*

He grabbed the bag from the backseat and headed for the two redheads in his life.

Cecily quickly disappeared inside, and to her credit, Fiona managed a smile as he approached. "Hi. Welcome."

"Thanks." He followed her across the threshold and closed the screen door. "Interesting tree," he said once they moved into the living room.

She shifted on her heels and her dress moved around her legs. "It's fiber-optic," she explained. "Cecily insisted."

"Saves having to store the decorations, I guess," he said

and passed her the brown bag he carried. "From the organic deli in town."

She peered into the bag and bit her bottom lip as she examined the contents of Brie and crackers and antipasto ingredients. "Great, that's my favorite spot."

"I know," he replied. "Evie mentioned something."

She looked nervous all of a sudden. "Wyatt, I want to—"

"Hey, guys," Cecily announced as she bounced back into the room with Muffin in her arms. "Can we watch a Christmas DVD?"

Fiona sucked in a long breath. "Good idea. You pick a movie, and I'll get the drinks and snacks started."

She took off and Wyatt dropped into the love seat. He certainly had no intention of going anywhere near the sofa. He doubted he'd ever be able to look at the paisley print again without seeing Fiona stretched out in seductive invitation. And he wished she'd stop wearing that sexy perfume. Damn scent hit him with the force of a sledgehammer every time she came near him.

It was close to ten minutes before she came back into the room. She did three trips and placed trays of food on the coffee table and drinks on the buffet nearby. He offered to help but she insisted she had it under control. She poured three glasses of something he couldn't distinguish, but which looked as if it had clumps of fruit in it, and placed them on the coffee table. When she was done, she sat in one corner of the sofa. Cecily sat in the middle and demanded he sit on the other side.

"You won't see the television from there," his niece complained. "I know how much you *looove* Christmas movies."

Wyatt looked toward Fiona. She smiled and flicked her gaze to the other end of the sofa. *Get a grip*. He moved and sat down, feeling light-years away from her.

"Not a fan, huh?" she asked and grabbed a handful of popcorn from the bowl in Cecily's lap.

"You could say that."

"Me, either," she admitted as the movie credits began to roll.

Cecily shushed them both and sat forward to pocket some chocolate. Then she slid off the edge, sat lotus-style in between the sofa and table, and began to graze on the selection of fruit and cheese and assorted food spread out in front of her.

Wyatt looked at Fiona. Being with her seemed incredibly normal. That was what struck him so hard. And so unexpectedly. She was easy to be with. Easy to like. What had started as physical attraction had morphed into something else. And the feelings were alien to him. He was somehow vulnerable.

Was that what mind-blowing sex did to a man's brain?

He reached across the back of the sofa and lightly touched her shoulder. She smiled as only she could. Wyatt wished he knew her better. He also wished he wasn't cynical and could trust what he was feeling. But he didn't. And he suspected Fiona knew as much.

Chapter Nine

Family.

That's what this feels like.

A mother, a father, a cheerful teenager plonked between them downing popcorn and laughing at a silly movie. Fiona knew it was a fantasy. But in that moment, it was real. And it was hers.

Wyatt's touch was mesmerizing. His hand stayed at her shoulder for a while, and he drew tiny circles with his thumb. She knew she shouldn't allow it. But it seemed right, somehow. When she moved to take her drink off the table, he pulled back.

Once the movie was over, Cecily insisted on opening a gift. Just one, she said, to tide them over until the following day. Her daughter's insistence that they follow the traditional Christmas protocol made her smile. Fiona sat on the love seat and summoned the heart to enjoy the celebration. Wyatt took a spot on an old chair next to the tree, and her daughter dropped onto the floor. Cecily opened one of the gifts Fiona gave her—a silver pendant in the shape of a dazzling unicorn. She adored it, thought it was the most beautiful thing she'd ever seen.

"It's one of a kind," Fiona explained. "My friend Mary-Jayne is a silversmith."

"A talented lady," Wyatt said and admired the piece.

"She's Evie's little sister. I'll get her to craft a pair of matching earrings," she told Cecily. "For your birthday."

Cecily groaned. "But that's ages away."

Fiona looked at Wyatt. "I know the date," she said and quickly changed the subject. "So, who's next?"

Cecily grabbed a gift from beneath the tree and tossed it toward her uncle. He squeezed the package. "Socks?"

Cecily laughed. "Nope. Fiona said they were off the list this year."

He mouthed a silent thank-you and tore open the gift. Not socks but a soft blue T-shirt she knew would look great on him.

"Now you," Cecily insisted and dragged the square package that was leaning against the wall.

Fiona rested the gift against her knees. They were both watching her—the child she loved and the man she had fallen hopelessly in love with.

The gift was from Wyatt, and as she pulled off the paper and realized what he'd given her, Fiona's eyes welled with tears. The portrait of Cecily was an exact likeness, framed in polished oak. "Oh...it's so..." She looked at Wyatt. "It's perfect. How did you—"

"Ellen," he explained. "My sister is the artist. She did this piece a few months back. I thought you might like it."

"I love it," she said quickly. *I love you.* "Thank you. It's more than I ever expected."

"Gosh, I look like you," Cecily said as she came behind Fiona and peered at the portrait. "Don't I, Uncle Wyatt?"

He kept his gaze locked with hers. "Yes. Double trouble."

Cecily laughed. It was such a heart-wrenching moment, and Fiona wanted to bottle up the memories. For another day, another time, when she was alone again.

"Who's up for supper?" she asked and blinked at the tears in her eyes.

"Not me," Cecily groaned out as she patted her full tummy. "Too much punch and popcorn. I think I'm going to crash for a while in the spare room."

She left with a hug for them both and took off down the short hallway.

"She exhausts me," Fiona declared as she slumped back in the love seat.

He grinned and checked his watch. "Nine-thirty," he commented. "And now we have no chaperone. Would you like me to leave?"

"No," she said in a rush and then exhaled. "I mean, we hardly need a chaperone."

He shrugged. "I'm not so sure."

Fiona did her best to ignore the simmering heat low in her belly. But in low-rise jeans and a black Henley shirt, he looked so good, so handsome, it was impossible to forget how passionately they'd made love only days earlier.

"I told you why I can't do this," she said quietly.

Wyatt stood up. "I know what you said. I'm just not entirely sure that's how you feel."

Fiona sucked in a sharp breath. Did he know she had fallen in love with him? *Am I that transparent?* "I have to put Cecily first. Not myself."

"So you said."

"You're leaving in ten days, Wyatt. I might come across as independent and self-sufficient, but the truth is I'm not the kind of woman who thinks it's okay to sleep with someone casually."

His expression narrowed. "I'm not indiscriminate, either, Fiona. I've had one brief relationship since I broke up with Yvette. I don't sleep around."

"I wasn't suggesting you—"

"I have no intention of ignoring you for the next ten days," he said quietly. "I'd like it if you showed me the same courtesy."

Shame weighed down her shoulders. He was right. She had been ignoring him. "I'm sorry. My only excuse is I'm afraid of messing things up with Cecily."

"You won't," he assured her. "Have some faith in yourself, Fiona. And trust Cecily."

"I've never been very good at trusting people."

Wyatt moved across the room and dropped onto the sofa. "Not surprising."

She shrugged. "I suppose. I did try to love my mother. But I didn't trust her to make the right choices." She gave a brittle laugh. "And she rarely let me down. I can't remember how many times I was dragged out of hotel rooms at dawn because she didn't have the money to pay the bill. Or how many cowboys she rolled over while they were asleep. I used to watch her steal money from their pockets and she'd tell me to be quiet when I begged her not to do it. Bad hotel rooms, short spells in one school or another... I never had the opportunity to make friends. And there was no point when we moved around so much. When she died, I think a part of me was...was..."

"Relieved?"

Fiona nodded and marveled at how easy it was to tell him things she'd always kept to herself. Not even Callie and Evie knew so much about her childhood.

This is it. This is trust. This is love.

"I'm not proud to think like that, but it's true. My uncle... well, he tried. He did the best he could, the best he knew how, I suppose. That's why it's so important I make the right choices now. I want Cecily to know I'm not a screwup."

"Acting on our mutual attraction doesn't make you a screwup, Fiona."

"Maybe," she said in a halfhearted sort of agreement. "All I know is that I am determined to be a good role model. I know in my heart your sister will always be her mother. I only hope I can be Cecily's friend, the woman she goes to when she needs guidance. Soon she'll be thinking about boys and love and sex. When she asks those questions, I want to be able to tell her that making love should be special...should be shared between two people who are *in love*."

Fiona looked at him, hoping, dreaming and wishing for some sign that he thought that, too. She'd made love with him because she loved him. Clearly for Wyatt it was little more than attraction. Mutual attraction, he'd called it. Not love. Only sex.

"You're right, of course," he said after a moment, and Fiona wished she knew what his impassive, locked-out expression meant. "And she should talk to you about that stuff."

"As long as I steer her in the right direction?"

His mouth twisted. "I want her to realize her potential. Be whoever she's meant to be."

"I want that, too. And again, I apologize for being shut down this week. We were both part of what happened. I didn't mean to make a bigger deal of it than it was. I don't want there to be tension between us. Especially since Cecily picked up on it."

"She did?"

"Yeah. She doesn't want us to fight. She doesn't like arguing." Fiona inhaled and met his gaze head-on. "Her parents fought in the few months before their deaths. I know you said it was nothing, but it meant something to Cecily. She's still disturbed by it."

"I'll talk to her," he said and shifted in his seat. "So, how about that supper you promised?"

"Hungry?"

He glanced at the remnants of food on the coffee table. "A man cannot live by popcorn alone. Allow me into your kitchen and I'll make you a sandwich you'll never forget."

Fiona laughed and then jumped up and straightened her dress over her hips. "Deal."

Fifteen minutes later, after she cleared away the scraps from the living room, Wyatt had loaded a plate with sandwiches filled with thick slices of ham and sweet pickles and a few with smoked turkey breast and cranberry jelly. He popped the plate in the center of the table, and Fiona grabbed two bottles of ginger beer from the refrigerator.

"Looks great," she said and sat down.

Wyatt grabbed a sandwich and devoured it in four bites.

There was an easy camaraderie between them. She liked it. Men usually made her nervous. But she had no nerves. Not even the underlying thread of sexual desire curling around the room made her tense. He wouldn't act on it; she knew that without question. He would respect her wishes. Wyatt oozed integrity by the bucket load.

"I guess we should talk about contact," she said after a few bites of her sandwich. "With Cecily. I would like to see her again on the next school vacation if that's okay with you."

He grabbed another sandwich. "You can see as much of Cecily as she wants."

Fiona's heart rolled. "Thank you for being so supportive. It means a lot to me."

"Cecily wants you in her life," he said around a bite. "Incidentally, you are welcome to visit Waradoon anytime. My mother will want to meet you. Sooner would be better than later."

Now Fiona was nervous. "Will she disapprove?"

"Of you?" He gave a lopsided grin. "Hardly."

Relief washed over her skin. "I'd like that."

Wyatt drank some ginger beer and patted his washboard-flat stomach. "I should probably check on Cecily. If she's crashed out, she may as well stay the night."

"Of course."

He stood and scraped the chair back. "Then I'll head off."

Fiona quickly got to her feet. "You could stay," she said and saw both his brows crank upward. "I mean, the sofa's pretty comfortable, and Cecily will want you to be here in the morning when she wakes up. And…I'd like that, too."

His mouth twisted and he went to say something, then stopped and took a moment. "If you're sure."

"I'm sure," she said quickly, before she had a chance to change her mind. "I'll get you a blanket and pillow."

He flexed his arms upward and stretched. The movement pulled the T-shirt up and exposed his belly. Fiona swallowed the sudden lump that formed in her throat. She'd touched him there, kissed him and reveled in his glorious skin. Her fingers itched as the memory swept through her blood.

Fiona took off to collect what he needed and detoured to check on Cecily. As expected, her daughter was asleep, snoring softly with Muffin curled in the crook of her arm. She called the dog, and once Muffin had jumped off the bed and shot past her feet, Fiona covered Cecily with a light blanket and flicked off the corner lamp.

Back in the living room, Fiona faced Wyatt.

I could so easily invite him into my bed.

The temptation heightened her awareness. She wanted him so much she could barely breathe. She quickly dumped the pillow and blanket on the edge of the sofa. "Are you sure you'll be—"

"I'll be fine. Go to bed."

His words had a profound effect on her senses. "But if you need—"

"Go to bed," he said again, deeper this time. "Before I forget my good intentions."

Fiona stepped back, her heart pounding. She wanted him so much. Needed him so much. Loved him so much. Denying it suddenly seemed foolish. "I want you to stay," she whispered. "With me."

And within seconds she was in his arms.

The sofa wasn't comfortable, as Wyatt discovered around 4:00 a.m. when he left Fiona asleep and made his way to the living room. Her big bed, with its colorful quilt and plump pillows, was a much more appealing option—especially since Fiona's lovely arms had been wrapped around him. But he'd been struck by a burst of doing the right thing. And that meant being settled on the couch when Cecily woke up.

So he stared at the ceiling for two hours, in between shooing off the dog that clearly wanted to curl up between his feet.

Last night, despite his best intentions, the moment she'd walked into his arms, Wyatt had crumbled. Her skin, her lips and her beautiful hair—he had no answer for the burning desire that consumed him whenever she was near him. He couldn't resist. No woman had ever had such an effect on him. There had been no words when they'd made love. Only touch and taste and an exploration of the senses. Each stroke more mind-blowing than the last.

Wyatt groaned and put the pillow over his face to muffle the sound. He swung his legs off the sofa and sat up. Sleep was out of the question. Television filled the next hour or so, and at dawn he heard Cecily's cheerful voice echoing down the hallway.

Fiona emerged about ten minutes later, and by then he was in the kitchen making coffee. Dressed in pale-gray-and-black, sweats she looked weary and sleep-deprived. And so beautiful his breath caught in his throat.

"Coffee. Mmm…lovely," she said and took the mug he offered.

Cecily was bouncing around within seconds. "Merry Christmas in July!" She hugged them both. "Oh, can we please open gifts first?"

Wyatt caught Fiona's gaze. There would be no holding back his exuberant niece and they both knew it. "Sure," Fiona said. "Lead the way."

It took about three minutes for Cecily to devour all her gifts and leave a pile of discarded wrapping paper in her wake as she danced on happy feet, clinging to the new cell phone he'd given her. A good idea he'd be sure to thank Fiona for suggesting.

Sharing gifts with Fiona seemed ridiculously intimate, and he knew Cecily watched them interact with keen interest. His niece was hoping, he suspected, to see their relationship develop into something more, something permanent. Wyatt knew she wanted to be a part of a traditional family unit again. And Fiona was her birth mother—in Cecily's young eyes it would be the perfect solution.

Would he consider it? When he knew it would mean a commitment and ultimately marriage? He couldn't deny his attraction for Fiona. And they were compatible in many ways. Not only between the sheets. He liked her and enjoyed her company. But his resistance lingered. He'd been played before. How could he be sure this wouldn't turn out the same?

"If it's not detailed enough, I can return it."

Wyatt shifted his attention to the moment. Fiona was

watching him as he handled the thick book on car restoration, and he remembered how he'd mentioned he had plans to one day rebuild the '67 Camaro his father had in the garage at Waradoon.

"It's great," he replied. "Thanks."

She looked at the book and grimaced. "You're difficult to buy for."

"I told you he had everything," Cecily chimed in as she took a second away from her phone. "Imagine trying to come up with something new every year...*sheesh*."

"Do you have everything?" Fiona asked quietly once Cecily returned to pressing buttons.

Wyatt held her gaze. "Right now...I think I do."

And suddenly Wyatt knew his orderly, practical life would be empty without Fiona Walsh in it.

The day had a surreal edge for Fiona. By midmorning she'd cooked breakfast, which they shared around the kitchen table, as they chatted through mouthfuls of fried ham and eggs. Afterward, Wyatt helped her wash the dishes. Before she had a chance to protest, Fiona found herself trapped between his chest and the kitchen counter and caught in a delicious liplock with him that was so passionate it made her heart surge. Of course, Cecily catching them in a clinch as she walked into the kitchen had Fiona pulling away so quickly she almost fell over. This made her daughter laugh, and Wyatt grab her with lightning-fast reflexes before she ended up in a twisted heap on the floor.

Her embarrassment aside, the time she spent with them both would become bottled memories she'd treasure forever. Cecily's animated happiness was almost too sweet to bear. And Wyatt... She wished she knew what the future held. Especially after last night. She'd spouted a whole lot of reasons why they couldn't get involved and then rushed into his arms again. Fiona cursed her lack of self-control. But still, he was such a wonderful lover—thoughtful and attentive, passionate and reverent. She'd discovered more about giving and receiving pleasure in the past week than she had in all her adult life.

But what was he feeling? She wanted to believe he genuinely cared for her and to believe it was more than a fling. His comments while they'd opened gifts that morning encouraged her to think he did. But without the actual words, how could she be sure? Assurance had never seemed more important. He liked her…she was savvy enough to figure that out. And they were good together in bed. *So good. Too good.* So good her hormones were running riot. But sex wasn't enough to sustain a relationship between two people who hardly knew one another. And with Cecily clearly hoping for it to happen, Fiona knew her daughter would be painfully disappointed if they started something that faded as quickly as it had begun. Cecily had endured enough disappointments, and Fiona wasn't about to add to the load.

By eleven she said goodbye and waved farewell to them from the front porch when they returned to the B and B to change clothes. There was a baby shower at Evie's parents' home that afternoon, and since they'd all been invited, they'd agreed to go together. Like a real family.

Exactly the family I've longed for.

But she needed reality. She also refused to let her imagination run away with wild ideas. After she showered and changed into a knee-length pale blue dress cut on the bias, Fiona waited for about ten minutes before they returned to pick her up.

Wyatt looked so good in chinos and a white shirt it stole her breath.

"Ready?" he asked as she opened the door.

"Yes," she said quickly. "I just have this to take." She

picked up a bag near the door. "Makings for a cheese-and-fruit platter and a gift for Evie and Scott's baby," she explained.

She didn't pull back when he grabbed the bag in one hand and took her hand with the other. Once Fiona had closed the door, he walked her to the car. Cecily was grinning from ear to ear in the backseat. *Oh, no...don't start thinking this is something real.* She wanted to say the words out loud. To herself. To her daughter. Knowing how it must look with their hands linked, Fiona pulled away as they reached the car and quickly ducked into the front seat. He placed the bag in the back and they headed off.

The trip to the Prestons' home took only a few minutes, and by the time they arrived, there were several cars parked outside. Cecily jumped out quickly before Fiona had a chance to move and took off to find Lily. Wyatt reached across and grasped her arm.

"Fiona?"

"Everyone's inside," she breathed. "Let's go—"

"I think we should talk."

She knew what was coming, didn't she? The talk. The let's-be-friends speech. She'd heard it before. Maybe she'd imagined his interest as being more than sexual? Whatever it was, she was going down fast. And she had to save herself.

"You want out?" she blurted and moved her arm.

"What?"

"From me...from whatever this is."

He frowned. "Why would I want that?"

Fiona shrugged. "Because it's less complicated."

"If I didn't want complicated," he said and grabbed her hand, "I wouldn't have come here to find you in the first place. I would have told Cecily to wait until she was eighteen and search for you then. But I did come here and we did meet... and we did connect."

Connect? God, she should be jumping out of her skin that

he wasn't backing out. Instead, her heart was thumping so hard she wondered if she would hyperventilate. She wanted more than a connection. She wanted *I love you*. He stroked her hand with his thumb and watched her with blistering intensity, and it wasn't enough. It would never be enough. She wanted the lot. She wanted him in every way possible.

"But you're leaving soon."

"Yes," he replied and kept stroking her skin. "I have to get back. The company, my family. It's all a long way from here."

Fiona nodded because she wasn't sure she could do anything else.

"So, come to Waradoon?"

"But I—"

"And soon. Let's see if this connection works somewhere else."

God, she was tempted. "Cecily would—"

"Think it's a great idea," he said, cutting her off without batting an eye.

Of course she would. Cecily wanted a family. With parents and siblings one day. She hadn't dared admit to her daughter that it was her dream, too. But what about Wyatt's dreams? His fiancée had cheated on him—could she expect that he'd want to get seriously involved with anyone?

"I don't know. I'll think about it."

He didn't look happy with her response, but after a second, he shrugged. "Sure. We should go inside, don't you think?"

Fiona agreed and quickly got out of the car. Wyatt retrieved the bags from the backseat and she waited for him by the bottom step. Once inside, she took the bags from him and headed for the kitchen and left Wyatt to his own devices, presumably to hang out with the rest of the men and talk about the stuff men seemed to be able to talk about even if they weren't well acquainted.

Callie was in the kitchen cutting thick slices of watermelon, and Evie was decorating a fluffy meringue. Both women eyed Fiona as she walked into the room, and Callie raised her brows. Fiona knew that look—knew her friend had something on her mind.

"What?"

Callie wasn't one to beat around the bush. "Cecily just made an appearance. Where's the gorgeous uncle?"

Fiona dumped the bags on the counter. "Outside. And I'd rather not—"

"She's onto you."

"Huh?"

Callie's mouth turned up at the edges. "Cecily. She and Lily have become firm friends. She told Lily that you and Wyatt were, and I quote, 'so doing it.'"

Fiona's cheeks burned. "Lily said that?"

"Yes. Our girls have been texting in the small hours. They've got quite the hotline going." Callie stopped her cutting.

Evie spoke. "So, is it true?"

Fiona opened her mouth in protest. But this was Callie and Evie. Her best friends. "We're...well...yes."

"Good for you," Evie said and smiled.

Callie didn't look so pleased. "I thought you didn't want to complicate things?"

"I don't. Anyway, it won't last," she said and despised how foolishly hopeless she sounded.

Callie looked at her. "You're sure of that?"

"I'm not sure of anything," Fiona admitted. "What I'm feeling. What Wyatt's feeling. If he's feeling anything at all. And with Cecily stuck in the middle, it's getting harder every day. I have absolutely no idea what I'm doing here."

Callie looked serious suddenly. "Well, considering what happened with her parents, I think you need to figure it out.

You can tell me to mind my own business, but I think the last thing that girl needs is more confusion in her life."

Fiona frowned. "What do you mean?"

"Well, despite her obvious exuberance for the two of you to be together, Cecily isn't entirely convinced any relationship can survive since she found out about her father's affair."

Fiona stilled, poleaxed by Callie's words. "Her father's *what?*"

"Affair," Callie said again and looked at her oddly. "She told Lily. I was sure she would have said something to you."

"No. Only that they were having some problems." The words left her mouth with a kind of static disbelief. "Are you sure that's what she said?"

Callie nodded. "He'd had an affair. Apparently they'd gone away together on a trip to work on their marriage. Since they were killed the day before they were due to arrive home, I guess no one will ever know whether they were able to work things out."

An affair?

Fiona couldn't believe it. Oh, not that Jim Todd had been unfaithful. But that Wyatt hadn't told her. She'd asked him about his sister's marriage, and he'd shrugged off her questions and shut her out. Deliberately. And she wouldn't stand for it. Not with Cecily stuck in the middle.

Fiona knew she had to start thinking with her head and not her heart.

Or I might lose everything.

And that, she thought with a resolute breath, was not an option.

Chapter Ten

Wyatt sensed the distinct change in Fiona's mood the moment she walked outside. She glared at him with a kind of unholy rage as she walked across to where Cecily sat by the pool. He wished he knew her better. He hung out with Noah and Cameron for a while and saw his chance to speak with her when she made her way back into the house. He followed her through the kitchen and into the front living room. She clearly knew he was behind her because her back was stiff with tension.

"Fiona, wait up."

She stalled about ten feet in front of him and turned. "What?"

He took note of her bright blue-gray eyes and lips pressed tight. "Exactly—what?"

She opened her mouth and then quickly clamped it shut.

"What's wrong?" he insisted.

"Now isn't the time to get into it."

"Seems like the perfect time."

"In someone else's home?" She shook her head. "I don't think so."

"So, all this sudden anger is aimed at me?"

She rocked back on her heels. "At myself," she said and flicked her hair in that way he could not ignore. "For being so gullible."

"Gullible?" Wyatt stepped closer and shut the sliding door. "What does that mean?"

"It means that I've become so wrapped up in *wanting* you I've forgotten why you're here. I've forgotten what I'm doing. I've also forgotten that I promised this would only be about Cecily."

Wyatt pushed past his frustration and tried to not sound impatient. "That's something of an old song, don't you think? We can't undo what's done."

Her blue-gray eyes flashed lightning. "Well, you would say that, considering you've been moving me around like a pawn on a chessboard."

He stared at her. "What?"

"Lying by omission is still lying," she said hotly, as if she couldn't get the words out quickly enough.

Annoyance ignited behind his ribs. He had no idea what she meant. "I haven't lied to you."

Both her brows shot up. "Really? So, if letting me think your sister's marriage was rock-solid, when we both know it wasn't, isn't lying, what is?"

Wyatt swayed fractionally. "What are you talking about?"

"You know exactly," she shot back. "Your sister and her husband were having a few problems, you said. Nothing serious. Since when is infidelity nothing?"

Infidelity? So, she knew. He wondered how much. "Since it's a private family issue and none of your business."

Wyatt knew it sounded harsh and dismissive. And he knew

she'd be hurt by his words. But he wasn't about to lay any Harper skeletons out for open discussion. The past was the past, and that was exactly where it would remain. Even if it meant shutting her out.

She took a heavy breath. "And that puts me in my place? Well, I'm pleased we've cleared that up. I'd hate to harbor the illusion that I was important enough to be privy to something about your family. Or you."

Her eyes flashed at him. He could have said something to assure her she was important. Or that she was quickly becoming the most important thing to him. Instead he stuck by his determination to keep the whole ugly mess from hurting any more people than it already had.

"What happened in my family has no bearing on your relationship with Cecily."

It sounded exclusive and they both knew it. "What about my relationship with you?" she asked, suddenly all eyes, all emotion.

Wyatt wasn't sure where their relationship was heading. It was too new. Too raw. And arguing about it wouldn't help. "It's nothing—"

"Nothing?" Her voice rose as she cut him off.

"If you'd let me finish—"

"Oh, we're finished all right," she said and glared at him. "We are absolutely finished. Over. Done. *Kaput.*"

"You're overreacting," he replied, harsher than he liked.

"What does it matter? We've already established that I'm nothing to you."

Wyatt expelled a frustrated breath. "That's not what I said."

"I know exactly what you—"

"Would you stop fighting? Just stop!"

They both stilled. Cecily had emerged from the hall and stood in the doorway, her eyes bright and her cheeks red.

When they said her name simultaneously, she shook her head with a kind of frantic denial.

"Just stop fighting…please," she implored and wrapped her thin arms around herself.

Guilt hit Wyatt in the center of his chest. He remembered those last few months before Karen and Jim were killed. It had been a tough time, and Cecily had been in the middle of it, as much as he knew his sister had done her best to shield her from seeing and hearing too much. "We were just—"

"Fighting," she wailed. "Arguing."

Fiona stepped toward her. "I'm sorry if you thought we were—"

"I heard you. I know what fighting sounds like."

"And you're right," Wyatt said quietly and tried to ignore the pain of Fiona's expression and the confusion on his niece's face. "But it wasn't about you. It wasn't anything to do with you. So nothing has changed for you, Cecily. Fiona and I are both here for you. That's all that matters."

"You were talking about my folks," Cecily said. "I heard. And I know what Dad did."

Did she? Wyatt wondered if she knew everything. If she knew the role he'd played in the whole sordid mess. Karen had blamed him often enough. When Wyatt had suggested that she and her husband take some time out to get their relationship back on track and see if they could make their marriage work, he hadn't imagined it would be the last time they'd speak.

"They loved you. Your dad loved you. Don't worry about anything else."

His niece shrugged and stepped back, away from Fiona, away from him. "I thought things would work out," Cecily said shakily. "This morning you guys were… Well, I thought we'd all be together and happy."

"Cecily," he said gently, "Fiona and I are friends and we'll do our best to remain friends. But relationships can be complex."

"I've already had the adult-relationships-are-complicated speech from her," she said and pointed a finger in Fiona's direction. "If it's so complicated, why did you sleep together in the first place?"

Wyatt saw Fiona turn pale and fought the urge to go to her. And Cecily looked as if she needed comfort, too. By chance and circumstance, they had become the most important people in his life. If Karen and Jim were alive, they would be doing this. They would be standing guard over the reunion between birth mother and daughter. And he'd be living his own life, perhaps only involved peripherally. But his sister was gone. It was his job to protect Cecily. And because he and Fiona were lovers, because they'd crossed the line from acquaintance into friendship and then into something way more intimate than he'd bargained for, he experienced a deep-rooted need to protect Fiona, as well. And knowing how important the moment was to both of the women standing in front of him, Wyatt quickly shouldered the responsibility.

"Because when you're falling for someone that's what people do. And sometimes guys can act like jerks when it comes to a beautiful woman."

Cecily's mouth opened in a rounded O.

Of all things Fiona might have expected Wyatt to say, that wasn't one of them. She stared at him and then glanced at her daughter. Cecily's face creased in a tiny smile.

"So, you guys are cool?"

"Yes," he replied quietly.

Fiona was so angry with him she hurt all over. But she wouldn't say another word in front of Cecily. She'd done enough damage to their relationship for one day.

"We're fine," she said flatly. "And friends, just as your uncle said."

"Good. Fighting sucks. What if you fight and then something happens and you never see that person again?"

So young and so smart. Her daughter was a remarkable young woman. She had some serious ground to make up after allowing her personal feelings for Wyatt to blur what was really important.

Fiona looked toward Wyatt for a bare second. *Because when you're falling for someone that's what people do.* Did he mean it? Was he really falling for her? Had he guessed she'd fallen completely and hopelessly in love with him? No. Impossible. He wasn't falling. She was *nothing* to him. He'd only said that to appease Cecily. More lies.

"How about you and I go and check out what Callie and Lily are doing?" She linked her arm through her daughter's and hoped Cecily would accept her embrace.

She did, thankfully. "Great idea. Are you coming, Uncle Wyatt?"

"No, you go ahead. I want to finish talking with Lily's dad about the school canteen project."

Fiona managed to look at him again. "He's going to help?"

"Looks that way," Wyatt replied.

"He has three kids at the school, so I'm not surprised."

Wyatt shrugged in a vague kind of way, which belied the tension radiating from him. They needed to talk and they both knew it. But now wasn't the time or place.

"Noah has contacts in the local building industry and can assist with organizing contract labor from this end," Wyatt said. "Your funds from Harper's should be cleared within thirty days, so once the plans are submitted and approved through council, the project can go ahead."

"Ooh," Cecily said with a burst of sudden excitement. "You'll have to come to the big Harper's charity ball next month. Won't she, Uncle Wyatt?"

His eyes regarded her with burning intensity. "Of course,"

he replied. "In fact, it's customary for a representative of the beneficiaries of the charity fund to attend. You could represent the school and accept your check on the night."

"Oh, I couldn't possibly—"

"It would be perfect," Cecily said excitedly. "You could stay at Waradoon and meet Nan and Pop and my aunts and everyone else. And don't forget Banjo. I really want you to see my horse. Please say you'll come and stay. We can go shopping for our dresses together. It's really fancy and so much fun." She turned her attention to her uncle. "Make her say yes, Uncle Wyatt."

He nodded. "You'd be welcome to attend."

It wasn't exactly the invitation from him she secretly craved. *I really want you to come with me* would have been better. Perhaps he already had a date? That thought made Fiona hurt all over. She cursed herself for being so foolish. They were finished. She was *nothing* to him.

"I'll think about it," she said, stiffer than she would have liked, and the disappointment on her daughter's face plunged into her heart like a knife. "I promise," she added. "Now, let's go and see Lily."

She steered Cecily from the room. There would be time later for recriminations. All she wanted was to enjoy the day with her daughter. And later, much later, she would think about how she would face Wyatt alone, knowing how little she meant to him and knowing he'd only said what he'd said to appease Cecily's concerns.

And it hurt more than she'd believed possible.

Fiona hadn't expected Cecily to want to stay the night at the Prestons'. But she and Lily had forged such a strong friendship, and Fiona didn't have the heart to deny her daughter's request. Wyatt didn't look happy about it but gave in when Cecily promised to be back at the B and B early the following morning.

The drive back to her house later that evening was thick with tension. She managed to avoid him for most of the afternoon and didn't say anything until Wyatt pulled the car into her driveway.

She grabbed her handbag and moved to open the door. "Well, thank you for the lift. Can you tell Cecily that I'll call her—"

"Fiona?"

She stopped moving when he spoke her name. "What?"

He expelled a sharp breath. "We need to talk, either now or later. I'd prefer now. I'd like an opportunity to explain my reasons for keeping my family's business private."

She knew why. She didn't need to hear it again. *Because I'm nothing to you.*

"Okay," she said as she opened the door. "Let's talk."

Minutes later they were inside. Fiona gave Muffin a moment's attention when the little dog bounded toward her, then she dropped her bags on the hall stand and headed for the living room. She heard Wyatt close the front door, and she was seated on the sofa by the time he'd traced her steps.

He remained standing, his shoulders tight and expression unreadable. "I didn't lie to you," he said quietly. "The fact is I didn't tell you about Karen and Jim's marriage problems because I didn't think it had any bearing on your relationship with Cecily."

Fiona drew in a breath. "You know, I'm not so naive I'd actually believe that hogwash."

He made an irritated sound. "So you're determined to think I did it deliberately?"

She nodded. "I think you did it because it was easier to keep me in the dark. It was easier to let me believe they were perfect."

"No one's perfect."

She shot up. "No? Well, you never gave me a chance, did you? Right from the beginning, from the moment we met and you told me about Cecily, I've been busting my behind trying to prove that I'm good enough…that I deserve to be a part of Cecily's life."

"I've never once asked you to aim for some perfect standard. In fact, I recall saying that Karen and Jim were *not* perfect."

"You didn't have to say anything either way," she snapped back. "It's been made clear to me that they were the faultless parents who loved Cecily. You made me believe they were flawless and as though I didn't have a hope of competing with that. So I tried to be myself…my very obviously *flawed* self and hoped that was enough."

"It is enough. Cecily is already attached to you."

"Because her perfect parents are gone. Don't you think I get that? If Karen were here, my relationship with Cecily would be very different."

Wyatt's gaze sharpened instantly. "What do you expect? She lost her mother. She's looking for that connection again."

"I know that. I know what she wants and I'm trying so hard to give it to her. But if I'd known I might have been doing this on an even playing field, I could have, I don't know, worked out a way to not seem so *desperate* to make it work out. But I haven't. I'm the screwup who gave her away, and I'll always be that person."

"You're not a screwup, Fiona."

"I am," she shot back. "I gave her up. I handed her over to strangers. I abandoned her. And I know, in her heart, a part of Cecily is always going to think that. She's always going to know they wanted her and I didn't."

"You can't change the past. Believe me, I know that. And I know my niece. She's grateful to have you in her life. You want to hear than Karen and Jim weren't perfect, that their marriage was busted and they were on the verge of splitting? Sure, I can tell you that. I can tell you Jim slept with another woman and it broke my sister's heart. So, now you know, does it change anything about your relationship with Cecily? I don't think so. Unless you want to keep using it as an excuse to hide behind."

Fiona's skin prickled. "What?"

"An excuse," he said again. "In case you mess up with Cecily. It's an easy out for you, isn't it?"

"That's not fair. I've never—"

"Oh, come on, Fiona, you've got that blueprint down pat. I've read the report, remember? The moves from one town to the next, short stints as a contract teacher, a few brief relationships with men you never see again once the relationship fizzles out. You can't hide from the truth when it's written in black-and-white."

Anger and humiliation crept over her skin. "Black-and-white?" she echoed, incredulous and so fired up she almost lunged at him and smacked his face. "You knew? I mean, you know about—"

"The accountant? The truck driver? The real-estate salesman?"

Put that way, it sounded like a long list, and shame filled her blood. "I was in a committed relationship with each of..." She paused, regrouped, tried to say the words without making herself feel cheap and indiscriminate. "What I meant is that I knew each of those men for well over six months before we moved our relationship to the next level. I've only once ever jumped into an intimate relationship without really knowing the person."

"You mean with Cecily's father?"

"I mean with you." Fiona pushed back her shoulders as the truth tumbled from her lips and she didn't care that he looked annoyed by her admission. "Actually, I didn't have a relationship with *him* at all."

Wyatt's eyes narrowed. "Then what was it? A one-night stand?"

Fiona's skin burned, and she felt as though her body were suddenly moving in exaggerated slow motion. If only it *had* been a one-night stand. As the color drained from her face, Fiona knew Wyatt was intensely aware of her altering demeanor. He was a smart guy. The truth teetered on her lips and she swallowed hard. "It was...it was..."

His expression changed quickly. She watched, both fascinated and mortified, as he worked out that something wasn't quite right. A familiar deep-rooted shame washed across her skin.

"Fiona?"

She turned away from the soft sound of his voice. After a few deep breaths, she found her voice. "Jamie Corbett."

"What?"

"That's what you wanted to know, isn't it?" she said and wrapped her arms across her chest. "You wanted his name. Now you have it."

"Corbett?" She heard the query in his voice. "Why does that sound so—"

"Familiar?" Fiona said on a shaky breath. "It would be if you read the report on my mother's death."

"I did," Wyatt replied steadily. "She was killed in a train-crossing accident alongside her twenty-two-year-old..." He stopped and took a few seconds. "Jamie Corbett was your mother's lover?"

Fiona shuddered. An image, like a speedy camera in reverse, flashed through her mind, and the memories leached into her skull. Shayne had gone out looking to score. Fiona was left alone in the grimy motel room they occupied with the young cowboy her mother had picked up in a bar a month earlier. He'd seemed friendly at first. So she'd smiled and crossed her legs as she sat propped up on the single bed she occupied. He'd joined her on the bed to play cards and they'd laughed together. She'd liked the attention, liked how he told her she was pretty and would grow up to be a real heart-breaker one day. He'd touched her ankle at first. Then her leg. When she'd pulled away, he'd grabbed her harder. Although still a virgin, Fiona had known enough about sex to realize what was about to happen.

"Fiona?" Wyatt's voice pulled her back into the present. "Are you saying that Corbett is Cecily's father?"

Emotion clutched her throat. "Yes."

He said her name softly. "Would you turn around?"

She did as he asked slowly, still holding her arms tightly around her chest. She could barely hold contact with his eyes. She focused on the tiny pulse in his cheek beating rapidly. She knew he was thinking, imagining and probably work-ing her out.

But he didn't speak straightaway. When she did meet his gaze, there was a somber realization in his blue eyes. "Fiona, what did he do to you?"

Fiona closed her eyes for a moment and sucked in a breath. She hadn't said the words out loud since telling her mother she was pregnant a couple of months later. And Shayne hadn't believed her. Instead, Fiona had been accused of trying to run interference in her mother's relationship with Jamie Corbett and she'd been quickly shipped off to her uncle.

The words clawed at her throat and she swallowed hard. "He took… He was…"

As her admission trailed off, silence stretched between them like brittle elastic. Finally, Wyatt spoke again. "Fiona, did he rape you?"

She shook her head and then nodded. "It was… Yes…I suppose…"

"Suppose?"

"Well," she managed to reply despite the hard lump in her throat, "I said no."

"And?"

Fiona didn't miss his quiet control and took a few moments before she replied. "And he said I'd asked for it. Said I wanted it. He said a lot of things." She dropped her arms and sat on the sofa. "Maybe in a way I did ask for it. I don't know what to think anymore. Shayne had left us alone in the motel room. I guess I was flattered at first… He paid me some attention, and with my mother the way she was, I was *starved* for it, if that makes sense."

It did make sense. But Wyatt could barely think straight as he absorbed what she was telling him. He pushed the building rage back down and tried to concentrate. "What did you do…after?"

She shrugged and looked so small and vulnerable, so alone, Wyatt had to force himself to remain where he was and not take her in his arms and offer her the comfort he suspected she desperately needed.

"My mother didn't believe me," she said softly. "When I found out I was pregnant, she accused me of trying to come between them. The next day I was sent to my uncle."

Wyatt clenched his fists. "You didn't press charges? You didn't make him—"

"I was fifteen," she said and drew in a heavy breath. "And afraid."

Rationally, and in that part of him that was civilized and logical, Wyatt understood. But that other part, the one that was fuelled by a powerful and instinctive urge to protect her, wanted to grind Corbett into the ground.

"And you've never told anyone what happened?"

She shook her head. "No. They were killed three weeks after I went to live with my uncle. Telling wouldn't have changed what happened. Once Cecily was born, I didn't have a chance to think about anything other than how I had to give my baby away."

Wyatt's insides tightened into knots and he experienced a deep-rooted pain behind his ribs. There were so many people who should have been held accountable for what had happened to her—certainly the lowlife who had brutalized her and the mother who hadn't given a damn. There was the great-uncle, too...and even Karen, who had insisted on a closed adoption, knowing full well that Cecily's birth mother was only fifteen.

"You were let down badly by your family," he said, more statement than question.

She shrugged. "I guess I've never really had a family. Now, because of Cecily, for the first time in my life I feel like I have a chance to have one. And I don't want to do anything to ruin that chance. We jumped into bed together after only a week. We gave in to the attraction, but at the end of the day it's just sex. And sex isn't enough to sustain a relationship, not even great sex." She sighed heavily. "Let's face it, if it was something more, you would have trusted me enough to tell me about your sister's marriage being in trouble, right?"

The truth knocked against his rib cage. He didn't trust easily. Somehow Fiona knew that. "Karen's relationship with Jim had nothing to do with you and Cecily. I know you've worked hard to develop a relationship with Cecily. It has a strong foundation now and will only become stronger the more time you spend together."

Her eyes moistened. "What if she can't forgive me for giving her up?"

"She can," he replied gently. "She has. She cares about you. And I care about you, Fiona. But after the way things ended with Yvette, I'm not about to rush into something without being certain it's going to last. The fact that Cecily wants to see us together makes it even more important to take things slowly. That's why I asked you to come to Waradoon to meet the family. We need time to get to know one another outside of the bedroom, don't you think?"

"But if it fades…I mean, if the attraction we have for each other disappears, what then? What do I do, Wyatt? With Cecily stuck in the middle, how do we push past that?"

"You're predicting failure before we've barely begun?"

Fiona let out a heavy breath. "Because that's what I do. I fail at relationships. I'm nearly thirty years old and the longest friendships I've had are with Callie and Evie and we've only known one another a few years. And you, I imagine, with your picture-perfect family and private-school education— I'll bet you have the same friends you made in kindergarten."

He didn't deny it.

Emotion glittered in her eyes. "You're right about me. Each time a relationship ends, I shut down. I shut down because I don't want to be friends when it's over. Maybe it's some hang-up from watching my mother get ditched by one man after the other and how she tried to cling to them afterward and made a fool of herself by trying to stay friends and keeping herself involved in their lives—even after they'd moved on."

Wyatt rocked back on his heels. "You're not your mother, Fiona."

The tears fell. She blinked a couple of times and drew in a shuddering breath so deep he felt it through to the marrow in his bones. Something uncurled in his chest, a strange and piercing pain that hit him with the sharpness of an arrow.

Wyatt wasn't sure how he ended up in front of her or how she ended up in his arms.

"But how do I ever tell her the truth, Wyatt?"

He held her close. "She'll understand. When you're ready, when she's ready…and I'll be there with you when you do."

"How can I be sure?"

He kissed the top of her head. "I know how much Cecily means to you and I'm not about to tear her out of your life. She's your daughter, Fiona. You're not alone anymore."

But Wyatt knew she didn't quite believe him.

Chapter Eleven

Saying goodbye to Cecily was the hardest thing Fiona had ever done. She'd had her three weeks and now it was over. Her heart felt as if it would shatter into a million pieces.

And saying goodbye to Wyatt just about tipped her over the edge. Exaggerated by the fact their relationship had gone from being lovers to Wyatt treating her like a protective big brother.

The intimacy was gone. He'd changed toward her. He was polite and caring and made an effort to spend time with her and Cecily, but she wasn't fooled. The politeness was excruciating. The friendliness made her want to scream. The most intimate thing he did was grab her hand to help her up the stairs at the information kiosk when they visited the local turtle rookery. She'd told him everything. Her deepest secret. And he'd pulled away. It hurt so much she wasn't sure how she managed to get through the last few days.

Of course, they would still have contact. He was Cecily's guardian, and any decisions about contact with her daughter would have to be approved by Wyatt. But their relationship had become so lukewarm it was barely recognizable.

On the day she had to say goodbye, all her energy was focused on staying calm. Cecily didn't need to see her tears. As it was, her daughter hugged her so tightly she had to choke back a sob. When Wyatt kissed her on the cheek, she'd swayed against him a little, remembering, wanting to feel the safety in his arms once more before he left her.

"Thank you for everything," she whispered against his jaw as she pulled back.

He raised a brow. "Everything?"

"For bringing Cecily here," she explained. "For giving me this chance."

"It's been good for Cecily. I owe you thanks for welcoming her into your life."

With her heart breaking, she'd waved them off outside the B and B, watching as the rental car disappeared down the road. Evie came up behind her and dropped an arm over her shoulder.

"You okay?" her friend asked.

Fiona swallowed the lump in her throat. "Yeah."

"She's a remarkable girl."

Pride swelled in her chest. "I know."

"And the tall drink of water?" Evie asked as one brow rose dramatically.

"It's over," she replied and blinked the hotness from her eyes.

"You're in love with him?"

She didn't bother to deny it. "Crazy, huh?"

"To fall in love?" Evie shook her head. "Not at all. You're going to see them in a couple of weeks, right?"

She nodded. "Yes, for the charity dinner."

Everything was organized. She'd fly down for four days while Mary-Jayne stayed at her house to look after Muffin, and Callie would care for Titan. Cecily insisted they go shopping for their dresses in the city, and she was looking forward to scouring a few high-end boutiques for just the right gown to wear at the charity dinner.

"So, if you decide to stay, I'll understand."

Stay? Had she considered it? To leave Crystal Point would be a wrench. She loved her job, her friends and her little house. But to be close to Cecily…the idea filled her with immense joy.

"My life is here, though."

"Home is where the heart is," Evie replied and squeezed her shoulders assuringly. "Your daughter needs you. And Wyatt, I suspect, needs you, too…even if he doesn't know it yet."

"So, Cecily tells me you and the birth mother got kind of close during the big visit?"

Wyatt glared at his sister. Ellen, as usual, always said exactly what was on her mind.

"She has a name. And it's none of your business."

"Ha—don't get all brooding and silent on me. I think it's great. Cecily certainly approves of the match."

The match? Was that what it was? Stupid. They hardly knew one another.

But he missed her like hell. And he walked around like a bear with a sore head. His family was too polite to really say anything intrusive about his increasingly obvious bad mood. Only Glynis, his assistant, told him to take a pill for whatever ailed him.

"Cecily wants a mother again," he remarked and smiled when Ellen's daughter grabbed hold of his knees and thrust a squishy, dog-eared picture book in his direction.

"What Cecily wants is a mother and a father who love one another."

Wyatt looked at his sister for a moment and then hauled not-quite-two-year-old Amy into his arms. "We'll see what happens," he said and flipped open the book as Amy pumped her chubby legs.

Ellen huffed. "Not all women are like Yvette."

He glanced up. "I know that."

"Well, you probably won't want to hear this, but it seems to me you've avoided getting serious with anyone since she, you know…"

"Cheated?"

Ellen shrugged. "That's an ugly word. But yeah, since she did that. And if this…I mean, if Fiona is someone you could feel strongly about, it would be a shame to ignore those feelings."

Wyatt raised a brow. "Have you been watching the Hallmark channel again?"

"You can scoff all you like. But I know you as well as anyone." She looked at the baby in his arms. "I know what you want. This," she said, motioning toward the baby, who was now chuckling so loud it made Wyatt smile. "A home, family…someone special to curl up to at night after working at Harper's for twelve hours a day."

Wyatt didn't look at his sister. As usual, Ellen made the complicated sound simple. "I'm not about to rush into anything."

"Like you did last time?"

"Exactly."

"Yvette was bad news for any man," she said bluntly. "You just got caught in the firing line."

"I asked her to marry me. I knew what I was doing."

"So you made a mistake…suck it up," Ellen said and grabbed her son Rory as he toddled toward her. She propped him on the seat beside her. "You think Alessio didn't make his fair share of mistakes before he came to his senses and realized he was in love with me? We all make mistakes, Wyatt. Even a man as infallible as you can notch up one or two."

Her words made him half smile. "Fiona's a special woman and I won't have her become one of those mistakes."

She grinned. "Well, who would have *thunk* it? You do have a heart beating beneath that all-work exterior."

"Funny. Take the munchkin so I can get out of here," he said and handed Amy over.

Ellen grabbed the baby and set her beside her twin brother, younger by less than ten minutes. "Cecily told me Fiona will be here for the charity dinner?"

"That's right," Wyatt said as he stood.

"I'm looking forward to meeting her."

"Grilling her, you mean?"

"I'll be on my best behavior," she promised. "She's a part of Cecily's life now, which means she's a part of our lives, too. And the school where she teaches is one of the beneficiaries of this year's list of charities?"

"That's right."

"An out-of-state recipient?" Her brows came up. "That's unusual."

"But not unheard-of," he replied. "It's a tiny school that needed help."

"I read your recommendation and pushed it through with the directors like you asked. I wasn't questioning their need, only your motives."

"There's no motive. Just a group of children who needed a new canteen."

"And Fiona?"

"Is a caring teacher who along with the rest of the faculty is grateful for Harper's generosity."

"Your generosity," Ellen corrected. "I'm not criticizing you. Actually, I think it's rather sweet. Romantic, even."

He rolled his eyes. "Definitely too much Hallmark. I'll see myself out."

As Wyatt drove back to Waradoon, he considered his sister's words. She was right, of course. He'd pushed for the funds for the school because he thought it would help Fiona. Helping Fiona was important to him.

More to the point, Fiona was important to him. And he didn't know what the hell to do about it. He'd kept away from her in that last week with some noble idea about giving Fiona undistracted time with her daughter. He hadn't expected that it would make him feel so damned lonely.

Fiona's flight to Sydney three weeks later was delayed by more than an hour. So by the time she'd checked herself off the aircraft and walked through the gate, she figured Cecily had been waiting impatiently for her arrival. Fiona heard her daughter's squeal when she spotted her. "I'm so glad you're here," Cecily said in an excited whisper as they embraced.

"Me, too," Fiona said and hugged her back, inhaling the familiar scent of Cecily's apple shampoo, and a surge of love warmed every part of her skin.

Someone cleared their throat and Fiona looked over Cecily's head. A smart-looking woman about sixty with brilliant blue eyes stood to the side.

"Hello," the woman said pleasantly and thrust out her hand. "I'm Janet Harper. You must be Fiona?"

"Yes. It's nice to meet you, Mrs. Harper."

"Oh, Janet," the other woman insisted. "I'm parked outside. Do you need to collect your bag from the carousel?"

Fiona nodded. "That would be great."

It took about ten minutes to grab her suitcase and walk from the domestic terminal. "We thought we'd go shopping before we head for Waradoon," Janet said as they placed Fiona's bag in the rear of the dark blue SUV. "I know a fabulous boutique in the bay area where I'm sure you'll find exactly the right dress for Saturday night. It's owned by the niece of a friend of mine. My daughter Ellen bought her dress there last week."

Fiona smiled and nodded. She was being railroaded and organized, but strangely, she didn't mind in the least. There was something incredibly likeable about Janet Harper. In her white capri pants and collared navy-and-white-striped long-sleeved polo, enough makeup to enhance her patrician features and sporting a silvery bob blunt to her neck, she was just as Fiona might have imagined Wyatt's mother to be.

Wyatt...

Her tongue burned with the urge to ask about him. But she didn't. She certainly didn't want to come across as a love-sick fool pining over a man who...who what? Liked her? Wanted her? Both pretty much summed up their brief relationship. She hadn't heard from him since he and Cecily had left Crystal Point except for one cursory email confirming the date for Cecily's next school-break visit.

After her emotional outburst, he'd backed off—just as she'd known he would. He'd said she wasn't alone. However, once he had returned home, Fiona had never felt more alone in her life. Only Cecily's daily emails or text messages and telephone calls kept Fiona from going quietly out of her mind. Of course, her daughter kept her updated on his movements, which seemed to be all about work and little else. She was reluctant to admit how pleased she was to hear that he spent most of his time at Harper's. Imagining him out doing whatever an unattached man did was too much to bear.

"We're delighted you could stay with us, Fiona," Janet said, cutting through her thoughts. "Cecily has talked of nothing else but you for the past two weeks."

"Aw, Nan," Cecily complained from the backseat as she

fiddled with her cell phone. "You're not supposed to tell her that."

"Well, I've thought of nothing else but Cecily for the past few weeks…so I guess we're even."

Cecily laughed loudly. "Not *just* me, I'll bet."

Fiona bit back the protest in her throat. Janet's watchful gaze was only a bend of the neck away, and the last thing she wanted to do was look guilty and acknowledge Cecily's announcement in any way whatsoever.

"Cecily tells me you grow orchids?"

It was a clumsy segue, and Fiona caught the edges of a smile on Janet's lips. But she wasn't about to enter into a conversation that had anything to do with the other woman's son. Even though Cecily looked as though it was all she wanted to talk about. It made Fiona wonder how much her daughter had told the Harpers about the three weeks she and her uncle had spent in Crystal Point. If the look on Janet's face was anything to go by, then it was clear Cecily had said more than enough. And curious relatives she could do without.

Thankfully, Janet answered her question and they spent the remainder of the drive discussing hobbies and nonwork pursuits. By the time they pulled into a parking space outside a very exclusive-looking store, Fiona knew everything about the older woman's golf swing and determination to get her husband back onto the green after his recent mild heart attack. Brought on, Janet insisted, by the grief associated with his daughter's death.

Half an hour later, Fiona was swathed in yards of luxuriously slinky emerald-green satin and knew she had found the perfect gown for the charity dinner. The color complemented her hair and complexion. The spaghetti straps, tightly boned bodice and floor-length skirt, which was ruched behind her knees, was just about the most gorgeous creation she'd ever seen and also had a ridiculously excessive price tag. Way too much for her teacher's salary.

"We'll take it," Janet insisted to the tall, pencil-thin young woman who had selected the magnificent gown.

Fiona protested immediately. "Oh, no. But could I see something else?" she asked as she touched the lovely fabric. "Maybe something a little less—"

"We'll take it," Janet said again and gently silenced her. "It's like it was made for you."

"Yes," Cecily agreed with a kind of two-against-one grin. "And you need shoes, too."

Fiona half turned toward Janet. "Mrs. Harper, I couldn't possibly afford such—"

"I insist," she said and passed something to the salesclerk. "Call that number and you'll reach my son's assistant. Glynis will give you the payment details."

Fiona's eyes popped wide when she realized what was transpiring. "I can't allow—"

"I'm under strict instructions," she explained, cutting her off. "There's no point in being stubborn about it. He always gets what he wants."

He got me into bed within a week.

Although she wasn't about to announce *that* fact to his mother.

Fiona nodded acquiescingly. She'd deal with Wyatt later. "Thank you. It's very generous of...everyone."

Janet patted her arm. "Good girl. And later," she said in a lower voice as she leaned forward and pretended to adjust the narrow strap, "you can tell me exactly what you've done to my son that's got him so wound up he can barely string a sentence together without snapping people's heads off."

"What I've done?" she echoed, mortified and confused. "I don't—"

"Later," Janet insisted. "And now," she said to the clerk, "let's match this dress with a wicked pair of heels."

And just like that, Fiona got sucked into the Harpers' world. And worse, was terrified she might get tossed out again when the weekend was over.

Wyatt drove to Waradoon Friday evening. As he eased the BMW into the driveway, the big house greeted him with welcoming warmth. And as always, the tension knotted in the center of his chest eased slowly. But not all the way. At least, not tonight.

He parked behind Ellen and Alessio's hulking SUV and killed the engine. After a couple of long breaths, he grabbed his iPhone and jacket and headed inside.

The moment he stepped across the threshold, he heard voices coming from out the back and the sound of splashing water. He made his way past the wide front entrance and down the hall. He found Rosa in the kitchen, creating a variety of homemade pizzas.

"They look good," he said and moved to swipe a slice from the pizza she'd just pulled from the wood-fired stove his mother had installed to complement the huge red cedar kitchen.

"You wait," Rosa scolded, her accent thickly Sicilian even though she'd lived in Australia most of her adult life. Nearly all of those years, she'd lived and worked at Waradoon along with her husband. "Enough for *esrebody*."

"Rosalie, you're breaking my heart."

"Ha," she scoffed. "You only hungry now because you don't eat in the city." She looked him over and grunted. "You too skinny. You need to work less and eat and make love more."

Wyatt laughed. "I'll see what I can do."

"I'm speaking serious. A man needs love—just ask my Silvio."

He looked at the pizza and winked. "If I promise to love more, can I have a piece?"

"You go," she said and shooed him off. "Your mama been expecting you for hours. And *Cecilia*. Everyone waits for you."

He laughed, saluted and headed outside.

Of course, the first person he spotted when he slipped through the door and onto the huge patio was Fiona. She stood at the far end of the heated pool, illuminated by the lights behind, poised and ready to dive into the water. The black high-cut bikini amplified the sheer luminescent beauty of her skin and her wet hair clung to her scalp. His body stirred, remembering…wanting.

Mesmerized, he watched as she took a long breath, bent her knees and pushed herself off the pool's edge. The dive was clean and swift, and within seconds she surfaced above the water.

"Aren't you a little overdressed for a pool party?"

Wyatt looked to his left. Ellen had approached, hair wet, a sarong wrapped around her bathing suit and both brows raised.

"I wasn't aware we were having a party."

"Mother's idea," she explained. "To keep the kids happy."

Wyatt spotted Alessio in the shallow end of the huge pool, a toddler in each arm, while their four-year-old son, Thomas, bobbed around in inflatable floaties. Cecily sat on the edge of the pool, laughing at something Fiona had said.

"I guess I'll go get changed."

"Good idea. And keep the X-rated thoughts under wraps until we've all gone home, will you?"

"What?"

"You know what I mean, Captain Obvious," Ellen said with a smile. "Incidentally, she's quite the hit. I approve."

Wyatt didn't respond. Instead he headed back into the house.

Fiona hauled herself out of the pool, wrapped a cotton sarong over her bikini and squeezed the water from her hair. Nerves set in as she padded around the edge of the pool and ignored Cecily's pleas to return to the water.

She headed for the patio and perused the drinks table.

She'd sensed Wyatt's arrival even before she saw him standing by the doors that led into the kitchen. He'd looked so good in his shirt and tie, a jacket flung over one arm, and it had taken every ounce of her self-control to remain where she was. She'd been anticipating his appearance for over twenty-four hours. A surreal twenty-four hours. The Harpers were something else. Friendly, noisy, loving…the kind of family she'd only ever imagined existed. Knowing Cecily had grown up surrounded by such warmth and caring somehow eased a portion of the guilt and grief that had lain in her heart for so long.

Janet Harper was an übergrandmother and clearly adored Cecily and the rest of her grandchildren. Her husband, Lincoln, or Linc as he preferred, was a handsome, older-looking version of his son. He was quiet and caring and sometimes seemed just a little sad. Fiona had thought he might resent her sudden involvement with his family, considering he'd lost his oldest daughter, and now she'd resurfaced and was very much a part of Cecily's life. But on the contrary, he couldn't have been more welcoming. The day before he'd given her a tour of Waradoon on the back of a quad bike, showing off his herd of Wagyu cattle and the small crop of grapevines he tended to.

Ellen, she'd discovered, was incredibly likable and her husband more good-looking than a straight man had any right to be. They were all remarkable people. Good people.

"Shall we have that talk now?"

Janet had come up beside her as she poured a glass of juice. Linc was at the barbecue turning burgers, and Ellen had returned to the water's edge to urge her family to leave the pool before they wrinkled up. Wyatt was nowhere to be seen.

"Oh, okay," she said quietly and took a sip.

"Are you and my son seriously involved?" Janet scooped out a ladle of punch into a glass. "I suppose I mean are you sleeping together?"

Fiona choked on a breath. "I can't talk about—"

"Enough said, then," Janet responded. "It's your business what you do. I just don't want to see anyone get hurt. I must say how happy Cecily is that you're here. We all are."

"You've been very welcoming. I appreciate it."

"You're part of my granddaughter's life," Janet replied. "It would be unwise to do anything other than welcome you here."

Fiona understood what she meant. "But not exactly easy."

"For me it's easier than I'd expected. But then, Karen wasn't my child. I mean, I loved her very much and she was very young when her father and I married. Her own mother had died when she was five. My husband, though, feels her loss deeply."

"I appreciate what you're saying. And I have no intention of trying to replace his daughter and her role in Cecily's life."

"Of course you do," Janet said with a kind of blunt gentleness that made Fiona straighten. "You are Cecily's mother. You carried her. You gave birth to her. That's a bond no one but a mother could understand."

"Yes," she said quietly. "It is a bond. I can hardly believe how strong it is sometimes."

"A mother's love is like none other." Janet's eyes strayed to the pool. "When I had Wyatt, when I held this tiny baby for the first time, I felt something so deep, so all-consuming. It was impossible to imagine I could love another human being so much. And it brought Linc and I closer together, made our love stronger."

Emotion tightened her throat. "I'm sure it did."

Janet nodded and patted her shoulder. "It must have been hard on your own, and being so young, I can only imagine. It was insensitive of me to say that. One day, I'm sure you'll have the opportunity to share the experience with the man you love."

Fiona felt as though two hands were wrapped around her heart and squeezing. "Mmm."

What could she say? *Guess what...the man I love is your son.*

"Karen loved Cecily very much. Above all others." When Fiona's eyes widened, Janet continued. "Yes, even Jim. But I suppose Wyatt has told you all about that."

He hasn't told me anything. "He said they had a few problems."

Janet nodded. "Karen was focused on Cecily. Jim worked long hours. They stopped communicating. To give them credit, I think they genuinely did want to make it work." Janet let out a long breath. "And perhaps they would have— if it hadn't been for that thing with Yvette."

Chapter Twelve

"Yvette?"

Fiona heard the word leave her tongue. A sickly feeling reached down low. Suddenly she wasn't sure she wanted to hear any more.

"Yvette and Jim," Janet said quietly. "A messy business. But families can be messy—even the happiest of families."

Yvette and Jim.

Wyatt's fiancée and his sister's husband. Fiona had seen a picture of the pudgy, nondescript man on the stairwell wall. *Yvette and Jim.* Was it possible? Of course, because Janet had told her so. It simply seemed impossible. Wyatt had told her his ex-fiancée had been unfaithful. And Jim had cheated on his wife. Imagining the two of them together, as realization dawned, brought a sour taste to her mouth.

Such betrayal. Her heart lurched for Karen Todd. Her insides ached for Wyatt.

Why didn't he tell me?

She hurt through to the marrow of her bones. His silence was another obvious example of how little she meant to him. If he'd cared, he would have trusted her. If he'd cared, he would have spoken to her over the past couple of weeks.

"He's always been a closed book," Janet said with more intuition than Fiona could stand.

She didn't want her life on show. Her dreams. Her wants. She couldn't bear Janet seeing her helpless and wishing for something she sensed would never be. She was in love with Wyatt. She didn't imagine she'd get past those feelings anytime soon.

"We're not…" She stopped and denied herself the sudden urge to tell this woman everything. Janet wasn't one of her girlfriends. She was Wyatt's mother. Her loyalty would lie with her son. "I'm here for Cecily. I have to be."

"I understand you want to do the right thing by your child." *Your child…*

Fiona blinked back tears from her eyes. "I do. I will."

"And you don't want to be derailed?"

Did this woman know everything? Fiona couldn't believe Janet had figured her out in a little over twenty-four hours. "No, I don't. And Wyatt…"

"Never lets anyone know what he's thinking? Or feeling?" The other woman smiled. "I know, it's infuriating. Don't be put off by it—underneath he's as vulnerable as the rest of us."

She smiled but didn't believe a word of it. "I think I'll go change now."

Janet nodded. "Good idea. Rosa will bring out the pizzas, and Linc will be serving his infamous burgers shortly."

Fiona smiled again and headed off in the direction of the guesthouse. The one-bedroom suite had a huge living area, bathroom and fully equipped kitchenette. It was attached to the rear of the main house and was luxury personified. Every detail, from the rich cream-and-coffee-colored furnishings to the wide French doors that opened onto a small patio with its own hot tub, to the freshly cut flowers and thick white comforter on the bed, which was piled with about a dozen pillows, made her feel as if she was staying at a five-star hotel.

She grabbed her green knitted dress off a hanger and changed in the bathroom. It took a few minutes to attack her hair with a dryer, and she finger-combed it for a moment before heading back into the living area. Her feet came to a stop when she spotted Wyatt outside, standing by the hot tub with his back toward the house.

The sun had all but gone down and the overhead light made his dark hair shimmer. He'd changed into jeans and a pale blue shirt, and her insides did their usual flip-flop. He really was too gorgeous for words. After a second, she walked across the room and slid the screen open a little.

He turned instantly. "Hey."

"Hi."

His gaze traveled over her slowly. "It's good to see you."

"You, too."

They were being so polite she wanted to scream.

"Are you comfortable here?" he asked, gesturing toward the guesthouse.

"Yes, very much."

"Cecily said you were sick yesterday. Are you all right?"

Fiona made a mental note to quiz her daughter on what to say and what not to say to people. Especially to Wyatt. "I'm fine. It was just a headache. I never travel well—even short trips."

"But you came anyway?"

"For Cecily—yes." She pushed the screen door back fully. "I've missed her."

And I've missed you, too.

His arms looked strong and safe, and Fiona fought the urge to fall into them. "Your family has been very kind to me."

"Just as well," he said quietly. "Or they might get a dose of your red-haired temper."

"What temper?"

He smiled. "Can I come inside?"

"Of course," she said and stepped aside. "It's your house."

"Actually, it's my parents' house," Wyatt said as he crossed the threshold. "But it's my home. At least for the moment."

Fiona glanced at him. "And your apartment in the city?"

He shrugged. "A place to sleep. I own some land about ten miles east from here, and I've been thinking I might build a house on it one day."

She wondered if he'd planned that while engaged to be married. Perhaps he'd wanted to build a home for his new bride? Now that his engagement was over, the "one day" he talked about was probably some faraway moment in the future.

"Fiona?" He moved closer, watching her with burning intensity. "What are you thinking?"

"That having a home base closer to the city will cut down your commute."

He looked skeptical. "That's it? Anything else?"

She took a breath, as deep as she could, and wrapped her arms around her waist. She wanted answers. "I'm wondering why you didn't tell me it was Yvette who had the affair with Jim."

Wyatt visibly paled. "How did you—"

"Your mother told me," she answered, cutting him off. "Without an agenda, I might add. I presume she thought you would have told me yourself. I'm guessing she thought we were more involved than we actually are," Fiona said and pushed back the pain knocking against her rib cage. "Cecily hasn't exactly been keeping anything a secret."

"No," Wyatt agreed. "She hasn't. Cecily wants you permanently in her life. If we were together, she'd get that."

"But we're not," Fiona said and figured there was no point in sugarcoating the situation. "Right? Because if we were, you certainly would have told me about how the woman you were going to marry slept with your sister's husband."

He went to say something, then stopped. Thinking, planning his words. "It's not a subject I enjoy talking about."

Fiona pulled back a frown. "Is that all I get?"

He stared at her for a moment and pushed his hands into the pockets of his jeans. "What's the point in rehashing the past? Talking about it won't change anything."

Janet had called her son a closed book. Fiona felt like shaking him. "Do you have so little trust in me? So little faith in..." *Us.* She longed to say it but couldn't.

He scowled. "It's not about trust."

"Of course it is," she retorted. "If you trusted me, you'd share something...anything." Fiona gripped herself rigidly. "My God, I feel like such a fool. I fell apart right in front of you. I told you everything. I told you things I've never shared with anyone else. And you held me and said I wasn't alone. Do you know how hard it is for me to talk about my past, especially Shayne and what happened that night? Do you know that I never, *ever* cry like that?" She swallowed the stinging emotion in her throat. "From the first moment we met, I've tried to be the truest version of myself. I had to be for Cecily's sake. I couldn't keep anything from you in the end. I knew I had to let you know me, so that you would let me know my daughter. I thought...I guess I thought I was getting the same honesty in return."

He let out an exasperated sigh. "What do you want me to say to you?"

She moved forward and placed her hand on his chest. It was their first touch in weeks, and she felt the vibration of his heart beneath her palm. "I want you to say what's in here. I want you to tell me what happened."

Wyatt stepped back and her hand dropped. "Tell you what? That I caught them together in my own apartment? That I wasn't supposed to be home that weekend but my meeting was canceled and I thought I'd surprise Yvette because I knew she was staying there overnight? Do you want to know exactly where I caught them? And what they were doing? It's not a pretty story. None of it." He pushed a hand through his hair. "Do you also want to know that I had to stop myself from smashing Jim in the face? And that after I'd hauled him outside, he begged me not to tell Karen?"

"Wyatt, I—"

"You wanted to know," he said bitterly. "Here it is…I found my fiancée in my bed having sex with my sister's husband."

Bile rose in Fiona's throat. "Wyatt, I'm so sorry. Did you tell Karen?"

He shook his head. "I gave Jim twenty-four hours to come clean with his wife."

"And did he?"

"Sure," Wyatt replied. "Then a bad situation got worse."

"I don't understand?"

He exhaled heavily. "Karen wanted someone to blame."

"Then she obviously blamed Yvette? Or her husband? He was the…" Fiona's voice trailed off when she saw Wyatt shake his head. "She couldn't possibly have blamed you."

"She did," he said flatly. "It was a messy time. Christmas, in fact."

"Cecily said something to me," Fiona told him quietly. "About how you didn't show up on Christmas Eve."

"She remembers that? I'm not surprised. There wasn't a lot of Christmas cheer going around at the time."

"But why did Karen blame you?"

He shrugged. "It's a no-brainer—I brought Yvette into the family. Karen needed to hold someone responsible."

"That's not altogether logical."

"It was to her. She was hurting. After the sting had left and once Yvette was out of my life, I understood Karen's reaction."

Fiona fought the need to go to him. But if he wanted comfort, he would ask her for it, wouldn't he? "Did you make peace with Karen before she passed away?"

"Mostly. We talked. She told me they were trying to rebuild their marriage."

"Is that why they were on holiday?"

He shrugged again, this time stiffer. "Karen asked me for advice. I suggested she work out what they enjoyed doing together. Rock fishing is what she came up with." When Fiona raised both brows, he continued. "Sex wasn't it, according to my sister. Which I guess explains why Jim fell for Yvette."

"And what was Yvette's excuse?"

"Boredom, narcissism…you can take your pick. For three months she did a good impression of caring about someone other than herself."

"You mean you?"

Another shrug. "I thought it was time I settled down. I was tired of coming home to an empty apartment. Yvette is the daughter of a business associate and we hit it off when we met. Or so I thought."

He didn't mention love, didn't say he was swept away by the other woman and had to make her his own. "You couldn't forgive her?"

"No. More for Karen than myself. My sister had a twenty-year marriage at stake. But as far as Yvette and I were concerned, I got over it. I got over her."

Ridiculously relieved, Fiona continued. "And Karen?"

"She…died."

She pushed her feet forward and moved in front of him. "That wasn't your fault."

His impassive expression was impossible to read. "It was

my suggestion she try to reconnect with Jim by doing something they enjoyed doing together."

Her fingers itched to bond with him and she touched his arm. "And still not your fault."

He grunted. "Can we talk about something else?"

"Sure," she said. "I was going to ask you if I could take Cecily to—"

"I meant you and me," he interrupted. "You in particular."

Fiona swallowed hard. "What… Okay…what in particular?"

"I just want to make sure my family isn't giving you the third degree. They can be intrusive at times, although with the best intentions. Ellen and my mother are—"

"They've been great," Fiona said quickly. "If they overstep sometimes, it's only because they care about you and Cecily. I'm an unknown quantity to them and it's natural they'd be curious."

His mouth thinned and he covered her hand with his. "According to Ellen, you're a hit anyway. I'm probably being overcautious."

Fiona's skin burned where he touched her. "I can do this. I want this, Wyatt. I want to be here for Cecily. I want your family to know I'm a good person and that I would never do anything to hurt Cecily." She stopped, paused, looked directly into his eyes. "Or anyone else."

"Fiona," he said and softly rubbed her hand with his thumb. "You are extraordinary. But I raced into the thing with Yvette without really knowing her. Because I was rash, a whole lot of people got hurt. I won't do that again, regardless of how much I…how strong the connection is here. I can't deny I'm drawn to you." He urged her closer. "Or how much I want you. Like right now, I just want to kiss you."

"But I thought…when you left Crystal Point we weren't… I didn't think you wanted this."

"I backed off, yes," he said on a sigh. "Because you wanted time with Cecily and our involvement was distracting you from that. I promised you three weeks where you could get to know your daughter."

"That's why I got the big-brother routine during that last week?"

He half smiled and leaned closer. "Yes. Just so you know, I don't feel the least bit brotherly toward you."

"I thought…I thought it was because of what I told you."

His expression narrowed. "Because of Corbett?" He shook his head. "Nothing you said made me look at you differently. You weren't to blame for that, Fiona. You were an innocent girl. *Innocent,*" he said again with emphasis as he grasped her chin. "And I will always be sorry I wasn't there to protect you."

She melted, as she knew she would. He kissed her with such searing passion and skill Fiona's knees threatened to give way. So she held on, gripping his shoulders with a kind of mad desperation. It had been forever since he'd kissed her with such intensity, and she craved his touch and possession as if it was a searing thirst.

Fiona thrust her fingertips into his hair and pulled him closer. She loved him so much. Wanted him so much. And she almost told him so. Almost. Something held her back, a lingering fear, from long ago, from now. From the very moment she found herself in. *No one has ever truly loved me. Why would Wyatt?* He wanted her, which was obvious. But if it were just sex? If it were only ever just sex…would that be enough?

"Fiona…" he muttered against her lips. "I want to—"

"Knock, knock!"

A tap on the door, and Cecily's chirpy voice acted like a bucket of cold water. They pulled apart like a pair of guilty teenagers, and Fiona pushed her hair back with a shaky hand.

"Sorry to interrupt," her daughter said with a cheek-splitting grin, "but Nan said that the pizzas are on the table and the barbecue is ready and everyone is waiting on you guys."

Wyatt stepped toward the door. "Thanks, kiddo. We'll be along in a minute."

Cecily grinned again, looking outrageously pleased. "Take your time."

Once she'd scooted off, Wyatt turned back to Fiona. "Are you okay?"

She shrugged. "I guess."

"It's not the first time she's caught us together. I daresay it won't be the last."

Fiona drew in a breath. "So, you want to continue?"

"Maybe not right now," he said and smiled. "But you're here for the weekend, right? So we'll see where this goes. There's no hurry, is there?"

Fiona smiled, but it didn't touch her heart. One weekend didn't make a relationship. Weekends were for lovers. Once she returned to Crystal Point, how often would they have an opportunity to one another? And how many long-distance relationships lasted? "No hurry," she said agreeably and tried to forget the ever-growing pain in her heart. He wanted slow. She wanted now. How could it ever work?

Over dinner, Wyatt felt the scrutiny of his family's curiosity more than ever. They did, he suspected, imagine they were watching a little romance unfold before their eyes. And maybe they were, but he didn't like their interference one bit. He certainly wasn't about to do anything obvious to encourage their notions.

Ellen's none-too-subtle comments about Fiona having more than one reason to visit Waradoon again had Alessio shushing her. Even Rae, who'd arrived late and made no apology, had cast her older sister a death stare. To her credit, Fiona took it in her stride. En masse, his family could be overwhelming… and Yvette had certainly complained about it on a number of occasions. The überexuberence his sisters displayed had become exaggerated since Karen's death. He suspected the girls did it for their father's benefit, overcompensating to relieve some of his grief. Wyatt understood, but he didn't want Fiona stuck in the middle of their games.

Because he liked her. And it wasn't simply because his libido had jumped off the Richter scale since he'd known her. Sure, he enjoyed making love to her. They were great in bed together. But he knew great sex wasn't enough to sustain a long relationship. She'd accused him of not trusting her and she was right. Yvette's betrayal still had a sting, and that sting made Wyatt question Fiona's motives, even if it were the last thing he wanted to believe. But what if she were cozying up to him simply to get close to Cecily? He knew how much she wanted a permanent relationship with her daughter. What would she do to get it? He didn't like how the thought made him feel.

Wyatt looked across the table and she met his gaze immediately, as though they were connected by some invisible force. *Stupid*. He was becoming way too sentimental. Her eyes asked him what was wrong, and he shook his head fractionally. He wasn't about to get into it over the dinner table.

She smiled and nibbled her lower lip a little. Her mouth glistened wetly, and Wyatt's body tightened instantly. He'd planned to spend the night at Waradoon. But maybe that wasn't a great idea. Spending the night with Fiona was out of the question. Yet spending the night with Fiona was exactly what he wanted to do.

With dinner over, Ellen and Alessio left by nine o'clock. Rae headed off to bed shortly after, muttering something about an early morning start drenching the neighbor's cattle, and Cecily bounded out of the room to hook up with Lily Preston on Skype. With only his parents and Fiona remaining in the front living room, everyone sipping coffee bar him, Wyatt could feel his mother's curiosity because she wore it like a beacon. Seeing him happily married off would thrill her to pieces. And it looked as though, just like Cecily, his mother considered Fiona a prime candidate for the role. He could see Janet's mind working in overdrive, planning a wedding, imagining more grandchildren.

But he wouldn't be pushed. Not until he was certain it would last. The lukewarm feelings he'd had for Yvette, mostly fuelled by physical attraction, waved in front of him like a red flag. He wouldn't be that shallow again. If Fiona had feelings for him other than desire, she didn't really show it. And with the idea she might be playing him just a little hanging around in the back of his mind, Wyatt knew he wasn't in any position to start thinking long-term. He didn't know her very well. And Yvette had proven his instincts sucked. What if it was just an act? She wanted her daughter—could he be sure she wouldn't do anything to get her? But as she watched him with her smoky blue-gray eyes, it made Wyatt want her all the more.

As if on cue, his parents bade them good-night. Within moments they were alone. Fiona remained on the sofa, cradling a coffee cup.

"Is everything all right?"

Intuitive to the core, he thought. "Yes."

"If it's not, I'd rather you just say so," she said on a breath. "Ever since we sat down to dinner, you've looked like you want to punch someone."

"Not exactly."

"Then what is it?"

"I want to spend the night with you," he said flatly. "And I can't."

She placed her empty cup on the side table and crossed her legs. "But it wouldn't be appropriate anyhow, would it? Considering your earlier speech about taking things slow."

"I guess not." As if he was going to get any sleep knowing she was tucked away in the guesthouse. It would be a better idea to go back to his apartment and stare at the ceiling. "I have to get back to the city. I have a meeting tomorrow."

"On a Saturday?"

He half shrugged and stretched the truth as far as his conscience would allow. "Sure. So I'll see you tomorrow night."

"Tomorrow?"

"At the charity dinner, remember?"

"Oh, yes." She sounded vague, not like herself. "Well, goodbye, Wyatt." She stood and grabbed her cup. "I'll take this to the kitchen and return to the guesthouse."

He watched her leave and felt like the biggest jerk of all time.

Fiona had never owned a more beautiful dress. The luxurious satin was decadent and cool against her skin, and the only underwear she wore was a black thong. Cecily helped with her hair and she did the same in return. Makeup went on with emphasis around her eyes using a smoky kohl pencil and a shimmering gloss on her lips.

"Wow," her daughter said when she was done and insisted Fiona twirl. "Totally hot. Wait until Uncle Wyatt sees you."

Fiona looked at her reflection in the long mirror. She hadn't seen Wyatt all day. After his announcement about returning to the city, she'd spent most of the day jumping between loving him and loathing him. Of course, loving had won out. But she remained angry. He could have stayed. Even if only to spend time together. Their relationship was going backward. Thankfully, the bond she'd created with Cecily was flourishing. She adored her daughter and cherished every moment she spent in her company.

"I gotta run," Cecily announced. "Thanks for doing my hair. But if I don't get into my dress in the next five minutes, Nan will come looking for me. See you at the dinner."

Fiona frowned. She'd assumed they'd be traveling together in her grandparents' car.

"But I thought—"

"You look great," Cecily said on a rush of breath and hugged her carefully. "See ya."

She disappeared through the door, and Fiona heard the security screen slide open and shut. After checking her hair and makeup, Fiona grabbed her small bag. It was six-thirty and the party started at seven. Figuring she'd better make her way into the main house or risk being left behind, she shut off the bedroom light and walked into the living room.

She stopped dead in her tracks.

Wyatt stood by the door, dressed in a tuxedo, and looked so gorgeous it stole her breath. His glittering gaze swept over her appreciatively as he dazzled Fiona with a smile.

And she fell in love with him all over again.

Chapter Thirteen

"Are you ready to go, beautiful?"

Fiona rocked backward and teetered on her ridiculously high heels. "I thought you were in the city?"

"I was. But I'm here now." He admired her again, lingering around her waist and then higher to where her breasts pushed upward and added a generous swell to her cleavage. "You look sensational."

She shuddered beneath his appraisal. "It's the dress."

"It's you. Not the dress."

"You paid for it," she said snippily, irritated that he was egotistical enough to turn up and imagine she'd been waiting for him. "The dress, I mean."

"It was clearly a great investment." He checked his watch. "But if we don't get moving, we're going to be late. My father is the emcee for the evening and he growls if people walk in halfway through one of his infamously poor jokes."

Minutes later, Fiona was buckled into the front seat of

Wyatt's BMW and waited until he'd started the engine before she spoke again. "So, is this a date?"

He glanced at her, pushed off the parking brake and grinned. "Yeah."

"You might have let me know."

He drove the car along the paved driveway. "I thought it was a given."

"And I thought I was traveling with your parents and Cecily."

"Even after I asked you to come with me?"

Fiona kept her gaze straight ahead. "That's not exactly what you said."

He shrugged. "Semantics."

"You're being a real jerk, you know that?" she said and suddenly wished he'd take her back to the house so she could rid herself of the beautiful dress and then flop onto the bed and cry her heart out.

He sighed. "I apologize. Let's start again. You look beautiful and I'd be honored to take you to the charity dinner tonight."

Oh, he was good. She got rid of her frown and sort of smiled. "Well, you don't look so bad yourself."

"So, friends again?"

Fiona wasn't going to let him off the hook as easily as he wanted. "I'll think about it. And only if you tell me why you really left last night."

He sighed heavily. "A momentary lapse of good sense."

"Try again."

"Are you sure you want me to say?"

She nodded. "I'm sure."

"Okay," he said in that maddeningly calm way she'd become familiar with. "It occurred to me that we've got to a certain stage fairly quickly."

"And you want to take things slow," she replied. "I get that."

"But we haven't. So I was wondering why. I mean outside of the fact we have this insane chemistry. I know you want to get close to Cecily and—"

Fiona snapped her neck sideways as the blood in her veins simmered. "What is it you think I'm doing?"

"I'm not sure."

But she was. She could put two and two together. And the number she came up with made her sick to the stomach. Suddenly it became altogether too clear what he meant. "Do you think I slept with you simply to stay close to my daughter?"

"As I said, I'm not—"

Fiona's insides burned. "I don't have sex for favors."

He groaned. "I'm sorry. Of course I didn't mean it like that."

"I'm not my mother. And I'm not your ex." Fiona fired off her shots as coolly as she could. "Not all women resort to trickery and manipulation. If you thought that about me, I'm surprised you let me anywhere near Cecily."

"I don't think that about you. Actually, I don't know what the hell I'm thinking. All I seem to do is say the wrong thing to you and that's certainly not my intention. So yeah, maybe I do have some lingering hang-ups from finding the woman I was going to marry in bed with another man. And that has made me cautious…and sometimes plain old suspicious."

It was quite the admission considering he was usually as emotionally impenetrable as a vault. Janet had said he was vulnerable beneath his no-nonsense, pragmatic exterior. At that moment, Fiona knew the other woman was right.

"O-o-kay. We agree you're not perfect?"

"Unanimously."

"And you believe that I didn't sleep with you out of some ulterior motive?"

"Yes."

Stupidly relieved, and just plain old stupid, Fiona wondered if they made bigger fools than her. "Good. Although, I'm curious about something. If you suspected I wasn't genuine, why did you say you wanted to spend last night with me?"

"I'm a jerk, not a rock. I enjoy making love with you, Fiona."

Except love has nothing to do with it. If he imagined her capable of manipulating him in such a way, he couldn't possibly feel anything other than desire, could he?

Thankfully, they pulled into a driveway and he announced they'd arrived at their destination. A huge gated arch loomed overhead and the words *Mariah Downs* were etched onto the timber in fancy writing. There were dozens of cars parked along the road and more vehicles closer to the huge home, which looked as if it had been plucked from a Southern plantation from years gone by. Once they reached the valet parking attendant, Fiona grabbed her bag and stepped from the car. It was still light and she watched as people arrived from a few directions, dressed up and ready to make an impression.

Wyatt handed the keys to the valet and grasped her elbow. "Let's go inside."

He explained that what was once a residence had been beautifully transformed into a working vineyard and luxury hotel. A curling staircase led upstairs, and the ballroom was large enough to accommodate several hundred people.

"It's amazing," she said as they walked across the foyer.

"The original owners were French and held most of the land around here. It was turned into a hotel about thirty years ago and has changed hands a few times since then. A friend of mine owns it now and has steadily restored the building and the vineyard in the last five years. It should start producing wine again in the next year or so. We usually hold this event in the city, but when Ellen suggested Mariah Downs, we all agreed."

The magnificent entrance, the huge staircase—Fiona's mind went into overdrive. It was exactly the kind of place she'd imagined in her secret dreams—the dreams where she was a bride and about to marry the man she loved. It was, she realized, the perfect setting for a wedding. In a flash of a second, she saw it all clearly—the beautiful white gown, Callie and Evie attending her, Cecily in a pale satin dress. And Wyatt…waiting at the altar and watching as she walked toward him.

He was looking at her, and she wondered if he saw the longing in her eyes. No…of course not. He couldn't possibly guess her secret dreams.

"What are you thinking?" he asked quietly.

Fiona wanted to shake off her silly fantasies, but the idea lingered. "That would be a lovely place to get…well, to get…"

"Married?"

She stared up at him and got drawn deeper into his gaze. "Yes."

He took her hand and rubbed his thumb across her knuckles. "And is that what you want?"

Fiona's breath caught in her throat. "Someday…I guess."

His eyes never left hers. "Someday soon?"

She shrugged her bare shoulders, almost dying inside. "I have to find myself a groom first."

He smiled and her. "I suppose that's usually the way it works."

If she wasn't so completely in love with him, Fiona would have laughed at his teasing.

Instead, she shook off her fantasies, managed a smile and moved her hand from his. "We should go inside."

He nodded and took her elbow again before leading her toward the door. Fiona faltered in the doorway and looked around. There were at least thirty large round tables in the ballroom, covered in stark white cloths and laid out with fine crystal and tableware. At the front of the room was a small stage and podium, and there were already a couple of hundred people milling around the tables, some sitting, some talking in groups. The men were dressed in tuxedos or suit and tie. The women wore an array of outfits, from classic ball gowns in satin and flowing organza to more modern cocktail-length dresses.

She couldn't help but notice how people hushed as they walked by. "People are staring."

Wyatt smiled and ushered her forward. "Because you look so beautiful. Relax and enjoy yourself."

She smiled back. But she knew the reason for the stares. This was the Harper Engineering charity dinner, and Wyatt *was* Harper Engineering. And she was his date. No wonder he'd forked out for the dress. He'd probably imagined she'd turn up in worn riding breeches and a grass-stained T-shirt.

By the time they were midway across the room, she heard Cecily's familiar voice calling her name. Her daughter was beside her in seconds. "This is our table," she said excitedly and pointed to a table at the front. "You're next to me. Uncle Wyatt's on the other side, of course."

Her joyous grin was incredibly infectious, and Fiona moved away from Wyatt for a moment and kissed Cecily affectionately.

"Shall we sit down, then?" Fiona suggested when she spotted Janet already sitting beside Alessio and Ellen. She managed a tiny wave and Janet gave her a discreet thumbs-up.

"I think you have to cruise the room first," Cecily said. "You know, 'cause you're Uncle Wyatt's date. And Pop will be making a speech soon."

True enough, Wyatt returned to her side. "Walk with me," he said and skillfully maneuvered her around the room. The consummate host, he worked the room and spent close to half an hour moving from one table to the next. Fiona was introduced to more people than she would ever remember, with Wyatt quietly explaining who they were before they reached each table. From workers at the main fabrication factory to mid- and high-level management, directors, colleagues, business associates and their respective spouses and several beneficiaries, he showed no preference and simply charmed everyone they spoke with.

By the time they returned to their table, most of the other tables were filled. The lights dimmed fractionally as Linc took the podium and welcomed everyone to the event.

"You did great," Wyatt whispered close to her ear. She felt his breath against her skin and shivered. "Now that's over, you can relax and have a good time. And collect your check for the school," he added and winked. "Although, now the whole room knows you're with me tonight, I'll probably be accused of preferential treatment."

Fiona hadn't considered that. "If you'd rather not—"

"I'm joking, sweetheart. People can think what they like. Relax and have some fun."

Sweetheart. Fiona almost swooned. Did women actually swoon anymore?

Wyatt ordered her a drink, and the room hushed as Linc began talking about the Harper charity fund and explained how the moneys raised through events like the dinner was used. From the school canteen in Crystal Point to new recliners in the pediatric ward at a hospital, every cent was accounted for. Linc spoke with pride at their achievements and cracked fractionally when he announced the creation of an educational scholarship developed in memory of Karen Harper Todd.

The family was clearly immersed in memories. Alessio had an arm draped around his wife's shoulder; Janet and Rae sat close. Fiona grabbed Cecily's hand and squeezed, sensing her daughter needed her strength as Linc talked about Karen. Unsure about open displays of comfort and affection, she placed her other hand on Wyatt's leg beneath the table.

When Linc was done, the audience applauded. Fiona removed her hand from Wyatt's thigh and released Cecily. There would be presentations later, but for now the first course was being served. The scallops sautéed in a decadent, creamy sauce were divine.

"Is everything okay?" Wyatt asked quietly as Fiona lingered over her food.

"Oh, yes. Delicious."

He looked at her mouth. "Mmm, it is."

"Almost as good as that spicy chicken you brought to my house, remember?"

"I remember."

"That night seems like such a long time ago."

"Do you think?" He leaned in closer. "You know, I almost kissed you that night."

"No way."

"Way. I wanted to."

She smiled. "That's why you left in a hurry?"

"Yep."

Fiona's heart contracted. They'd come a long way since that evening. "I probably would have kissed you back."

"Too bad for me, then," he said, closer now. "You can make it up to me later," he said and proceeded to spear the scallop she was toying with. He raised the fork to her mouth, and after a second's hesitation, she took the bite.

The move was oddly intimate, and Fiona didn't miss the surprised looks from the family, Janet and Ellen in particular. She ignored her embarrassment and focused on her meal. By the time the plates had been cleared, Linc had returned to the stage and began the first of several presentations. Fiona's was the third name to be announced, and she collected the check on behalf of the school. She kept her thank-you speech short, mentioning the Harper family and how much the support meant to her small school.

When the presentations were over, the second course arrived. Supremely conscious of the man beside her and of the fact that they were being scrutinized by countless pairs of eyes, Fiona did her best to concentrate on her food and respond to her daughter's animated chatter. But she could feel their curiosity in bucket loads. Did they approve of her? Did she measure up as Cecily's mother…or as Wyatt's…whatever?

By dessert she was so wound up she barely tasted the raspberry brûlée.

"Something wrong?"

He'd asked quietly and she raised her shoulders. "Do you do this kind of thing a lot?"

"Eat? I try to squeeze it into my daily routine."

Fiona let his lame humor pass. "I mean these events…the dressed-up, everyone-primped-and-looking-beautiful kind of thing?"

"Once a year," he replied. "Why?"

"I feel a bit out of my league. I'm a no-frills sort of person and—"

"You're easily the most beautiful woman in the room," he said, silencing her effectively. "But I understand what you're saying. I do this because it's important to my father. It's his night, really. He's always been the philanthropist in the family, and even more so since he's retired."

"You took over the business at a young age?"

"At twenty-four. Dad had suffered his second heart attack. So, I stepped in and he gradually handed over the reins."

"Did you ever want to do anything else?"

"Sure, I would have liked to work outside of the company a little longer than I did, simply for experience. But it wasn't to be. Harper's is third generation. As you can see from to-night, a lot of people rely on the business for their livelihood. We employ hundreds of staff and contractors, and if the company went down, a whole lot of people would go down with it. Including everyone at this table."

It seemed like a monumental responsibility. She'd never doubted he worked hard, but understanding why spiked her admiration. And her love. He really was a remarkable man. Fiona experienced a strong surge of feeling. Her eyes clouded, longing grew, need for him uncurled low in her belly and in her heart.

"You know," he said softly, for her ears only, "if you keep looking at me like that, I might have to book a room at this hotel tonight."

It sounded like a blissful idea. "I'd like that."

Wyatt's insides were jumping all over the place. She looked as if she *knew* him. Really. Deeply. In ways he'd only imagined existed. His chest tightened as he recognized the intensity of his own feelings. Every part of him was attuned to her, aware of her on a level he'd never experienced before. He wanted her. Longed for her. Needed her. And it shocked him to the core.

He hadn't truly *needed* anyone before.

He almost blurted it out. Almost. He needed time to process. To think. To figure out what came next.

Wyatt remembered his glib comments before they'd entered the ballroom, about marriage and weddings. She'd looked hurt by his remarks. He hated that he'd done that. Hurting Fiona was the last thing he wanted to do.

"Fiona," he said quietly. "There's something we should talk about. I need to tell you how I—"

"Fiona?"

It was Cecily's voice that interrupted him. He watched as his niece grabbed her mother's arm and gently pulled her around in the chair. They spoke for a second in hushed voices before Fiona briefly turned back toward him.

"Would you excuse us?" she said as she stood.

Wyatt glanced at his niece, who looked unusually serious all of a sudden. "Is there a problem?" he asked.

Fiona shook her head as she ushered Cecily to her feet. Now wasn't the time to explain Cecily thought she had her period. "Girl stuff. Won't be long."

Fiona calmed Cecily down the moment they got into the powder room and gave her daughter a gentle talk about preparedness and keeping a diary to ensure she avoided any unexpected mishaps regarding her monthly cycle. Once Cecily had headed off into the cubicle, Fiona touched up her lip gloss. Several other women came and went, most smiling, and one commented on the loveliness of her gown.

Waiting for her daughter, she felt like a mother in the truest sense of the word, thankful she had what Cecily needed tucked in her purse, even though her own cycle was like clockwork.

Except...

Fiona stilled. *Clockwork.* Always.

Except this month. She did a quick mental calculation.

Oh, God. I'm late.

Not by much. A few days. Five at the most. But enough to get her thinking. Enough to get her worried.

Could I really be pregnant?

Fiona considered other possible signs. Sure, she had a few headaches. And her stomach had played up once or twice. But she'd put that down to nerves and anxiety.

A baby? Wyatt's baby?

The notion filled her with both apprehension and joy. They'd been mindful of protection every time they'd made love. There was, of course, that time in the kitchen when they'd improvised. And once in the shower they'd almost forgotten before it was too late.

But…pregnant? And if she were having Wyatt's baby, what would it do to their relationship? He wanted to go slowly. On the drive to the dinner, he'd questioned her motives. Would he suspect she'd gotten pregnant to trap him? And Cecily? How could she expect her daughter to understand? If she were pregnant, she would absolutely have the baby. No question about that. But how would she explain to her daughter her intention to keep this baby, when she'd given her away?

"So, you're Wyatt's new squeeze?"

Fiona snapped out of her baby trance and jerked her head around. A woman stood by the sink. Tall and thin, she had raven-black hair and brown eyes—the word *exotic* came instantly to mind. Her black gown amplified her svelte body. She couldn't recall being introduced to the other woman.

"Excuse me?"

"Wyatt. Tall, rich, ridiculously good-looking and great in bed—of course you know who I mean. He is quite the catch. And the family certainly looks like they approve. I've never seen Janet smile so much. Even the frosty-faced Ellen seems to agree." She clapped her hands a couple of times. "Well done, you."

Fiona's instincts kindled and she had a sudden bad feeling. "Do I know you?"

"By reputation, I'm sure."

Uh-oh. Her burgeoning suspicions were confirmed when Cecily came out from the cubicle. "What are you doing here, Yvette?"

"Don't stress, kid—I didn't crash the party," she said, sounding almost bored. "I paid for my ticket like everyone else." She looked toward Fiona. "My father does business with Wyatt. We have a table."

"Uncle Wyatt wouldn't want you here," Cecily said and stepped a little closer toward Fiona.

"Well, Uncle Wyatt doesn't always get what he wants."

Cecily pushed back her shoulders. "Leave my…leave Fiona alone."

Bless her, Fiona thought, but knew it was time to take charge. "Come on, let's get back to our table."

The other woman's eyes widened, and she raised her brows as her gaze flicked from one to the other. "Oh, of course, I get it now. The same red hair, the same freckles. You're the mysterious birth mother?"

Fiona grasped Cecily's arms and urged her toward the door. "There's nothing mysterious about me at all. Now, if you'll excuse us?"

"Has poor Karen been replaced already?"

Cecily gasped. "You can just go and—"

"That's enough, Cecily," Fiona said and steered her forward. "Go back to the table. I'll be along in a moment."

Her daughter shook her head. "But I can't leave you—"

"Go," she insisted. Once Cecily disappeared through the doorway, Fiona turned her attention completely toward the other woman. "If you must be a spiteful witch, I'd appreciate if you didn't do it in front of my daughter."

Fiona took a fortifying breath, brushed past her and walked out the door.

But the other woman clearly wasn't finished with her yet.

When she was out of the powder room and on her way back to the ballroom, Yvette came up beside her quickly and spoke again. "Oh, don't get all lioness on me… I didn't mean to upset the kid. I always liked Cecily. Thank God she's nothing like her mother." She looked at Fiona and shrugged. "I meant her *other* mother. Looks like you landed nicely on your feet, though. Cecily and Wyatt in one swoop of your net. I admire your tactics. You're pretty and smart—no wonder

Wyatt can't keep his eyes off you. I've been watching you from my dark little corner of the room." Then her gaze narrowed. "It won't last, you know."

Fiona knew there was little point in rattling the other woman's cage, knew the best thing to do was continue walking, but she couldn't suppress the rising anger in her blood. She stood perfectly still on her heels. "What did you say?"

"They're different to us regular folk. They're a unified front."

Loyalty surged through her veins. "Because they're a close family who care about one another?"

"Because they close ranks," Yvette said bitterly. "You might be in favor now, but there will come a time where you'll do something wrong and they will cast you out without a backward glance."

"That's a little dramatic, don't you think?"

"I've been there."

Loyalty turned into a fierce desire to protect. Not only Wyatt. All of them. Because the Harpers were good people who loved her daughter dearly. And Wyatt was the man she loved and she'd protect him with her dying breath. "You betrayed Wyatt. You betrayed his sister. What did you expect? Forgiveness?"

Yvette's eyes shadowed over. "I expected exactly what I got—nothing. From Wyatt, from Jim…from all of them. And then Jim was dead and no one asked me how I felt. No one cared how I felt. I didn't matter."

"They lost a daughter," Fiona said, stronger, more resilient. "They were grieving."

"So was I. My engagement was broken. Wyatt didn't—"

"That's enough. You cheated, you got caught. And here's some advice for you—when you agree to marry one man, you don't have sex with someone else. You're supposed to be in love with that person. And when you love someone—

when you *truly* love someone—you don't betray them. You give them your whole heart and take their whole heart in return. And you protect that heart with everything inside you."

Yvette opened her mouth to speak and then clamped it shut. She looked over Fiona's shoulder and gasped. Fiona spun around. Wyatt stood behind her, an odd look on his face.

And Fiona knew, without a doubt, that he'd heard everything, and she was completely and totally busted.

Chapter Fourteen

"Of course, my favorite part was when you were wiping the floor with what's-her-name."

Fiona was back in the guesthouse. Her lovely dress was hanging behind the bedroom door. And Cecily kept talking nonstop. Wyatt had driven them home once the dinner ended, and of course after Yvette's none-too-discreet exit from the event. Oddly, Wyatt hadn't said anything to her. He'd even danced with her a couple of times when the music had begun, Yvette and her own outburst seemingly forgotten.

Of course, the fact he hadn't booked them into a hotel suite for the night made her think he was simply biding his time. She knew him well enough to suspect scenes weren't his thing. No doubt an argument between his date and ex-fiancée wasn't the picture of professionalism he expected from her.

She owed him an explanation.

And I have to tell him I could be pregnant.

In the drama of Yvette's confrontation, she'd forgotten that little detail for about five seconds.

"You should scoot off to bed," she told Cecily as she cleansed her face in the en suite bathroom and ignored her comment about Yvette. "I'll see you in the morning."

"But you were amazing," she said with a grin. "Just think, Uncle Wyatt almost married that awful woman."

Fiona couldn't stop thinking about it. "Well, he didn't. Now, bed."

Cecily didn't budge. "So, are you Uncle Wyatt's girlfriend now?"

It was a question she had no idea how to answer. She was going home tomorrow and didn't know when she'd see Wyatt again. A long-distance relationship certainly wasn't in her future. Considering the quiet way he'd said good-night to her a little over an hour earlier, she wasn't sure he would be in her future at all.

"We're friends."

Cecily's brows came up. "Friends don't usually make out, though, do they?"

Her daughter smiled at her, and Fiona couldn't help grinning. "No, I guess they don't."

Cecily laughed delightedly. "You were right—relationships *are* complicated. I'll bet you and Uncle Wyatt can't wait for me to start dating." She shuffled off the bed and gave Fiona a long hug. "Maybe by then you guys will have worked your own love life out. 'Night, Ma."

Ma. Fiona's heart rolled over. When Cecily had asked if she could call her that sweet word, Fiona had almost burst into tears. It was more than she'd ever hoped for. Her daughter's courage astounded her.

But how will she react if I have to tell her I'm pregnant?

It was a huge leap. She had no idea how her daughter would react, and it scared her. She didn't want to lose the relationship they'd come to share.

Once Cecily had left, Fiona, in her nightgown, padded

from the bedroom into the small kitchenette. She wanted tea and was filling the kettle when the French doors rattled.

She knew it would be Wyatt. He still wore his suit, but the tie was gone. Earlier that evening he'd said he had something to tell her. Add her passionate outburst, and she was certain they had plenty to discuss.

And then of course there's the whole maybe-I'm-having-your-baby thing.

How would he react? He was an honorable man—would he want to do the *honorable* thing? In her heart she suspected he would. What then? Did she dare take whatever he offered, even if he didn't mention love? Could she? She opened the screen. He walked inside and shut the door once he was in the room. He looked tense. His shoulders were unusually tight. Was he angry with her? Unsure, Fiona jumped in. "Wyatt, I'm so sorry about making a—"

"Shh," he said, silencing her. "Be quiet. And come here." It was a deliriously seductive command. One she couldn't resist. She moved across the room and he drew her against him. "Now I can do what I've wanted to do all night."

He kissed her deeply, drawing a response from her starved lips. Fiona's arms curled over his shoulders and she melted. Oh, how she melted. No matter what her future held, she would always remember the deep tenderness of his kiss and the soft caress of his hands against her skin. *No matter what.* Jeepers…time to come clean.

"Wyatt, I have to tell you—"

"Later," he said against her mouth. "Right now, I need you."

Then have me, her heart sang. He needed her. Maybe that would be enough. He lifted her up and carried her into the bedroom. Wyatt got out of his clothes with lightning speed and she did the same. They made love quickly, using touch to transcend words, finding pleasure so powerful she felt it through to her very soul. Every touch, every kiss, spoke volumes. He moved over her and possessed her completely, and for those precious moments, they were one, unified by a mutual need. Afterward they held one another, and Fiona stroked his back, her body warm and glowing with a lovely lethargy.

"I thought you wanted to go slow?" she said once her breathing returned to normal and as she snuggled into him.

"Clearly I think too much."

She grinned and pressed a kiss against his throat. "Sometimes. So, what are you thinking now?" she asked huskily and curved her fingers over his hip and then lower still.

He grabbed her hand and laughed as he rolled her over onto her back. "That I'm going to kiss you again."

"I thought you might be angry with me."

He placed his hands on her shoulders. "For what?"

"Making a scene tonight. Embarrassing you. Not minding my own business—take your pick."

He reached up and brushed her cheek with the back of his hand. "Cecily told me what happened. I know Yvette can be confrontational."

Fiona sighed. "I feel a little sorry for her. I mean, I know she did something really terrible, but maybe she genuinely did care for Jim?"

"Maybe," he said vaguely.

"Sorry, I shouldn't interfere. And I apologize for reacting to her insults. I should have walked away."

He stared down into her face. "Promise me something—never change who you are."

Her throat closed over. *Tell him now about the maybe baby.* Only, she didn't want to break the tender moment. She didn't want the feeling to end. He'd said he needed her, now…

tonight. *A few hours won't make any difference. I'll tell him in the morning.*

"I promise," she whispered and kissed him with every ounce of love in her heart.

Wyatt woke up alone. He heard Fiona moving around the guesthouse, making coffee if his nose were any judge. It was still early. A sliver of dawn light cut through the space between the curtains. He rolled over and stared at the ceiling. He felt oddly at peace. Happy.

Watching her go into battle in his defense had been one of those moments in his life when the full impact of the situation had hit him with the force of a freight train.

And he knew what he wanted.

Fiona.

Time suddenly wasn't an issue. He wanted to jump, and jump fast. Seeing her go into battle for him had made it all so clear. Fiona was nothing like Yvette. She was strong and proud and honest to the bone.

Suddenly, nothing else mattered but making her his own.

He got up and pulled on the trousers she'd laid on the end of the bed and wrestled into his shirt, not bothering with the buttons. There was a bag on the floor, half-packed, and he remembered she was leaving today. He certainly didn't want her to go. But if she did, they'd try a long-distance relationship for a while. He'd do whatever he had to.

Wyatt found her in the living room, on the sofa, a steaming mug in her hand. In her satin nightgown, she looked sleepy and tousled. Adorable. He wanted to drag her back into bed and make love to her all over again. "'Morning," he said easily.

She offered a tight smile. "Hi."

"Have you been up long?"

She nodded, suddenly grave. "We really need to talk."

"Sure." Wyatt stood behind the sofa and tried to ignore the rapidness of his heartbeat.

He noticed her hand shake as she placed the mug on the coffee table. She drew in a long breath and looked as if she had something serious to tell him. "I'm late."

Late? He almost stupidly said, *For what?*

"Late?"

"Late," she said again, solemn. "And I'm *never* late."

He took about two seconds to figure out what she meant and asked her straight out, "You're pregnant?"

She gave a little shrug. "I might be. I'm about five days overdue."

Two things struck Wyatt simultaneously. First, a gut-wrenching shock and then a kind of unbelievable elation, which sent his head spinning into some far-off stratosphere. Pregnant? A baby? *His* baby? "When will you know for sure?"

"Um, today, I guess. I could do one of those home tests."

"Then let's go and buy one."

Fiona glanced at the clock on the wall. "It's not seven o'clock. Nothing will be open yet."

She had a point. There were no all-night pharmacies within a twenty-mile radius. "We'll wait until the stores open."

She nodded and he watched as she twisted her hands together. She said his name softly. "I didn't do this deliberately."

He knew that. "It takes two people to make a baby. I'm not about to accuse you of anything."

Her mouth creased. "I wanted to tell you last night."

Wyatt shrugged. He wasn't about to get hung up on six hours. "It's okay, Fiona. In my eagerness to make love to you, I didn't exactly give you a chance to tell me anything."

She drew in a shuddering breath. "You're not angry?"

Wyatt shook his head. "Why would I be?" he asked, then realized what he'd thought was tension holding her shoulders so tight was, in fact, raw emotion. Emotion she was hanging on to by a thread. "Fiona, why would you think that?"

She looked up, all eyes, all feeling. "Because this is such… such a *disaster.*"

A disaster? "Since when is a baby a—"

"Since I have no idea how I'm supposed to tell my daughter," she said and cut him off. "Since I've tried so hard to take this giant leap forward with Cecily and now I have to explain that, if I am pregnant, I have every intention of keeping this baby. How do I tell her that, Wyatt? How do I tell her I want this baby…when I didn't…when I gave her up?"

He rocked back on his bare heels. Complicated just jumped off the Richter scale. "She'll understand."

"You don't know that."

"I know Cecily. And this situation is hardly the same as when you were fifteen. For one, I'm not—"

"But what if she thinks I love this child more?" she shot back and looked at him through eyes shimmering with tears. "And what if she's right? What if I do love this baby in ways I haven't yet—"

"Fiona," Wyatt said as he charged around the sofa and sat down. "Cecily knows how you feel about her. You're imagining the worst without good reason."

"But you don't know…" She shook through a ragged breath and he folded her hands within his. "You don't know how hard I've tried to be her mother. How much I want to be her mother. How much I want her to know she's the most important thing in the world to me."

"I do know," he said gently and felt her tears right through to his soul. "You've been incredible with her. You *are* incredible with her." Wyatt touched her face and wiped away her tears. "She needs you in her life. Permanently. The truth is I'm not cut out to be a single parent, Fiona. And for the first time in eighteen months, I feel like I'm not alone in this."

She stilled. "What are you saying?"

He went for it. Feetfirst. Jumping when he'd thought he'd never want to jump again. "Marry me, Fiona?"

Stillness turned into stone. She looked shocked. Even appalled. "I...can't... I couldn't do that."

Can't. Couldn't. Not exactly the response he'd hoped for. "You can," he insisted.

She shook her head. "I won't marry someone because I'm pregnant."

Someone? As if he was no one in particular. He didn't like that statement one bit.

"You're pregnant?"

He knew that voice. Cecily! They both turned toward the door. His niece stood beneath the threshold, one hand still on the doorknob. Fiona spoke. "Cecily, I—"

"You're really pregnant?"

"We're not sure," Wyatt said quietly. "But when we do know, we'll make sure you hear about it first."

Fiona moved away from him and stood. "I'm sorry, Cecily. I know you must be disappointed in me."

She said the words with such a heavy heart that all Wyatt wanted to do was haul her into his arms and kiss some sense into her. Cecily, bless her, didn't seem the least bit let down.

"I'm not disappointed," his niece said and chuckled. "Although...I might be if you turn down Uncle Wyatt's proposal. You guys should get married—then we could be a real family."

Thanks, kid. At least someone was in his corner. "Cecily," Wyatt said as he got to his feet. "Would you leave us alone for a minute?"

"Sure," she replied. "Take all the time you need." She looked at Fiona and grinned before she headed back through the door.

Once he was sure she'd gone, Wyatt spoke. "See, no problem."

Fiona glared at him. "I'm not going to put my daughter in the middle of this."

"She *is* in the middle of it, Fiona." He took a couple of steps and reached for her, taking her hand within his. "She's right here, part of this, part of *us*."

Fiona shook her head. "People don't get married because of pregnancy these days. I won't trap you."

"I'd hardly call this a trap."

She pulled away and stood, pushing her hair from her face. "You know, you're just about the most honorable man I've ever met. And because you have so much integrity, it would be wrong of me to take advantage of you like that. Because I have integrity, too, Wyatt. *If* I am pregnant, we'll discuss access and all the things that need to happen when two people have a child together. Until we know for sure, there's nothing else to say."

Her rejection stung like a slap to the face. He tried another tactic. "What about Cecily? You heard her...she wants this."

She stared at him, all eyes. "I explained the situation as best I—"

"If you won't marry me for *our* child," he said deliberately, as annoyance settled behind his ribs, "then marry me for *your* child."

"What?"

"Give Cecily what she wants. Two parents, together...add in a baby brother or sister and she'll be over the moon." He jumped up. "You know it's what she wants to happen. You can give it to her. You could be with her every day. You won't have to leave this afternoon. You gave her up once. You handed her over to strangers and missed out on the first fourteen years of her life. Well, here's your chance to be a part of the rest of it."

She looked so wounded Wyatt wanted to snatch the words

back. Hurting Fiona wasn't on his agenda. And he was hurting her now. But damn it, she was hurting him, too.

"No. And now I'd like to be alone for a while," she said quietly.

"Fiona, when two people have feelings for—"

"Exactly," she snapped. "When *two* people have feelings. Not one person. I think it's fairly obvious that any feelings here are all on one side. Now please leave me alone."

He saw her chin go up, defiant, angry and wounded at the same time. One-sided feelings? What did that mean? That she didn't care? He could have sworn she did. Despite the uncharacteristic coldness in her voice, he pressed on. "You know I'm right about getting married."

"All I know is that my mother married Eddie Walsh because she was pregnant. And I don't want to be that kind of woman."

He wanted to reassure her that she was nothing like her mother. But she looked as though she was about to collapse, and if she was pregnant, the last thing she needed was stress. "I'll… Sure. I'll leave you alone. Promise me you'll think about it?"

She clutched her arms to her chest. "There's nothing to think about. We don't even know if I'm pregnant."

Then marry me anyway.

But he'd had about as much rejection as he could take.

It took about sixty seconds to grab the remainder of his clothes and shove his feet into the dress shoes. When he returned to the living area, he noticed she hadn't moved. Wyatt didn't bother saying anything and strode from the guesthouse.

By the time he reached the pool area, he'd calmed down. His parents were there, seated under the annex, sipping coffee and sharing the morning paper. If they were surprised to see him emerge from the direction of the guesthouse, half-dressed, a thunderous expression on his face, they didn't show it.

He stopped by the pool gate and watched them. In their own world, together, they shared something unique. A bond, he knew, which grew stronger with every touch, with every moment they spent in one another's company. A bond that would never be broken. And they had been married for thirty-five years, through loss, grief, joy. Through it all. Together.

It was simply…love.

At that moment, like a lightning bolt searing across his skin, Wyatt realized that he did believe in love and didn't just want and need Fiona… It was more than that. Much more. He loved her. Wholly. Completely. And for the entire time he'd been trying to convince her to marry him, not once had he said the words.

And that just wouldn't do.

Fiona had no intention of waiting around to pee on a stick with Wyatt breathing down her neck. If she were pregnant, she wanted to be on her own turf when she found out. She was going home. She would go back to Crystal Point and figure out her next move. A thousand miles away from him.

She marched to the bedroom, making special effort to not look at the crumpled bed.

Marry him? Yeah, right. She wasn't a charity case. She could do it on her own. She pulled jeans and a T-shirt from the dresser and shoved the rest of her clothes into her case.

The jeans still fit. Ha…she probably wasn't pregnant at all.

Not that she'd be showing at just a few weeks along. But still… That only made her burst into tears like some kind of hormonal wreck.

Fiona quickly pulled herself together and rubbed her face. She'd have plenty of time to cry when she was alone, tucked up in her little house with only Muffin for company. But she had Callie and Evie and M.J. Her friends would support her. And she'd see Cecily during school breaks. It would be enough.

But inside, in the deepest part of her heart, she was breaking. She wasn't sure how, but the past few days had somehow blurred into a real life. *My real life.* It was as though, by miracle or chance, she finally belonged somewhere and to someone. And not just Wyatt or Cecily but to all the Harpers. They'd embraced her, shown kindness and consideration. She felt accepted, understood and part of something real. Silly, perhaps, but after only a few days, they actually felt like family.

The family she'd never had. And the family she'd always wanted.

Which was why she'd *had* to turn down Wyatt's proposal. Marrying him to make a family wouldn't be right. Tempting…but dishonest. And she wasn't like that. Besides, he hadn't said anything about loving her. They'd made love—which was about physical need and not enough to sustain a marriage. She wanted his love. Nothing else would do for her. More to the point, perhaps for the first time in her life, Fiona believed she deserved love.

She touched her belly, and tears filled her eyes again. She wanted Wyatt's baby so much. If she were pregnant, she vowed to love and cherish his child with all her heart. Knowing Cecily wasn't upset about the idea of a new baby only made her cry more. Her daughter possessed a generous, forgiving spirit, and she said a silent thank-you to Karen Todd for nurturing her into such an amazing person. She owed it to the other woman's memory to always do right by the daughter they both loved.

Still crying, Fiona collected her things from the bathroom and made the bed, ignoring the memories flashing through her mind when she recalled what she had done with Wyatt between the sheets only hours before. When she was done, she grabbed her bag and left the room.

Only, she hadn't expected to find Wyatt standing in the center of the living room, still wearing his unbuttoned shirt. He stared at her. She dropped her bag and stared back and suddenly didn't care that he saw her tears.

"I was thinking," he said quietly, deeply, almost uncertainly, as if his voice might break, "that if you don't want to marry me because we might have made a baby together... even though having a baby with you would just about be the greatest thing I could imagine happening..." He paused, took a breath. "And if you don't want to marry me even if it would make Cecily really happy, and after everything she's been through, she deserves all the happiness we could give her... If that's not enough...I was thinking that maybe..." He stopped again and swallowed hard. "Maybe you'll marry me because I love you."

Poleaxed, Fiona's feet stuck to the carpet. She stared at him, into him, through to his soul. "I... But I..."

"Of course, if you don't love me—"

"I do," she said on a rush and hardly dared to breathe in. So, she'd gone and done it now. "I do love you."

"I think I know that now," he said, so quiet, so still. "Last night...last night I watched you defend me so courageously to Yvette. I listened while you talked about love and I knew you would only do that if you loved me."

Completely outed, Fiona knew there was little point in denying it any longer. "I'm sorry, Wyatt. I didn't mean to fall in love with you. Right from the beginning, I knew it was supposed to be just about Cecily. But the more time we spent together the more I couldn't stop thinking about you, and suddenly I had all these feelings inside me that I didn't know what to do with. And then we made love and it just got...worse."

"Worse?"

She shrugged. "Stronger. But I—"

"Do you know when I first fell in love with you?" he asked softly as he came toward her and took her hands. "I didn't recognize it for what it was at the time. That day we went walking toward the beach, remember? We were talking and you were laughing and I remember all I wanted to do was hold your hand. Like this," he said and linked their fingers intimately.

Fiona's heart almost burst through her chest. "You really love me? You're not just saying that because you think I might be pregnant? You didn't say anything before—"

He raised her hands and kissed her knuckles. "I was an idiot before. I'm in love with you, Fiona. But if you don't want to get married, I can wait until—"

"Oh, I do," she said, happy, delirious, terrified. "I want to marry you so much." She looked up, still uncertain. "But you said you wanted to go slow?"

He urged her closer and his bare chest was warm where they connected. "I don't want to go slow. I want you beside me every day. All the fears I had about rushing into something again, about making a mistake...you know what? That stuff doesn't matter to me anymore. I made a big mistake with Yvette. One I can't take back. I shouldn't have proposed marriage. I wasn't in love with her." He sighed resignedly. "Maybe she knew that. Maybe that's why she ended up with Jim. I don't know, and frankly, I'm tired of thinking about it. I only want to think about you. About us."

Us. Fiona's heart sang. Tears came again. "No one has ever loved me."

His eyes glittered and he wrapped his arms around her. "I love you. I want you. I need you."

"You said that last night," she reminded him, safe, secure. "I thought it was about sex."

Wyatt grabbed her chin and tilted her head back. "I *love*

making love to you. But that's part of loving someone, I guess. I love everything you are, everything we'll be together."

"Will your family be okay with it?"

He smiled and kissed her gently. "My family, especially my parents, adore you," he said against her mouth. "And will love you even more when we supply them with the first Harper grandchild to carry on the family name."

She eased back. "But what if I'm not pregnant? Will you still want to—"

"If it's meant to be, it will happen," he said and kissed her again. "We don't even have to find out today if you don't want to. I can wait. I want to have kids, Fiona, but we have time to get to know one another first. Although, I can't imagine anyone knowing me as well as you already do."

He was right about that. They had a strong connection, apparent from the very first. And nothing, she knew in her deepest heart, would ever break it. "I'll never knowingly hurt you, Wyatt. You have my promise."

"I know, sweetheart. And I want you to have a beautiful wedding—everything you've ever dreamed it to be."

"Mariah Downs," she whispered. "You knew what I was thinking about that, about us?"

"I knew," he said and kissed her forehead gently. "I want that, too. So, we'll get married there and I'll take you anywhere you want to go for a honeymoon. When we get back, I want to build you a house on that land I told you about so Cecily can come live with us, and I can drive home every night and see your lovely face when I walk through the door. And you can bring your dog and that horse you cherish."

Muffin? Titan? "I'll have to move," she said in a vague kind of way. "Again."

"Do you mind?" he asked as his expression narrowed. "Leaving Crystal Point, your job, your friends…will you be able to do that?"

Fiona wrapped her arms around his waist. "I've moved before. I can do it again. And anyway, my friends are in Crystal Point. But my family is here."

Wyatt's embrace tightened. "You're right. The both of us... Cecily—" his hand dropped to her belly and he splayed his palm over her "—and this tiny life we might have made together."

"You'd really be happy if we had a baby? I mean, so soon?"

He smiled. "We can add to our family whenever you're ready and as many times as you'd like."

Fiona's heart almost burst through her rib cage. All her old fears somehow disappeared. Along with the lingering resentment she had for the mother who hadn't really wanted her. Shayne was forgotten. Jamie Corbett was forgotten. In her arms stood her future. The past suddenly seeped away.

"Three more kids," she said, laughing and crying, too. "Shall we go to the store and buy one of those tests?"

Wyatt grinned and looked so happy it brought fresh tears to her eyes. "Absolutely. But let's tell my folks and Cecily we're getting married first."

He grabbed her hand and they walked from the guesthouse, laughing and kissing.

And into the kind of love Fiona had always wished for.

Epilogue

Fiona pulled the satin wrap around her waist and sat on the edge of the bed. Her gown looked beautiful hanging on the closet door and she let out a long, wistful sigh.

This is my wedding day.

The guesthouse at Waradoon had become her home for the past two months, and she would continue to live with the Harpers until the new house was built. She preferred it this way. Wyatt's city apartment had every luxury but it was too far from Cecily. For now he commuted back to Waradoon on Friday and returned to the city each Monday. Of course, she missed him terribly, but they both wanted what was best for Cecily.

Muffin yapped and Fiona grinned. "And yes, it's far from you, too."

"You should have started getting dressed, Ma," Cecily said in a slightly despairing voice as she raced into the bedroom. "You don't want to keep Uncle Wyatt waiting, do you?"

Fiona stood and smiled. "It's tradition for the bride to keep the groom waiting," she said and hugged her daughter, who seemed to have cornered the market on pre-wedding jitters. "And Callie and Evie will be here soon to help me get into my dress."

Cecily managed a smile and gently pulled back. "Don't crease me," she said and brushed at the pale lavender satin dress she wore, "or Nan will have a fit."

Fiona adjusted Cecily's strap. "You look so beautiful."

Her daughter looked up, eyes glistening. "Thanks."

"Is something wrong?"

Cecily shook her head. "Just happy. And…and a bit sad."

Fiona understood. Her daughter's world had changed so much in a matter of months. "Are you thinking about your parents?" she asked gently.

Cecily shrugged. "I guess. Sometimes I wish…I wish my mother could have met you."

"I wish that, too."

Cecily drew in a tight breath. "I'd just like her to know that things have, you know, worked out…for you and Uncle Wyatt. And for me."

She grabbed Cecily's hand and squeezed assuringly. "You know what? I think she knows."

Cecily's lip wobbled. "Maybe you're right. And I think she'd be really happy that I'm going to have a little brother soon."

Fiona smiled and instinctively laid a hand on her belly. "Brother? You could be getting a sister."

She shrugged again. "Either is good."

Fiona agreed. At not quite four months along in her pregnancy, she wasn't quite showing yet, but she'd certainly battled the dreaded morning sickness during those first couple of months. Thankfully, she was now over feeling unwell and absolutely loved being pregnant.

At that moment, Callie came into the room, clapping her hands together. "Okay, it's time to get ready. The limo will be here in ten minutes."

Evie arrived, and as she dressed in her beautiful organza-and-lace gown and was attended by her daughter and closest friends, Fiona experienced such an acute sense of happiness she had to fight back tears. *I won't cry. Not today.* But moisture quickly filled her eyes.

Thankfully, Callie was on hand with a tissue. "No more tears," her friend said and watched as she carefully dabbed at her eyes, "or we'll have to redo your mascara."

"No more. I promise," Fiona said and quickly pulled herself together.

Evie smiled and patted her arm. "Good—or we'll all start blubbering."

They all laughed, and it was another twenty minutes before they were in the car and on their way.

When they reached their destination, Fiona took a few deep breaths and waited wordlessly as Callie and Cecily fiddled with her veil and train and then walked with her toward the huge doorway of the beautiful estate home. To be married at Mariah Downs was truly a dream come true. The foyer had been turned into an altar hosting dozens of covered chairs and countless floral arrangements. Her friends and several work colleagues from Crystal Point were there, as were the Harpers and their extended family. As she stood beneath the threshold and waited for the music to begin, she spotted Wyatt by the stairway. He looked handsome in his dark suit as he spoke quietly to Alessio, who stood at his side as best man.

And then the music started and he turned. As Evie and Callie made their way up the aisle in turn, she met his gaze and her heart rolled over. The love she saw in his eyes took her breath away.

Cecily grasped her arm. "Come on, Ma, it's time."

Wyatt had suggested she walk down the aisle with her daughter, and Fiona had felt the rightness of it through to her bones. When they reached the altar, Cecily took Fiona's small posy bouquet and gave her uncle a beaming smile as she stepped in beside Evie and Callie.

Fiona turned toward Wyatt and he took her hand.

"Hey, beautiful," he said softly. "You made it."

"I made it," she whispered.

"*We* made it," he said and gently squeezed her fingers.

Every ounce of love she had for him rose up and she reached out to grab Cecily's hand, linking them all together. "Yes, we certainly did."

* * * * *

WEALTHY AUSTRALIAN, SECRET SON

MARGARET WAY

CHAPTER ONE

The present

IT WAS an idyllic day for a garden party. The sky was a deep blue; sparkling sunshine flooded the Valley; a cooling breeze lowered the spring into summer heat. A veritable explosion of flowering trees and foaming blossom had turned the rich rural area into one breathtakingly beautiful garden that leapt at the eye and caught at the throat. It was so perfect a world the inhabitants of Silver Valley felt privileged to live in it.

Only Charlotte Prescott, a widow at twenty-six, with a seven-year-old child, stood in front of the bank of mirrors in her dressing room, staring blindly at her own reflection. The end of an era had finally arrived, but there was no joy in it for her, for her father, or for Christopher, her clever, thoughtful child. They were the dispossessed, and nothing in the world could soothe the pain of loss.

For the past month, since the invitations had begun to arrive, Silver Valley had been eagerly anticipating the Open Day: a get-to-know-you garden party to be held in the grounds of the grandest colonial mansion in the valley, Riverbend. Such a lovely name, Riverbend! A private house, its grandeur reflected the wealth and community standing of the man who had built it in the 1880s, Charles

Randall Marsdon, a young man of means who had migrated from England to a country that didn't have a splendid *past*, like his homeland, but in his opinion had a glowing *future*. He'd meant to be part of that future. He'd meant to get to the top!

There might have been a certain amount of bravado in that young man's goal, but Charles Marsdon had turned out not only to be a visionary, but a hard-headed businessman who had moved to the highest echelons of colonial life with enviable speed.

Riverbend was a wonderfully romantic two-storey mansion, with a fine Georgian façade and soaring white columns, its classic architecture adapted to climatic needs with large-scale open-arched verandahs providing deep shading for the house. It had been in the Marsdon family—*her* family—for six generations, but sadly it would never pass to her adored son. For the simple reason that Riverbend was no longer theirs. The mansion, its surrounding vineyards and olive groves, badly neglected since the Tragedy, had been sold to a company called Vortex. Little was known about Vortex, except that it had met the stiff price her father had put on the estate. Not that he could have afforded to take a lofty attitude. Marsdon money had all but run out. But Vivian Marsdon was an immensely proud man who never for a moment underestimated his important position in the Valley. It was *everything* to him to keep face. In any event, the asking price, exorbitantly high, had been paid swiftly—and oddly enough without a single quibble.

Now, months later, the CEO of the company was finally coming to town. Naturally she and her father had been invited, although neither of them had met any Vortex representative. The sale had been handled to her father's satisfaction by their family solicitors, Dunnett & Banfield. Part of the deal was that her father was to have tenure of the Lodge—originally an old coach house—during his lifetime, after which it would be returned to the estate. The coach house had been converted and greatly enlarged by her grandfather into a beautiful and comfortable guest house that had enjoyed a good deal of use in the old days, when her grandparents had entertained on a grand scale, and it was at the Lodge they were living now. Just the three of them: father, daughter, grandson.

Her former in-laws—Martyn's parents and his sister Nicole—barely acknowledged them these days. The estrangement had become entrenched in the eighteen months since Martyn's death. Her husband, three years older than she, had been killed when he'd lost control of his high-powered sports car on a notorious black spot in the Valley and smashed into a tree. A young woman had been with him. Mercifully she'd been thrown clear of the car, suffering only minor injuries. It had later transpired she had been Martyn's mistress for close on six months. Of course Martyn hadn't been getting what he'd needed at home. If Charlotte had been a loving wife the tragedy would never have happened. The *second* major tragedy in her lifetime. It seemed very much as if Charlotte Prescott was a jinx.

Poor old you! Charlotte spoke silently to her image. *What a mess you've made of your life!*

She really didn't need anyone to tell her that. The irony was that her father had made just as much a mess of his own life—even before the Tragedy. The *first* tragedy. The only one that mattered to her parents. Her father had had little time for Martyn, yet he himself was a man without insight into his own limitations. Perhaps the defining one was unloading responsibility. Vivian Marsdon was constitutionally incapable of accepting the blame for anything. Anything that went wrong was always someone else's fault, or due to some circumstance beyond his control. The start of the Marsdon freefall from grace had begun when her highly respected grandfather, Sir Richard Marsdon, had died. His only son and heir had not been able to pick up the reins. It was as simple as that. The theory of three. One man made the money, the next enlarged on it, the third lost it. No better cushion than piles of money. Not every generation produced an heir with the Midas touch, let alone the necessary drive to manage and significantly enlarge the family fortune.

Her father, born to wealth and prestige, lacked Sir Richard's strong character as well as his formidable business brain. Marsdon money had begun to disappear early, like water down a drain. Failed pie-in-the-sky schemes had been approached with enthusiasm. Her father had turned a deaf ear to cautioning counsel from accountants and solicitors alike. He knew best. Sadly, his lack of judgement had put a discernible dent in the family fortunes. And that was even before the Tragedy that had blighted their family life.

With a sigh of regret, Charlotte picked up her lovely hat with its wide floppy brim, settling it on her head. She rarely wore her long hair loose these days, preferring to pull it back from her face and arrange it in various knots. In any case, the straw picture hat demanded she pull her hair back off her face. Her dress was Hermes silk, in chartreuse, strapless except for a wide silk band over one shoulder that flowed down the bodice and short skirt. The hat was a perfect colour match, adorned with organdie peonies in masterly deep pinks that complemented the unique shade of golden lime-green.

The outfit wasn't new, but she had only worn it once, at Melbourne Cup day when Martyn was alive. Martyn had taken great pride in how she looked. She'd always had to look her best. In those days she had been every inch a *fashionista*, such had been their extravagant and, it had to be said, *empty* lifestyle. Martyn had been a man much like her father—an inheritor of wealth who could do what he liked, when he liked, if he so chose. Martyn had made his choice. He had always expected to marry her, right from childhood, bringing about the union of two long-established rural families. And once he'd had her—he had always been mad about her—he had set about making their lifestyle a whirl of pleasure up until his untimely death.

From time to time she had consoled herself with the thought that perhaps Martyn, as he matured, would cease taking up endless defensive positions against his highly effective father, Gordon, come to recognise his family responsibilities and then pursue them with some skill and determination.

Sadly, all her hopes—and Gordon Prescott's—had been killed off one by one. And she'd had to face some hard facts herself. Hadn't she been left with a legacy of guilt? She had never loved Martyn. Bonded to him from earliest childhood, she had always regarded him with great affection. But *romantic* love? Never! The heart wasn't obedient to the expectations of others. She *knew* what romantic love was. She *knew* about passion—dangerous passion and its infinite temptations—but she hadn't steered away from it in the interests of safety. She had totally succumbed.

All these years later her heart still pumped his name.
Rohan.

She heard her son's voice clearly. He sounded anxious. "Mummy, are you ready? Grandpa wants to leave."

A moment later, Christopher, a strikingly handsome little boy, dressed in a bright blue shirt with mother-of-pearl buttons and grey cargo pants, tore into the room.

"Come on, come on," he urged, holding out his hand to

her. "He's stomping around the hall and going red in the face. That means his blood pressure is going up, doesn't it?"

"Nothing for you to worry about, sweetheart," Charlotte answered calmly. "Grandpa's health is excellent. Stomping is a way to get our attention. Anyway, we're not late," she pointed out.

It had been after Martyn's death, on her father's urging, that she and Christopher had moved into the Lodge. Her father was sad and lonely, finding it hard getting over the big reversals in his life. She knew at some point she *had* to make a life for herself and her son. But where? She couldn't escape the Valley. Christopher loved it here. It was his home. He loved his friends, his school, his beautiful environment and his bond with his grandfather. It made a move away from the Valley extremely difficult, and there were other crucial considerations for a single mother with a young child.

Martyn had left her little money. They had lived with his parents at their huge High Grove estate. They had wanted for nothing, all expenses paid, but Martyn's father—knowing his son's proclivities—had kept his son on a fairly tight leash. His widow, so all members of the Prescott family had come to believe, was undeserving.

"Grandpa runs to a timetable of his own," Christopher was saying, shaking his golden-blond head. She too was blonde, with green eyes. Martyn had been fair as well, with greyish-blue eyes. Christopher's eyes were as brilliant as blue-fire diamonds. "You look lovely in that dress, Mummy," he added, full of love and pride in his beautiful mother. "Please don't be sad today. I just wish I was seventeen instead of seven," he lamented. "I'm just a kid. But I'll grow up and become a great big success. You'll have *me* to look after you."

"My knight in shining armour!" She bent to give him a

big hug, then took his outstretched hand, shaking it back and forth as if beginning a march. "Onward, Christian soldiers!"

"What's that?" He looked up at her with interest.

"It's an English hymn," she explained. Her father wouldn't have included hymns in the curriculum. Her father wasn't big on hymns. Not since the Tragedy. "It means we have to go forth and do our best. *Endure.* It was a favourite hymn of Sir Winston Churchill. You know who he was?"

"Of course!" Christopher scoffed. "He was the great English World War II Prime Minister. The country gave him a *huge* amount of money for his services to the nation, then they took most of it back in tax. Grandpa told me."

Charlotte laughed. Very well read himself, her father had taken it upon himself to "educate" Christopher. Christopher had attended the best school in the Valley for a few years now, but her father took his grandson's education much further, taking pride and delight it setting streams of general, historical and geographical questions for which Christopher had to find the answers. Christopher was already computer literate but her father wasn't—something that infuriated him—and insisted he find the answers in the books in the well-stocked library. Christopher never cheated. He always came up trumps. Christopher was a very clever little boy.

Like his father.

The garden party was well underway by the time they finished their stroll along the curving driveway. Riverbend had never looked more beautiful, Charlotte thought, pierced by the same sense of loss she knew her father was experiencing—though one would never have known it from his confident Lord of the Manor bearing. Her father was a handsome man, but alas not a lot of people in the Valley liked him. The mansion, since they had moved, had undergone very necessary repairs. These days it was superbly maintained, and staffed by a housekeeper, her husband—a sort of major-domo—and several ground staff to bring the once-famous gardens back to their best. A good-looking young woman came out from Sydney from time to time, to check on what was being done. Charlotte had met her once, purely by accident…

The young woman had left her Mercedes parked off the broad gravelled driveway so she could take a good look at the Lodge, screened from view by a grove of mature trees. Charlotte had been deadheading the roses when her uninvited visitor—brunette, dark-eyed, in a glamorous black power suit worn with a very stylish snow-white ruffled blouse—had near tumbled into view on her very high heels.

"Oh, good afternoon! Hope I didn't startle you?" she'd called, the voice loud and very precise.

Well, sort of, Charlotte thought. "You did rather," she answered mildly. The woman's greeting had been pleasant enough. The tone wasn't. It was seriously imperative. Charlotte might as well have been a slack employee who needed checking up on. "May I help you?" She was aware she was being treated to a comprehensive appraisal. A head-to-toe affair.

The young woman staggered a few steps further across the thick green grass, thoroughly aerating it. She had to give up as the stiletto heels of her expensive shoes sank with every step. "I don't think so. I'm Diane Rodgers, by the way."

"Well, hello, Diane Rodgers," Charlotte said with a smile.

Ms Rodgers responded to that with a crisp look. "I've been appointed by the new owner to oversee progress at

Riverbend. I just thought I'd take a look at the Lodge while I was at it."

"May I ask if you're an estate agent?" Charlotte knew perfectly well she wasn't, but she was reacting to the tone.

"Of course I'm not!" Ms Rodgers looked affronted. An estate agent, indeed!

"Just checking. The Lodge is private property, Ms Rodgers. But I'm sure you know that."

"Surely you have no objection to my taking a look?" The question was undisguisedly sarcastic. "I'm not making an inspection, after all."

"Which would be entirely inappropriate," Charlotte countered.

"Excuse me?" Ms Rodgers's arching black brows rose high.

"No offence, Ms Rodgers, but this is *private* property." The woman already knew that and didn't care. Had she tried a friendly approach, things might have gone differently.

As it was, Diane Rodgers was clearly on a power trip.

She gave an incredulous laugh, accompanied by a toss of her glossy head. "No need to get on your high horse. Though I expect it's understandable. You couldn't bear to part with the place. Isn't that right? You're the daughter of the previous owner." It was a statement, not a question.

"Why would you assume that?" Charlotte resumed deadheading the exquisite deep crimson Ecstasy roses.

"I've *heard* about you, Mrs Prescott." The emphasis was heavy, the smile *knowing*—as if Charlotte's secret was out. She had spent time in an institution. Possibly mental. "You're every bit as beautiful as I've been told."

"Beauty isn't the be all and end all. There are more important things. But may I ask who told you that?" There was a glint in Charlotte's crystal-clear green eyes.

"Sorry, that would be telling. You know yourself how

people love to talk. But being rich and beautiful can't prevent tragedy from occurring, can it? I hear you lost a brother when you were both children. Then a husband only a while back. Must have been frightful experiences? Both?"

Charlotte felt her stomach lurch. Who had this remarkably insensitive young woman spoken to? Someone she'd met in the village? Nicole, Martyn's younger sister? Nicole had always resented her. If Ms Rodgers's informant *had* been Nicole she would have learned a lot—most of it laced with vitriol.

A moment passed. "I'm sure you heard about that too, Ms Rodgers," Charlotte said quietly. "Now, you must excuse me. I have things to do. Preparations for dinner, for one."

"Just your father and your son, I'm told?"

It was more or less a taunt, and it bewildered Charlotte. Why the aggression? The expression on Ms Rodgers's face was hardly compassionate. Charlotte felt a wave of anger flow over her. "I must go in, Ms Rodgers." She folded her secateurs, then placed them in the white wicker basket at her feet. "Do please remember in future the Lodge is off-limits."

Diane Rodgers had intended to sound coolly amused, but she couldn't for the life of her disguise her resentment— which happened to be extreme. Who *was* this Charlotte Prescott to be so hoity-toity? She had well and truly fallen off her pedestal. At least that was the word. "Suit yourself!" she clipped, making too swift an about turn. She staggered, and had to throw a balancing arm aloft, making for the safety of solid ground.

Everyone appeared to be dressed to the nines for the Open Day. Filmy pastel dresses and pretty wide-brimmed hats were all the rage. Women had learned to take shelter from the blazing Australian sun. Sunscreen. Hats. Charlotte recalled how her mother had always looked after her skin, making sure her daughter did the same. Early days. These days her mother didn't talk to her often. Her mother didn't talk to *anyone* from the old days. Certainly not her ex-husband. Her parents had divorced two years after the Tragedy. Her mother had remarried a few years after that, and lived in some splendour in Melbourne's elite Toorak. If she had ever hoped her mother would find solace in her beautiful grandson, Christopher, she had been doomed to bitter disappointment. There had only been *one* boy in her mother's life: her pride and joy, her son Matthew.

"Mummy, can I please go off with Peter?" Christopher jolted her out of her sad thoughts. Peter Stafford was Christopher's best friend from day one at pre-school. He stood at Christopher's shoulder with a big grin planted on his engaging little face.

"I don't see why not." Charlotte smiled back. "Hello there, Peter. You're looking very smart." She touched a hand to his checked-cotton clad shoulder.

"Am I?" Peter blushed with pleasure, looking down at his new clothes. Christopher had told him in advance he was wearing long trousers, so Peter had insisted his mother buy him a pair. His first. He felt very grown-up.

Christopher hit him mildly in the ribs. "You know Mummy's only being nice."

"I *mean* it, Peter." Charlotte glanced over Peter's head. "Mum and Dad are here?"

Peter nodded. "Angie too." Angie was his older sister. "We had to wait ages for Angie to change her dress. I liked the first dress better. Then she had to fix her hair again. She was making Mum really angry."

"Well, I'm sure everyone has settled down," Charlotte offered soothingly. She knew Angela Stafford—as difficult a child as Peter was trouble-free. "We're all here to enjoy ourselves, and it's a beautiful day." Charlotte placed a loving hand on top of her son's head. "Check in with me from time to time, sweetheart?"

"Of course." He smiled up at her, searching her face in a near-adult way. "If you prefer, Pete and I can stay with you."

"Don't be silly!" she scoffed. "Off you go." Christopher— her little man!

The boys had begun to move away when Peter turned back. "I'm very sorry Riverbend is going out of the family, Mrs Prescott," he said, his brown eyes sweetly sympathetic. "Sorry for you *and* Mr Marsdon. Riverbend would have come to Chris."

Charlotte almost burst into tears. "Well, you know what they say, Peter," she managed lightly. "All good things must come to an end. But thank you. You're a good boy. A credit to your family."

"If *he* is, so am I!" Christopher crowed, impatiently brushing his thick floppy golden hair off his forehead. It was a gesture Charlotte knew well.

She turned her head away. She had to keep her spirits up. Her father was deeply involved in a conversation with the rotund, flush-faced Mayor. The Mayor appeared to be paying careful attention. The Marsdon name still carried a lot of clout. She walked on, waving a hand to those in the crowd who had stuck by her and her father.

Her parents' separation, and subsequent divorce, had split the Valley. Her beautiful, very dignified mother had chaired most of the Valley's charity functions, opening up the grounds of Riverbend for events much like today's. She had been well respected. Her father had never approached that high level of Valley approval, though he was supremely unaware of it such was his unshakeable self-confidence.

The Tragedy had torn her mother to pieces. Her father, grief-stricken, had managed to survive.

What exactly had happened to *her*? She had grown up knowing her mother loved her, but that Matthew, her older brother, the firstborn, was the apple of their mother's eye— her favourite. Her mother was the sort of woman who doted on a *son*. Charlotte hadn't minded at all. She had adored her brother too. Matthew had been a miraculously happy boy. A child of light. And he'd always had Rohan for his best friend. Rohan had been the young son of a single mother in the Valley—Mary Rose Costello.

Mary Rose, orphaned at an early age, had been "raised right" by her maternal grandmother, a strict woman of modest means, who had sent her very pretty granddaughter to the district's excellent convent school. Mary Rose Costello, with the Celt's white skin and red hair, had been regarded by the whole community as a "good girl". One who didn't "play around". Yet Mary Rose Costello, too young to be wise, had blotted her copybook by falling pregnant. Horror of horrors out of wedlock or even an engagement. The odd thing was, in that closely knit Valley, no one had been able to come up with the identity of Rohan's father. Lord knew they had all speculated, long and hard.

Mary Rose had never confided in anyone—including her bitterly shocked and disappointed grandmother. Mary Rose had never spoken the name of her child's father, but everyone was in agreement that he must have been a stunningly handsome man. And clever. Rohan Costello, born on the wrong side of the blanket, was far and away the handsomest, cleverest boy in the Valley. When Mary Rose's grandmother had died, she'd had the heart to leave her granddaughter and her little son the cottage. Mary Rose had then worked as a domestic in both the Marsdon and Prescott residences. She'd also done dressmaking. She had, in fact, been a very fine dressmaker, with natural skills. It was Charlotte's mother who had encouraged Mary Rose to take in orders, spreading the word to her friends across the Valley. So the Costellos had survived, given her mother's continuing patronage.

Up until the Tragedy.

People were milling about on the lush open lawn that stretched a goodly distance to all points of the compass, or taking shelter from the sun beneath the magnolia trees, heavy with plate-sized waxy cream flowers. Children were playing hide and seek amid the hedges; others romped on the grass. The naughty ones were running under the spray from the playing fountain until some adult stopped them before they got soaked. Everyone looked delighted to have been invited. A huge white marquee had been erected, serving delicious little crustless sandwiches, an amazing variety of beautifully decorated cupcakes, and lashings of strawberries and cream. White wine, a selection of fruit juices and the ubiquitous colas and soft drinks were also provided. No one would be allowed to get sozzled on alcohol that afternoon.

Charlotte had a few pleasant words with dozens of people as she threaded her way through the crowd. Her smile was starting to feel like a glaze on her face. It wasn't easy, appearing relaxed and composed, given the melancholy depths of her feelings, but she'd had plenty of practice. Years of containing her grief had taught control, if nothing else. Years of going down to breakfast with the Prescotts, a smile glued to her face, after another fierce encounter with Martyn. At such times he had hit her. Lashed out. Nowhere it would show. That would have caused an uproar. Though spoilt rotten by his mother and sister, his father would swiftly have taken him to account. Domestic violence was totally unacceptable. A man *never* hit a woman. It was unthinkable. Cowardly.

Only Martyn, who had turned out to be a bully, had desperately wanted what she could never give him. Her undivided love. He had even been jealous of Christopher. Had he ever dared lift a hand to her son she would have left him. But as it was, pride had held her in place. It wasn't as though she could have rung home and said, *I'm up to the neck with this marriage. I want out. I'm coming home.*

Her mother had been endeavouring to make a new life for herself elsewhere. Her father at that stage would have told her to "pull her socks up" and make her marriage work. It was only after Martyn had been killed and the scandalous circumstances were on public record that her father had welcomed her back—lonely, and totally unused to running a house. That was women's work. He'd detested the cleaning ladies who came in from time to time. His daughter would take over and cook him some decent meals. Such was his Lord of the Manor mentality. Besides, he loved his little grandson. "Chip off the old block!" he used to say, when Christopher unquestionably *wasn't.*

He took it for granted that Charlotte would stay, when she knew she could not. But when would the right time arrive? Christopher was now seven. No longer a small child.

Everyone was agog to meet the new mystery owner. So far he hadn't appeared, but an hour into the afternoon a helicopter suddenly flew overhead, disappearing over the roof of the mansion to land on the great spread of lawn at the rear of the house. Ten minutes later there was a little fanfare that got everyone's attention. A tall man, immaculately tailored with a red rosebud in his lapel, followed by no less a personage than Ms Diane Rodgers in full garden party regalia, came through the front door.

Even at a distance one could see this was someone quite out of the ordinary. He moved with lithe grace across the colonnaded verandah, coming to stand at the top of the short flight of stone stairs that led to the garden. His eyes surveyed the smiling crowd as he lifted a hand.

Immediately, enthusiastic clapping broke out. Here was their host at last! And didn't he look the part! They were just so thrilled—especially the children, who had stared up in wonderment at the big silver helicopter with its loud whirring rotors.

How is Dad going to handle this? Charlotte thought.

Her father revealed his class. He strolled out of the crowd, perhaps with a certain swagger, to greet the CEO of the company that had bought the ancestral home. "Come along, Charlotte," he commanded, as he drew alongside her. "It's just you and me now. Time to greet the new owner. I very much suspect he's more than just a CEO."

Unfailingly, Charlotte supported her father.

"My, he *is* a handsome man." Her father pitched his voice low. "And a whole lot younger than I would have expected," he tacked on in some surprise. "I fully antici-pated someone in their late forties at least. Hang on—don't I know him?"

Charlotte couldn't say whether he did or he didn't. Even with the broad brim of her picture hat the slanting sun was in her eyes. But she did manage to put a lovely welcoming smile on her face. They were on show. Anyone who was anyone in the Valley was ranged behind them—every last man, woman and child keen observers of this meeting. This was an historic day. The Marsdons, for so long lords and ladies of the Valley, now displaced, were expected to act with grace and aplomb.

Except it didn't happen that way.

"Good God, Costello—it *can't* be you?" Vivian Randall bellowed like an enraged bull.

He came to such an abrupt halt Charlotte, slightly behind him, all but slammed into him, clutching at his arm to steady herself. She saw the blood draining out of her father's face. A hard man to surprise, he looked utterly pole-axed.

She, herself, had felt no portent of disaster. No inkling that another great turning point in her life had arrived. She couldn't change direction. She was stuck in place, with such a tangle of emotions knotted inside her they could never be untied.

There wasn't a flicker of answering emotion on the man's striking, highly intelligent face. "Good afternoon, Mr Marsdon," he said suavely, coming down the stone steps to greet them. Effortless charm. An overlay of natural command. His voice was cultured, the timbre dark. An extremely attractive voice. One people would always listen to. "Charlotte." He turned his head to look at her. Blazing blue eyes consumed her, the electric *blueness* in startling contrast to his colouring—crow-black hair and brows, olive skin that was tanned to a polished bronze. The searing gaze remained fixed on her.

She was swamped by an overwhelming sense of unre-
ality.

Rohan!

The intervening years were as nothing—carried away as if by a king tide. The day of reckoning had come. Hadn't she always known it would? Her heart was pumping double time. The shock was devastating—too excruciating to be borne. She had thought she had built up many protective layers. Now she was blown away by her own emotional fragility. She tried to get her breath, slow her palpitating heart. She felt as weak as a kitten. She raised one trembling hand to her temple as a great stillness started to descend on her. She was vaguely aware she was slipping sideways…

No, no—don't give way! Hold up!

"Rohan!" she breathed.

He was as familiar to her as she was to herself. Yet he had never given a hint of warning—right up until this very day. It was cruel. Rohan had never been cruel. But it was abundantly clear he wanted to shock her far more than he wanted to shock her father. He wanted to stun *her* to her very soul. She read it in his dynamic face. Revenge, smoothly masked. But not to her. She knew him too well. So long as there was memory, the past lived on. One might long to forget, but memory wouldn't allow it.

Her pride broke.

"You do *this* to me, Rohan?" She knew she sounded pitiful. The immediate world had turned from radiant sunshine to a swirling grey fog. It smothered her like a thick blanket. Her ears seemed stuffed with cotton wool. She was moving beyond complete awareness, deeper into the fog, oblivious to the strong arms that shot out with alacrity to gather her up.

A little golden-haired boy ran out of the crowd, crying over and over in a panic, "Mummy…Mummy… Mummy!"

His grandfather, beside himself with sick rage, tried to catch him. The boy broke away, intent on only one thing: following the tall stranger who was carrying his beautiful mother back into the house.

This was the new owner of Riverbend! By now everyone was saying his name, turning one to the other, themselves in a state of shock.

Rohan Costello.

Fate had a way of catching up with everyone.

CHAPTER TWO

Silver Valley, summer fourteen years ago

IT WAS one of those endless afternoons of high summer—
glorious months of the school vacation, when the heat sent
them racing from the turquoise swimming pool in the mansion's grounds into the river. It meandered through the
valley and lay in a broad glittering curve at Riverbend's
feet. They knew they were supposed to keep to the pool
that afternoon, but it wasn't as though they weren't allowed
to take frequent dips in the river. After all, their father had
had a carpenter erect a diving dock for their pleasure. Prior
to that they had used a rope and an old tyre, fixed to stout
branches of a river gum to swing from.

She was twelve, and very much part of the Pack of Four,
as they had become known throughout the Valley. She
didn't feel honoured to be allowed to tag along with the
boys. She *was* one of them. All three boys were inseparable
friends: her older brother Mattie, Rohan—Mrs Costello's
son—a courtesy title insisted on by their mother, because
Mrs Costello was really a miss, but who cared?—and
Martyn Prescott, young son of the neighbouring estate,
High Grove. Charlotte was their muse.

Although she would have died rather than say it aloud,
Rohan was her shining white knight. She loved him. She

loved the burning blue looks he bent on her. But these days a kind of humming tension had cut into their easy affection. Once or twice she'd had the crazy desire to kiss him. Proof, if any were needed, that she was fast growing up.

Rohan easily beat them into the water that day, striking out into the middle of the stream, the ripples on the dark green surface edged with sparkles the sunlight had cast on the river. "What's keeping you?" he yelled, throwing a long tanned arm above water. "Come on, Charlie. You can beat the both of them!"

He was absolutely splendid, Rohan! Even as a boy he had a glamour about him. As her mother had once commented, "Rohan's an extraordinary boy—a born leader, and so good for my darling Mattie!" In those early days their mother had been very protective of her only son.

"Won't do him a bit of good, wrapping him in cotton wool." That irritated comment always came from their father, who was sure such mollycoddling was holding his son back.

Perhaps he was right? But their mother took no notice. Unlike her young daughter, who enjoyed splendid health, Matthew had suffered from asthma since infancy. Mattie's paediatrician had told their anxiety-ridden mother he would most likely grow out of it by age fourteen. It was that kind of asthma.

That fatal day Charlotte remembered running to the diving dock, her long, silver-blonde hair flying around her face. It was Martyn who had pulled her hair out of its thick plait. It was something he loved to do. Most of the time she rounded on him—"How stupid, Martyn!" was her usual protest as she began to re-plait it.

"You look better that way, Charlie. One day you're going to be an absolute knockout. Mum and Dad say that. Not

Nicole, of course. She's as jealous as hell. One day we're going to get married. Mum says that too."

"Dream on!" she always scoffed. Get married, indeed! Some husband Martyn would make.

Mattie always laughed, "Boy, has he got a crush on you, Charlie!"

She chose not to believe it. She didn't know then that some crushes get very crushed.

Rohan never laughed. Never joked about it. He kept silent on that score. The Marsdons and the Prescotts were the privileged children of the Valley. Certainly not Rohan Costello, who lived with his mother on the outskirts of town in a little cottage hardly big enough to swing a cat. Their mother said the pair would have to shift soon.

"Rohan is quickly turning into a man!"

At fourteen, nearing fifteen, it was apparent the fast-growing Rohan would easily attain six feet and more in maturity. Mattie, on the other hand, was small for his age. Rohan was by far the strongest and the best swimmer, though she was pretty good herself—but built for speed rather than endurance.

Totally unselfconscious, even with her budding breasts showing through her swimsuit and her long light limbs gleaming a pale gold, with Rohan—her hero—watching, she made a full racing dive into the water, striking out towards him as he urged her on, both of them utterly carefree, not knowing then that this was the last day they would ever swim in the river.

Years later she would shudder when she remembered their odd near-total absorption in one another that summer afternoon. A boy and a girl. One almost fifteen, the other twelve.

Romeo and Juliet.

Martyn appeared angry with them, sniping away. Jealous. Mattie was his normal sweet self. At one stage he called out that he was going to swim across to the opposite bank, where beautiful weeping willows bent their branches towards the stream.

"Stay with us, Mattie," Rohan yelled, cupping his hands around his mouth.

"What's the matter? Reckon I can't do it?" Mattie called back, sounding very much as if he was going to take up the challenge.

"'Course you can!" she had shouted, always mindful of her brother's self-esteem, undermined by his sickness. "But do like Rohan says, Mattie. Stay with us."

Mattie appeared persuaded. He turned in their direction, only then Martyn yelled, his voice loud with taunt, "Don't be such a cream puff, Marsdon! Are you always going to do what Mummy says? Are you always going to stick by Rohan's side? Rohan will look after Mummy's little darling. Isn't that his job? Go for it, Mattie! Don't be such a wimp!"

"Shut up, Martyn!" Rohan roared, in a voice none of them had ever heard before. It was an adult voice. The voice of command.

Immediately Martyn ceased his taunts, but Mattie confounded them all by kicking out towards the opposite bank, his thin arms stiff and straight in the water.

"Perhaps we should let him?" Charlotte had appealed to Rohan, brows knotted. "Mummy really does mollycoddle him."

"You can say that again!" Martyn chortled unkindly. Everyone in the Valley knew how protective Barbara Marsdon was of her only son.

"I'm going after him." It only took a little while of watching Mattie's efforts for Rohan to make the decision. "You shouldn't have taunted him, Martyn. You're supposed to be Mattie's friend. He's trying to be brave, but the brave way is the safest way. Mattie doesn't have your strength, or mine. He isn't the strongest of swimmers."

"He'll make it." Martyn was trying not to sound anxious, but his warier brain cells had kicked in. Rohan was right. He shouldn't have egged Mattie on. He went to say something in his own defence, only Rohan had struck out in his powerful freestyle while Charlotte followed.

Martyn chose to remain behind. He thought they were both overreacting. Mattie would be okay. Sure he would! The distance between the banks at that point wasn't all that wide. The water was warm. The surface was still. There was no appreciable undercurrent. Well, not really. The waters were much murkier on the other side, with the wild tangle of undergrowth, the heavy overhang of trees, the resultant debris that would have found its way into the river. For someone like Rohan the swim would be no more than a couple of lengths of the pool. But for Mattie?

Hell, they could be in the middle of a crisis, Martyn realised—too late.

One minute Mattie's thin arms were making silver splashes in the water, and then to their utter horror his head, gilded by sunlight, disappeared beneath the water.

All of a sudden the river that had taken them so many times into its wonderful cool embrace seemed a frightening place.

"Oh, God—oh, God!" Charlotte shrieked, knowing in her bones something was wrong. "Get him, Rohan!" she cried hysterically.

"Come on, don't be stupid, Charlie. He's only showing off," Martyn shouted at her, starting to feel desperately worried. The traumas of childhood had a way of echoing down the years. Martyn felt shivers of prescience shoot into his gut.

Charlotte ignored him, heart in her mouth. Martyn never was much good in a crisis. It was Rohan who knifed through the dark green water with the speed of a torpedo.

She went after him, showing her own unprecedented burst of speed. "God—oh, God!" Tears were pouring down her face, lost in river water.

There was no sign of Matthew. She knew he wouldn't be playing games. Matthew was enormously considerate of others. He would never frighten her, never cause concern to the people he loved. He loved her. He loved Rohan, his best friend. He wouldn't even have caused dread to Martyn, who had taunted him either.

"Mattie…Mattie *Mattie…!*" She was yelling his name at the top of her lungs, startling birds that took off in a kaleidoscope of colour.

Rohan too had disappeared, diving beneath the dark green water. She followed his example, fear reverberating deep within her body. Lungs tortured, she had to surface for air. As she came up she thought she saw something shimmering—a *shape* moving downstream. She went after it. Rohan beat her to it. She was screaming in earnest now. Rohan was cradling a clearly unconscious Mattie like a baby, holding him out of the water in his strong arms. A thin runnel of blood was streaming off Mattie's pale temple.

Fate could swoop like an eagle from a clear blue sky.

"I'll tow him to the bank," Rohan shouted to her. His voice was choked, his handsome young face twisted in terror. 'I'll try CPR. Keep at it. Charlie—get help."

But Mattie was gone. She *knew* it. Lovely, laughing Mattie. The best brother in the world.

A swim across the river. She could have done it easily. Yet Mattie might have plunged into a deep sea in the black-ness of night. There was no sign of Martyn either. He must have run back to the house for help. She thought she might as well drown herself with Mattie gone. There would be no life at Riverbend now. Her mother would most likely go mad. She knew her father would somehow survive. But her mother, even if she could get through the years of annihilating grief, wouldn't stay within sight of the river where her adored Matthew had drowned. She would go away, leaving Charlotte and her father alone.

Except for the gentle shadow of Matthew Marsdon, who would always be fourteen.

The whole tragic thing would be blamed on someone. Her inner voice gave her the sacrificial name.

Rohan.

Rohan the born leader, who would be judged by her parents, the Prescotts, and a few others in the Valley resentful of the Costello boy's superior looks and high intelligence over their own sons, to have let Matthew Marsdon drown.

Such an intolerable burden to place on the shoulders of a mere boy. A crime, and Rohan Costello was innocent of the charge.

The present. The garden party.

Rohan Costello had returned to the scene of his childhood devastation. That showed passion and courage. It also showed that the cleverest boy in the Valley had become extraordinarily successful in life. Matthew Marsdon's tragic death had locked the daughter, Charlotte, and Costello even more closely together. Eventually they'd gone beyond the boundaries, but that had never been known, or if suspected never proved. What *was* known was that the Tragedy had never driven them apart—even when Charlotte's parents, in particular her mother Barbara, had burned with something approaching hatred for the boy she had in a way helped nurture.

There had only been one course left to the Costellos. Mother and son had been virtually driven out of the Valley, the sheer weight of condemnation too great.

The brutality of it!

People could only wonder if Rohan Costello had returned to Silver Valley to settle old scores? The past was never as far away as people liked to pretend.

Charlotte's faint lasted only seconds, but when she was out of it and the world had stopped spinning she was still in a state of shock, her body trembling with nerves. She was lying on one of the long sofas in the drawing room, her head and her feet resting on a pile of silk cushions. Her hair had all but fallen out of its elegant arrangement. She was minus her hat and, she noted dazedly, her expensive sandals.

Rohan was at her head. Christopher was at her feet. Diane Rodgers and a couple of her mother's old friends stood close by. Her mother's friends' watching faces were showing their concern. Not so Ms Rodgers, whose almond eyes were narrow. There was no sign of her father, but George Morrissey, their family doctor, hurried in, calling as he came, "Charlie, dear, whatever happened?"

Morrissey had brought the Marsdon children into the world, and Charlotte had always been a great favourite.

"How are you feeling now?" He sat down beside her to take her pulse. A few more checks, and then, satisfied there was nothing serious about the faint, he raised her up gently, while Rohan Costello, the new owner, resettled the cushions as a prop at her back.

"The heat, George," she explained, not daring to look up at Rohan, who had so stunningly re-entered her life. What she wanted to do was seize hold of her little son and run for her life. Except there was no escape. Not now. "I must be going soft."

"That'll be the day!" the doctor scoffed.

"Mummy?" Christopher's lovely olive skin had turned paper-white. "Are you all right?"

"I'm fine, darling." She held out a reassuring hand. "Come here to me." She tried hard to inject brightness into her voice. "I love you, Chrissie."

"Mummy, I love you too. You've never fainted before." He clutched her hand, staring anxiously into her face.

"I'm fine now, sweetheart. Just a little dizzy." She drew him down onto the spot Dr Morrissey had readily vacated, putting a soothing arm around him and dropping a kiss on the top of his golden head. "I'll get up in a minute."

"Give it a little longer, Charlie," Morrissey advised, happy to see her natural colour returning. He very much suspected extreme shock was the cause of Charlotte's faint. Incredible to think young Costello had become so successful. Then again, not. Rohan Costello *had* been an exceptionally bright lad.

"This *is* a surprise, Rohan," he said, turning to hold out his hand.

Rohan Costello took it in a firm grip. The doctor could hardly say, given the circumstances of Rohan Costello's departure, *Welcome back to Silver Valley*!

"It's good to see you again, Dr Morrissey," Rohan answered smoothly. "You were always kind to my mother and me."

"You were both very easy to be kind to, Rohan," Morrissey assured him with genuine warmth. "And how is your mother?"

"She's doing very well, sir," Rohan responded pleasantly, but it was obvious he wasn't going to be more forthcoming.

"Good, good! I'm very glad to hear it. Do you intend to spend much time in the Valley, Rohan?" Morrissey dared to ask. "You must have become a very successful businessman?"

Rohan gave him a half smile that bracketed his handsome mouth. "I've had a few lucky breaks, Doctor."

"I think it would have more to do with brain power. You were always very clever."

George Morrissey, the keeper of many secrets, turned back to take another look at Charlotte and her precious boy. What a beautiful child Christopher was, with those glorious blue eyes! One rarely saw that depth of colour. He had delivered Christopher Prescott, Charlotte's baby, who had come a little early. He was sure everyone had believed him. He was the most respected medical doctor in the Valley. After the tragic death of Charlotte's young brother Matthew, and the flight of her mother from the "haunted" Valley, he had become very protective of Charlotte Marsdon, who had gone on to marry a young man who in his opinion had simply not been worthy of her. Martyn Prescott—who himself had met a tragic fate.

Christopher too wanted to talk to the tall stranger—the man who had carried his mother so effortlessly into their house. Well, *his* house now. And it seemed to suit him just fine. Christopher was very thankful the *right* person would have ownership of Riverbend. He looked just the sort of man to look after it.

Christopher stood up, wondering why his mother was trying to grab hold of his arm. He held out his hand, as he had been taught. "Hello, I'm Christopher. We used to live here."

"I know that, Christopher," the man answered quietly, moving in closer.

The man's blue eyes made contact with his own, and Christopher felt transfixed. "Do you know Mummy?" He didn't see how the man could, yet those vibes he seemed to have inherited from someone told him this man and his mother knew one another well. It was a mystery, but there it was!

Charlotte put her feet to the floor, unsure if she could even stand, still not looking at Rohan but acutely aware that the full force of his attention was focused on her and her son. "Mr Costello is a very busy man, Chris," she said. Christopher was so sharp. "We mustn't keep him from mingling with his guests."

"No, Mummy." Christopher nodded his head in agreement, but continued with a further question. "*How* do you know my mother?" It seemed important he find out. Perceptive beyond his years, he felt the tension between his mother and the tall stranger. He couldn't figure it out. But it was *there*. Mummy was nice to everyone, yet she wasn't being exactly nice to Mr Costello. Something had to be worrying her.

"Your mother and I grew up together, Christopher," Rohan explained. "I left the Valley when I was seventeen. I'm Rohan. No need to call me Mr Costello."

"Oh, I'd like that," Christopher said, his cheeks taking on a gratified flush. "We thought you were going to be pretty old. But you're *young*!"

"Your mother has never mentioned me?"

Christopher shook his blond head. "Did you know my dad died?" He edged closer to the man. It was like being drawn by a magnet. It sort of *thrilled* him. He felt he could follow this man Rohan like the disciples in Bible stories had followed their Master. It both pleased and puzzled him.

"Yes, I did, Christopher. I'm very sorry." Rohan's voice was gentle, yet his expression was stern.

"There's just Mummy and me now." Christopher felt the sting of tears at the back of his eyes. He had loved his dad. Of course he had. One *had* to love one's dad. But never like he loved his mother. What was really strange was that he cared for his grumpy old grandfather more than he had cared for his dad. "And Grandpa, of course," he tacked on. "You must have known my dad and Uncle Mattie?"

"Oh, darling, not all these questions!" Charlotte spoke with agitation. He had sussed out enough already. Something had happened to Christopher of late. He was picking up on vibes, on looks and words that appeared to him laden with meaning. He was growing up too fast.

For once, Christopher didn't heed her. "Uncle Mattie is still around," he told Rohan, staring up at him. He was really surprised by the way he felt drawn to his man. "I often *feel* Uncle Mattie around."

Rohan didn't laugh or deride his claim. "I believe it, Christopher," he said. "I feel Mattie too, at different times. He would have *loved* you."

"Would he?" Christopher was immensely pleased. Uncle Mattie would have loved him! He was liking Rohan more and more. "Mummy said I looked like him when I was little." He continued to meet Rohan's amazing blue eyes. They glittered like jewels. "Do I?"

Rohan considered that carefully. "You might have, Christopher, when you were younger. But not now."

"No." Christopher shook his blond head, as though his own opinion had been confirmed. "I don't look like anyone, really," he confided.

Oh, yes, you do!

Charlotte kept her head down, her heart fluttering wildly in her breast. Christopher's face had changed as the baby softness had firmed and his features became more pronounced. Heredity. It was all so *dangerous*.

It was Diane Rodgers who located Charlotte's expensive sandals, then passed them to her in such a manner as to suggest a hurry-up. There was a faint accompanying glare as well. Charlotte bent to put her strappy sandals back on, then made an attempt to fix her hair. She felt totally disorientated. And there was Christopher, chattering away to Rohan as if he had known him all his young life. It almost broke her.

"Here's your hat, love." A familiar face swam into view. Kathy Nolan—a good friend to her mother and a good friend to her. "It's beautiful."

"Thank you, Kathy." Charlotte took the picture hat in her hand.

"Feeling better now, love?" Kathy Nolan was very fond of Charlotte.

"Much better, thank you, Kathy. I'm so sorry I embarrassed you all. The heat got to me."

Kathy, a kindly woman, let that go. A beautiful breeze was keeping the temperature positively balmy. Charlotte had fainted because Rohan Costello was the last man in the universe she would have expected to buy the Marsdon mansion, Kathy reckoned. To tell the truth she felt a little freaked out herself. Rohan Costello, of all people! And didn't he look *marvellous*! Always a handsome boy, the adult Rohan took her breath away. Many people in the Valley—herself and her husband certainly—had been unhappy when the Costellos had left after Rohan had completed his final year at secondary school. Later they had learned he was their top achiever. The highest category. No surprise.

Poor Barbara had never made allowances for the ages

of the other children when Mattie had drowned. It had been a terrible accident. With all the care in the world, accidents still happened. Yet Barbara had gone on a bitter, never-ending attack. So very sad! Loss took people in different ways. Bereft of her son, Barbara Marsdon had been in despair. That inner devastation had brought about the divorce. The marriage had been beyond repair. Barbara had told her she'd doubted her ability to be a good mother to Charlotte. She wasn't functioning properly. That had been true enough. Charlotte was to remain with her father.

Yet here was Rohan Costello, back in the Valley. Not only that, taking possession of Riverbend. Fact is far stranger than fiction, Kathy thought.

Diane Rodgers, looking very glamorous in classic white, with a striking black and white creation on her head, spoke up. "Would you like me to help you back to the Lodge, Mrs Prescott? No trouble, I assure you."

At the sound of those precise tones, Christopher swung back. "Mummy has *me*," he said, not rudely—he knew better than that—but he didn't like the way the lady was speaking to his mother. It didn't sound gentle and caring, like Mrs Nolan. It sounded more like teachers at his school when the kids weren't on their best behaviour.

"Wouldn't you like to stay on, Christopher?" Rohan suggested. "I'm sure you have a friend with you. I'll run your mother home."

Christopher considered that for a full minute. "I won't stay if you don't feel well, Mummy," he said, his protective attitude on show. "Peter will be okay."

Charlotte rose to her feet, hoping she didn't look as desperate as she felt. "Sweetheart, I don't want you to bother about me. I don't want *anyone* to bother about me. I'm fine."

"You're sure of that, Charlie?" Morrissey laid a gentle hand on her shoulder.

"You mustn't let me keep you, George." Charlotte gave him a shaky smile. "I know you and Ruth will love wandering around the grounds. They're in tip-top condition."

"That they are!" George Morrissey agreed. He turned back to the tall authoritative figure of the adult Rohan Costello. "I'd be delighted if you'd say hello to my wife, Rohan. She'd love to catch up."

"It would be a pleasure." Rohan gave a slight inclination of his handsome dark head.

The doctor lifted a hand in general farewell, then walked off towards the entrance hall.

"You must allow me to run you back to the Lodge at least, Charlotte," Rohan said, with a compelling undernote she couldn't fail to miss. "I'll make sure Chris gets home."

"Thank you, Rohan," Christopher piped up. "Can't take the helicopter, I suppose?" he joked, executing a full circle, arms outstretched. "Whump, whump, whump!"

"Not that far." Rohan returned the boy's entrancing smile. "But I promise you a ride one day soon."

Christopher looked blown away. "Gee, that's great! Wait until I tell Peter."

"Maybe Peter too," Rohan said.

"That'd be *awesome*! So where's Grandpa?" Christopher suddenly asked of his mother. "Why didn't he come into the house?"

"He may well be outside, Christopher," Rohan answered smoothly. "Why don't you go and see? Your mother is safe with me."

"Is that all right, Mummy? I can go?" Christopher studied her face. His mother was *so* beautiful. The most beautiful mother in the world.

"Of course you can, darling." Charlotte summoned up a smile. "I want you to enjoy yourself."

"Thank you." Christopher shifted his blue gaze back to Rohan. "It's great to meet you, Rohan." He put out his hand. Man to man.

Rohan shook it gravely. "Great to meet you too, Christopher," he responded. *At long last.*

Many things in life changed. Some things never did.

CHAPTER THREE

THEY were quite alone. It was terrifying. Was she afraid of Rohan? That simply couldn't be. But she was terrified of the emotions that must be raging through him. Terrified of the *steel* in him. Where had her beautiful white knight gone? A shudder ripped through her. This was a Rohan she had never seen.

The village ladies had gone back outside, to enjoy the rest of the afternoon. Diane Rodgers had hovered, but Rohan had given her a taut smile and told her in his dark mellifluous voice to go and take a look at the roses. They were in magnificent full bloom. Ms Rodgers looked as though she had been planning something entirely different. One would have had to be blind to miss Ms Rodgers's keen interest in Rohan. And who could blame her?

The pulverising shock had not worn off. Nor would it for a long time. Now she felt an added trepidation, and—God help her—the old pounding excitement. He looked wonderful. *Wonderful!* The man who had loved her and whom she had loved in return.

Rohan.

She saw how much she still loved him. No one else had ever mattered. But now wasn't the time to fall apart. She had to keep some measure of herself together. "I can walk back to the Lodge," she said, although her voice was reduced to a trembling whisper. "You don't have to take me."

"*Don't* I?"

The slash of his voice cut her heart to ribbons.

God—oh, God!

Recognition of the trouble she was in settled on her.

He took hold of her bare slender arm, pulling her in to his side. "He's *mine*, isn't he?" he ground out. His tone was implacable.

She wasn't up to this. She was a lost soul. She was acutely aware of the pronounced pallor beneath his golden-olive skin. He was in shock too. She wanted to touch his face. Didn't dare. She felt sorrow. Guilt. Pity. Remorse. Her heart was fluttering like a frantic bird in her breast. She had to try to evade the whole momentous issue. She needed time to *think*.

"I don't know what you're talking about, Rohan." She allowed a fallen lock of hair to half-shield her face.

"Is that why you're trembling from head to foot?" he answered curtly. "Christopher is *mine*. My child—not Martyn's."

She tried to disengage herself, but didn't have a hope. He was far too strong. "Are you insane?" Her voice shook with alarm.

"God!" Rohan burst out, his breathing harsh. "Don't play the fool with me, Charlotte. He has *my* eyes. My nose. My mouth. My chin."

Your beautiful smile. The habit you had of flipping your hair back with an impatient hand.

"He's going to get more and more like me," Rohan gritted. "What are you going to do then?"

"Rohan, *please*," she begged, hating herself.

He took no pity on her. It was all he could do not to shake her until her blonde head collapsed against his chest.

Despite himself, he was breathing in the very special scent of her—the freshness, the fragrance. He could breathe her in for ever. He was that much of a fool.

"How could you do this, Charlotte? It's unforgiv-able what you've done. No *way* is Christopher Martyn's child."

"Please, Rohan, *stop*!" She shut her eyes tight in pain and despair. She was still light-headed.

"You made the decision to banish me from your heart and your head," he accused her. "You know you did. No love in a cottage for Charlotte Marsdon. God, no! Poor Martyn was always crazy about you. You were the ulti-mate prize, waiting for him. Did he *know* the child wasn't his?"

Years of unhappiness, pain and guilt echoed from her throat. "How *could* he know?" she shouted. "*I* didn't."

"What?" He took a backward glance through the mansion, then led her away into the splendid book-lined library.

Her father had taken his pick of the valuable collection of books. Even in her highly perturbed state she could see their number had been replaced.

"You mean you were having sex with us *both*?" Rohan asked, looking and sounding appalled. "Oh, don't tell me. I don't want to know," he groaned.

She had to turn away from the anger flashing in his blue eyes. "It wasn't like that, Rohan. You were lost to me. Forever lost to me.'

His brief laugh couldn't have been more bitter or disbe-lieving. "You're lying again. You *knew* I would never let you go. I had to make something of myself, Charlotte. I had to have something to offer you. All I needed was a little time. I told you that. I believed you understood. But, no, you got yourself married to *Martyn* in double-quick time. Poor gutless Martyn, who went around telling everyone who would listen that *I* had goaded Mattie into trying to swim the river. Martyn was the golden boy in the Valley, not me. I was Mary Rose Costello's bastard son. Yet I thought the world would freeze over before *you* ever gave yourself to Martyn."

"Maybe he *took* me, Rohan. Ever think of that?" She threw up her head in a kind of wild defiance, though she was on the verge of breaking down completely.

"What are you *saying*?" There was fire in his eyes.

Rivers of tears were threateningly close. "I don't know *what* I'm saying." Her heart was labouring in her chest. "I never thought I would lay eyes on you again."

"Rubbish!" he responded violently. "You *knew* you would see me again. With Martyn gone. I've given you enough time to recover.'

"There would *never* be enough time." Her green eyes glittered. "What do you expect me to say? Welcome back, Rohan?"

A great anger was running in his veins. Whatever he had expected, it had never been *this*. He had learned early that she and Martyn had had a child—a boy. The agony of it, the pain of loss and betrayal, had nearly driven him mad. Day and night, month after month, year after year he had fought his demons. Charlotte and Martyn. Now he was confronted by the staggering truth. Christopher wasn't Martyn's at all. Christopher was *his*.

How terrible a crime was that? And what about the precautions she was supposed to have taken? "You're a cheat and a liar, Charlotte," he said, low-voiced and dangerous. "And I fully intend to prove it. You told me you loved me. You promised to wait for as long as it took. Why not? We had plenty of time. You were only eighteen. I hadn't even turned twenty-one. *I'm* Christopher's father. Don't look away from me. Don't attempt more lies. I *will* push this further."

"A threat?"

"You bet!" he said harshly, even though to his horror the old hunger was as fierce as ever. Would *nothing* kill it? She was even more beautiful—her beauty more pronounced, more complete. Charlotte who had betrayed him. And herself.

"Please, Rohan, I don't need this now." There was anguish in her face and in her voice. "I can walk back to the Lodge."

"Forget it. I'm driving you. Has your father the faintest clue? Or is he still hiding his head in the sand?" He compelled her out of the comfortable elegance of the library and back into the arched corridor, making for the rear of the house, where a vehicle was garaged and kept for his convenience.

"Dad loves Christopher very much." There was a trembling catch in her voice.

"Not what I asked you," he said grimly.

They were out in the sunshine now. The scent of the white rambling rose that framed the pedimented door and climbed the stone wall filled the air with its lovely nostalgic perfume. More roses rioted in the gardens, and lovely plump peonies—one of her great favourites.

"Chris did have a fleeting look of Mattie for a few years," she offered bleakly. This was the age of DNA. There was no point in trying to delude Rohan. What he said was correct. Christopher would only grow more like him. Hadn't she been buffeted by the winds of panic for some time? "Now that he's lost his little-boy softness the resemblance has disappeared. He has our blond hair."

"Isn't that marvelous?" he exclaimed ironically. "He has the Marsdon blond hair! God knows what might have happened had his hair been crow-black, like mine. Or, even worse, *red* like my mother's."

"I loved you, Rohan." The words flamed out of her.

In response he made a strangled sound of utter disgust. "You must have wept buckets after you decided to drop me. But there's intense satisfaction in my being rich. Daddy turned out to be a real loser with his lack of financial acumen. I had nothing. Too young. Martyn stood to inherit a fortune. Must have ruined your day when you lost him. How come you're living with your father? Didn't Martyn leave you a rich woman?"

"Sad to say, no. It's none of your business, Rohan."

"I beg to differ. It's very much my business. Martyn's father was too smart to let go of the purse strings. And your mother? The self-appointed avenger?"

"My mother has settled—or tried to settle—into a different life. I don't see much of her. She has little interest in my beautiful Chrissie."

"*Our* beautiful Christopher," he corrected curtly, usurping her as the single parent.

"He's not Mattie, you see," she continued sadly. "Really there was no one else for my mother."

Rohan's striking face was set like granite. "She loved you in her way. Of course she did."

"Not enough," she answered simply.

"I think I might find that a blessing," Rohan mused. "Your mother keeping her distance from my son. Your mother is deeply neurotic. She would never accept *me* in any capacity. Not in a hundred lifetimes."

She couldn't deny it. Rohan had been chosen as the scapegoat. She had been the daughter of the family—a girl of twelve. Martyn Prescott the only son of close friends. It had to be Rohan Costello—Mary Rose's boy. "My mother has been steeped in grief, Rohan. Dad has soldiered on."

"Good old Vivian!" Rohan retorted with extreme sarcasm. "The fire's not out in the old boy either. Did you hear the way he bellowed my name?"

Charlotte flinched, defending him quickly. "It was cruel not to let us know."

"Cruel?" Rohan's brilliant eyes shot sparks. "The hide of you to talk of cruelty! I can't believe *your* treachery! I've missed out on the first seven years of my son's life, Charlotte. First words. First steps. Birthdays. The first day at school. How can you possibly make it up to me for that?"

"I can't. I *can't*. I'm so sorry, Rohan. Sorry. Sorry, sorry. Do you want me to go down on my knees? I've raised Christopher as best I could. He's a beautiful, loving, clever child. He's everything in the world to me."

"So that's okay, then, is it? He's everything in the world to *you*. What about *me*? I never held my newborn son in my arms. I was robbed of that great joy. Tell me, how did you manage to put it across Martyn? Or didn't you? It's common knowledge he had a young woman in the car with him. It's a great mercy she wasn't killed or injured as well. Tell me—did he fall out of love with you? Or did he get sick of what little affection you could show him? You didn't love him. Don't tell me you did."

"I married Martyn and what came of it?" she said. "He's dead."

"You weren't responsible for that." He reacted to the pain in her face.

"Wasn't I?"

"So he had a tough time? Why did you do it, Charlotte? The money, the position?"

"I was *pregnant*, Rohan."

"By *me*!" he exploded. "Why didn't you contact me? God knows, I had the right to know."

"I wasn't sure whose child I was carrying, Rohan." Her voice was that of the frightened, isolated young girl she had been.

"Oh, poor, poor you! It couldn't have taken you all that long to find out!"

"Too late," she acknowledged, remembering her shock. "Martyn never did find out. Christopher has changed quite a lot in the past eighteen months."

"I'm not getting this at all," he frowned. "What about the Prescotts?"

"They have their suspicions. Nicole hates me. Always did, I think. We don't see much of them."

"Another plus! So when did you decide to seduce Martyn? I mean have sex with him. Clinch your position in his life."

"I don't want to talk about this, Rohan," she said, in a tight, defensive voice. "It's all over and done with."

"Not by a long shot. I can see you're badly frightened, and you should be. I have every intention of claiming my son."

She stood paralysed. "You can't do that to me."

"Can't I? I *can*, by God!" There was strain and a world of determination in his striking face.

"You can't take him from me, Rohan. You can't mean that. He's my life. I adore him."

"Who would take any notice of *you*? You were supposed to have *adored* me, remember? I don't intend to take our son from you, Charlotte. Unlike you, I do have a heart. *You* are part of the package." He let his eyes rest on her. Beautiful, beautiful, unfaithful Charlotte. "I want you *and* our son. Our boy can't be separated from his mother."

Jets of emotion shot through her. "In the same way you needed to have Riverbend?" she challenged.

"Perhaps I hated to see such a magnificent estate go to

rack and ruin." He shrugged. "I have plans for Riverbend, Charlotte. Plans for the vineyards, a winery, olive groves."

She accepted he had plans without hesitation. "You own the estate—not the company Vortex?"

"I *am* Vortex—and a couple of other affiliated companies as well. And I own Riverbend, lock, stock and barrel. Your father has done virtually nothing in the way of improvements since your grandfather died. I don't particularly dislike your father. I never did. It was your *mother* who was truly horrible to us. You know—your mother—the *great* lady." His eyes glittered with blue light.

"There are big turning points in life, Rohan," she said in a pain-filled voice. "My mother was never the same person after we lost Mattie. Feel pity for her. I do. Mattie's death blasted her apart. God knows how *I* would continue if anything…if anything—" She broke off in deep distress.

"Oh, stop it." He cut her off ruthlessly. "Nothing is going to happen to Christopher."

"God keep him safe. I've loved and protected him. Taken care of him all these years."

His voice carried both anger and confusion. "Martyn— how did he feel? Of course you always could twist him around your little finger."

"I can't talk about Martyn, Rohan." She focused her gaze on the massed beds of Japanese hybrid petunias—white in one, rosy-pink in another.

"You couldn't have let him down worse than you did me," he said bleakly. "He had *no* suspicions?"

She brought her green gaze back to him. Was he aware she was *devouring* his marvellous face, feature by feature, marking the changes, the refinements of maturity. *Rohan. Her Rohan.* "I told you. I can't talk about this."

"Maybe not today, but you will," he insisted. "You saw

Christopher with me, Charlotte. He accepted me on sight. I won't let him go. You either."

She took in his unyielding expression. "You want to punish me?"

"Every day," he admitted with a grim smile. "My perfect captive—my golden Charlotte, Martyn Prescott's *widow*." His tone was quiet, yet it lashed out at her. "Now, there's no need for you to go into a mad panic. I realise we've both had a tremendous shock today. I'll handle this from now on. You don't have to do or say a thing. I'll be making frequent trips in and out of the Valley. Plenty of time to establish a truly poignant renewal of our old romance. The whole Valley knows how close we were at one time. This will be our second chance. Isn't that wonderful? A second chance. I'm certain you'll have the sense to fall into line."

She found the strength to launch her own attack. "It doesn't really look like I have an option. And Diane Rodgers? What about her? Will you keep her on as your mistress?"

His black brows drew together. "Don't be so ridiculous. Diane is a highly efficient PR person. Nothing more."

"Perhaps you should tell *her* that." She stared at him directly—only he didn't appear to be taking on board what she said.

"God, isn't it *good* to be back in Silver Valley?" he enthused with great irony. "Let me return you to Daddy, Charlotte. We'll take the Range Rover. You've got an awful lot to think about, haven't you? Don't worry about *our* son. I'll bring him safely home."

Of course he would. She trusted him. "All I want is Christopher's happiness," she said.

His magnetic smile turned deeply mocking. "I think I can guarantee that. As for *us*—we're just going to have to work very hard at our respective roles."

"You won't say anything to Christopher?" In her agitation she grasped his arm.

He looked down at her elegant, long fingers. "What do you take me for? I won't be telling him our little secret until I'm sure—*we're* sure—he can handle it."

"Thank you, Rohan." She removed her hand—she knew he wanted her to—overcome by relief and gratitude. Rohan had suffered so much as a boy it would have been impossible for him to heap grief on any child, let alone his own son.

It was her own actions that gave her the most pain. What she had done to Rohan was beyond forgiveness. There was little comfort in the knowledge that she had believed at the beginning she was carrying Martyn's child. She had been taking the pill when she and Rohan had been together, that first year at university in Sydney. A necessary precaution against her falling pregnant. They'd both been so young. Rohan had begged her to give him time to make something of himself so he would be in a position to offer marriage. Growing up as he had, with the social stigma of not knowing who his father was, he'd been intent on doing everything just right.

Yet despite that she *had* fallen pregnant. And by Rohan. She had been certain for some years now. It had taken her over-long to realise the contraceptive pill's efficacy could be put in jeopardy if a woman experienced a bout of sickness like a bad stomach upset. That had happened to her around about that time. A chicken roll at a campus picnic. She and a girlfriend had been very sick for twenty-four hours following the picnic. One had to be so careful in the heat. Chicken was about the worst food there was.

As for Martyn! Even now she couldn't bear to think about that night when he had totally lost his head. All these years later she was still left with mental bruising—far worse than the physical bruising Martyn had left on her unyielding body. The monstrous reality of it was that Martyn, her friend from earliest childhood, had taken her against her will. There was a word for it. She studiously avoided it. But she remembered the way she had thrashed about as she'd tried to stop him. It had only excited him further—as though he'd believed she was playing a game. The comforting arm he had initially offered her had turned swiftly into the arm that had so easily overpowered her. Afterwards he had begged for forgiveness in tears, citing that he'd had too much to drink.

He *had*. But into their marriage he had told her, with triumph in her eyes, that her pregnancy had been a sure way of getting her away from Rohan.

"You know Rohan will never be in a position to reinvent himself. I mean, he's really poor. It'll always be a long, hard hike for him to get ahead. Probably twenty years. What you need is the life you were born to. A guy like me to lean on."

How could she have leant on Martyn when he hadn't even been able to stand up for himself?

It had been the worst possible start to a disastrous marriage that should never have happened. Only in those days she had been literally terrified of bringing further trauma to her already traumatised parents. Facts were facts. She'd been pregnant. Martyn was the father. They'd been too young, but he'd adored her. In a way she had brought it all down on herself.

Her father had given them a lavish wedding at Riverbend. He had spent a fortune. The Prescotts had been over the moon at that time, with the union of the two families. She'd been seen, even then, as a steadying influence on Martyn.

Many times she had thought she would go to her grave

not telling anyone the truth of what had really happened that awful night. She had so trusted Martyn, and he had been obsessed with taking control of her body. What was going to happen now was quite another matter. Rohan was back. Rohan was indisputably in charge. Christopher would not remain very long not knowing who his real father was. Not that much longer and everyone in the Valley would know. Had Christopher inherited Rohan's raven locks instead of the Marsdon blond hair they would know already. Christopher was fast turning into a dead ringer for his father.

Her father stormed into the entrance hall of the Lodge just as she stepped inside the door. Rohan had dropped her off outside. He knew about the side entrance to the Lodge, of course. It had been an excruciating short ride. Both of them utterly silent, yet unbearably aware of each other. She couldn't even find the courage to ask about his mother. Mrs Costello had always been lovely to her. They had embraced in tears the day she and Rohan had left the Valley.

"Not your fault. Never your fault, Charlotte."

Getting herself married to Martyn Prescott was. It had wrecked their friendship. It had wrecked lives.

So there she was, on what was supposed to have been a picture-perfect day, with her heart slashed to ribbons.

"That was Costello, wasn't it?" A great helpless anger seemed to surround Vivian Marsdon like a cloud.

"You know it was, Dad." She moved past him into the living room, sinking dazedly into an armchair. Her father followed her, remaining standing. He would think that gave him the advantage. "No point in working yourself up. It's not going to do a bit of good. And, really, you can't yell at Rohan. Not ever again. You'll get more than you bargained for. We *all* will. The old days are over—the days when you and Mum attacked Rohan and Mrs Costello at every opportunity.'

"That fire-eater!' Vivian Marsdon snorted, his expression tight.

"And good for her!" Charlotte felt her own anger gather. "All Mrs Costello did was defend her son."

"*Miss* Costello, thank you."

"Don't be so sanctimonious! Maybe she was like a tigress defending her young? Good on her! I admired her immensely for taking on my high and mighty parents. She was driven to it. You were both so cruel. Mum was by far the worst."

"Your mother was off her head, Charlie. I mean she was completely out of it. We had lost our only son. What *did* you expect of us?" he asked, his voice a mix of shame and outrage.

"I expected wisdom, Dad. Compassion, understanding. Not a blind allocation of the blame. It was a terrible freak accident. We're not the only family to have lost loved ones in tragic accidents. Families suffer all over the world— the rich and the poor alike. Please sit down, Dad. Better yet, calm down. Can I tell you, not for the first time, it was Martyn who was at fault? It was Martyn who goaded Mattie into swimming the river. Rohan and I called him back. He *was* coming back. But Martyn wanted to wind Mattie up. Throw down a challenge. Rohan went after Mattie, but Mattie wouldn't stop. He was trying to prove something."

Vivian Marsdon recoiled in near horror. "What *is* this?"

"The *truth* of that terrible afternoon, Dad. The truth you and Mum wouldn't listen to. But you surely heard the version Martyn, coward that he was, put about."

"I—don't—believe—you." There was a kind of delirium

in Vivian's deep, cultured voice. "You worshipped young Costello. You would always be on his side. You would lie for him if you had to."

"What does it matter now, Dad? I give up. Let's say the fault lay with Fate." Charlotte put a hand to her pounding head. "You've only ever believed what you wanted to anyway."

Her father panted with outrage. "To think you would malign your late husband! Poor, dead Martyn! You're still looking to clear Costello, of course."

"You're right about that!" she declared. "All those years ago you and Mum turned on us with deaf ears. You had your own agenda. Martyn was a Prescott. Rohan was a nobody. Only that was far from true, wasn't it? Rohan was always destined to be somebody. Even Mum said it when she was still sane. The two of you made him your scapegoat."

Vivian Marsdon's chin quivered with rage. "He was the ringleader of your silly Pack of Four. You were just a girl. Martyn always played the fool. It was Costello who had to pay for his extreme negligence, his lack of supervision."

"How brutally unfair! Mattie, Martyn and Rohan were all of an age. Why should *Rohan* have to pay?"

"Because we'll never get our son back—that's why," her father thundered. "Don't you understand that? Losing Matthew broke up our marriage. Your mother couldn't bear to stay here. She couldn't bear to be with me though I shared her pain."

"Of course you did, Dad, but never to the same degree. Mum will rake over the ashes of that terrible day until she dies. I wonder how Reiner copes? Sometimes he must feel like he's in prison."

Her father slumped down heavily. "Who cares about Reiner? God knows how your mother married the man.

We'll never get Matthew back. I'll never get *her* back. But we have our splendid little Chrissie. Where is he, anyway?" He stared around, suddenly becoming aware his grandson hadn't yet come home.

"Settle down, Dad," Charlotte begged wearily. "He's with Peter. I'm not going to chain him to me, like Mum did with Mattie. Christopher and Peter are sensible boys. They're only down the drive. "

"He should have come home with you, none the less," Vivian maintained.

He was very seriously disturbed by Rohan Costello's shock return to the Valley. And that wasn't the only reason for his sense of anxiety. What was the effect it was going to have on Charlotte? He wasn't such a fool he didn't know Rohan Costello had once been everything in the world to his daughter. Was Rohan Costello's desire *now* for revenge?

"Chris is enjoying himself, Dad. Don't worry about him. And whatever you do," she added with heavy irony, "don't worry about me—the child who survived. Mum told me in one of her black fits of depression she wished *I* had been the one to die."

Vivian had to steady himself by gripping the sides of his high-backed armchair. "She didn't. She *couldn't*." He was sincerely shocked.

"Sorry, Dad. She *did*. She didn't have to say it anyway. We both knew Mattie was the light of Mum's eyes."

"But, Charlie, dear, she loved you." He was shaking his fair head as though he couldn't believe her disclosure.

"Only as long as Mattie was around." Charlotte took the last clip out of her hair and shook its gleaming masses free.

Vivian Marsdon's tanned skin had gone very white. "Well, *I* love you, Charlotte. *You* were my favourite. I loved

Matthew, of course. But you were my little girl—always so clever and bright and full of life. Your mother wrapped poor Matthew in cotton wool. It was a big mistake, but Barbara would never listen to me."

"She listened to no one when it came to Mattie. It was Rohan who encouraged Mattie to be more outgoing. And look where it got him."

Her father flinched. "It will be impossible to make peace with Costello. Too much history, Charlotte," he said. "I'm tormented by the past. Only the young can spring back from tragedy."

She exhaled a long breath. "If you *can't* make peace, Dad, you will have to learn to be civil. We're going to be seeing a lot of Rohan. He's staying in the Valley for some time."

"So what did he say?"

"That he's going to make Riverbend, its vineyards and the olive groves, the best in the Valley. He's going to produce fine wines and the finest olive oils. He's got big plans."

"Good luck to him, then," her father said, sounding hollowed out. Vivian Marsdon knew Costello would achieve everything he had ever wanted. And didn't that include Charlotte, his daughter? "Oh, God, I feel wretched," he mumbled. "I started my married life with such high hopes. I wanted to be loved and admired like my father. I wanted to be a great success. I thought I had inherited his business brain. I didn't, sad to say. I've had to come face to face with the cold, hard facts. I never listened. I made terrible mistakes. It cost us all. And I had to live with your mother's chronic obsession with Mattie and his health."

"Don't upset yourself, Dad. We won't talk about Mattie any more. It's too painful."

"Indeed it is. But we have our Chrissie—the best boy in the world. He's amazingly bright."

Like father. Like son.

"I know *you* were always a top student, Charlie," her father continued, "but Martyn definitely wasn't. He couldn't even get a place at university. He was spoiled rotten—born lazy. Unlike Gordon. Christopher has an exceptionally high IQ. I was thrilled when he was classed as a gifted child."

"And you've brought him on wonderfully, Dad," she said gently. "I'm so grateful you take such an interest in him."

Her father's thick eyebrows shot up. "Good God, girl, he's my grandson."

"Please remember that, Dad," she said very quietly. "Mum has little or no time for him."

Vivian Marsdon moaned in distress. "Her loss, my dear. Chrissie used to look like Matthew, but he doesn't any more. Still, he's a Marsdon. My eyes have faded somewhat, but they used to be very blue. Did you ask Costello how he's made his money? He owns the place outright, doesn't he?"

Charlotte nodded. "He *is* Vortex. I wasn't about to question him, Dad. I don't have the right."

"Blasted revenge—that's what it is." Vivian Marsdon was back to railing. "He's lived to get square. I tell you, I was shocked out of my mind to see him."

"And *I* wasn't?"

"The arrogance of him!" Marsdon fumed. "Always had it—even as a boy."

Charlotte expelled a long breath. "Not arrogance, Dad. Rohan was never arrogant. Rohan *is* what he is. Someone truly exceptional. By temperament a born leader."

Vivian Marsdon drew a deep sigh. Who could deny it? Many a time he had wished for a son like Rohan Costello, at the same time feeling guilty at the very thought. It was as if he were brushing his own son Matthew, a beautiful, sunny-natured boy, aside.

"Well, Costello—unlike me—obviously knows how to make money," he said finally. "But doesn't that prove how little he actually cares about you? You were supposed to be such great friends. Inseparable at one time. He surely could have notified you? Let you know beforehand. Not shocked us both. If that isn't revenge, what is?"

She had absolutely no comeback to that.

CHAPTER FOUR

MONDAY morning. School. The same primary school they had all attended as children. She followed her normal routine, picking up Peter Stafford and his scratchy little sister Angela along the way. Angela was such an unpleasant child sometimes it was hard to believe the two were related.

As always, Charlotte arrived in comfortable time, allowing the boys to settle before classes began. There was welcome shade beneath a flowering gum twenty yards from the front gate. She moved her Mercedes smoothly into the parking spot left by a departing Volvo. The driver, her friend Penny, wiggled a hand out of the window. Penny's little one, Emma, was only in pre-school. Charlotte had been the first to marry and fall pregnant. Or rather the other way about. She wouldn't be the first or the last. But it certainly made her the youngest mother of a Grade 3 child.

"Thank you, Mrs Prescott." Dear little Peter never forgot to thank her, while his sister dashed away without a backward glance.

She watched the boys shoulder their backpacks. "It's always a pleasure, Peter." She smiled affectionately at him. "Now, you two have a good day and I'll see you this afternoon." She touched a farewelling hand to Peter's shoulder, dropped a kiss on her son's head.

"See you, Mummy," Christopher said, his face lighting up with his wonderfully sweet smile.

It tore at her heart. Rohan had smiled at her like that. Once. Christopher's hair was a gleaming blond, like hers, but he didn't have her creamy skin. He had Rohan's olive skin. In summer it turned a trouble-free gold.

She stood watching a minute more as they ran through the open double gates, meeting up with a group of their friends. All weekend Christopher had been as happy and excited as any young boy could be at having met Rohan, who now owned Riverbend. Things might have been a little different had he taken a dislike to the new owner. As it was, he appeared thrilled. It had been Rohan said this; Rohan said that.

She had thought her father might fly off the handle, but oddly enough he'd listened to his grandson with an attentive smile. He would be thinking Christopher was missing his father. That was Martyn. So far her father suspected nothing. She knew her father would always love Christopher, no matter what. But the inevitability of Christopher's real paternity coming out scared her to death. There had never been a scandal attached to the Marsdon name. Martyn had blotted the Prescotts' copybook. She wasn't thinking of herself. She was thinking, as always, of her son. And her father. God knew what her absent mother would make of it! She shuddered to think.

She was about to return to her car when she became aware that a tall, lean, stunning young man, wearing jeans and a navy T-shirt with a white logo, was heading straight for her. Only now could she see the estate's Range Rover a little distance down on the opposite side of the road. He must have been waiting for her.

She stood stock still, willing her heart to stop racing. Her body, which had been calm enough, was now assailed by tingles. She watched him swiftly cross the road. Rohan had always been graceful, beautifully co-ordinated. He hadn't just excelled in the classroom, he had been the Valley's top athlete. Many of the boys had been gifted young sportsmen—Martyn had been a fine swimmer, tennis and cricket player. He had wanted to study sports when he finished high school, but he hadn't had the marks. Poor Martyn. His father had put him to work. Well, in a manner of speaking. Martyn had wanted for nothing.

Except *her*. Unrequited love did terrible things to a man.

"Good morning, Rohan." She knew she sounded very formal, but she was concentrating hard on marshalling her strength. "You wanted to see me?"

"I thought we could have a cup of coffee." He was studying her as intently as she was studying him.

"I really don't have the time."

"I think you do. A cup of coffee and a friendly chat. Won't keep you long. I've checked out the village. Stefano's?"

She nodded. "It's the best."

"So I'll meet you there?"

Her nerves were drawn so tight they were thrumming like live wires. "I can't imagine not doing what you want, Rohan." She turned away before he could form a retort.

At that time in the morning it was easy to find a parking spot in the main road, outside the popular coffee shop with its attractive awning in broad white and terracotta stripes. Stefano's was owned and run by an Italian family who really knew their business. Coffee was accompanied by selections of little cakes, mini-cheesecakes and pastries. Stefano's also served delicious light lunches. Charlotte and the friends who had remained loyal to her had been frequent customers since the café had opened almost a year before.

This morning she was greeted with a beaming, "*Buon giorno*, Carlotta—Signor Costello." Stefano was a large man, almost bear-like in appearance, but very light on his feet.

"*Buon giorno*, Stefano."

It only then occurred to Charlotte that the de Campo family would have been invited to the Open Day. Obviously Stefano, the grandfather and head of the family, had met Rohan that day. Hence the big flashing smile and the use of his name.

Stefano took their orders after a few pleasantries: long black for Rohan, cappuccino for her, and a small slice each of Signora de Campo's freshly baked Siena cake—a great favourite with the customers.

Charlotte looked across the table, set with a crisp white cloth and a tiny glass vase containing a single fresh flower—a sunshine-yellow gerbera, with an open smiling face. "So, how can I help you, Rohan?"

He just looked at her. He wanted to keep looking at her. Never stop. Her beautiful blonde hair was drawn back from her face, a section caught high with a gold clasp, the rest of her shining mane hanging down her back. She was dressed much as he was, but in a feminine version: jeans—white, in her case—with a pink and white checked shirt, white trainers on her feet. She was wearing no make-up apart from a soft pink lipgloss, so far as he could see. She always had had flawless skin.

"How's Christopher?"

So many emotions were cascading through her. "Full of his new best friend. It's been Rohan this, Rohan that, all weekend," she told him.

"How did your father take that?" His gaze sharpened.

"To be honest—"

"For a *change*," he cut in.

She gave a small grimace and looked away from him into the sunlit street. Two of the school mothers were going into the bookshop opposite. Other villagers were strolling past the coffee shop, one commenting on the luxuriant potted golden canes that flanked the front door.

"Dad loves Christopher," she said, turning her head slowly back to him. "I told you that. He listened and smiled."

"Good grief!" Rohan leaned back in his comfortable chair, eyes sparkling with malice. "Maybe there are miracles after all!"

"One likes to think so. Here comes Stefano."

"Gosh, why the warning?" he asked sardonically. "I thought we looked perfectly relaxed—not raring for a fight."

"*You* might feel relaxed. I don't."

"Charlotte, you look perfectly beautiful and quite normal. A good actress, I guess."

Stefano set the tray down on an adjacent empty table, then unloaded their coffee, placing it before them. The panforte followed, heavily dusted with white icing sugar and showing roasted nuts and a succulent mix of candied peel.

"*Grazie*, Stefano." Rohan nodded in acknowledgement. "This looks good."

"*Altro?*"

"*Nient'altro, grazie.*" Charlotte answered this time, giving the courtly proprietor a warm smile.

It was the first genuine smile Rohan had seen from her in a very, very long time. It wasn't directed at him. He saw Stefano flush with pleasure. Charlotte had never been fully aware of her own beauty and its power.

The coffee was excellent. Stefano glanced back and Rohan gave him the seal of approval with a thumbs-up. Stefano was a great *barista*, and it wasn't all that easy. He savoured another long sip, then leaned back. "I'm having a few guests this coming Saturday. Probably they'll all be here by late afternoon, and will stay over until Sunday. Ten of us in all. Counting you, of course."

She hoped her composed expression didn't change. "Who needs *my* acceptance?" She turned out her palms.

"Come on," he jeered softly. "In the old days you were someone very special in my life. You're about to be reinstated."

She saw the glint in his eyes. "I'm absolutely rapt about that, Rohan. This is blackmail, you know."

His voice hardened. "You'd do well to remember the reason. Try the cake. It looks delicious."

"So what am I supposed to *do*?" she asked after a moment.

"Nothing too onerous. I've given my housekeeper the night off. Ms Rodgers will be looking after the catering. All you have to do is look beautiful and come to dinner Saturday night."

"That's all?" Part of her wanted to tell him she didn't much like his PR woman. She hoped Ms Rodgers wasn't going to play hostess at Riverbend. She didn't think she could take seeing Diane Rodgers sitting where her mother had always sat.

"That's all—apart from an impromptu little after-dinner concert." He raised a black brow at her.

"I'm sorry, Rohan. I'm out of practice." She wasn't. She loved her piano. She was a very good pianist—just like her mother. She had started teaching Christopher the very day he'd shown interest. He'd been five. "Besides, there's the little matter of a piano."

"Solved," he said. "I've had a new Steinway installed. "Even out of practice—which I doubt—an hour or two on that would set you right.'

She had a flashback to the Open Day, when she had fainted. Used to seeing a concert grand in the Drawing Room, in her bemused state she had thought it hers.

"Just a couple of party pieces?" he suggested. "I want to show you off. I intend everyone to know we're back to being *very good friends*!"

Very good friends? "Aren't you rather rushing it?" There was a defiant look in her eyes.

"Not at all." He shrugged. "My friends know I grew up in Silver Valley. They will learn it was your father who sold me Riverbend."

"They don't know now?"

"Only Diane."

"Of course—Diane. Sounds like she runs your life. Am I to take it she'll be a guest at dinner?"

"You know the rules, Charlotte. Even numbers." His tone was sardonic.

"So you have someone for me?"

"I have someone for Diane," he corrected. "*You're* my certain someone, Charlotte. God knows, I've waited all these years, never considering for a moment what you'd been up to."

"Formal or informal dress?" Stoically she ignored his taunting.

"Why, formal—what else? Your parents' dinner parties were always formal. My mother—you know, the hired help—used to tell me how everyone dressed up. How beautiful your mother always looked, the splendid jewellery she wore. In those days my mother thought the world of Mrs Marsdon, the Lady of the Manor."

It gave Charlotte an opening, if nothing else. "How *is* your mother? I wanted so much to ask."

"So why didn't you?'

"I knew right off to exercise extreme caution around you. You've changed, Rohan."

"Alas, I have!" he drawled. "Let me see. Who could have changed me? Changed my life?"

"Fate is as close as I can get." She picked up her coffee before it went cold.

He gave her an insouciant smile. "I have to return to Sydney this afternoon. Back Friday night. I have business meetings lined up."

She gave him an enquiring look. "Dare I ask what line of business you are in?"

"Why not?" He leaned forward. "You remember I was a computer whiz kid?"

"Absolutely. You were a whiz kid at everything," she admitted wryly.

"You might also remember I was searching desperately for a way to make money so I could offer marriage to the girl I *then* loved." The steely glint was back in his eyes. "I was always into computer science, I had a special flair for it. Then it struck me that the quickest way to make money was to try to break into entertainment software. I'd done well enough with educational software, but decided to take the risk of moving to games. Sometimes they don't take off. Mine did. I've never looked back. In no time at all the money started to flow in. I have three companies now that handle multiple software programs. I hire the right people. My employees are all young and brilliant at what they do. I've built businesses around what I and my staff enjoy. They also have the opportunity to buy shares in our companies—share in the profits. They all want to get rich too."

"So you've made millions?" she asked, not at all surprised. He had energy and enterprise written all over him.

"The *reason* I wanted to make millions," he told her tersely, "was to keep *you* in the style you were accustomed to. And, of course, to make life much better and easier for my mother. Which, needless to say, I have."

"And I'm glad, Rohan. Truly glad. Your mother deserves her slice of good fortune. But why ever did you want Riverbend?"

He gave an elegant shrug of his shoulder. Whoever his father was, he must have been a fascinating man. "Simple. I'm always on the lookout for something else. I got started on real estate investing. Real estate, as you know, is one of the best ways to create wealth. Better yet hold on to it for the family I intend to have. Christopher is our *first* child. Hopefully I'll get to hold our second-born child in my arms. It was a dream of mine to have our child."

"It was *our* dream, Rohan." There was no mistaking the injured look in her lustrous green eyes.

"Odd way you went about it."

They were so utterly engrossed in each other they failed to notice the small, dumpy young woman who strode with single-minded purpose to their table.

"Well, well, well!" Nicole Prescott said, her tone coated with layer upon layer of meaning they were obviously meant to guess at.

Charlotte realised at once that Nicole's seeing them together had greatly upset her. Every muscle in her own stomach clenched, as though steeling for the blows that might come. Rohan stood up, looking perfectly self-assured, and at six-three towering over the diminutive Nicole. Nicole could easily have looked so much better, but Charlotte had learned to her cost that Nicole much preferred her image of messy, prolonged adolescence.

"Mind your own business, Charlotte. We can't all look like you!" How many times had she heard that?

"Well, well, well, to you too, Nicole," Rohan said suavely. "Tell me—were you after coffee, or did you see us through the window?" He gave her a brilliant look that fell short of contempt. He had never liked Nicole Prescott. Had little reason to.

A tremor shook Charlotte's whole body. Nicole had always been such an abrasive person, with an oversized chip on her shoulder. It had made her very hurtful. Over the years Nicole had developed such a badly done by expression it had set like cement. Did she intend to make a scene? Nicole was given to hurling insults. She was even cruel. She had done her best to blacken Rohan's name—though, knowing her brother, she must have had serious doubts about Martyn's version of events that fatal afternoon. It all went back to Mattie.

"You just never could keep away from each other," Nicole hissed, literally seething with resentment.

Rohan pitched his voice low, but it carried natural authority and the capacity to act on it. "I would advise you not to make an enemy of me, Nicole."

"That's right—you're *rich* now," she sneered.

"And I have big interests in this valley."

Nicole blinked. *Big interests?* Hadn't her father hinted at some such thing? Not just Riverbend, then? She forced herself to look away from Rohan Costello's burning blue gaze. It transfixed her. Bluer than blue. She heard her mother's voice in her head, *"We don't know. We don't know."* Always handsome, Rohan Costello had matured into the sort of man women couldn't take their eyes off. She had to concentrate now on Charlotte—the weak link.

She had hated beautiful Charlotte Marsdon all her life. So unfairly blessed. Beauty, charm, brains. She had the lot. Everyone loved her. Well, *she* hated Charlotte. Had hated her even when she'd followed Charlotte down the aisle to join her besotted brother in unholy matrimony—she the shortest and the plainest of the bridesmaids. Beauty gave a woman such power. Martyn was the one who had inherited all the looks. As a kid he had nicknamed her Mousy. It still stuck in some quarters. But she had triumphed over her nondescript looks by developing a tongue sharp enough to cut.

They hadn't been invited to the garden party. She and her mother had fumed over that. They were the Prescotts. Not a family to be ignored. Small wonder they were furious. Her father had simply made the comment, "What did the two of you expect?"

It was like that these days. Two against one. She and her mother against her father. He was so unbelievably *tolerant*. And he had never had much faith or pride in her adored brother. She would never forgive him for that.

"You knew about all this, didn't you?" She rounded on Charlotte with the barbed accusation. "You knew he'd bought Riverbend. You knew he'd had us barred from the garden party."

"Wrong on both counts, Nicole," Charlotte said. It was news to her. There was no guarantee Nicole wouldn't start spewing venom any moment now. Out of the corner of her eye she could see Stefano, looking their way rather anxiously.

"I *know* you," Nicole spat. "I know the two of you. Your history. I know how you broke my brother's heart."

"And we know *you*, Nicole," Rohan responded in a warning voice. "You and Martyn. *Unfortunately*. If you want a cup of coffee I suggest you consider going elsewhere."

There was a daunting edge to his voice. "We've only just settled in, and Stefano is looking this way with concern."

"Forget him!" Nicole snapped out, but the hard challenge was causing her to crumple like soggy tissue paper. "How's my nephew, by the way?" She shot Charlotte a look of utter loathing.

Charlotte thought her heart might go into spasm. Christopher had to be protected at all costs. She looked beyond Nicole with her puffy cheeks to Rohan, who had made the slightest move forward. "Why don't *we* go?" she suggested quickly. "Nicole is beyond hope."

"*I'm* beyond hope?" Nicole's face took on high colour. She was the one to do the taunting, launch the insults. Not lovely, ladylike Charlotte.

"Probably you know it," Rohan suggested suavely. "I'd go now, Nicole, if I were you. Remember you're a *Prescott*!"

That stopped Nicole more effectively than a jug of cold water. She backed off abruptly, saying scornfully as she went, "Your poor mother—the *cleaning lady*—never did teach you any manners, did she?"

Rohan laughed, as though genuinely amused by the comment. "I've never heard my mother swear—yet *your* mother drops the F-word in every other sentence. I bet you do too."

For once Nicole had no reply. She spun about, and then took off like a bat out of hell.

Rohan sat down again with an exaggerated sigh. "What a gentle little soul she is! A helicopter could spot that chip on her shoulder. All in all, the Prescotts were blessed with their children, wouldn't you say? Nicole's jealousy of you is downright pathological.'

"That's what makes her dangerous, Rohan."

He looked across at her, seeing her distress. "It's okay. Stop worrying. What can she actually do?"

"She's already seized on Christopher's resemblance to you," she said in a deeply concerned voice.

"Christopher's relationship to me *must* come out." His tone hardened.

"But you promised!"

"And I meant it." Frowning, he looked truly formidable. "Nicole and her dreadful mother—how in God's name did you ever live with them?—can suspect all they like. They don't *know*."

"They could offer to take him for a weekend. This is the age of DNA testing." Fear was lodged like a heavy stone against her heart.

"Isn't that good?" he countered with the utmost sarcasm. "Tell them *no*. You've already said they've seen little of you since Martyn's death."

"I like Gordon—Martyn's father. He's the nice one of the family."

"Wasn't Martyn nice enough to marry?"

"Martyn's dead." She veiled her eyes.

"Well, his death is one less cross for you to bear," he pointed out rather callously. "I'm sorry Martyn had to die so young, Charlotte. Once we were friends, until he turned on me with a vengeance. Anything to protect himself. He really was gutless. We both know he had a foolhardy streak that was always going to get him and sadly other people into trouble. You could have divorced him."

"Then I really would have been in trouble." She reacted with an involuntary shudder.

He sat forward, staring at her in consternation. "What is *that* supposed to mean?" His eyes blazed.

She didn't answer. She had said too much already. Did

anyone get through life unscathed? Women particularly? Vulnerable women with children to protect?

"Were you afraid of Martyn? What he might do?"

She shook her head.

"If you ever try to leave me, I'll kill you and the boy."

Martyn's final words to her had played over and over in her head. By now they were driven deep into her psyche. "I must go, Rohan," she pleaded. "There are things I have to do at home."

"You're going to have to talk to me some time." He rose to his splendid height, extracting a couple of notes from his wallet.

She stood up more slowly. "There are some things you don't need to hear, Rohan."

His steely determination—the determination that had turned him at under thirty into a multimillionaire—was well in evidence. "That, Charlotte, is an answer I don't accept."

Life for Charlotte had become an endless series of hurdles.

CHAPTER FIVE

SOMEONE on Rohan's staff was to pick her up at ten to seven. Drinks in the library. Dinner in the formal dining room. Diane Rodgers was handling the catering. Diane Rodgers would be sitting down to dinner. Swanning around Charlotte's former home.

"Why are you doing this?" her father asked, for the umpteenth time.

It wasn't as though she had a choice. "Rohan insisted."

"And you jumped?"

"Only some of the time." She had no protection from Rohan.

"You look *beautiful*, Mummy." Christopher caught his mother's fingers. He didn't like it when Grandpa had words with his mother. "I love it when you let your hair down." He looked up admiringly at his mother's thick golden hair. He was used to seeing her hair tied back, but tonight it fell in lovely big waves around her face and over her shoulders. "I love the dress too," he enthused. "I've never seen it before." It was a long dress of some shiny material. It deepened the colour of his mother's green eyes and made her lovely skin glow.

"You love *everything* about your mother," Vivian Marsdon said with an indulgent smile. He too loved seeing his daughter looking her best. As a boy, like Christopher, he had taken great pleasure in seeing his own mother dress up for an occasion. "You *do* look beautiful, Charlotte." He paused for a moment, considering. "Why don't you wear your grandmother's emeralds?"

"Goodness me, Dad, I don't want to overdo it!" she exclaimed. Her mother had taken the beautiful jewellery her husband had given her, but Grandma Marsdon's jewellery was off-limits. It was to remain in the family.

"Well, I *want* you to," Vivian Marsdon decided. "Damned strangers swanning around in our house." Eerily, he echoed her thoughts.

"You swore, Grandpa," Christopher turned to look at his grandfather. "You know the rules. Swearing isn't allowed." He figured it was time to get one back at Grandpa.

"I'm sorry, son," Vivian apologised. "I'm a bit upset. I'll take the emeralds from the safe, Charlotte. I'd like you to wear them. Keep the flag flying, if you like. I'm sure the other women will be wearing their best jewellery."

"Probably, Dad," she conceded. "But it might be a mite hard to top Gran's emeralds."

"Well, you have the beauty and the style," he said, already moving off to his study, where the safe was installed. "Besides, they'll go perfectly with that dress. Green is your colour."

Rohan, looking devastatingly handsome in black tie, greeted her at the door. "Ah, Charlotte! You look a vision of beauty!"

She brought herself quickly under control. It wasn't easy when she was on an emotional see-saw. Fear. Elation. She couldn't get over having Rohan back in her life. It was like some impossible dream. Her love for him had never lost its intensity, even through the unhappy years of her marriage. She had given up the love of her life for Martyn, whose actions had determined the course of all three of their lives. She rarely let her mind travel back to Martyn's unwitting part in Mattie's tragedy. She had never, ever upbraided Martyn for it. Only for his part in denouncing Rohan to anyone who would listen. Martyn hadn't been a strong character. He had known that and suffered for it.

Now Rohan's brilliant eyes glittered over her and touched on the emeralds, no more dazzling than her eyes. He bent his dark head to brush her cheek. Her heart turned over. The clean male scent of him! He took the opportunity to murmur in her ear. "Ah, the famous Marsdon emeralds. They look glorious! But no more than you!"

"Why, thank you, Rohan." She had become fairly adept at pretending cool composure. "That's what Dad was hoping for. 'Fly the flag' were his exact words."

"And how triumphantly it's unfurled! Come on in." He took her hand, his long fingers curling around hers. Electricity shot up her arm, branched away into her throat, her breast, travelled to the sensitive delta of her body. She felt the impact of skin on skin at every level. "Meet my guests," he was saying smoothly. "I'm sure you'll like them, and they you. Still think losing Riverbend is tragic?" His downbent head pinned her gaze.

"Not any more. I only wanted it for Christopher anyway."

"Then your prayers have been answered," he returned sardonically.

Diane Rodgers had marked their entry. Immediately she was seized by a jealousy so powerful it was a wonder she didn't moan aloud. She felt so completely engulfed by it, it was like drowning in mortal sin. If there was such a thing. They looked *perfect* together. Stunning foils for each other. Charlotte Prescott looked *beyond* glamorous—and looking glamorous was her own crowning achievement. Up until now she had thought she looked terrific in her short mesh and sequin dress. Hell, she *did* look terrific. But Mrs Prescott looked *fabulous*—a walking, breathing, real-live beautiful woman. The long dress, clinging and dipping in all the right places, put her in mind of the emerald silk number Keira Knightley had worn in the movie *Atonement*. If that weren't enough, a magnificent diamond and emerald necklace was strung around her neck like a glittering tie, caught by a big dazzling emerald clasp of God knew how many carats. The full length of the separate strands dipped into her creamy cleavage.

Hell!

Diane looked furtively about her. She had an idea she might have exclaimed aloud.

She couldn't have. No one responded. Not that they were looking in her direction. They were staring at the beauty on Rohan's arm. One thing offered a grain of consolation. Mrs Prescott's late husband—a bit of a playboy, she'd heard—had been having an affair at the time of his fatal accident. A young woman had been with him in his luxury Maserati. The miracle was she hadn't joined her boyfriend. So the beauteous Mrs Prescott hadn't been able to hang on to her husband! She had lost him. Diane half believed that gave her hope.

The only other times she had seen Charlotte Marsdon, her long hair had been confined. Now it billowed away from her face, revealing matching diamond and emerald earrings. Who the hell could compete with that? It was utterly demoralising. Her mood turned from super-confident to darkly brooding.

"Geez, isn't she *fan-taas-tic!*" Sam Bailey turned his smooth brown head to give her a cat-like grin.

Diane Rodgers was tempted to crack him on the nose;

instead she met his look head-on. "Gorgeous!" she agreed, feeling as if she was under siege.

She had never much liked Sam Bailey. Now she hated him and his playful little taunts. At least she *thought* they were playful. She'd been certain she'd been keeping her wild infatuation with the dead sexy Rohan under wraps. Apparently not. Rohan Costello had got right under her skin at first sight, and she prided herself on her street cool. Were they all laughing at her? God, that would be catastrophic! She couldn't ask Sam—he was making a bee-line for his boss and the exquisite Mrs Prescott. What a hell of a pity the husband was dead. But playboys given to driving fast cars sadly tended to die young.

Diane had done an impressive job of handling the arrangements. Charlotte awarded her top marks. If she hadn't exactly done things herself, then she had the knack of gathering together the right people. The flower arrangements in the entrance hall and the main reception rooms were stunning. A quartet of sumptuous yellow roses, their lovely full heads massed in crystal bowls, were set at intervals along the dining table. She had never seen the impressive gold and white dinner set before, but she recognised Versace. The dinner plates were flanked by sterling silver flatware. Georgian silver candlesticks marched apace. Trios of exquisite crystal wine glasses were set at the head of the dinner plates.

Food and drink turned out to be superb, as did the efficient and unobtrusive service from two good-looking, nattily uniformed young waiters. Perfectly moulded smoked salmon and prawn timbales topped with a slice of cucumber and a sprig of coriander for starters; a choice of beef fillet with wild mushrooms and a mushroom vinaigrette or chicken with peaches and vanilla; crêpes with walnut cream and butterscotch sauce or chocolate cherry liqueur cake. It was a truly elegant and satisfying feast.

Conversation flowed easily, ranging over a number of interesting and entertaining topics—all non-divisive. Charlotte found it much easier than she had anticipated. She had never been to Riverbend as a guest. Rohan presided at the head of the table, she to his right. The guest of honour. She wondered what they all thought. Curiously, she felt relaxed—even with Diane Rodgers shooting her many a burning look of appraisal that bit hostile.

She had attended countless dinner parties over the years, but she found herself enjoying Rohan's quick-witted and amusing guests more than most. It was obvious they thought the world of him. Their friend as well as their boss. They were all of an age. Three of the young men and two of the very attractive young women, not including Diane Rodgers, worked for Rohan. Two of the young men were computer whiz kids and had brought their girlfriends along.

Rohan's guests knew better than to start asking leading questions. Except for Diane who, over coffee and liqueurs in the Drawing Room, decided it was high time to throw the cat among the pigeons. For starters there was the enthralling subject of their shared childhood. Charlotte's and Rohan's.

"I bet Rohan was an A-grade student," she said, setting down her exquisite little coffee cup so she could lap up the answer.

Charlotte smiled, wondering where this was going. "The cleverest boy in the Valley," she said, without looking at Rohan. "We all knew he was going to make a huge success of himself."

"Whereas you settled for being a wife and mother?" Diane said, her voice full of womanly understanding. "Possibly the best job of all. You must have been very young when you had your gorgeous little boy. He's—what? Seven?"

"Yes, he is. And he *is* beautiful," Charlotte agreed, hoping Diane would stop. Rohan might look perfectly at ease, lounging back in his armchair, but she knew him so well she could sense a growing turbulence.

"You married another one of your childhood friends—Martyn Prescott, I believe?" Diane pressed on where angels would fear to tread. "Isn't that right? What were you called again? The Gang of Four?"

Charlotte's heart plunged. She was certain Diane Rodgers had talked to Nicole Prescott. "The *Pack* of Four, Diane. But I think you already knew that."

Rohan broke in crisply. "I'm sure Charlotte doesn't want to continue the interrogation, Diane. But *I'm* rather interested to know who told you about the Pack of Four."

Diane's colour deepened. "Gosh, I can't remember," she said, with an innocent blink of her heavily made up dark eyes. "I thought it was a lovely story, anyway. I'm sorry if I've upset you, Charlotte. I just wasn't thinking." Her voice dripped apology.

"That's quite all right, Diane." Charlotte maintained her cool calm. Maybe Diane was on the level? Anything was possible. "I lost my husband eighteen months ago," she told the table. They murmured their sympathy, all of them embarrassed by Diane's insensitivity. At least three of the guests could have told Charlotte that Diane Rodgers could be obnoxious.

"Sorry. So sorry." Diane pressed a hand to her mouth, then thought she had nothing to lose. "I know you've had more than your fair share of tragedy."

Down the table, Sam Bailey rolled his eyes. "Is that silly bitch into annihilation? If she doesn't shut her mouth soon she could just find herself out of a well-paid job," he muttered to his girlfriend, who was in total agreement. They all knew Diane Rodgers was highly effective—she was devoted to their boss and very capable—but the dumbest person on the planet could diagnose an attack of monster jealousy when they saw it.

Some time later, Charlotte took her place at the piano—to delighted applause.

"Do you want the lid up?" Rohan asked, aware Diane had upset Charlotte. Which meant she had upset him, too. Anyone would think he'd been sleeping with Diane, so apparent was her jealousy.

"Not right up," Charlotte said. "I don't want to rocket my audience out of the room." Spacious as the Drawing Room was, this was a nine-foot concert grand.

"This just gets better and better!" Sam exclaimed, settling onto one of the sofas beside his girlfriend and taking her hand. He was blown away by the magnificence of Riverbend. For that matter blown away by the beautiful daughter of the former owner. There was quite a story there.

"I'm a little out of practice," Charlotte turned on the long piano seat to confess. "I've chosen the lovely 'Levitski Waltz'. You may not know the name, but I'm sure you will know the melody, and a couple of shortish pieces from Albéniz's *Suite Española*."

"*Olé!*" Irrepressible Sam essayed a burst of flamenco clapping. Rohan's Charlotte was simply sensational. Why not? So was his boss.

Charlotte waited until they were all seated comfortably, Rohan at their centre. Then she turned back to the Steinway. She was certain Rohan would have had it tuned to perfect pitch after it had been shifted into the house.

To be on the safe side she made a short exploration of the beautiful instrument's dynamics.

"What the hell is she doing?" Diane had to ask the question, feeling a stab of dismay. She wasn't into classical music. She fluffed out her shiny bob. "Is that it?" she whispered to the young woman beside her.

"Get real!" was the astonished response. "Charlotte is just warming up."

"Yeah—I was just having a little joke," said Diane, trying to prove she was as clued-up as the rest of them. She knew Rohan loved classical music. She had seen many of his CDs. Piano, violin, opera singers, symphony orchestras. You name it. Difficult when she had a passion for rock. Something *hot*!

When at last the beautiful, talented Mrs Prescott's little recital came to an end Diane muttered to herself, *"Thank you, God!"* She felt sure Charlotte had been showing off. Closed eyes. Bowed head. That business with her raised hands. *Showing off.* The waltz hadn't been too bad. But she'd had no compulsion to tap her toes at the Spanish numbers. Needless to say that smart alec Sam the sycophant had. It had really pained her to mark the expression on Rohan's handsome face. It suggested he had been transported to some celestial plain. Okay, he adored classical music. Probably that was his only fault.

The party broke up around twelve-thirty. Rohan's guests started to make their way upstairs, having told Charlotte how much they'd enjoyed meeting her and congratulating her on her lovely performance at the piano. Rohan's Charlotte was a true musician.

Last in line, Diane bit her lip so hard she very nearly drew blood. "I hope you enjoyed yourself, Charlotte?" she said, with a bright hostess look.

"Very much so." Charlotte smiled. "I must congratulate you on arranging everything so beautifully, Diane."

"All in a day's work!" Diane's expression turned suitably modest. "I'll say goodnight, then. Will we be seeing you tomorrow?" It wasn't as though the Prescott woman didn't have plenty of time to squander, she thought.

"I doubt it," Charlotte replied lightly. "Goodnight, Diane."

"Goodnight." Diane revved up a smile even though she was so angry. "Goodnight, Rohan."

God, he had to be the sexiest man on the planet. Maybe too sexy for his own good? She had an overwhelming urge to grab him and press him to her throbbing bosom. She had convinced herself she was worthy of Rohan Costello, although she knew he came with a warning. This was a guy who broke hearts. Not intentionally, was the word. But he hadn't been serious about any one of the highly attractive young women he had dated in the past. It distressed her terribly to have Charlotte Prescott, the widow, re-emerge.

Rohan gave her the smile she adored. Did he have any idea how sexy he was? "Goodnight, Diane. Everything went very well."

"Why, thank you!" Diane saw herself as the very image of indefatigable efficiency. She waggled her fingers, then started to move off towards the grand staircase, carrying the heavy weight of jealousy. She paused and turned back for a moment, focusing her gaze on Charlotte. "Look, why don't we catch up some time, Charlotte?" she suggested, making it sound as though they had hit it off wonderfully well. Kindred spirits, as it were.

"You want to keep her under observation?" Rohan asked suavely.

Diane wasn't sure if that was a joke or not. Rohan was such a man of mystery.

Charlotte was kinder. "I'll keep it in mind, Diane."

"Lovely!" Diane threw in another brilliant hostessy smile.

They remained silent until they saw Diane moving gracefully up the staircase on her very high heels.

Charlotte felt rather sorry for Diane. She didn't blame her for falling for Rohan. He was magnetic enough to draw any woman. She had caught Sam Bailey in particular having little snickers at Diane's expense. Diane wasn't liked, it seemed. But she *was* efficient. And very vulnerable where her boss was concerned.

"Now, there's a woman who would like to own you," she said wryly.

"Good thing she hasn't told *me*," was Rohan's brisk reply. "Will we walk back to the Lodge, or won't your evening sandals take it?" He glanced down at her beautifully shod narrow feet. "We can go through the garden. Or I can drive you."

"The drive might be safer."

"Oh, don't be ridiculous!" His tone was derisive. "Nobody said anything about sex," he taunted.

"But you're planning on having it soon?" She rounded on him, lustrous green eyes sparking a challenge.

"Well, we always were compatible in that area," he said, taking her arm. "So—a walk, or the Range Rover?'

"The garden," she said. "It's quickest and the easiest."

His brilliant gaze moved searchingly over her, as though he could uncover her every thought, her every secret. "I can't promise I'll make a point of sticking to the paths."

She put a hand to her throat, as though her heart had suddenly leapt there. Punishment she deserved. The day of reckoning wasn't far off. And then there was Rohan's mother, Mary Rose, deprived of her only grandchild.

Mea culpa!

* * *

A lovely soothing breeze lapped at her hair and her skin, at the fluid long skirt of her evening gown. It wrapped her body and caressed her ankles. The familiar scents of a thousand roses and creamy honeysuckle hung in the air. Above them the stars glittered and danced in a sky of midnight blue velvet. This wasn't wise. But then she had never been able to command wisdom. An aching throb was building up fast in her body.

"Shouldn't you have brought a torch?" she asked, afraid she was revealing too much of her inner agitation.

"For *you*? For *me*?" He gave an edgy laugh. "We know every inch of this place. Don't twist away from me."

"Ah, Rohan!" She gave vent to a deep tremulous sigh that managed to be incredibly seductive. For all their time apart, she was still in thrall to him. Once married to Martyn, she had tried very hard to exorcise Rohan's powerful image. Only it had haunted her every day of her life. And then, as her adored little son had grown older, Rohan's features and mannerisms had begun to emerge! The *fear* she had felt when that occurred! The outright panic. God help her—she had married the *wrong* man! Martyn wasn't the father of her child.

How horrendously rash she had been. She hadn't allowed herself enough time. Only back then she hadn't known what else to do. So young. Pregnant. And she couldn't think Martyn, her friend from childhood, wicked for having physically overcome her. She'd known before they had started out to a rock concert that evening how badly Martyn wanted her. For years he had wanted to be more than just her friend. Only there had always been Rohan. Rohan—who couldn't offer the financial security and the lifestyle he could.

So Martyn had watched and waited for *his* moment.

When she'd realised she was pregnant how she had longed for a wise, loving mother to turn to—a mother full of unconditional love, full of advice as to which course she should take. Her father hadn't been ready for any more shocks. Her escape routes had all been cut off. There had seemed no other course than to pay for her mistake.

Rohan's hand on her tightened, startling her out of her melancholy. "You know it's cruel in its way," he began conversationally. "One can kill trust, respect, write off the crime of betrayal, but one can never kill sexual attraction. I want you very badly—which you damn well know. But then, ours was a very passionate relationship, wasn't it, Charlotte? While it lasted, that is."

Even as he spoke, he could feel the hot blood coursing through his veins. How could he punish Charlotte? Countless times he had longed to be in a position to do so. He had even bought Riverbend, putting in an outrageous offer almost as soon as it came on the market. Revenge on the Marsdons? Revenge on Charlotte who had betrayed him with Martyn, of all people? The only massive impediment was that he wanted her no matter what she did. Charlotte had taken possession of the deepest part of his being.

They walked through a tunnel hung with lovely wisteria towards the summer house, designed as a small Grecian-style temple portico. It glowed whitely ahead. The four classical columns that supported the stone structure were garlanded with a beautiful old-fashioned rose that put out great romantic clusters of cream and palest yellow fragrant blooms, with dark green glossy leaves. Her mother had used to call it the Bourbon rose.

She had a feeling of being inwardly lit up with desire—languorous on the one hand, on the other highly alert. The radiance she felt was so intense it surely must be showing in the luminescence of her skin. She stumbled just a little in her high-heeled sandals. He gripped her arm.

"Oh, Lord!" came from Rohan under his breath. "You were the *world* to me." He hauled her very tightly into his arms. "I lived for you. For our future together."

She was desperate to make amends. "Rohan, I thought—"

He cut her off. "I *don't* want to hear. Remember how we used to come to this place? In secret? This was our shrine, remember? The place of our spiritual and sexual exploration."

"Rohan, I loved you with all my heart."

"Yet you betrayed me."

"I told you. I deserved punishment." She was trembling so badly she needed his tall, lean body to balance her. So much she'd had to endure over the past years. She wanted to cry her heart out. Swear that what she would confess would be the truth, the whole truth, and nothing but the truth.

His grip was fierce and unrelenting. "Well, I have you *now*," he breathed, taking a silky massed handful of her hair and tilting her face up to him. "Come on, Charlotte. Kiss me like you used to."

It was a taunt, a torment. Never an invitation. As in everything he took the initiative. "You're never going to go away, Charlotte."

"No." She was breathless.

"Say it."

"I'm never going to go away. I'll never leave you."

"As if I haven't heard that before." His voice was unbearably cynical. "Only this time we have our son."

Oh, Rohan, hold me. Hold me.

It was an old, old prayer for when she was in a hopeless, helpless situation.

He let go of her long hair, his hands moving to cup her face, his fingers pressing into the fine bones of her skull.

His kiss fell intently on her mouth. Only she confounded him by opening it fully, like a flower to the rain, admitting his seeking tongue to the moist interior. There was no end to sensation, the rush of desire, the rediscovery of rapture. No end to the richness, the incredible *lushness* of sensual pleasure. She reached up naked arms to lock them around his neck. Their darting tongues met in an age-old love dance. She could feel his hands on her, trembling. This had to be a dream from which she never wanted to wake. The first time since the last time she had come blazingly alive. More extraordinarily, the bitterness she knew she had caused, the torture of years of thinking himself betrayed, were nowhere. Not in his mouth. Not in his hands. Profound passion came for them at an annihilating rush.

His hand sought and found her breast, forefinger and thumb stimulating the already tightly budded nipple.

She moaned in mindless rapture, throwing back her head as he kissed her throat.

Oh, the depths of passion! Not even suffering could blunt them.

She could feel herself dissolving. He her captor; she his. She yearned for him…yearned for him… This was her once-in-a-lifetime great love. Desire beat like a drum. It gained power. Surrender would come swiftly behind it. Soon all sense of place would vanish with their clothes. Passion demanded flesh on flesh.

Somehow she found the strength to put a restraining hand over the caressing hand that was palming the globe of her breast. Another second of this and she would be lost to the world.

He must have felt the same way, because he stopped the arousing movement of his hand, letting his hot cheek fall against hers, encountering the wetness of her tears. He savoured them, licking them off with his tongue. They had both been moving with tremendous momentum towards the point of no return.

"All right," he acknowledged, trying to subsume his own near-ungovernable arousal. "I want you for the *night*. Not just minutes out of time."

"Rohan, I can't—"

He cut her off. "You'll have to come to *me*," he said, his voice picking up strength and determination. "Not here. Not Riverbend. I realise the difficulties. But Sydney. Next weekend I've been invited to a big charity function. You'll come as my partner. I'll leave it to you to explain it to your father and Christopher."

She tried to focus on rearranging the bodice of her beautiful silk gown. The flesh of her breast still tingled from his touch. At the very portal of surrender she had pulled back, though she knew her sex-starved body would have no peaceful rest that night.

"It would upset Dad quite a bit," she managed after a while.

"Do you think that bothers me?" His answer was full of disdain. "Your fine, upstanding parents gave my mother and me hell. The only person I'm concerned about is Christopher. I'm only guessing, but I think he'll take it rather well. You're a beautiful young woman, Charlotte. You can't go the rest of your life alone. Or were you planning on living with Daddy for ever?"

"I don't deserve that, Rohan," she shot back. "It's been very difficult. Martyn's death. Dad so sad and lonely. He needed me, Rohan. I couldn't refuse him. I went on to finish my Arts degree externally. I didn't give up. I know I could get myself a halfway decent job in the city, but here in the Valley it would be difficult. No teaching jobs, for instance. All taken. Then there's the fact Chrissie loves the Valley. He loves Dad. I'd hate to uproot him, and I'd have the difficult job of finding a suitable minder for holidays and after-school hours. Not easy!"

"No." He saw the difficulties. "But you don't have to worry now. That's all been taken care of. Our son needs his father."

"I can't let you browbeat me, Rohan." Out of the blue Martyn and his treatment of her popped sickeningly into her mind.

But Rohan was no Martyn.

"*Browbeat* you?" He looked down at her, aghast. "As if I would or could. You want me as much as I want you. That was always the way. Who do you think you're kidding, Charlotte?"

She could feel the tears coming on again. "I've had no *self*, Rohan! Do you understand? No *self*."

He was shaken by the very real agony in her voice. "Did you think you could learn to love Martyn?" He was trying desperately to understand.

"I *loathed* him!" She thrust away. This was dangerous. She had to get home.

"Loathed him?" Rohan was stunned. "What did he do to make you loathe him? Martyn was mad about you. You *loathed* him? Come on, now. I need to know why."

She tossed back her long mane that tumbled in gleaming disarray over her shoulders, struggling hard to come up with an answer that might stave off a confrontation. "You know Martyn wasn't the strongest of characters. His mother pampered him all his life. Rendered him useless. I don't want to talk about Martyn. He's dead, and in some way I am to blame."

He stood stock still, wishing she were under a spotlight so he could look deep into her eyes. "You couldn't possibly have been frightened of Martyn?" He was forced to consider what he had never considered before. Martyn had adored Charlotte. He would never have hurt her. Would he? "I know he could be a bit of a bully, but you could always handle him. Remember how he bullied that little Thomas kid? I threatened to knock the living daylights out of him if he didn't lay off the kid. First and last time I ever threatened anyone. When you married Martyn you put yourself in the Prescotts' power. And Martyn's father was always a decent man."

"The past is past, Rohan," she said, low-voiced. "Neither of us can change it."

"So you *won't* talk?"

"There's nothing to talk about any more," she insisted. "If I could undo the past I would."

Rohan groaned like a man desperate for peace of mind. "I'm not following this at all. If you seriously believed Martyn was Christopher's father—and that's *your* story— you were having sex with both of us."

"I was so *alone.*" *Unprotected. Isolated.* "You took that computer job in Western Australia. It couldn't have been further away. I know they offered you a lot of money, but that meant you were gone for the entire summer vacation. I was without you for the best part of four months. I can't talk about this any more, Rohan. I betrayed you. I betrayed myself. I made a terrible mess of my life. But I'm begging for a ceasefire. You've told me what you want. I understand. I want to make it up to you for your suffering."

Rohan raised a staying hand. "Oh, be damned to that, Charlotte!" he said, very sombrely. "Thing is, you *can't.* I understand your wanting the continuation of your privileged lifestyle. Pregnancy would have made you very vulnerable. You were so young. But I can't forgive you for depriving me of my son, depriving my innocent, hard-working mother of her grandson. You do well to cry. Now, I'd better get you home. Daddy will be waiting up for his golden girl."

CHAPTER SIX

Just as she feared, her father made strenuous objections to her spending the following weekend in Sydney.

"You've always been in Costello's power!" he ranted. "You'd think the boy was some powerful sorcerer. He's always had your heart and your mind."

How true! She and Rohan had connected from early childhood on some profoundly crucial wavelength. "He's not a *boy* any longer, Dad," she pointed out. "He's very much a man. I'm twenty-six, remember? I want a life."

"Not with Costello." Vivian Marsdon violently shook his head. "Never with Costello. The idea is *monstrous*! What would it do to your mother?"

Charlotte's caught her father's eyes. "Do you mean the mother who so cherishes me and my little son?" she asked with considerable pain. "Mum took herself out of our lives. Why should I now worry what *she* thinks?"

"Because you always did and you always will. We both care. I still love Barbara. And you still love your mother, no matter how badly she let us down."

"What about Christopher, Dad?" Charlotte asked heatedly. "*You'll* always love him? No matter what?"

Vivian Marsdon frowningly picked up on her words. "No matter what? What are we talking about, here? Have you formed some new understanding with Costello?"

"There's so much you don't know, Dad. At the heart of it is the sad fact you never *wanted* to know. If Rohan could get me at the snap of a finger, why do you suppose I married Martyn?"

Vivian Marsdon's thick sandy blond eyebrows drew together in a ferocious frown. "Because he loved you. God, Charlie, he was *madly* in love with you. You were all things to him. I scarcely need mention he was in a position to offer you far more than Costello ever could. Security counts with a woman."

"You mean what he could offer *at the time*? It wasn't Martyn's money anyway. The truth is, Dad, Martyn and I lived off his father. They wanted it that way. I wasn't allowed a job outside organising social events. And there was nothing, absolutely nothing, I could do."

Vivian Marsdon stumbled back into his vast armchair. "I don't believe this."

"That's because you've spent your life hiding your head in the sand. It's safer down there."

"It's what I *believed*, Charlie, but I see now I was wrong. I was fearful for your mother's sanity. I couldn't bring myself to take a stand against her. God, I loved her. She was my *wife*. We were happy in the old days. Before our darling Mattie died."

"I know, Dad." Charlotte bowed her head. Nothing good had come out of Mattie's tragic death. But for years of her childhood up until that point it *had* been a magic time. And most of that magic had been due to Rohan Costello.

"But *you* don't have to be alone, Charlie. You're a very beautiful, highly intelligent young woman. You're *my* daughter. A Marsdon. That name still carries a lot of clout. I could name a dozen young men in the Valley desperate to pound their way to your door."

She laughed. "Not a few of them you didn't frighten off, Dad. Good thing I wasn't interested in any of them."

"Why would you be?" he snorted. "Ordinary. Ordinary young men. Costello *isn't*, whatever else he is. He's bought Riverbend on *your* account!" He said it as though he had hit on an invisible truth.

"Rohan bought Riverbend because he's a very astute businessman. It's prime real estate, Dad. The most beautiful estate in a beautiful prosperous valley. Rohan has big plans."

"And they surely include you," Vivian Marsdon said with a sinking heart.

"That upsets you so dreadfully, Dad?"

He looked across at her mournfully. "I couldn't bear to lose you and Chrissie, Charlotte. I have no one else."

"But you won't be losing either of us, Dad," she said, with a burst of love and sympathy. "As long as that's what you want, I would never deprive my boy of his grandfather. He *loves* you."

"He does. God has blessed me. And I love my grandson with all my heart. He's a wonderful little boy. He's going to make his mark in the world. And I didn't think much of Costello's trying to buy the boy's affection by taking him and young Peter for that helicopter ride."

"Oh, come on now, Dad. They were absolutely thrilled. Chris had all the kids madly envious when he told them about it at school. Chris went with Rohan very willingly."

Vivian Marsdon sighed. "I ask you—how did it happen? You'd think Christopher had known him all his life," he added with amazement. "Of course a helicopter ride is a sure way to get to a seven-year-old's heart."

"See it as Christopher learning new things, Dad. He's

only a little boy, but he's a good judge of a person's character. Children see very clearly."

"Especially the latest in helicopters," Marsdon grunted. "It sounds very much to me as though you and Costello have an agenda of your own. How did it happen in such a very short time? I mean, he's only just back in your life. You fainted when you saw him, you were so distressed. Are you really over your husband? What will the Prescotts think if you two get together?"

Charlotte's clear voice hardened. "The only Prescott you have any time for, Dad, is Gordon Prescott. Don't pretend you respected Martyn."

Her father shifted uncomfortably. "I truly believe the only reason he was unfaithful to you, Charlie, was because you didn't love him as he wished."

"Dad, you could be right." Her expression was a mix of self-disgust and sorrow. "I have to tell you I never loved Martyn. It was all a big cover-up. I was pregnant when I married him."

Her father gave vent to another deep sigh. "Yes, well… All the more reason for you to have tried very hard to make a go of it."

"I *did* try, Dad. Not easy pretending you love someone when you don't."

Vivian Marsdon sat with a mournful expression carved into his handsome face. "Your mother didn't beat about the bush with me. She took off."

"It was Riverbend—the river, Dad." She tried to console him.

"Yet we still see Mattie walking by the river, don't we?" He lifted his head to give her the saddest smile. "The river doesn't torture us. In mysterious ways it comforts us. Mattie is close by. Our Chrissie feels Mattie's presence. I never thought much about a *soul* until we lost Mattie. But now

I'm certain we do have one. Never thought much about God. Unlike your mother, I now know there is one. Mattie's *spirit* is here. And it's not a sad one. Wherever he is, Mattie is happy. Remember that strange woman who came to stay outside the village some years back? Always dressed like the old idea of a gypsy? She stopped me once to ask the name of the other child who was with little Christopher and me."

"I remember your account of the incident vividly. The woman claimed she saw a blond boy, on the frail side, aged about fourteen, walking along with you."

"That's right." Vivian Marsdon covered his face with his hand. "It shocked me at the time, but then I realised someone must have told her about Mattie in the village."

"That *could* have happened, Dad, but I don't think it did. She'd only just arrived. Besides, it would have been very cruel to approach you in that way, and you saw no sign of her being anything like that. She kept herself to herself while she was living in that old cottage that had belonged to a relative, and the very last thing people did was bring up our family tragedy. Everyone knew the grief and suffering it had brought down on our heads. Who knows? Maybe she did have a genuine gift. I'm open-minded about such things. You are too. We all *see* Mattie. He's not a trillion miles away. Some part of him is still here, in the place where he lost his mortal life."

"Your mother couldn't bear the thought," Vivian Marsdon said. 'But it comforts me to think that woman might have been saying it the way she saw it."

"Me too." Charlotte reached out for her father's hand.

"You're a good girl, Charlie. *My* girl." He took his hand-kerchief from his pocket, then strenuously blew his nose. "So, you're going to Sydney for the weekend?"

"I am."

"Have you told Chrissie?"

"Not before I'd spoken to you."

Vivian sank further into his armchair. "I have the feeling he won't have any objection. There could be another helicopter ride in store for him."

Charlotte waited until she had dropped off Peter and his little monster of a sister at their front gate. Peter stood and waved. Angela, as was her custom, ran inside without any acknowledgement of the ride. Then she waited until Peter too was safely inside his front gate. They watched him walking up the short drive.

"Gosh, she's an awful kid!" Christopher made a funny whooping noise. "The rudest kid I know." He was amazed by Angela's behaviour. "Do you suppose she's going to spend her whole life in a bad mood? Peter tells his mother how rude she is, but even Mrs Stafford doesn't seem able to get Angie to say thank you."

"Hopefully it's just a phase." Charlotte patted her son's small hand. The shape of it was Rohan's. "I've something to ask you," she said, keeping her eyes on the road. Safety was all-important. Martyn had been such a careless driver, even when he'd had her and their precious child on board. "Rohan has asked me to be his partner at a big charity function in Sydney this coming Saturday night."

"Really?" Christopher's radiant blue eyes grew huge. "Gee, he's a fast worker," he said, with real admiration.

"If you don't want me to go, I won't." Charlotte meant it.

Christopher laughed. "Don't be silly. I think it's great! I really like Rohan. I want him to be our friend. He's so clever. He'd make a great teacher. He knows tons of things. More than Grandpa, I think. I'd never say that to Gramps, though. Rohan knows all about vineyards and olive groves too. He has lots of plans for Riverbend. He told me I could be in on all of them. Honestly, Mum, I can't think of anyone better than Rohan to go out with. It's sad, the way you're always stuck at home. You looked so beautiful the other night. Rohan thought so too."

"Did he tell you?" She felt the heat in her cheeks.

"Sure he told me. He told me all about when you were kids. You were the greatest friends. He told me really, *really* nice things about you and Uncle Mattie."

She bit her lip. "And about your—father? About Daddy?"

"No, not about Daddy," Christopher admitted. "But Rohan is so easy to talk to I nearly told him I didn't think Daddy liked me."

"What?" Charlotte felt her every nerve in her body stretch to breaking point.

"I *didn't* say anything," Christopher swiftly reassured her, suddenly looking upset. "But Daddy didn't like me much, did he? Not like Grandpa loves me. Nothing like *you* love me. You love me to bits!"

"You can bet on that!" Charlotte spoke with great fervour. "But Daddy did love you, Chrissie," she said, deeply distressed.

"No, Mum." He shook his head. "I don't want you to tell a big fat lie to make me feel better. None of them seemed to care about me. Maybe Grandfather Prescott did. He was always nice. But Grandma Prescott and Nicole—they sure weren't very nice to me. Especially Nicole. I reckon Angela will grow up to be a person just like Nicole. Then there's Grandma Marsdon. She doesn't want to see me. Maybe she thinks you shouldn't have had me in the first place?"

"Christopher, my darling boy! You've been thinking all these things?" She was shocked and appalled. Her son was only seven years old, but already he was weighing up things in his head like an adult.

"Don't worry about it, Mummy." His expression turned protective. "I don't actually care about them any more. Some of the kids tease me about how you and I live with Grandpa. They say things like, 'Why doesn't your mum get married again?' That sort of thing. It annoys me a bit, but it makes Pete *really* angry. He's my friend."

Charlotte's heart gave a great lunge. "You've never told me any of this before. I thought you told me everything?" She felt very sad.

"I didn't tell you because I knew it would upset you. But Rohan's *great*!" Enthusiasm was renewed. "I'm wishing and wishing you two hit it off."

So without even trying Rohan had found a powerful ally.

In his *son*.

Charlotte found as much excitement in the helicopter ride as Christopher would. It was fantastic to see the beautiful rural landscape become a cityscape unfolding beneath them. With the helicopter's wraparound glass the visibility was everything one could wish for, and the Harbour looked magnificent on that special Saturday morning.

It was impossible for her not to feel a surge of pride at the first sight of their beautiful capital city and the iconic "Coathanger"—which was what Sydneysiders called the Sydney Harbour Bridge. The world's largest steel arched bridge, it linked the Sydney CBD and the South and North Shores, with their famous beaches. And down there, jutting out into the sparkling blue waters of Bennelong Point, was one of the great wonders of the modern world: the Sydney Opera House, its famous roof evocative of a ship at full sail.

It couldn't have been more appropriate for the Harbour City, Charlotte thought, though the distinguishing "sails" had cost a great fortune and a whole lot of heartache. But there it was today, in all its splendour. Probably the nation's most recognisable image.

Their pilot Tim Holland, a very experienced and highly respected pilot, was retained by Rohan for personal *and* company use. On Rohan's instructions he took them on a short joyride to increase Charlotte's pleasure. Yachts were out aplenty. The Harbour bloomed with a profusion of white sails. Below them a crowd swam and frolicked in the legendary Bondi surf. Others lay out on the golden sand, sunbaking. Charlotte hoped they were slathered in sunblock. Sydney was Australia's oldest, largest and most culturally diverse city. It was also the most exciting, with an unmatchable *buzz*. She could feel her spirits, for so long down, soaring.

Rohan used his state-of-the-art headset with its voice-activated microphone to speak with her and their pilot, Tim. The headsets enabled them to easily communicate.

"American Airmen during the Second World War flew a couple of Kittyhawks under the Bridge. Not to be outdone, the following year a *flight* of RAAF Wirraways did their own fly-under. These days tourists and locals love climbing it. I've made the Bridge Climb three times. By day, at twilight, and by night."

"It can't be for the faint-hearted?"

"Well, there are safety precautions, of course. One has to give a blood-alcohol reading, for a start. Then there's the Climb Simulator, to get an idea of what one might experience. But the view is worth it a million times over. It's absolutely breathtaking."

"Like now!" she replied. "Christopher would find this the most marvellous adventure."

"He'll see it." Rohan spoke matter-of-factly. He might have issues with her, but he had bonded with his son on sight. Such was the power of blood.

A company limo was standing by to take them the short distance to her city hotel, beautifully positioned between the Opera House and the Harbour Bridge. She had insisted on checking into a hotel, even though she knew she would be spending the night with Rohan at his Harbourside apartment. That was their agreement. But she had promised Christopher she would ring him from her hotel when she arrived, and tell him of all the excitement of the helicopter flight. Plus there was the fact she wanted to offer at least token resistance to Rohan's command of events.

He accompanied her to her luxurious room, looking around him as if to assure himself everything was up to scratch. "You know as well as I do, Rohan, this hotel has a reputation for excellence," she protested mildly. "But I suppose as you've paid for it you're entitled to check out the mod-cons."

"Thank you for thinking of that, Charlotte," he returned suavely. "I have a little trip planned for us this afternoon after lunch."

"It can't top the flight. That was wonderful. I'm going to ring Chrissie in a minute. He's the main man in my life."

"He's now the main man in *my* life as well. What I have in mind, my beautiful Charlotte, is to take you on a visit to my mother."

She was taken by complete surprise.

"Remember, I do have one?" he said, sardonically. "One of these days I might even go in search of my father."

She slumped onto the bed, staring up at him. "Have you found out who he is? Your mother told you?"

"Miraculously, *yes*. A huge step for mankind. She

hadn't told a soul—including the grandmother who reared her—but…"

"But, what?"

He lowered his lean length into an armchair, facing her. "I'm surprised you haven't guessed, Charlotte. You were always so intuitive. I was in rather a mess when I found out you'd married Martyn. But that was nothing to finding out you'd borne him a child. My mother was very worried about me. She decided at long last she was going to tell me what had happened to her when she was very young."

"Are you going to share it with me?"

Tension snapped and hummed as if overhead electricity wires were strung across the room.

"Why not? My father is Italian. Who would have thought it? I had always assumed he was Australian. But my birth father was born and lived in Rome. He and a few of his well-heeled student friends were tripping around the world, enjoying a university vacation. The Opera House, apparently, was a must-see for him. He was an architectural student, and the Opera House is a magnet for architects as well as millions of people from around the world. It was Jorn Utzon's *tour de force*, after all. He met my mother while the two of them were wandering around the plateau. He was taking photographs for his own records. They got to talking. That was the start of it! He was something of a polyglot, which no doubt helped. Apparently he spoke fluent English, French—and Italian, of course. My mother thought him the most fascinating human being she had ever met in her life. She fell for him hook, line and sinker. Whether he was just taking advantage of a pretty girl in a foreign country, I don't know. She says *not*. But she knew their romance couldn't last. Too much against it. He was from another country and a totally different background, obviously wealthy."

"Yet she took enormous risks?"

"A lot of us make mistakes when we're young, Charlotte," he said dryly. "I don't have to tell *you* that. He swore he would write to her, but he never did. Once he was home again among his own people his holiday romance would soon have faded away. Happens all the time." He gave a cynical shrug.

"But you know his name?"

There was a slight flare to his nostrils. He looked every inch a man of high mettle. "I do. He's most likely married, with grown-up children. He wouldn't be all that happy to discover he'd left an illegitimate son in far-off Australia. It would upset the apple cart. No, Charlotte, I'm the product of a short, sweet encounter. Maybe he remembers my mother now and again. She must have been very pretty. She still is."

"I believe it!" Very pretty, with lovely Celtic colouring that hadn't got a look-in with Christopher. "You're upset, Rohan?"

"Am I not supposed to be?" he challenged. "You're so good at analysing people, Charlotte."

"I'm good at analysing *you*," she returned with some spirit. "Don't be bitter."

"My dear Charlotte, I'm *managing* my bitterness. You know, in some ways you and my mother are alike. Both of you have lived your lives withholding vital information. Both of you took it upon yourselves to decide the outcome of your pregnancies. My mother told no one. You decided to go with a great lie."

She flushed at the hardness of the gaze. "So you're going to take it out on me for ever?"

"No. Let's forget about it." He rose lithely to his feet. "Worse things have happened at sea. I have a couple of things I need to attend to. I'll pick you up in an hour.

Remember me to my son, won't you? Tell him I'll organise another trip for him. His friend Peter too, if he likes. Mattie always thought of me whenever there was a trip on offer."

"Mattie worshipped you."

He sighed deeply. "Matthew should have been allowed to run wild when we were kids, but your mother insisted on cooping him up. I find that truly sad."

Neither of them spoke for a moment, both lost in the past. Charlotte was the first to recover. "I must tell you something that now appears not all that amazing. Christopher says he wants to be an architect when he grows up. He's seen the Opera House many times. We've been out on the Harbour. He thinks the sails are like the rising waves of the Pacific. He used to draw them over and over, lamenting he could never get them right. Dad's been happy to buy books for him. He's told him all about the brilliant young Danish architect who had no computer to work with, no internet, just a drawing board. Christopher is very good at art. His skills are way beyond his peers, according to his art teacher."

"Good grief!" Rohan looked surprised. "I can draw myself. You'll remember that? But these days we have all the technology we need to hand. I never thought of becoming an architect, even if we'd had the money. But *Christopher*!"

"I guess blood will out," she said quietly.

"Then we have to see he realises his dream." Rohan turned brisk. "We'll have lunch, then we'll go and see my mother. I bought her a very nice apartment at Point Piper." He named one of the most sought-after areas to live in Sydney. "It has everything going for it. The best north-facing Harbour views, easy access to the city, exclusive shops and restaurants, ocean beaches nearby."

She caught him up at the door, laying a detaining hand on his arm. "Does she know about Christopher?" Her green eyes were huge with concern.

"Don't panic," he said quietly. "She *would* if she ever laid eyes on him. But no, Charlotte, I'm not cruel. My mother knows I've bought Riverbend. She knows I went after *you*, seeing as I don't seem capable of staying away," he said with a degree of self-contempt. "And I've told her we're back together again."

"What did she say to that?" Her expression grew more anxious.

His strong arms encircled her waist as he drew her to him. He dropped a light kiss on her mouth—not soft, but subtle—lingering over it as though there were no better way for the two of them to communicate. "What makes me happy makes my mother happy," he said when he lifted his head.

"But she knows how much I hurt you. She must know that I…" Her voice faltered, gave out.

"Unquestionably it will be a great shock to her to find out Christopher is *my* son, not Martyn Prescott's. But you can be sure of one thing. She will welcome Christopher, her *grandson*, with open arms."

"If not me?" There was great sadness and regret in her tone. Mary Rose of the flame-coloured hair had adored her son, her only child. She would feel very strongly about what had been done to him to this day.

"Lucky for you, my mother has a very loving heart, Charlotte. A great blessing when *your* mother gave herself up to obsession."

"She didn't know how to control it!" she responded, with a show of heat. "She didn't know how to properly *love*! She's not the only one."

"Indeed she isn't." He dropped his encircling arms, his face grim. "Some of it must have rubbed off on you."

She swung away, her body quaking with nerves. Once she had been a very spirited young person—full of life, full of a bright challenge. But all the stuffing had been knocked out of her. "I'm having second thoughts about staying, Rohan," she warned him.

He glanced very casually at his handsome gold watch. "I'll pick you up in the foyer. We might as well have lunch here. The restaurants are very good. Then on to my mother's. All that has happened you'll find she'll forgive you, Charlotte. After all, like you, she's a woman with a past."

"The last word as ever, Rohan?" she countered.

He spun back, his low laugh sardonic. "It was *you* who had the last word, Charlotte. But times have changed." He reached only a few inches to pull her back into his arms. "What about letting yourself go for a minute?" he challenged, his blue eyes alight. "See it as practice, if you like. *Kiss me, Charlotte*. The sort of kiss that will carry me right through the day." His hands slid gently down her shoulders. "Remember how we used to sleep together naked, our limbs entwined? My arms around the silky curves of your body. The scent of your skin was wonderful! Peaches and citrus and something subtly musky too. God, how I loved you! I could never get enough of you. So kiss me, Charlotte. It's a simple thing."

Only it wasn't simple at all. It was as terrifying as taking a leap off the edge of a cliff. She *wanted* to kiss him. Kiss him deeply. She wanted to hold his dark head with her hands. She wanted to express her profound sense of loss and grief. In the end she lifted herself onto her toes, touching her lips to his. It was a feather-light kiss, so gentle, her hand caressing the side of his face. His darkly olive skin had a faint rasp from his beard.

He opened his mouth slightly to accommodate her. Immediately she slipped the tip of her tongue into the cavity, brushing it over his fine white teeth and the inside of his upper lip. He tasted wonderful. Her body was reacting very strongly. The kiss deepened into something *real*. The fever of it, the never-to-be-forgotten rapture… The time they had *wasted*!

His hand slid down the creamy column of her neck, pale as a rose, closing on the small high mound of her breast. The sensitive coral-pink nipple was already erect, like a tiny budding fruit.

"Is this kiss *real*?" he drew back a little to ask. To taunt? "It seems real to me."

"Rohan, don't let's fight. I only want us to become closer."

"Well, we do have tonight." His handsome head descended and he began to kiss in earnest. So deeply, so ravenously, that after a while she fully expected both of them would simply topple to the floor, captives of passion.

It was beautiful. It was agonising. It was a language both of them spoke perfectly…

Then suddenly his hands on her shoulders were firm. He was holding her away, male supremacy absolute. "Some things can't be crushed, can they?" he muttered ironically. "It's the same as it used to be, our lovemaking."

"You sound like it's a curse." She could barely speak for the thudding of her heart and the turmoil in her flesh.

"Some curse!" he said with a twisted smile. He dropped his hands, becoming businesslike. "I'm sure you've brought a dress to wear this afternoon. Not that I don't love the jeans and T-shirt. You have a great body. But a dress, I think. I'm sure my mother will agree you're even more beautiful now than you were as a girl. God knows, your grace and beauty turned me inside out."

Charlotte touched him with a trembling hand. "Let's try to be kind to one another, Rohan."

He thought that over for a tense moment, then flashed his white smile. Their son's smile. "Why not? For old times' sake, if nothing else."

They were actually outside the door of Mary Rose Costello's luxury apartment. Charlotte was in a daze of apprehension, trying to grapple with the speed of recent events. The force of her beating heart was stirring the printed silk of her dress. She was seeking forgiveness, but she didn't know how she could begin to deserve it. She wasn't the only one haunted by the events of the past. So was Rohan—and his mother. If Mary Rose Costello even suspected she had a little grandson who had been denied to her…

Dear God!

Rohan took her hand, his long fingers twining with hers. "Just like the old days," he said sardonically, standing back a little as his mother opened the door to them. Her expression was composed, but it had to be said a shade austere.

Charlotte just escaped making some little exclamation. Mary Rose Costello, a woman well over forty, looked a good ten years younger—as pretty and polished a woman as one could hope to see. Her former shock of copper-red hair was cut short and beautifully styled. Her complexion was the genuine redhead's classic alabaster. Not a wrinkle in sight. She looked rich and cared for down to her pearly fingertips. Petite and slight as ever, she was wearing a lovely cool maxi-dress—white splashed with small flowers.

Mary Rose Costello looked back at Charlotte keenly. There was no welcoming smile on her face. No big hello. *Maybe she might flatly refuse to let me in?* Charlotte agonised, worried her treacherous knees might buckle. Maybe Mary Rose would start to vent her stored-up rage? Charlotte half expected it. Perhaps would have *preferred* rage to a false welcome. Still, she made the first move.

"Mrs Costello." She held out her hand. "I only learned from Rohan of this visit today. You don't have to ask me in if you don't want to." She wasn't going to cry, but she felt very much like it. Instead she bit the inside of her lip.

Mary Rose took a few seconds to respond. "You and my son have reunited, Charlotte. It's only natural I should agree to his request to invite you." A moment's hesitation, then she stepped forward, drawing the taller Charlotte into a short hug. "Come in, my dear. You must remember I was always very fond of you."

"I'm so grateful, Mrs Costello." Charlotte didn't look back at Rohan.

"My son looks after me in style, as you can see." Mary Rose flashed a proud loving smile in Rohan's direction. "But I do own and run a successful boutique in Double Bay. I was always very interested in fashion, if you remember? I'll show you over the boutique one day soon."

"Thank you. I'd be interested to see it. I remember all the lovely dresses you used to make." She was in peril of mentioning her mother, who had been so good and then so very vengeful towards the Costellos. She was feeling unreal. It was getting to be a constant state of mind.

"Come along, darling," Rohan said with the greatest show of affection, taking hold of Charlotte's nerveless arm and guiding her into the living room.

All for his mother's benefit, of course. Charlotte was fully conscious of that. They needed to present a united front. This was the first step. The more difficult ones were to follow.

"Please do call me Mary Rose, Charlotte." Mary Rose

indicated they should both take a seat on one of the richly textured cream sofas. The seats were separated by a long black lacquer coffee table holding several coffee table books and an exquisite arrangement of pure white hippeastrum heads, packed into a simple but elegantly-shaped white porcelain vase.

"How very beautiful!" Charlotte remarked, loving the purity of the arrangement.

"We have a wonderful young florist in the area, fast becoming known." Mary Rose had expected Charlotte to notice. "She really brings the beauty of even a few flowers to life. I must show you her beautiful white butterfly orchid in a pot. She put the pot into a bed of bright green moss inside a glass vase like a large tumbler. I love white flowers."

"As do I." Charlotte looked around the living room, grateful for a little breathing space. How did one go about having a conversation when all the important issues had to be avoided like the plague? The living room was spacious, and elegantly decorated, with many imaginative touches and a small collection of very fine art. "I recognise the work of that artist," she said, naming a painter famous for her abstracts. One of her large canvases hung above the white marble mantel—dramatic, but beautifully calm.

"Rohan bought it for my birthday," Mary Rose said, with the sweetest smile she reserved for her son.

How would she smile at her grandson? *Would* she smile?

"It makes a balance for the panoramic views, don't you think, Charlotte?" Rohan was acting lover-like to the hilt. "I had a landscaper come in to make a little green oasis on the balcony."

"What I can see of it is stunning." Small-talk was going a little way to helping her relax. Through the open sliding glass doors she could see many beautiful plants growing in planter troughs. An eye-catching green flowering wall had been integrated into the design.

"My lovely lush sanctuary." Mary Rose smiled. "It's amazing what they're doing these days with apartment balconies. You look very beautiful, Charlotte." Mary Rose took a seat on the opposite sofa.

"Thank you." Charlotte responded quietly. She had never been comfortable with comments on her physical beauty. It was all in the genes anyway. There were many other things besides regular features.

"The last thing Charlotte is is vain." Rohan caught Charlotte's hand, carrying it to his mouth. He did it so beautifully he might well have meant it. Only they were putting on a show for his mother.

"May I say how wonderful *you* look?" Charlotte offered, in a sincere compliment. She didn't dare withdraw her hand from Rohan's. No telling what he might do next.

"I have to admit to a little hard work. I go to a gym twice a week. My son likes me to look my best. And of course I have to look good for the boutique. My clients expect it."

"Not a lot look as good or as youthful as my mother," Rohan said.

"That I well believe."

Was it going to be this simple? Charlotte thought. On the face of it she appeared to be accepted and forgiven. But then Mary Rose didn't know she had been deprived of her grandson—shut out of his early life, the precious infant and toddler years.

Inevitably the conversation, just as she'd dreaded, had to come around to Martyn. "I was very sorry to hear of his premature death." Mary Rose's face contorted slightly. "He was your husband. It must have been awful for you and for little Christopher. Rohan has told me what a remarkable little boy he is. Would you have a photo with you? If so, I'd love to see it."

Heart hammering, Charlotte opened her handbag, taking out her wallet. She had been meaning to replace the small photo of Christopher at age five with a current one. Now she was glad she hadn't. Christopher's blond curls clustered around his head. He was smiling. He looked like an angel. "This was taken a couple of years ago," she said, removing the photograph and handing it across to Mary Rose—her son's paternal grandmother.

Mary Rose started forward to take it. Her gaze rested on it for quite a while, then she lifted her copper head slowly. "You won't believe this, but he looks a bit like my Rohan when he was younger. Rohan didn't start out with dark hair, you know. It was fair for a few of those early years. Of course your boy has inherited the Marsdon blond hair," Mary Rose said, retaining her searching expression. "He's as beautiful as you are. He must be a great joy to you. But I can't see he looks much like you at this stage, Charlotte. Or Martyn." She frowned.

"He keeps changing." Charlotte felt the pulse beating in her temple.

"I must meet him." Mary Rose handed the photo back. "And your mother and father? How are they?"

"Didn't Rohan tell you?" Charlotte turned her head to look into Rohan's fire-blue eyes.

Rohan didn't answer. He waited for his mother's response.

Mary Rose shook her head. "I never really wanted to go there, Charlotte," she said. "Those years after you lost your brother and my son lost his dearest friend were very hard on all of us. The way my son was blamed by your mother broke my heart. But as a mother I understood she was out of her mind with grief. Still, it was a very painful time. Thank God my son has moved on. So have I. And here you are again, back in my son's life—as I often felt you would be, despite all the odds. Rohan tells me you and he are planning to get married very soon?"

She fixed her hazel gaze on Charlotte's face, with no attempt at lightness. This was the young woman who had broken her beloved son's heart. She had rejected him so she could have it all. Or so it had seemed. But even then, Mary Rose realised, some part of her had questioned Charlotte's motivation. Charlotte Marsdon had never been one to cause pain. The daughter of privilege, she had always been her lovely graceful self with everyone. Social standing hadn't come into it.

"Yes." Charlotte sat, her slender body taut, a whole weight of emotion in her eyes. "I want you to forgive me, Mrs Costello—Mary Rose. We need your blessing. *I* need your blessing. Finally I get to do the right thing." She stopped before she burst into tears.

"Then you *have* my blessing." Mary Rose Costello was herself holding back tears. "You need to get a life for yourself, Charlotte. For yourself and for your son. It's terrible, the loss of all the good years. Take it from someone who knows."

CHAPTER SEVEN

CHARLOTTE recognised any number of people as she entered the huge function room on Rohan's arm. From somewhere a small orchestra was playing classical music. It was barely audible above the loud hum of conversation and laughter. The glassed-in walls, the lighting, the profusion of flowers and green plants, the women's beautiful evening dresses all lent the grand ballroom of one of Sydney's most glamorous venues for social and charity events an exotic look—rather like a splendid conservatory. Tonight's function was to raise funds for a children's leukaemia foundation, and there was a heart-warming turnout.

Many people had marked their arrival. She was aware that heads were turning in all directions.

"Ah, there's Charlotte Prescott back on the scene. You remember her husband? A bit of a scandal there. And isn't that the new mover and shaker she's with? Rohan Costello?"

Charlotte acknowledged the people she knew with a little wave and a smile. Her mother had been a great fundraiser.

A woman's face stood out in the crowd—if only because of the cold distaste of her expression and the rigidity in the set of her head and shoulders. It was Diane Rodgers, looking very elegant in black and silver. Her dark eyes focused quite alarmingly on Charlotte and then moved on to Rohan. But Rohan had his head turned go the side, saluting a colleague.

Thank God Ms Rodgers wasn't seated at their table, Charlotte thought, wondering if Rohan had anything to do with it. Diane Rodgers was an assertive go-getter. It was painfully obvious she had convinced herself she had a real chance with Rohan, and her bitter disappointment over the destruction of her daydreams had turned to loathing of her perceived rival. Unrequited love could be a terrible business.

Rohan knew everyone at their table, and swiftly and charmingly made introductions. Charlotte was greeted warmly. Waiters appeared with champagne. The evening was underway.

Charlotte gazed around her with pleasure. The ballroom, which had one of the most spectacular views of Sydney Harbour, was a glitter of lights. The circular tables placed all around the huge room had floor-length cloths of alternating pastel blue, pink and silver. The chairs were tied with broad bands of silver satin. Small arrangements of blue hydrangeas or posies of pink roses acted as centrepieces. Massed clouds of pink, blue and silver balloons were suspended from the ceiling. The huge screen up on the dais showed the logo of the charity in the familiar colours.

Guests had really dressed up for the occasion. Men in black tie, women wearing the sorts of gowns one saw flipping over the pages of *Vogue*. Everyone had the sense this was going to be a most successful evening, for a very deserving charity. Charlotte was pleased to see some of the richest and most powerful men in the country seated at tables not far from them. That could only mean a great deal of money would be raised.

Hours later, after a very successful evening, it was time to go home. Just as Charlotte had expected, Diane Rodgers, dark eyes glowing like coals, was lying in wait for Rohan.

"Won't be a moment," Rohan told Charlotte with a wry smile.

"That's okay."

A beaming, portly elderly man was making for Charlotte, calling her name in a delighted voice. Charlotte held out her hand to ex-senator Sir Malcolm Fielding. "How lovely to see you, Malcolm." She held up her cheek for his kiss. Malcolm Fielding had gone to school and university with her grandfather. They had always remained good friends. In the old days Malcolm and his late wife had been frequent visitors to Riverbend.

"Your mother is here, dear—did you know?" Malcolm Fielding looked about, as though trying to locate Barbara in the moving throng.

"No, I didn't," Charlotte answered, calmly enough, though her feelings were rapidly turning to blind panic. *Her mother!* She was lucky if her mother ever answered one of her calls.

"An impressive lady, your mother," said Malcolm. "And still a handsome woman. A bit chilly though, dear. Even her smile, wouldn't you say? Terrible tragedy about young Mattie, but Barbara might be reminded she still has *you.* I was totally blitzed when your parents separated. But tragedy can sometimes do that to people."

He looked over Charlotte's shining blonde head. "Oh—a bit early, but there's my ride!" he exclaimed. "Can't keep them waiting. A flawless event, wouldn't you say, Charlotte? All the more because we met up." He kissed her cheek again. "I couldn't help noticing the young man you're with," he added roguishly. "Costello is making quite a name for himself. No relation to our ex-treasurer. Don't forget to remember me to your father, now. Tell him to give me a ring. We'll have lunch at the club."

"Will do, Sir Malcolm." Charlotte smiled, although a feeling of alarm was invading her entire body. Had her mother seen her with Rohan? Why was she so surprised her mother was in Sydney? She had spotted many a Melbournite who had flown in to attend this big charity function.

To calm her agitation she started walking along with the happy, chattering crowd towards one of the arched doorways that led onto the street. She knew Rohan would follow fairly soon. Outside, limousines were starting to cruise, picking up their passengers. The headlights picked up the multi colours of the women's dresses and the brilliance of their jewellery.

Charlotte was just slowing her steps so she wouldn't get too far ahead of Rohan when a woman's firm hand caught her from behind.

"One moment, Charlotte."

Charlotte turned back to face her mother.

I'm scared of this woman, she thought. *Scared of my own mother. Or of the bitter, backward-looking woman my mother had become.*

She wanted to run, but knew she had to stand her ground. "Good evening, Mother," she said courteously. "Is Kurt with you?" Kurt Reiner was a decent enough man. Very rich, of course.

"Forget Kurt!" Barbara Reiner snapped explosively. "He's somewhere. At the moment I don't give a toss where." Barbara Reiner's haughty face with its classic features had become marred over the years by a perpetual expression of malcontent.

"I didn't see you. It was such a big turn-out. Malcolm Fielding told me you were here. You look very well." Her mother wore vintage Dior, black lace, with a double string of South Sea pearls around her throat and large pearl pendant drops.

"The emeralds, I see!" She showed bitter disappointment that they weren't hanging from her own neck.

"Dad gave me permission to wear them."

"Well, he would, wouldn't he? He always did indulge you." Barbara's narrowed glance darted back to where Rohan was standing with the Premier and his wife. They were about to enter the back seat of a Rolls-Royce. "Tell me that's not Rohan Costello?" Fury streaked across Barbara's cold, distinguished face.

"Why ask a question when you know the answer?" Charlotte replied quietly. "You know perfectly well it's Rohan. Does anyone else look like him? Besides, you must have taken note of his very generous donation."

"So he's done well for himself." Barbara gritted her teeth. "He's got himself a *life*. Unlike my dead boy."

They would never rise above their family tragedy. "Nothing but Mattie. Nothing but Mattie," Charlotte moaned. "It's about time you pulled out of your tortured state of mind, Mum. Matthew would never have wanted it."

Barbara lifted a hand as though about to strike. "Don't you *ever* tell me how to live my life, Charlotte. I will mourn my son until the day I die. The agony will never go away."

"I understand that, Mum." Charlotte hastened to placate her. "But Dad and I grieve too. We loved Mattie."

"No one grieves like a mother," Barbara shot back.

"What would you do if you lost your boy? Go on—tell me. Losing a child is the worst blow a woman can ever suffer in life."

"You don't have to tell me that, Mum. I adore my son. But I can never forget that you once told me it was a pity it wasn't me who'd drowned instead of Mattie." Charlotte gave her mother a look of incurable hurt. "You don't have any deep regrets over that? You'd have got over *my* death, wouldn't you? Probably completely. Please let go of my arm."

Barbara had the grace to comply. "I've only just heard Costello was behind the purchase of Riverbend." She said it as though a monstrous deal had been done.

Charlotte began to walk away from the crowd. Quite a few people had been looking their way. Her mother was forced to follow. The breeze off the water caught at Charlotte's long blonde hair and the hem of her exquisite white chiffon gown. "Please keep your voice down, Mum. It's very carrying."

"Of course it is. Clarity and resonance has stood me in good stead. What I really feel like doing is screaming my head off." Barbara was visibly struggling for self-possession. "You're back with him, of course. The boy's his, isn't he? Your father might be a fool, but you can't fool me, Charlotte. I've always had my suspicions. You were pregnant by Costello, yet you married poor Martyn. What a terrible injustice! Did you ever get around to telling him his son was really Rohan Costello's child?" Barbara's demeanour showed frightening aggression.

"No, I didn't. Never!" It was hard to maintain control. "It might shock you, but I believed when I married Martyn he *was* the father of my child."

"I didn't come down in the last shower!" Barbara gave a contemptuous laugh. "You chose to marry *money*,

Charlotte. I understand that at least. Only a foolish woman thinks she can live on love alone—or what passes for love. A driving lust was all you had for Costello."

"Lust?" Charlotte was compelled to swallow down her anger. "What *is* to become of you, Mum? You're deeply neurotic. You need help."

Even in the semi-dark it was possible to see Barbara's flush. "Don't go too far, my girl," she warned. "What would have happened had your husband lived?" There was challenge in her voice. "When you think about it, you were cheating on both of them. Fancy that! Your father's saintly *angel*, with her long blonde hair, having sex with two young men at the same time. I can only marvel!"

"Marvel away!" Charlotte invited, chilled to the bone though the night was warm. She leaned in close to her mother. "I didn't have sex with Martyn, Mum. He *forced* sex on me." It was a measure of her upset that she revealed what she had never revealed before.

Her mother, who had been glaring at her, drew back with a fierce bark of laughter. "I—don't—believe—you."

"Why not, when you're so smart?" Charlotte was close to despair. She had just confided what she'd thought wild horses wouldn't drag out of her. "Things got out of hand. I begged him to stop but he wouldn't. *Couldn't*. I had to live with him. So I learned to think of it that way."

"As well you might!" Barbara drew further back in disgust. "Martyn was totally in love with you, you little fool! It's clear to me you must have led him on," she raged. "You know what you are?"

"Do tell me." Charlotte stood fast. It seemed as if mother-daughter love had gone for ever.

Rohan, unnoticed by both of them, was now only a few feet away. "Charlotte!"

"Don't attempt to drag Rohan into this," Charlotte warned, able to gather herself now Rohan was returning.

"I can and I *will*," Barbara stated forcefully.

Charlotte's heart pumped double-time.

"Good evening, Mrs Reiner," Rohan said.

He looked the very image of a staggeringly handsome and highly successful young man about town, but Barbara stormed towards him as though he were a deadbeat. "You two deserve one another, you know. Do you think I'm a fool?"

Rohan answered with complete self-control. "I certainly don't think you're a fool, Mrs Reiner. So what's the point of acting like one? I'm sure you don't really want to draw attention to yourself. *You're* the one with the fine reputation, after all."

Barbara's coiffed head shot back. "Kindly treat me with respect, Costello," she said, with shocking arrogance.

"Maybe I'll do that when you do the same for me," Rohan replied suavely. He took Charlotte's trembling arm, aware of just how much punishment Charlotte had taken over the years. Barbara Marsdon had been unbelievably cruel to her daughter. "We'll say goodnight, Mrs Reiner. I see you've been giving Charlotte hell. Nothing new in that."

Barbara's stare was malignant. She took in his impressive height and physique, the way he held himself, the self-assuredness, the cultured voice, his stunning good-looks. And those *eyes*! Mary Rose Costello's illegitimate child had come a long way. There was no sign of remorse in him—no plea for forgiveness. Didn't he know Mattie's death had nearly killed her? There was no reality any more. No normal life. Sometimes she thought it would have been best had she drowned with her son. And to think Rohan Costello was back into their lives! He still wanted

her daughter! That couldn't be allowed. As for the boy...
A bitter resentment rolled off Barbara in waves.

"So confident," she said icily, as though he had no right
to be. "And haven't you grown inches? But you'll be hearing more from me, Rohan Costello. That I can promise."

"Then please do keep it civil, Mrs Reiner." Rohan retained his low, even tone. "I wouldn't want to take action
against you."

Barbara didn't deign to answer. She turned away, trying
to get her ravaged face in order before she went back to
her husband. How she wished something horrible would
happen to Rohan Costello! So arrogant, so challenging, and
far, far too confident. As for her daughter! She was going
to reserve a little time and place for Charlotte...

"God, I think we could do with a couple of major tranquil-
lisers after that brush with your mother." Rohan put out his
hand to signal his approaching limousine driver. "What do
you suppose she knows about hiring hit men?"

"Don't laugh, Rohan." Charlotte's beautiful face was full
of upset. She was bitterly regretting her admission about
Martyn. She knew she would have to pay for it somewhere
down the line.

"So what do you want me to do? Buy a suit of armour?
Your mother ran out on you and your father. She should
not be allowed to interfere in your life. And she had better
consider that *your* life is *my* life."

CHAPTER EIGHT

THEY were inside Rohan's penthouse apartment up in the clouds within twenty minutes. This was the second time Charlotte had been inside. As she'd promised to stay over-night she'd left her suitcase there before they had gone on to the function.

"I'm going to pour myself a stiff Scotch." Rohan reached a hand to a bank of switches. "What about you?"

He looked back at her. She looked supremely beautiful, but with a *fragile* overlay that didn't surprise him. He felt rattled himself. Some women were born martyrs. Barbara Marsdon-Reiner was one of them. The incredible thing was that in the pre-Mattie Tragedy days Barbara had been a nice woman. Obviously her whole mode of thinking had altered drastically after the terrible experience of losing her son. Her loathing of *him* hadn't gone away. It still held sway.

"I'll have a brandy." It was all Charlotte could think of. "A good French cognac, if you've got it."

"Which one of them *isn't* good?" he asked with a touch of humour.

They moved through the entrance hall with its stunning gold and white marble floor. An important seascape hung above an antique black and gold commode. The large living room beyond matched up with the hall in its refined opulence. Very European.

"Go sit down while I take a look." He walked away to a well-stocked drinks trolley, with an assortment of crystal decanters, and bent over it, checking. "You're in luck. I've the best of the best Hennessy and a Rémy Martin. One or the other should do the trick. Both nearly sent me broke."

"The Rémy Martin." Her father's choice. Budgeting, so far as her father was concerned, didn't include fine wines and brandies.

She felt shot through with desolation. The awful way her mother had attacked Rohan! Unforgivable. By her mother's lights Rohan Costello should have been one great big failure in life. Instead he had made an outstanding success of himself.

Unable to settle, she drifted about the living room. "If I hadn't thought it before, I think grief has unhinged my mother," she offered sadly.

"You only *think*?" Rohan's dark head lifted. "Did she seem dangerous to you?" He wasn't entirely joking.

"Oh, don't say that!" She gave an involuntary shudder.

"Then what would you say?"

"Dad's lucky to be out of it?" She managed a wry laugh.

"You bet he is." Rohan continued fixing their drinks, fighting down the powerful urge to simply go to her, sweep her up in his arms and carry her into the bedroom.

How many times had Martyn Prescott swept her up in his arms? Hundreds? He couldn't bear to think about it. Not now.

"*You're* lucky too," he said. "And don't let me start on how lucky our son is. It's a good thing Grandmama doesn't want to see him. You'd have to think very seriously about that, Charlotte. I sure do. After tonight I wouldn't want her around him. Up until your mother's appearance it had been a brilliant night. We didn't really need her to mess it up."

She sighed deeply, turning to face the floor-to-ceiling sliding glass doors. The apartment had stupendous views of the Harbour and city on three sides. Glorious by day, it was absolutely breath-taking by night. A wonderland of glittering multi-coloured lights. This was very much a *man's* apartment. It had the feel of an exclusive gentlemen's club. She ran her hands appreciatively over the back of a black leather armchair. A custom-built sofa nearby was upholstered in a knobbly black and gold fabric of striking design. So easily did Rohan fit into these luxurious surroundings they might have been his heritage.

"My mother is one of the despairs of my life." She sank into the sofa. "She defeats me. I've loved her throughout all our traumas, but I can no longer cope. My mother still hates you. Can you believe it?"

"Charlotte, do please pay attention. Some old hatreds never die. Let's forget about your dear mother. I have it in my heart to spare a thought for poor old Reiner. He can't be a happy man."

"Maybe he drinks himself into oblivion when Mum sinks into one of her moods."

Rohan had to laugh, though he was deeply affected by the sadness in her face. Charlotte's *blondeness* and the pure white chiffon of her dress made her a vision of femininity against the lushly dark background of his sofa. She was removing the glorious Marsdon diamond and emerald earrings, putting them down on the coffee table. He watched her shake out her hair.

"Lord, those earrings are heavy," she sighed. "So is the necklace."

"Leave it," Rohan ordered, as she put up her hands to the clasp.

Adrenalin made a mad rush into her veins. "Why? Have you something erotic in mind?'

"Haven't *you*?" His blue eyes glittered. "We're so good at it."

"Old history, Rohan."

"Really?" His handsome mouth curled. Her cool touch-me-not look was incredibly sexy. "You still enjoy being kissed." He handed over a crystal brandy balloon, containing a good shot of cognac. "There's the same old excitement."

"So why don't *you* feel better about the whole thing?"

He didn't answer. Her beauty made its own light, he thought. She didn't need diamonds and emeralds. "I'll feel better when I know the whole story," he said eventually. "Mind if I sit beside you?"

"Oh, Rohan!" She was searingly aware of the devilment in his eyes.

"Relax, Charlotte." Instead he took an armchair. He had undone his black tie, letting it dangle against the snow-white of his dress shirt. He looked like a man one could only dream about.

"I love where you live." She took a slow sip of the cognac, feeling the subtle fire.

He flicked a careless glance around the living room. "It cost a good deal of money. But I'm happy with it."

"So how much time are you going to be able to spend at Riverbend?" She fixed her gaze on the contents of her brandy balloon as though it contained the answer. "Is it your intention to instal me there with Christopher?" Her eyes swept up to study him. The slant of a downlight gilded the planes and angles of his arresting face. Her heart turned

over with the endless love she couldn't find the courage
to put voice to.

"You mean do I intend to instal my wife and son there?"
he asked dryly. "The answer is yes. *I* have no heritage.
No background I can speak of. My biological father is a
mystery man. He has played no part in my life. My mother
and my grandmother had nothing. Mum had to work hard
to survive. I was smart enough to gain scholarships and
bursaries to secure my education. I want Christopher to
retain his Marsdon heritage."

"Only *you* have made it possible," she told him qui-
etly. "Life is very strange. Matthew should have inherited
Riverbend. And his children, had he lived to have them.
Now you say my son—"

"*Our* son," he corrected firmly.

"Will inherit?"

"Isn't that a comfort, Charlotte?" There was a tautness
in his voice.

"Beyond comfort, Rohan. My poor father raced through
his inheritance. I think he still doesn't quite know how it
happened. Losing Mattie blighted all our lives. But Dad
would have continued to make his ill-advised investments
even if Mattie had lived. So in the end Mattie would still
have missed out."

"I'm certain Matthew would have approved of his little
nephew as heir."

"He would." Charlotte was assailed by what might have
been. "Mattie would have loved him."

"Mattie would have given his life for you, Charlotte.
You were very close. I never heard a cross word pass between you. Yet you used to tell Martyn off left, right and
centre."

"He deserved it." Charlotte curled her fingers tightly

around her crystal glass. "It only takes one tragedy to affect so many other lives."

"Undoubtedly—but it doesn't come close to explaining how you came to choose Martyn over me. Every teacher, every tutor, all my classmates voted me the one most destined to succeed. You know. You were there. All I needed was a little time. As it turned out, *very* little time. I hit on a huge money-maker. It wasn't going to be my be-all and end-all. No way! But my every thought was for *you*, for our future together."

"Not all dreams have happy endings, Rohan," she said with a melancholy expression.

How could she ever tell Rohan that Martyn, their friend from childhood, had raped her? Such a hideous word she hesitated to think it, let alone give it voice. It was all too degrading. Rohan would be speechless with anger—some of which would have to fall on her for having given Martyn opportunity.

"Even now, my mother will do her utmost to break us up," she added.

"She won't succeed," he said, with absolute belief in himself. "I'm thinking an April wedding. We'll honeymoon in the European spring. Five months will give you time to get back into practice for loving me. It's a lifetime when a man wants a woman as desperately as I want you. You led me down the garden path, Charlotte, from when we were kids. We might not get the happy ending we talked about, but we do get another chance. We'll be together with our son."

She should have told him there and then that he was all she had ever wanted. Why didn't she? What was stopping her from saying, *Rohan, I love you. I've never stopped loving you. I was in despair when I had to marry Martyn. I truly believed I was carrying his child.* But she knew

Rohan's mind was focused on very different reasons. Getting back what he had once had was all that mattered to him now.

"What are you thinking about?" Rohan's voice brought her out of her reverie.

Her poignant smile tore at his heart.

All the awful stuff locked up inside her. The years with Martyn.

He'd *had* to have her. But oddly he'd never got her pregnant. She hadn't always taken precautions, believing she had a moral duty to give him his own child and his parents a *real* grandchild.

"I was thinking one has to pay for past sins," she said, bitter tears at the back of her throat.

"Not surprising, when the past is where it all began," he said quietly. "Come to bed."

The note in his voice, the look in his eyes, turned her limbs liquid. There was a *burning* along her veins. She didn't think she could move at all, or even draw breath, though her heart was soaring, lifting on wings.

Come to bed.

Could they really reclaim what they'd had? Passion was ravishing. Trust was something else again. Any relationship would flounder without trust.

"Finish your cognac if you think you need it."

She looked back at him across the space of seven years. The times they had been in each other's arms. The secret meetings. The secret language they'd used to communicate with one another. She thought of the passionate lovemaking, the delirious lovemaking, the soft, sweet lovemaking, of the times they'd been content to make each other laugh. They had been so *young*.

He had taken her virginity, himself a virgin. The first time for one had been the first time for the other. Only they had been quickly done with the kissing and the teasing. They had been driven to move on. Unfulfilled rapture was one thing, but there was too much physical pain involved if overwhelming desire couldn't find release.

How, then, could he believe for a moment she had sold herself to Martyn? How could he think her capable of such treachery? Shouldn't he be working his way through to some answers?

You're not helping him, chided the voice in her head.

How could she help him? My God, Martyn had done a job on her. She couldn't speak for the shame.

"Charlotte? Are you coming?" He held out his hand.

Her answer was little more than a whisper. She picked up her crystal balloon, took a last fevered gulp. Heat coursed down her throat, past her breasts into her stomach, then into the delta between her legs. That was where she wanted him—to make her cry out in rapture. She wanted other children. *His* children. Siblings for her darling Christopher.

He went to her, drawing her to her feet. Then his arms closed around her as if they were going to dance. Maybe he had some romantic ballad in his head? He must have, because he danced her around the quiet room, all the while staring down into her face.

She made an aching sound in her throat. There had been such heartbreak. But there was always *hope*. How could the intense love they had shared ever go entirely away? The space between them was throbbing with a sexual desire that had only picked up momentum.

"I want you so badly," he said, in an overpowering rush.

"*Want* is one word. Please tell me another."

"I *need* you." He kissed her cheek very softly.

"Can't you keep going?"

He was clasping her so tightly their bodies seemed

fused—his hard with desire. "What is it you want to hear? That I'll love you for ever and a day?"

"You used to tell me that." Her sadness was immense.

"The past is another country, Charlotte." He kissed the dip behind her ear.

"But you know how unpredictable life is." She lifted imploring green eyes. "Good things happen. Bad things happen. Life-altering things."

"We were supposed to face them together. I used to *dream* I would get you pregnant."

An incredible intimacy bonded them. "You *did*," she said softly.

"But you married Martyn."

"My mistake. I had to live with it." The opening was there again. A brave woman would have taken the hurdle. Only once more she balked. "Those years are over, Rohan. They were full of pain."

Frustration caught him by the throat. He wanted to shake the truth out of her. He had difficulty not doing it. "So why can't you *tell* me the whole story? Don't I have a right to know? Were you frightened of how your parents—your mother—would react? Knowing them, I can appreciate that. Was there *safety* and *security* in marrying Martyn? Pleasing your parents?"

Charlotte swallowed painfully. "Does it matter now?" The trouble was he was judging Martyn by his own standards. Martyn fell far below them. Martyn had been ill-equipped for not getting his own way, even by force. He had thought taking her was his right. Would the truth help her here?

"Okay. I'm done with talking."

Rohan's voice echoed his tension. He released her abruptly, so hard with desire he wanted to pull her down onto the rug and cover her there and then. His hunger was so strong. He wanted his body over hers. He wanted to forget those years when he'd thought his life had been smashed. If they had any chance at all he had to forget his bitterness, clamp down on his frustration. He had her now. He could so easily spoil things. Martyn had won her. But Martyn was gone.

She was a lightweight in his arms.

He carried her down the passageway to the master bedroom, cool from the air-conditioning. He let her body fall gently onto the luxurious bed. She bounced against its springiness before half rolling away from him.

He lowered himself onto the bed beside her, one hand on the slope of her bare shoulder, turning her back to him. "'While the one eludes, must the other pursue.' Browning, I think." He stared down into her river-green eyes. "I'm not looking for the right wife to live with, Charlotte. I've had other women. Nothing easy about being celibate. But I've never been able to wipe you out of my mind. Never lost my vivid memories of you. Attractive women came and *went*. All because of *you*. I found I didn't want a woman I could live happily enough with. I want a wife I can't live *without*. And that, Charlotte, is *you*. I know you never loved Martyn."

Her long hair glittered against the mix of gold, chocolate and black silk cushions that adorned the bed. That much she *could* admit. She *had* never loved Martyn.

"I'm trying so hard to understand."

"Then you'll use up all your understanding." Her defensive walls had been too long in place. "Make love to me, Rohan." She pressed a hand to her aching breast. "At least you *want* me."

"As you want me."

It was a statement not to be denied.

"Maybe we should let go of the past?" he suggested quietly.

"I want that too."

He turned her over, putting a hand to the long covered zipper on her evening dress. His nimble fingers unzipped her in one smooth movement before turning her back to him. "One thing, Charlotte." There was severity in his expression. "Never, *never* lie to me again."

A flush travelled all over her flawless skin. "I have never lied."

He dismissed that with a wave of his hand. "*Promise* me. Say it. *I'll never lie to you again, Rohan.*"

"Then you must say that to me too." Her eyes glowed as green as the ocean.

He didn't say a word. Neither did she.

Instead he began slowly to lower the bodice of her gown, revealing her small breasts, the white of roses. "Having our son hasn't changed your body," he said very quietly, his eyes gliding all over her as she lay on his bed. "Your breasts are still as perfect, the nipples coral-pink. See how they swell to my fingertips? Your waist is as narrow…" He began to peel the white chiffon dress further down her body like a man enthralled, listing his observations as he went. "Your stomach just as taut." He palmed his hand over it, circling and circling, moving lower, until he let his long fingers sink into the triangle of fine blonde hair at her core. "Remember all the crazy things we used to do?" His eyes were a perfect electric-blue. "Your body was my body. My body was yours. Two bodies. One beating heart. One soul."

She shivered to his touch. Beyond answering. She would picture how they'd been when she was dying. So young. Alone together. Without inhibition. Heat was sizzling up through her skin. Her whole body went into spasm as his fingers sought and then touched on an acutely sensitive spot. Her trembling legs fell apart. She wanted to lift them, wrap them around him, bind him to her. She wanted to make it up to him for every moment of those years of heartbreak.

His mouth came down on hers with a ravenous hunger, opening it up fully to his tongue. "Good," he muttered into the brandied sweet honey of her mouth. "Because we're going to do all of them again."

Love could bring either agony or ecstasy. Sometimes it brought both entwined.

The last time he had made love to her they had made a baby. A beautiful baby. Christopher.

Only she hadn't told him that momentous thing. It was beyond making sense of.

Within a week of that most memorable night Barbara Reiner decided it was high time to pay her daughter a visit. Vivian would most probably be at Riverbend—at the Lodge, of all places. Talk about a headlong fall from grace! Vivian was such a fool—always hiding his head in the sand. And to think he had sold the Marsdon ancestral home to Rohan Costello! It defied belief. But then Vivian was notorious for making horrendous decisions.

Silver Valley was only a few hundred miles from Sydney, but she certainly didn't intend to drive herself. She commandeered Kurt's Bentley and his chauffeur for the afternoon. Kurt had dared to rumble a tiny protest. Apparently he needed the car. But she had raised her eyebrows and told him to call a cab. She was looking forward to the trip. She knew Costello was in Sydney. She had rung his office, pretending she was a friend. No way did she want Costello anywhere on the scene. She didn't want him around to back up her daughter.

The boy would be at school. Rohan Costello's son. She could remember the precise moment when she'd first had her suspicions. She had been trying to give Charlotte some advice, and the boy—way too protective of his mother—had turned and given her such a piercing look of appraisal, with near-adult intelligence, she had been truly astonished. She had been judged and found wanting. It had suddenly dawned on her that she had seen that very look before. And those *brilliant blue eyes* didn't fit into the family, did they? Vivian had blue eyes, of course, but even as a young man they had never had that depth of colour, never mind the intensity of regard. She didn't actually *know*. She'd just had a gut feeling.

That was when she had started ignoring the boy. Others might find that extremely harsh, but they hadn't suffered like she had. And there was her daughter—the survivor. Charlotte hadn't learned her lesson. Costello was back in her life. There was going to be a scandal, but she had gone beyond caring. Anything to get back at Costello. He might have passed himself off in society, but his very humble beginnings were bound to come out. And there was the way poor Martyn had been treated! The only thing that would guarantee her silence was for Charlotte and Costello to split up. She presumed he didn't know the child was his. Any woman could pull the wool over a man's eyes. Men missed so much!

Charlotte couldn't remember the last time Christopher had had a day off school, but he—like a number of children and adults in the Valley—had caught a twenty-four-hour bug that had been doing the rounds. Mild enough, she had nevertheless decided to keep him at home for the day. Rohan had picked out some suitable computer games, so that would keep him occupied in his room.

It was a room any boy would envy. It housed his computer, a television, and a bookcase packed with a range of books on subjects that interested him. Not many boys Christopher's age shared his wide-ranging interest in learning and getting "the facts", but that was the way his mind worked. She had nearly fainted when his headmaster had made the chance remark, "The only other child I can remember as extraordinary as your boy, Mrs Prescott, was Rohan Costello."

One day Christopher would have to know the truth. But she recognised with gratitude that Rohan was as committed as she to giving their son time.

Christopher was actually the first to spot the Bentley sweeping up the driveway. It was after lunch. He ran back down the stairs, calling out excitedly to his mother, "Mummy, Mummy—I think maybe it's Grandmother in a Bentley."

Vivian Marsdon strode into the entrance hall. "Good God, surely not!"

"That will cost you, Grandpa!"

"Well, knock me down with a feather." Vivian changed tack, a huge frown on his face. "What do you suppose she wants?" he asked of his equally transfixed daughter.

"Maybe she's dropping in with goodies?" Christopher burst out laughing at his own joke.

Goodies, indeed. Charlotte felt only alarm. "Go back upstairs, darling. Stay in your room like a good boy."

"Can't I stay here?" Instinct told Christopher his mother and grandfather were preparing for trouble. They might need his help.

Vivian Marsdon confirmed his hunch. "There's something wrong with this. Why didn't she ring? I hope she hasn't got that b—husband of hers with her."

"Another fifty cents, Grandpa," Christopher reminded him, as the swear words started to come thick and fast.

"All right, all right. I'll pay up. Your mother is right. Go upstairs, Chrissie. Please don't come down until I come to get you."

Christopher took his mother's hand. "Won't it make you feel better if I stay? Grandmother doesn't worry me. She has no feelings for me."

Vivian Marsdon was aghast. "My dearest boy, your grandmother *loves* you. She just doesn't know how to show it."

Christopher gave his grandfather a kindly look. "It's okay, Grandpa. I don't miss her either."

"If I hadn't given up smoking I'd consider lighting up a cigar."

"Cigars are for celebration, aren't they?" Christopher asked.

"They're also an excellent way to soothe a man's nerves."

Charlotte smiled down on her son. "Do as I say, darling. Go back upstairs. Grandpa and I will take care of this."

Obediently Christopher turned away. "How do you know you can?" he paused to ask. "Grandmother is a serious pain in the a—"

"That will do, Christopher," Vivian Marsdon held up a warning hand. "I've told you not to use that crude expression."

"Sorry, Grandpa. By the way, she's by herself in the back seat. A chauffeur is driving. He's wearing a uniform with a hat."

"Dear Lord!" Vivian Marsdon rolled his eyes heavenward as Christopher disappeared up the stairs. "This is like waiting for a bomb to go off. Barbara has developed such a taste for doom and gloom, all she has left is her dark side."

Charlotte bowed her head in silent agreement. Her own concerns were intense. Today of all days, when Christopher was by chance home from school, her mother had arrived.

Barbara took tea before she launched into the reason for her unscheduled visit.

"It's about the boy," she said, setting down her fine bone-china cup.

"His name is Christopher," Vivian reminded his ex-wife testily. "The boy…the boy…I very much resent your calling your grandson that."

"So what do *you* call him?" Barbara asked, with a wild flash in her eyes.

Vivian stared back, utterly perplexed. "What on earth are you talking about, Barbara?"

Barbara's eyes shot to her daughter, who was looking very pale. "I see you haven't told your father?" she said, totally without sympathy.

"No one tells me a thing—how would I know?"

"Why are you doing this, Mum?" Charlotte asked. "Have you absolutely no compassion? No love in your heart?"

Barbara's tone was hard. "Don't try to turn the tables on me, Charlotte. I can't bear to be part of this…this… conspiracy," she cried, looking the very picture of self-righteousness.

Vivian Marsdon, provoked beyond measure, suddenly gave vent to a roar. "What the hell is this? Is it supposed to be some sort of trial, with you the judge and the jury, Barbara?"

She glared back at him. "Your golden angel betrayed us all," she said, riding a bitter wave. "She married poor

Martyn Prescott, knowing she was carrying Rohan Costello's child."

Vivian Marsdon's handsome face turned purple. *"W-h-a-t?"*

"Doesn't that make you feel good?" Barbara hurled at him. "Charlotte—your perfect girl—was having sex with both of them. She might have thought at the beginning it was Martyn's child—got her dates wrong—but it wouldn't have taken her long to wake up. The boy is enormously bright, I grant you. And poor Martyn was an idiot."

"You be very careful with what you're saying." Vivian Marsdon looked formidable. "If this is some vicious scheme from an old woman—"

"Old? *Old!*" For a moment Barbara looked as if she was going into cardiac arrest. "Why, you silly old man—I'm three years younger than you."

"And you're not looking good, Barbara. You're taking on the persona of the Wicked Witch of the West."

To Barbara it was a hard slap in the face. "For you of all people to say that! You loved me madly."

"And how much did you love *me*?" he countered, his mood abruptly shifting. "You never loved me, Barbara, did you? It was the Marsdon name. The Marsdon money."

Barbara gave him a vicious smile. "Which you promptly lost."

"Just like it's now the Reiner money—poor old fool," Vivian continued, as though she hadn't spoken. "By now he must know you're crazy."

Barbara threw up her hands in frustration. "We were supposed to be talking about your daughter and the things she got up to."

Vivian gave her a look of utter contempt. "You surely can't think you can turn me against my daughter? You can't think you can turn me against my beloved grandson? I don't give a damn who Chrissie's father is. My daughter Charlotte is his mother, and *I'm* his grandfather."

"Costello is his *father*!" Barbara shouted. "So that's your answer, is it? You don't mind that Rohan Costello is the boy's father? Rohan Costello—who let *our* boy drown?"

"Oh, Mum!" Charlotte moaned in despair, thanking God Christopher was far away in his room.

Vivian Marsdon was so angry he was temporarily unable to speak. "I should have stopped you, Barbara," he said grimly after a few moments. "I shouldn't have let you crucify young Costello and his mother—a struggling young woman you had once helped. Losing Mattie has deranged you. You desperately needed counselling at the time. I should have seen you got it. Instead I let you wreck your mental health and the Costellos' lives. Rohan was *not* to blame for Mattie's death. It was a tragic accident. I've long since accepted that."

"So he's not so bad. Is that it?" Barbara asked, breathing heavily. "You can adjust?"

"I may need a little time." Vivian turned to his daughter. "It's true, Charlie?"

"Of course it's true," Barbara cut in. "I don't go around making up stories."

"Keep out of this, Barbara," Vivian Marsdon warned. "I'm running out of patience with you."

Barbara gave a shriek of horror. "Patience? I just got here."

Charlotte ignored her mother. "Yes, Dad. But I believed when I married Martyn I was carrying his child."

"What else do you need, Vivian? A blasted DNA report?"

"Shut up, woman," Vivian Marsdon thundered, shocked

at his ex-wife's vindictiveness. "If you can't shut up then I'll show you the door." He had never sounded so authoritative.

Barbara Reiner reeled back in her chair. "I—beg—your—pardon?" She could scarcely believe her ears.

"Please...please stop. Both of you," Charlotte begged. "Marrying Martyn was a huge mistake, but I didn't know what else to do at the time. It wasn't as though you were here for me, Mum. I didn't have the guts to tell Dad I was pregnant. I didn't have the guts to go it alone."

"Go it alone?" Barbara repeated with scorn. "You took all the comfort you could from poor Martyn, though, didn't you? So much for your endless love for Costello!"

Charlotte met her mother's hard, accusatory gaze. "I *did* go to Martyn for comfort. I was missing Rohan terribly. We'd been friends all our lives."

"And you used him," Barbara condemned.

"I suppose I did." It had never for a second entered her head to abort her child. But she couldn't have turned to Rohan when she was carrying Martyn's child. There'd be no way out of it. She'd married Martyn.

"That's it. That's enough, Barbara," Vivian Marsdon said sternly. "How could Charlie go to you? Her mother? You were never the soul of comfort at the best of times. You spent all the years of Mattie's life dancing attendance on him."

"Because he was delicate, you ignorant fool!"

"The bitter truth was you spoonfed him. You would never listen to me—"

Charlotte cut in. "Please keep your voices down. I couldn't bear for Christopher to hear you."

"He won't hear us, Charlie." Vivian reached out to pat her hand. "His bedroom is too far away."

"Just as well." Charlotte shuddered. "What did you hope to achieve, Mum, by coming here?"

Barbara straightened her shoulders. "I need your word, Charlotte, that you won't marry Costello. I couldn't live with that. If you give me your promise there's no more to be said. You can carry on with your charade."

Charlotte stared back at her mother in wonderment. So wonderfully elegant on the outside, a total mess within. "I'm afraid there's no question of that. Rohan recognised his son the instant he laid eyes on him."

"Did he really?" Vivian Marsdon turned to his daughter, showing his shock.

"As per usual, Vivian, you've had your head in the sand," his ex-wife said contemptuously. "The boy will grow into the image of him. Those blue eyes, for a start. One rarely sees eyes like that. Are you *really* prepared to create a great scandal, Charlotte? For Costello? He's making quite a name for himself in the city. An illegitimate child won't help. Or the mother of his child marrying his childhood friend. What about the Valley? The news would shock the entire district. God alone knows what the Prescotts will think, let alone *do*."

"They'll do nothing," Vivian Marsdon said, his eyes on fire.

"They won't have to. There are few things Nicole and her mother like better than airing their suspicions," Charlotte said. "Rohan and I are prepared to wear it all. One can't hide the truth for ever."

"Just another nine-day wonder," Vivian Marsdon said with a hopeful smile. There would be a scandal. No question. But it was high time he came out on the side of his long-suffering daughter. "Good God, woman, Costello has bought Riverbend. He has big plans for it. Christopher is his son and heir. Christopher will one day inherit his birthright. Think of that. The wheel of fortune has turned full circle. Marsdons planted the first vines in the Valley, the first olive groves. We won't just be selling our harvested crops. I've heard Costello is planning to build a new winery. Bring in all the best people. I believe he's already having talks with the von Luckners—father and son. Remember old Konrad predicted young Rohan would have a splendid future?"

That was true. The von Luckners were members of a very posh clan from Germany, who had migrated shortly before the First World War to get away from Europe.

"Who told you, Dad?" It was no secret the von Luckners were in need of a big inflow of cash to expand and continue the late Erich von Luckner's bold vision.

"My dear girl, people tell me things. Always have. I am a Marsdon—a community leader."

"So, you're all going to finish up *friends*?" Barbara cried out in disbelief, appalled that things weren't going as she'd planned.

"There are worse things than friends, Barbara. Like ex-wives." Vivian glanced down pointedly at his watch. "Shouldn't you be getting back to poor old Reiner? I suppose he let you have the Bentley without a whimper?"

CHAPTER NINE

AFTER Barbara had left, acting as though she was cut to the quick by their refusal to heed her warnings, father and daughter returned to the living room, their hearts heavy.

"This is my fault," Charlotte said, her psyche so wounded by years of blame she sought not one ounce of sympathy for herself.

"Of course it isn't," groaned her father. "Was that *really* the woman I married?" he asked in genuine wonder. "What's bugging her most, do you suppose? The fact that you're going to marry Rohan Costello? That's he's Christopher's father? Or that you slept with poor old Martyn too? She always did take his side, you know. She believed Martyn's version of events over yours. Rohan never defended himself."

"He didn't have to, Dad. Rohan was an innocent victim. I was only with Martyn *once* before we were married." She turned her beautiful eyes on her father. There really had to be something wrong with her. Post-traumatic stress? That was a popular diagnosis. Terrible things happened, yet they were never mentioned. Abuses of all kinds. Perhaps she should get a big sheet of cardboard and write *Rape* on it? It wasn't going to trip off her tongue.

"What awful luck! It's women who pay the price, isn't

it? Women who get hurt the most. We weren't there for you, Charlie. And you were so young."

She couldn't bear to talk about it any more. Had she been able to depend upon a loving, wise mother, her life might have turned out differently.

Charlotte turned her head, as though her son might suddenly appear. "It's a wonder Chris hasn't come downstairs," she said, with a puzzled frown. "He would have seen the Bentley leave."

"We did tell him to remain in his room. He's a good boy, and a highly intuitive one. He knew there was going to be trouble. Barbara doesn't care how many casualties there are in her one-woman war."

"I'm so sorry, Dad."

"Oh, for God's sake, Charlie! It's your parents who should be sorry. You've had some very difficult episodes in your life. Mostly because we failed you—your mother and I. We failed the Costellos. We failed Martyn. He should have been made to retract his damaging statements. It's a wonder you have any love left for me."

Did one ever lose the capacity to love a parent? Even a bad one? "Plenty of love!" Charlotte rose to her feet, dropping a kiss on her father's silver-streaked blond head. "I'll look in on Chris, then make us both a strong cup of coffee."

"I'll get things going." Vivian stood up. On the surface he was calm enough; underneath he was full of intense regrets about his own past behaviour and horror at his ex-wife's lack of compassion. "Did you hear the way that woman spoke to us?" he huffed. "I'll tell you this: she won't put a foot inside the door again."

"Try to put it out of your mind, Dad," Charlotte advised.

"With Mattie gone, love is something Mum *cannot* provide. I think of her as not being in her *right* mind."

"One wonders if she ever was."

All was quiet inside when Charlotte knocked on her son's door. "It's me, Chris. You can come out now, darling. Sorry it took so long."

She waited for him to come to the door, full of questions. Gifted children had many advantages. They also suffered disadvantages. They recognised too much, too early. Maybe he was taking a nap? He hadn't been feeling one hundred per cent, but as usual he made no complaints.

"Chrissie?" She knocked again, and then when she got no response, opened the door.

The room was empty. She sucked in her breath. He had to be in the bathroom just down the hall. Maybe he'd been sick again? She hoped not. She had thought the short bout of vomiting the night before was over.

"Chrissie, love?" She knocked on the bathroom door. "Are you sick again?"

Again no response. She opened the door, taking in the empty white and turquoise tiled bathroom at a glance. Where was he? It was too early for her to be worried, yet she felt a chill run right through her body. Was it possible Christopher had crept down the stairs to listen in on the adult conversation? Would he do that? Had he heard his grandfather's lion-like roar? That would have put him on the alert. Christopher was a great one for knowing the facts. Why had his grandmother come visiting? They rarely saw her. Why had his grandfather shouted in that angry voice?

It was possible—more than possible—her son had decided to find out. Christopher was no ordinary child.

Oh, God! Oh, God! Was it happening all over again? A missing child? A mother's worst nightmare short of a child's confirmed death. Swiftly she got a hold on herself, trying to think things through. She had to accept now that he *had* listened in. Made the choice to run. Run where? Could he have gone to Peter's place? Could he have sought the comfort of his best friend? She hurried away to put a call through to Peter's house. Pray God he was there. Peter would be home from school by now.

Rohan's secretary, Shona, appeared at the door, her pretty face without its usual dimpled smile. "I know you told me to hold your calls, Rohan, but I think you'll want to take this one. It's Charlotte. She sounds very distressed."

"Right, put it through." He was scheduled to meet up with one of his more important clients, but if there was anything wrong with Charlotte he would cancel.

Under fifteen minutes later he was in the air, the company helicopter heading for Riverbend. Children were life itself to their parents. He had found Charlotte. He had found his son. Nothing would be allowed to put their future in jeopardy. He knew Charlotte's fears were gaining momentum with every passing hour, but what he had seen of his son gave him hope. A boy under tremendous stress, he had gone off on his own. Maybe he should have told his mother first. But he had needed to do some thinking alone. He had a strong feeling Christopher had inherited his temperament.

The instant she heard the *thrump-thrump* of the rotors Charlotte was flying out through the door, feeling as though if anyone could find Christopher it would be Rohan—his father. She hurled herself at him, the bone-deep stabs of fear abating to a level she could bear. It was torture to think her seven-year-old son had had to run away to counteract the shock and the grief he must have felt as powerful deceptions were exposed. Would she ever be the same for him again? Would his great love for her, his faith in her, change?

Rohan caught her up, pulling her close into his body. Her anguish couldn't have been more visible. "I spotted the police car and the scouters from the air," he said, his cheek against her thick curtain of hair. "There are a lot of people out there, all up and down the riverbank."

The river.

A half-forgotten poem sprang disturbingly into his head.

Whoever said happiness is the light shining on the water?
The water is cold and dark and deep.

There could *never* be another drowning. That was his belief, and it was strong. He wasn't about to panic. Mattie wouldn't allow it. Mattie who had ceased to be and yet lived on.

"Practically the whole village is out." Charlotte's willowy body was shaking like a leaf. "Where *is* he, Rohan?" She stared up into his brilliant eyes as though he alone knew the answer.

He took her firmly by the shoulders. "Wherever he is, Charlotte, he's *safe*. He loves you far too much to do anything silly. He's a clever, thoughtful child. He wants to be by himself right now. He wants to sort everything out in his own mind. I used to go off by myself, remember?"

"Yes, you did." She felt a flutter of hope.

"I can tell you one thing," Rohan said grimly. "Your

mother will never be allowed near Christopher again. Where's your father?"

He put his arm around her waist, leading her back into the house. She was trying so hard to be brave. That was the thing! Charlotte *was* brave. And she had never been one to tell even the smallest lie. It wasn't a matter of degree with Charlotte. A lie was a lie was a lie! Even now her inexplicable action in marrying Martyn brought him to near breaking point. Only he didn't have the time now for all the convolutions of his mind.

"Dad is out searching," Charlotte said. "He's tremendously upset. I shouldn't say this, but I'm feeling near hatred for my mother. She provoked this thing. Dad went off in a sick rage. He loves Christopher."

"I know. There are too many people searching the riverbanks. Christopher isn't there."

She lifted her eyes to him, tears welling. "But how can we be sure of that, Rohan? What Chrissie learned would have destroyed all his certainties about life. About me—his mother. About *you*—his real flesh-and-blood father. He's only a little boy, no matter how intelligent. What he overheard would have been shocking to his ears. Who knows what a child in shock will do?"

He bent to stay her quivering mouth with a kiss. "Mattie won't let Christopher fall in the river."

Her expression totally changed. "You're saying that as though Mattie is still alive and breathing."

"So what if he isn't? He's still out there. Somewhere. Parallel universe—who knows? I continue to feel a spiritual connection to my childhood friend. I don't go around analysing it. It just *is*. Christopher wouldn't do anything so radical, anyway. He knows Mattie's story. He's a child with deep feelings. He's trying to understand what he heard. Weigh it up. I'll get the Sergeant to direct more searchers to the vineyards and the olive groves. But somehow I don't think he's there. The old winery?"

"It's been searched. The house has been searched from top to bottom." She meant the Riverbend mansion.

"Right—well, I'm off!" He spoke with immense purpose.

"I'm coming with you." A tear ran down her cheek. She dashed it away. She would search until she dropped down dead.

Only Rohan wasn't having it. "I know how hard this is for you, Charlie, but you must stay here," he said with quiet authority. "For all we know Christopher could work his way back. We don't want him returning to an empty house."

"But, Rohan—he must have heard all the commotion." She was ready to argue, her nerves strung taut. This was her son. *Their* son. "The noise of the chopper arriving. I'm so frightened. I've spent so many years of my life frightened."

No time either for him to question *that* shock admission. *Years of her life frightened?* He knew next to nothing about her life with Martyn. She wouldn't tell him. "Well, I'm here now." He let her body slump against him, feed off his strength. "And I won't be back until I find our son. Trust me, Charlotte."

"With my life!" She looked up at him, her heart in her eyes. "With our son's life. Forgive me, Rohan. I've made so many mistakes. And now our son knows them." A sound of agony escaped her lips. "He thought me perfect. He won't any more. Rohan, he mightn't even *love* me any more. The thought is too dreadful!"

He took her beautiful, agonised face between his hands. "Christopher can no more stop loving you than I can." He spoke not gently, but with some force. Enough force to close out certain fears from her mind. "What you have to do is remember you're at the very *centre* of our lives. Hold the thought close. I'll find him." He bent his head and kissed her hard.

It had been dark for well over an hour. Wherever Christopher was, he surely must have heard their raised voices. The whole area was ringing with the echoes of his name. People, truly chilled by the turn of events, were loath to return home. Even Gordon Prescott, deeply distressed, had called in to the Lodge to express his concerns, then set out with Charlotte's father, friends from childhood. The searchers would come out again at first light, but the darkness was complete.

Were the Marsdons jinxed? For that matter the Prescotts?

Both families, so closely entwined, had suffered tragedies, and that was the question people were asking themselves. The atmosphere all along the riverbank had struck many a soul as extremely spooky. They all knew Matthew Marsdon's tragic story. They had been given instructions where to search. Every last man and woman hoped they would be the one to find the boy safe. But the more time that elapsed, the more fearful the searchers became. A seven-year-old child in peril! It struck at the heart of every parent.

Why had the boy taken off? All they had been told was that he had most probably overheard a family argument and become upset. Quite a few people had seen the big Bentley driving through the area, the ex-Mrs Marsdon sitting regally in its back seat, a uniformed chauffeur up front. Once a very highly regarded woman, Barbara Reiner as she was now had taken a nosedive in the popularity stakes. The love and attention she had lavished on her son had left her only daughter out in the cold. Small wonder

Charlotte Prescott's marriage hadn't worked. The feeling at the time had been that it was a marriage of convenience. And some reckoned she'd just *had* to be pregnant when she walked reed-slim down the aisle. What did it matter anyway? Charlotte Prescott was a beautiful young woman. Inside and out. Her son had to be found.

Alive.

Rohan didn't know the moment the answer to the question of Christopher's whereabouts came to him. Was it Christopher's guardian angel whispering in his ear? Or Mattie? Or maybe Mattie had been elected for the job?

He commandeered one of the search vehicles, a utility truck, and sped off. It didn't make a lot of sense, but that didn't matter. He had the strong conviction Christopher had headed off to the cottage where Rohan and his mother had lived. He thought now he had made some comment about it to Christopher—about the place where he and his mother had lived for the first seventeen years of his life.

As if a button had been pushed, there was a shift in his thinking. He remembered how he had pointed out his grandmother's old cottage to Christopher from the helicopter. The cottage had long been empty. He knew the land—not valuable—had been bought for future development, but so far nothing had happened. The timber structure appeared to be settling down into the earth. The white picket fence had a great many broken teeth. The corrugated iron roof, once a bright red, was thickly sown with dead foliage from the overhanging canopy of trees. What had been the small front and back gardens were overrun by long grass and vegetation gone wild. It was a veritable jungle now. The old cottage where he had grown up on the wrong side of the tracks was an abandoned old derelict.

There was no moon tonight. It was as black as only

country black could be. No street lights to pierce the darkness. He had a heavy-duty torch with him on the passenger seat. Would his boy be shrinking from the darkness? Would he be sitting frozen with fear of snakes? Would he be desperately regretting what he had done?

Rohan drove the utility truck right through what had been the front gate, jamming on the brakes at the base of the short flight of steps. He swung out of the vehicle, leaving the headlights on.

"Christopher!" he shouted, running up onto the verandah, hoping the old boards would take his weight. "It's me. It's Rohan. You must come out. You're a responsible boy. Your mother is sick with worry. So is your grandfather. People have been searching for you for hours. Come out now. You're quite safe. I'm here now. I'll never leave you again. That's my solemn promise, Christopher. Come out, son. We need to get you home."

The front door lay open, hanging on its hinges. Vandals? Or simply years of no one caring what happened to the place. Having accomplished so much, Rohan was having difficulty accepting he and his mother had ever lived in such a place—but then his mother had kept the cottage spotlessly clean. He had helped her put in a vegetable garden at the back. He had cut the grass while his mother had looked after the beds of perennials around the picket fence.

He moved into the house, shining the torch down the hallway that ran from front to back. God! He could cover it in less than half a dozen paces.

"I know you're here, Christopher," he called, gentling the urgency of his voice. "I know you're frightened. But there's nothing to be frightened about. I used to run off myself when I was a boy and things got too much for me to handle. I know how you feel. But your mother and I want you to come home. Please, Christopher. There are always things in life we have to face. We have to swallow our fears. Find our courage. Come out now. Let me see you. We can confront what is worrying you together."

Rohan didn't even consider he was talking to an empty old house. Christopher, his son, was here somewhere.

A moment later a small boy stumbled out of what had been the kitchen and into the hallway, vigorously rubbing his eyes. "I'm a real sook," he announced, in a quavery voice he tried hard to make stronger. "I've been crying."

Rohan thought he would never forget this moment. Huge relief bubbled up in his chest. He moved towards his son, feeling such a rush of love he couldn't begin to describe it. "Grown men cry, Christopher," he said, unbearably touched by the way this small boy was trying to hold himself together. "There's no shame in shedding a few tears. Come here to me."

"I wanted to see where you'd lived," Christopher explained, starting towards the wonderful man he had been drawn to on sight. "Are you my *real* dad?" he asked, realising with a pang of sadness that he had been having difficulty remembering the man he had once called Daddy for some time.

Rohan reached for his son, fragile as a bird in his strong grip. He lifted him high in his arms. "I *am* your father, Christopher," he said. "I am so very, *very* sorry for the confusion that's gone on." That surely couldn't be the best way to put it to a child? Rohan agonised. *Confusion?* He could hardly say he hadn't even known he existed until very recently. "I *want* to be your father. I want to do everything I can for you and your mother. How does that feel?"

Christopher had already reached his decision. He buried his hot, sweaty little face in his father's neck. "Real *good*!" he said.

* * *

Rohan used his mobile to have the search called off. News that young Christopher Prescott had been found safe and sound flew around the network. And Rohan, in a matter of days, was to make a sizeable and very welcome contribution to the Valley's Search and Rescue Team.

All's well that ends well—was the general view. One had to keep a close eye on kids. They created problems without meaning to. Sometimes awful things happened in communities. This, by the grace of God, wasn't one of them. Lots of people believed in guardian angels. Young Christopher Prescott obviously had one. And Rohan Costello, absent so long from Silver Valley, had managed to channel that guiding light.

They were safe. Both of them were safe. Christopher and Rohan. The joy of it swamped her. The exterior lights lit up the garden, and the Jeep had barely come to a stop when Christopher opened the door and jumped out onto the gravel.

"Mummy!" he cried, as though the sight of her had put his world right.

The love in her son's voice, the expression on his dirty, tear-streaked face, told Charlotte that whatever she had done her seven-year-old son was one person who wasn't going to hold her to blame.

"Chrissie!" She caught him to her, hugged and patted him hard, folded him into a mutual display of love. "Thank God you're safe."

Christopher pulled back a little, tilting his head. "It was Rohan who found me." He slanted his rescuer, who stood leaning against the Jeep, a beaming glance.

"Of course it was." Charlotte breathed in air. Breathed, *breathed*. Of course she'd known her little son would come back to her. Hadn't she?

She turned her head, binding Rohan to her with a glance. He had made the decision to remain on the periphery, clearly giving them a minute together. Her father, who had been positioned behind her at the front door, anxiously awaiting their arrival, had joined in the reunion, his long arms now making a cocoon around his daughter and his grandson.

"Christopher, you must never run off and scare us again," he scolded, making a sudden change of direction now the boy was safe. "We're endlessly grateful to you, Rohan," he called to the tall, handsome, self-contained young man standing apart. "It's a miracle you thought of the old cottage. Christopher could have been out all night. Come in, come in," he invited, with the warmth of a man who had decided to put the traumas of the past behind them. "Let me get you a well-deserved drink."

"It was so dark I couldn't see a thing," Christopher announced. "Rohan said I have to apologise to everyone who came out to search for me. Of course I will. But I never thought people would be going to look for me. Only you and Grandpa, Mummy. Rohan wasn't coming back until the weekend. He told me before he went away."

"God only knows—" Vivian Marsdon started in exasperation, then stopped. "There was a good chance your mother wouldn't have been able to contact Rohan, Christopher," he said after a moment.

"Let's drop it for now." Charlotte tapped her father's shoulder. "Chris needs a nice long shower, and when he's done he can have something to eat. Then bed."

"My stomach is groaning. I feel really hungry. There was no water at the cottage either. I'm sorry everyone was worried, but I wanted to go somewhere I could think."

His grandfather frowned. "You might have had to spend the night there, my boy."

"I think I fell asleep, but I can't be sure."

"Well, no harm's done." Rohan intervened smoothly. "I'll have that drink, Mr Marsdon, if it's okay?" He moved into the pool of light.

"Please, please—it's Vivian," Vivian Marsdon insisted, waving a welcoming hand. "I'll join you."

Charlotte and Rohan exchanged wry glances at her father's dramatic turnaround. "I'll take Chrissie off," she said. "Could you make him a sandwich, Dad? He can have a glass of milk with it."

"Put some Milo in it, please, Grandpa?" Christopher requested.

He turned his blond head to address his saviour, who just happened to be his father. He didn't know how it had happened, but he was sure his mother would explain it properly to him. He had a feeling Rohan wanted to hear too. Was it *confusion* that had put his grandmother into such a terrible spin? He hadn't waited on the stairs to hear all she had to say. The awful grating sound in her voice had made him feel sick. He had just wanted to get away from the house.

"You're going to wait for me, aren't you, Rohan?" He held his small body very still, awaiting his hero's answer.

"Yes, I am, chief!" Rohan gave his son a reassuring smile.

Christopher beamed. "Oh, good! Rohan and I are mates, Mummy. I'm his mate. He's my mate." He turned to Rohan, giving him a confidential man-to-man look. "I'll keep calling you Rohan for a while—just like you said, Rohan."

"Good thinking!" Rohan touched his fingertips to his forehead in a tiny salute.

Christopher burst out laughing, then sobered abruptly. He shot his mother an apprehensive look. "Grandmother's gone, hasn't she?"

"Too right she has!" his grandfather answered, his deep

voice rising, the vein in the middle of his forehead twitching away. "And she won't be coming back in a hurry."

"Does she know I ran away?" Christopher asked as his mother led him off.

"She will when she checks her e-mails." Vivian Marsdon smiled grimly. "Go along now, Christopher. You've worn us all out."

Charlotte and Rohan walked into Riverbend's entrance hall hand in hand, although both were aware of the intense strain between them. Christopher had been found. The danger was over. But she knew there were many questions that were going to be asked. The problem was she didn't know how she was going to answer Rohan, let alone find acceptable answers for their son. Highly intelligent Christopher might be, but he was still only a boy of seven. Plenty of time for him to find out how babies were made.

He had fallen asleep almost as soon as his head hit the pillow. Her father, who had put in some deeply harrowing hours searching for his grandson, had joined Christopher with his sandwiches, substituting a nice drop of Laphroaig for milk and a couple of teaspoons of Milo. Rohan had accepted a single malt whisky, but declined a chicken sandwich. He had contacted his housekeeper at the house, he explained. Dinner would be waiting. He had turned his dark head to invite Charlotte to join him—a naturally commanding young man, who wasn't going to accept a refusal.

She'd had absolutely no idea what response her father would make. He was a man of the old school who regarded himself as the head of family, to be deferred to no matter what one's age or status in life. Would he say it might be best if she remained at home? As it was, she had every intention of returning to the Lodge late. Christopher might very well awaken during the night. He had, after all, suffered his own trauma.

Instead Vivian Marsdon now walked them to the front door, where he paused to look at the younger man, his expression that of a man who had set aside time to put a nagging concern in order. "I want to tell you, Rohan, I deeply regret what has gone before." He fetched up a great sigh. "I can't, of course, change anything. None of us can. But I allowed my wife to control the whole terrible situation surrounding Mattie's death. Like a fool, I couldn't see what was under my nose. I'd very much appreciate it now, Rohan, if we could be friends?" He held out his hand, the tone of his deep, rich voice absolutely sincere.

This was the moment when Rohan would be well within his rights to reject an overture that had come far too late. Instead, without a moment's hesitation, he took Vivian Marsdon's hand in a brief, firm grip. "I'd like that, sir."

"Good. Good." Vivian coloured, fiercely pleased. He bent down to kiss his daughter's cheek. "Go along now, Charlie. Enjoy dinner. Relax your nerves. I'm sure you two have lots to talk about. I'll leave the light on for you."

"Thanks, Dad." Charlotte gave her father a lovely tender smile. "Chris was pretty much exhausted, but I'd like to check on him during the night."

"Hungry?" Rohan led the way past the grand reception rooms to the state-of-the-art kitchen.

"Not really, thank you, Rohan." Hours of the most intense anxiety had shocked hunger out of her.

He studied her intently, noting the haunted expression in her green eyes, the way she held her slender body taut. "Better have something all the same." He was reminded of the way she had looked on that long-ago terrible day at the river. Both of them had suffered more than their fair share of grief.

"I shouldn't stop too long." Her eyes were stinging. What must he think of her? Rohan had always been her greatest friend. He had made her happier than anyone else in the world. He had been her truly glorious lover, was the father of her child. But she couldn't rid herself of the thought that she had lost his trust for ever. That weighed very heavily on her.

Louise Burch, the housekeeper, came bustling through the swinging kitchen door, leaving tantalising aromas in her wake. "Good evening, sir. Good evening, Mrs Prescott. I should have met you at the door," she apologised, sounding a little short of breath. "I was just coming to check."

"Don't worry about that, Louise. Roy not home yet?" Roy Burch had been one of the searchers.

Louise's face lit up with a smile as she turned to Charlotte. "All of us are so happy and relieved young Christopher has been found, Mrs Prescott. Boys are such scamps. Roy went off with some of our friends to have a celebratory drink. I was going to join them."

"Then you mustn't wait," Rohan said immediately. "Charlotte and I can manage."

Louise Burch adopted her professional manner. "Thank you so much. There's roast chicken just out of the oven. Pesto and mascarpone sauce. Little chat potatoes, beans, and baby peas from the garden. I'll wait and serve up."

"No need for that, Mrs Burch," Charlotte intervened with a smile. "You go off now. My father and I are enormously grateful to all the good caring people in the Valley. I will be telling your husband that when I see him. There's no need for you to look after the two of us."

"Well, if you say so." Louse Burch glanced from one to the other. What beautiful young people they were!

"We *do* say so, Louise." Rohan gave her an easy smile.

Louise blushed. Talk about sex appeal! "Then thank you so much. That's very good of you."

"Not at all. And we'll clear away afterwards, so you're not to worry," Charlotte said.

Moments later, apron folded away, Mrs Burch took her leave. "By the way, I made a plum cake with plum syrup," she told them with a bright smile. "One of my specialities. Plenty of ice cream and whipped cream in the fridge."

"Thank you, Louise," said Rohan. "I'll probably have a very large slice."

Louise Burch went off beaming. She and her husband were more contented than they had ever been, looking after Mr Costello. He was the best boss in the world, and their bungalow in the grounds couldn't be more comfortable. Silver Valley was absolute heaven after their last job, with a demanding old matriarch. They had made friends in no time.

Charlotte Prescott, a widow, was so beautiful—and so young to have a seven-year-old child to rear alone. Wouldn't it be wonderful if she and Mr Costello made a match of it? A grand house like Riverbend needed a lady like that. Apparently Mrs Prescott's father had fallen on hard times and had had to sell the estate. If those two beautiful young people got married Charlotte Prescott would never have to leave her old home…

"Let's eat in here," Rohan said.

"Rohan?"

"No talk. I need to feed you first. Sit down before you fall down. I can get this."

He pulled out a chair for her at the long granite-topped table before moving away, super-efficient in everything he did. She watched him walk over to some impressive-looking refrigerated wine-storage cabinets, the contents on full view through the glass doors. He pulled out a bottle of white wine, showing her the label.

"Fine. Fine…" She glanced at it, looked away. It was an award-winning Chardonnay. She was trying hard not to let the tension inside her break the surface. "Not much dinner for me, Rohan." Under his smooth control, he too had to be fighting powerful feelings.

"When did you last eat?" He found glasses, then poured the perfectly chilled wine, passing a glass to her.

"When did *you*?" she countered.

"Around seven this morning. I don't often get a chance to stop for lunch, so at the moment I'm hungry. Charlotte, you didn't answer *my* question."

She stared up at him with troubled eyes. "I can't seem to find the right answers to your questions."

"That's because you're hiding so much."

She was wearing a soft georgette top of pastel colours, with an ankle-length matching skirt. The top had a low oval neckline that allowed just a glimpse of cleavage. The fabric clung to her small high breasts and showed off her taut torso and tiny waist. She looked like a top model—especially with her long blonde mane loose. He didn't think he could ever let her cut her hair. It was too beautiful.

"You don't trust me," she said sadly.

"I *half* trust you." He softened it with a smile.

"Well, that's better than nothing. But lack of trust ruins relationships, Rohan. Anyway, I made afternoon tea for my mother. I don't remember eating anything, but I did have a cup of tea."

"We won't talk about your mother." He was busy cutting

slices of tender white chicken breast. "Not for the moment anyway."

She had to be content with that.

As it turned out, he didn't appear to have an appetite either—though they had no difficulty finishing the bottle of wine. Both ate little of what otherwise would have been a delicious meal.

"Well, we can't disappoint Mrs Burch," Rohan said later, eyeing the plum cake. The table was cleared, dishes rinsed and stacked in the dishwasher. "You'll have to join me in a slice. It looks good."

"She's a good cook. Very good."

"I wouldn't have hired her otherwise. She's rather passionate about food. I like that." He cut a large slice and then, before Charlotte could voice any protest, cut it in two, giving Charlotte the narrow end, and pouring a little plum syrup over both sections. "All right. *Eat* that."

"You're ordering me about?"

"Yes," he said crisply, then sat down again.

She took hold of her cake fork. "You want to talk to me, don't you?"

"Charlotte, my love, I've *tried* talking to you." The expression in his eyes was hard; a mocking smile curled his mouth.

"You must think I'm pathetic."

He laughed without humour. "Would you like some cream?" He stood up.

"No, thank you."

"Well, I'll have some. I need sweetening up." He went to the large stainless steel refrigerator standing side by side with a matching freezer. "Second thoughts—ice cream. Seriously—won't you join me?"

"You're enjoying this in a weird sort of way, aren't you?"

"The hell I am! We've both had a shock. I'm trying my level best to be kind." He pointed to her plate.

"Okay, okay." She handed it up to him. It might even make her feel better.

He laid a nicely turned dessertspoonful of vanilla ice cream on it.

Charlotte made herself eat. Actually, it was lovely.

When they were finished he took the plates and cutlery from her, rinsed them, then put them in the dishwasher, turning it on. Finally he disposed of the empty wine bottle.

"You're very useful in the kitchen." She gave in to a wry little laugh.

"Just one of my many talents. I'm pretty useful in the bedroom as well. And you don't hold back there, do you, Charlotte? Believe me, you're the best of the best. The cool, cool, touch-me-not is an enormous turn-on. Charlotte hiding her passionate nature."

The passionate nature only you unlocked, she thought. What a tremendous burden would be lifted from her if she could give voice to her heart!

You must help me, Rohan. I'm a damaged woman.

Seriously messed-up, too young, and with no one to turn to, to ease her out of it. It happened so much in life. She'd thought she didn't have a choice. She'd taken the wrong direction. She had married the wrong man.

"Would you like coffee?"

Rohan was desperate to make some breakthrough.

He loved this woman. Nothing could change that. Not even the fact she had rejected him for Martyn Prescott, who'd been able to give her every material thing in life. Her decision had troubled her deeply. Unfortunately one

always paid in the end for bad decisions. He still wanted
Charlotte very badly, and wondered whatever had happened to something called pride. Maybe love and pride
didn't go together? He had been committed to Charlotte
Marsdon from childhood. They were the legendary childhood sweethearts.

She stood up, her graceful body set in determined lines.
"I should go."

"In a little while. You might consider *I* won't be able
to rest until I hear what your mother had to say. What my
son overheard."

"He didn't tell you?" She bent her shining head, almost
as if in prayer.

"I didn't like to question him. It was enough to have him
safe. If you must know, I think Christopher is as confused
as I am. That was the fool word I had to use with him.
Confusion. Isn't that a sick joke? There was *confusion*
over who exactly was his father. Well, at least he knows
now—and he seems pretty happy about it. So thank God
for that! Let's go back into the living room. You're going
to have to open up a little, Charlotte. If only for our son's
sake."

He came around to her, taking her firmly by her upper
arms.

For a split second she was elsewhere. A different time.
A different place. A very different man. Bad memories
surfaced, caught her up so strongly she visibly cringed.
Then, realising what she had done—this was *Rohan*—she
took a great gulp of air.

Rohan stared at her, astounded. "I can't possibly be hurting you." Nevertheless he slackened his grip. "For God's
sake, Charlotte, what's *that* all about?"

She put her hand to her mouth. She was a mere heartbeat

away from telling him the whole shocking story. Only then she would lose his respect.

"You just *cringed* from me." Rohan tried very hard to speak gently. "Surely you didn't think I was about to hit you?"

"Of course not." She cursed herself for her involuntary action. "To tell the truth, I don't know what I'm doing."

"Charlotte, I wouldn't *dream* of hurting you."

"Rohan, I know that." She gave a desperate little moan, spent with emotion, letting her head fall forward against his chest.

"What am I going to do with you?" He began to rock her light body as if she were an inconsolable child. He'd used to think it quite possible to die of love for Charlotte. He still did. "You can't put me off, Charlotte." He lifted her chin, seeing his reflection in her eyes. "Tell me exactly what Christopher heard. Only then will I take you home. It's up to you. I need to be able to combat the fears my son has. We can't keep our history under wraps for much longer. Your father might have had blinkers on, but anyone with a sharp pair of eyes in their head will recognise me in Christopher. We both know that. It's all going to come out."

"I know." There was absolute certainty in her voice.

"You say that like you're in despair." He was grappling with the sexual hunger that had started to roar through him. "Don't you *want* the world to know Christopher is my son?"

She pressed her fingers against his mouth. "Rohan, the news will shock so many people. I don't really count my ex-in-laws among them—" she laughed raggedly "—but I must tell you I'm *elated* Chrissie has taken the revelation you're his real father in his stride. It has to be some deep primal recognition. But he must be wondering how it all

happened. How I married Martyn. How we are Prescotts.
And there's Martyn's tragic accident. Sooner or later someone is going to tell him there was a young woman in the
car with the man he thought was his father. God, *I* can't
handle it all. How can *he*? He's seven years old."

"Well, he's doing fine so far," Rohan pointed out tersely.
"Come into the living room. We can work it out together,
Charlotte. Life is full of revelations. People have to live
with them every day. Betrayed people. I want to marry
you. I'm going to marry you. Christopher should never be
parted from his mother, and he's my son. We can't go our
separate ways. That's not possible. I want to look after you
both. Maybe it isn't happening the way I always planned,
but it *is* happening. And soon."

He didn't say a word until she had finished telling him of
her mother's visit. "She couldn't have been more unpleasant—"

"Vicious, don't you mean?" His fire-blue eyes blazed.

"She didn't know Christopher was at home." Of all
things, she was now defending her indefensible mother.
"The *one* day he misses school, my mother turns up."

"Christopher said he ran off before he heard the lot."

"He heard more than enough," she said painfully. "He
heard my mother say I had sex with you *and* Martyn."

"Well, you did, didn't you?" he challenged bleakly.
"Does he know what 'having sex' means?"

She was so upset she averted her face. "The things he
knows *amaze* me. I don't know if he's got right down to
the '*hows*'. Dad is very involved in his education. They do
a lot together. But Dad would never get into that particular
area. He would regard Chrissie as far too young. It's all
history, geography, the moon, the stars, the earth—things
like that."

"Oh, Charlotte!" He felt close to defeat. "What happened to us?"

A great swath of her hair fell forward against her cheek. "I'm not proud of myself, Rohan. But I have to ask you to take pity on me. I can't take any more tonight. Tomorrow, maybe."

"Okay. I'll take you home. I have to go back to Sydney in the morning. I have an important meeting I had to cancel today. You'll be all right? I'll come back as soon as I can. We have to decide what's best to do. Your father has had a big shock too."

Charlotte gave a little sob. "There's no accounting for reactions. He did get a shock, but he's over it already. My mother's *performance* guaranteed that. You know, he's wasted years pining for her."

His mouth twisted at the irony. "Well, now he's seen her true colours. Your father is a handsome, virile man. He should remarry."

"Maybe he might now. Lord knows there are several very attractive eligible women in the Valley who would jump at the chance of becoming the second Mrs Marsdon. The years that one wastes!" She lifted her eyes to his. They were full of tears.

"Charlie, don't do this," he groaned, his voice deepening with emotion. "I hunger and thirst for you. I want to keep you here, but I can't. Don't cry. *Please.* You cry, and I warn you my feelings will get the better of me."

"So take me home," she burst out wildly, and yet she surged towards him.

He caught her as she all but threw herself at him, trying to suppress the raging fire of desire before it got totally out of hand.

"Rohan, I'm so *afraid*!"

"Of what? *Tell* me." He felt overwhelmingly protective.

"Of the things that might happen."

"So we've got a fair bit of explaining to do?" He thought that was what she meant. Gently he smoothed damp strands of her hair from her face. "We'll do it together. We speak to the Prescotts together. You clearly think they've had suspicions for some time. Did you love Martyn? Just a little? It's okay to tell me."

Once she'd had a good deal of affection for Martyn. As had he. Martyn Prescott had been an integral part of their daily lives.

"Who said anything about my loving Martyn?"

She'd shocked him with her throbbing answer. The *sob* in her voice. The sheer force of *repugnance* in her face. The stormy expression that swept into her lustrous green eyes took him totally unawares.

He stared down at her. "You blamed him for all the women? Martyn wasn't *really* a womaniser. He was obsessed with *you*. Perhaps he went after comfort elsewhere when you couldn't give him what he wanted?'

"Don't think I didn't try!" Her response was fiery. "I married him. I told you—I thought my unborn child was his. I thought I had a duty to marry him. You were thousands of miles away, on the other side of the continent. Four months can be an eternity. You thought money was important to me. It wasn't. *You* were. You have the mindset of a man who thinks his main job in life is to offer the woman he loves security."

"Well, isn't it?" He caught her beautiful face in his two hands, her hair a golden cloud around her face.

"No—no!"

He'd had enough. More than enough. Heart hammering,

he stopped her mouth with his own, taking a firm and desperate hold on her as though he would never let her get away. Only she returned his deep, passionate kiss, pressing her body ever closer against his, her own hunger, longing, love, hot and fierce.

"Charlotte!" At the fervour of her response, his hand moved to her breast. He knew the flimsy top would come off easily. Next the skirt. He belonged to this woman and no one else. She belonged to him.

Both of them had caught fire. Their mouths remained locked until they had to draw apart just to catch breath. There was no question of stopping. No question of saying *no* to the ecstasy on offer. They only had to come together for the fires of desire to crackle, burn, and then within moments turn into a raging inferno.

He drew her down onto the rug where they stood.

CHAPTER TEN

CHRISTOPHER, surprisingly none the worse for the traumatic events of the day before, insisted on going to school.

"I have to tell everyone I must have been delirious to do anything so stupid." He had worked out his explanation in advance. "I *did* have a high temperature, didn't I. Mummy?"

"Well, it didn't get to the scalding stage, but, yes, your temperature *was* higher than normal for some hours."

"Then that will have to do." He could never tell anyone the things his dreadful grandmother had screeched. He was still trying to figure them out.

"I'll come into school with you," Charlotte said. "Your headmaster turned out to search for you. So did the other teachers. I won't ever forget that."

Christopher looked more mortified than gratified. "I never knew people were going to search for me," he said unhappily. "I'll never do anything so stupid again."

She had to see the very calmness of his reaction had a great deal to do with his extraordinary emotional bond with Rohan. Rohan had come for him. Rohan had found him when no one else could. Rohan was now established as his *real* father, and that greatly reinforced Christopher's support base. Whatever the shock waves, they clearly hadn't overwhelmed their son. Christopher, a male child, saw

Rohan as supremely strong and capable. A father he could look up to. Two parents clearly *were* better than one. She agreed with that at every level.

The big dilemma actually centred around *her*. She had to go to her ex-in-laws and tell them exactly how it had been. She would not expose Martyn. She had no wish to bring extra pain on the Prescotts who, apart from Gordon, had never really treated her as "family". Every one in the Valley knew of the intense bond between her and the young Rohan Costello. Martyn came in second best. It didn't sit well with Mrs Prescott or Nicole, who had grown up un-wavering in her jealousy of the young woman who became her sister-in-law. Charlotte always had the feeling Nicole would have been hostile towards her even if there had been no Rohan. Perhaps she had made Nicole feel wanting in the femininity stakes.

Mrs Ellory, the Prescotts' long-time housekeeper, greeted her at the door, remarkably pleased at seeing Charlotte again. She had been told when Charlotte was due to arrive, as Charlotte had rung ahead to ask if it would be convenient if she called in.

The answer from Mrs Prescott couldn't have been more direct. "Yes," she'd said, and hung up.

"And Christopher? He's all right this morning?"

Charlotte smiled, remembering how kind Mrs Ellory had been to her little boy. "Insisted on going to school."

"Amazing what children get up to," Mrs Ellroy said. "But all's well that ends well. Mrs Prescott and Nicole are waiting for you in the Garden Room, Charlotte. Go through. I'll be bringing morning tea directly. Lovely to see you, Charlotte. I've missed you and young Christopher."

"We've missed you too, Mrs Ellory." It was perfectly

true. Sometimes she had thought "Ellie", as Christopher had called her, was her only real friend in the house.

When Charlotte walked into the Garden Room, with its beautiful display of plants and hanging baskets, neither her ex-mother-in-law nor Nicole spoke.

So that was the way it was going to be.

It was extremely unnerving, but she had to steel her resolve. If she and Rohan were to marry in a few months' time there were facts all of them had to contend with. No matter how badly she wanted to be away from here, she had no option but to pay the Prescotts the courtesy of letting them know of her plans. Though nothing had been said, Charlotte felt in her bones Mrs Prescott had come to realise Christopher wasn't her grandson. But at the beginning Martyn had been so obsessive about her. It had been as though she was the only girl in the world who could make him happy. And what Martyn wanted, Martyn got.

Rohan concluded his meeting much earlier than expected. A successful deal had been struck, with big gains for both sides. There were other pressing matters that needed his attention, but he was feeling uncommonly anxious. He knew he and Charlotte had to confront the Prescotts. They had a need and a *right* to know what he and Charlotte had planned. Charlotte believed the Prescotts already knew Christopher wasn't Martyn's child, but it would have to be stated at their meeting. Secrets might take years to come out, but they rarely remained secret for ever. In their case, with Christopher so closely resembling Rohan, discovery was imminent.

He picked up the phone, requesting that the company helicopter—on stand-by—be ready for a return flight to the Valley. He needed to be with Charlotte. He felt deep inside him that life with Martyn had damaged her. That the once highly eligible and attractive Martyn Prescott, admired by many young women in the Valley, while full of fun and good company, had apparently not matured into a strong character. He had never apologised to him or his mother for the damaging scenario he had come up with for that tragic day on the river. That was the problem with Martyn. He couldn't accept responsibility for his actions. Martyn had made life far harder for Rohan and his innocent mother. He had turned Charlotte's mother against them. The outright lies and the half truths had left unresolvable griefs.

The Prescott housekeeper, Mrs Ellory, was passing through the entrance hall of High Grove as Rohan approached the front door. Vivian Marsdon had directed him there.

"Charlotte wanted to assure them Chrissie is safe. Also to thank Gordon, if he's around, for his efforts," Marsdon had said.

That piece of news had hit Rohan like an actual blow. "You shouldn't have let her go, sir. I told Charlotte when she decided it was time to talk to the Prescotts I would go with her. How long ago did she leave?"

"Not five minutes." Vivian had been thoroughly flustered. "That's why I'm so very surprised to see *you*. We thought you were staying in Sydney."

"I had concerns. Intuitions. Anyway, I can't stop. I'm going after her. Could I borrow your car?"

"Of course. I'll get the keys."

"Well, this *is* a day for nice surprises." Mrs Ellory came to the door to greet him. "You look marvellous, Rohan. I couldn't be more thrilled you're back in the Valley. People are quite excited by your plans. More jobs. More prosperity."

"I'm glad to hear that, Mrs Ellory," Rohan said, and, getting to the point, "Do you know where Charlotte is?"

"They're in the Garden Room—at the back of the house." She looked into Rohan Costello's blazing eyes. The boy Christopher had eyes like that. "I probably shouldn't say this, but I'm glad you're here. Charlotte needs support in this house. Do you want me to take you through?"

"I'll go the back way, Mrs Ellory. It's shorter."

"And you'll be able to gauge how things are going," she whispered back. "I only stay for Mr Prescott, you know. Mrs Prescott has turned into a very bitter woman. As for Nicole…!" She rolled her eyes.

Rohan gave her quick salute, then ran down a short flight of stone steps. He could hear raised voices as he rounded the side of the house.

Nicole. Such a difficult creature, Nicole. Martyn had inherited all the looks and the charm in the family.

"You're the very *opposite* of the way you look and sound!" the jealous and insecure young woman was lashing out.

"Oh, Nicole, do be quiet," her mother cut in sharply, as if to a child. "You brought nothing but suffering to my son, Charlotte. You couldn't face the world pregnant and unmarried, and Costello was nowhere around. But Martyn *was*. Martyn adored you. God knows why, when you were so involved with Costello. And Costello was dirt-poor. He had nothing. His mother struggled just to put food on the table. I paid her more than she was worth."

"Are you *serious*?" Charlotte countered, in a clear, firm voice.

Rohan knew perfectly well the right thing to do was to go in and announce himself. Instead he stood frozen, able to hear perfectly but unable to be seen. Maybe in staying where he was he could make some sense of everything that had transpired. Charlotte was keeping so much from him. It might advantage him to stay where he was until it became obvious she needed his help.

"You never overpaid *anyone*, Lesley. A plain statement of fact. You were tight-fisted with everyone but Martyn. Nicole missed out. You owed her far more time and attention. Gordon was the kind, generous one—"

"None of your business any more," Lesley Prescott cut her off, affronted. "So, you and Costello intend to marry?"

"That's what I've come to tell you, Lesley. You have a right to know."

"Oh, how simply wonderful that you think so!" Lesley Prescott crowed. "May I ask when the great day is to be?"

"Early next year."

"No doubt with your son as pageboy?" she sneered. "You take comfort where you can find it, don't you, Charlotte? Costello has made quite a name for himself now."

"You know he's Christopher's father?"

There was a terrible note in Lesley Prescott's voice. "We didn't *know* at the beginning. We knew you and Martyn were dating when Costello wasn't around. You used my son."

"I didn't *use* Martyn," Charlotte said sadly. "I thought he was my friend—"

"And threw in a little sex," Nicole broke in with malice. "You'd been getting plenty with Costello. You must have missed it when he was away. Martyn was there. He was stupid enough to stay in love with you. That's what you do, isn't it? *Use* men."

High time to announce his presence, Rohan decided— only Charlotte's answer riveted him to the spot.

"It was Martyn who used *me*, Nicole."

No mistaking the utter gravity of her tone.

"Which means exactly what?" Lesley Prescott barked out. "You got caught out, didn't you? You never meant to fall pregnant by my son. It was always Costello you wanted."

"Always," Charlotte agreed. "How could I possibly have turned to Martyn after Rohan? Martyn was a liar. Lying was part of his nature. And it started early. It was Martyn who challenged Mattie to swim the river."

"Oh, yeah!" Nicole burst out, ample chest heaving.

"You knew your brother more than you care to admit, Nicole. You *know* he hit me. Not in the early years, but towards the end, when he was so unhappy. You *know*, but you don't dare speak the truth in front of your mother."

Lesley Prescott's face, like Charlotte's, was showing the depth of her upset. "Now it's your turn to lie," she cried. "My son would *never* do such a thing. I never saw any evidence of abuse. It wouldn't have been tolerated. Martyn adored you, even when he was off with women hardly more than prostitutes."

"It doesn't matter now, Lesley. I'm sorry I told you." Charlotte gave vent to a weary sigh.

"If my son struck you, you must have deserved it." Lesley Prescott launched into mitigation. In truth, she was shocked by the idea Martyn might have struck his beautiful wife. "You were withholding your marital obligations. You weren't a proper wife to him. Did you never consider he had saved you from a scandal? He *married* you. He thought the child was his. We all did.'

"I did too, Lesley," Charlotte responded soberly. "I was so ill-informed in those days I made a huge mistake. Rohan remains the love of my life. I was on the pill when I was with him. We couldn't afford for me to fall pregnant. I didn't realise at the time things can go wrong. I had a bout of sickness that interfered with the efficacy of the pill. I didn't know then. I know now."

"So you didn't take the pill with Martyn? Is that it?" Lesley scoffed, unable to abandon the pretence that her son had been perfect.

"With Rohan away, I stopped. There was no reason to keep on taking it until Rohan returned."

"What a risk you took with Martyn, then!" Lesley said bitterly. "You fed off his admiration and love. You seduced him, didn't you?"

"You were missing all that hot sex." Nicole, who had never had sex—hot or cold—laughed crudely.

"Do shut up, Nicole. Get a life. *Do* something about yourself," Charlotte told her—not without pity. She turned to her ex-mother-in-law. "I'm truly sorry, Lesley, for all the tragic things that have happened. I grieved for Martyn too, you know."

Lesley glared at her darkly. "Rubbish! In the olden days, Charlotte Marsdon, you would have been burned at the stake."

Something in Rohan snapped. He moved swiftly, the heart torn out of him.

"Look me in the face and tell me you're lying!" Lesley Prescott was crying. "You seduced my son. You probably got a huge kick out of it. After all, he worshipped the ground you walked on. You had to have *him* too."

Charlotte spoke so quietly Rohan could barely hear what she was saying. Then it hit him with horrified amazement.

"Martyn raped me."

He staggered as if at a king hit.

Martyn, their friend from early childhood, had raped her?

Inside the room Lesley Prescott was going berserk, also

horrified by *that* word. "Liar!" she shouted, waving her arms wildly in the air.

"What do *you* think, Nicole?" Charlotte gave the younger woman a chance to redeem herself. "You're the *one* person who knows what Martyn was like. Rohan doesn't know. I was too ashamed to tell him."

"Good!" Nicole actually looked a little crazy. "Why didn't you watch out for him, you fool?"

Lesley Prescott made a yelping sound, rounding on her daughter, astounded. "What in God's name are you talking about?"

"Wake up, Mum," Nicole said with undisguised contempt. "You and your Martyn. Your can-do-no-wrong son. Martyn was a bastard. I *knew* he was hitting Charlotte. It must have been awful for her. I *knew* he'd forced sex on her. He *told* me. He boasted about it. How else was he going to get her away from Rohan Costello?"

So there it is, Rohan's inner voice said. *The direst of secrets revealed.*

Hot blood rose like a tide, forming a red mist before his eyes. *His beautiful Charlotte.* He hadn't been there to protect or defend her. She would have trusted Martyn. If Martyn weren't dead, he thought he would kill him.

Eyes ablaze, Rohan rapped hard on the glass door with his knuckles, startling all three women. They turned their heads in unison, all three appalled.

"What a contemptible creature you are, Nicole," he said. "In your own way you're as guilty as your cowardly brother. Time to go, Charlotte." He issued the command. "I told you not to come here without me. These people have never done you any good."

Lesley Prescott felt intimidated to the bone. When exactly had young Rohan Costello become such a commanding figure? "How dare you come into my home unannounced?" she asked hoarsely.

"That wasn't my intention, Mrs Prescott. Only one never knows what one might learn by staying out of sight. I'd intended to announce myself—only in following your riveting conversation I have been able to learn the truth. Charlotte was protecting your sick bully of a son, Mrs Prescott. Think of the nobility of that. She kept silent. A mother herself, she didn't want to hurt *you*. You can only blame yourself for provoking her now. And I'm glad. Because now we have the truth of why Charlotte married Martyn. She believed herself pregnant by him. She believed marrying him was the proper course to take. Her parents failed her. *I* failed her—going so far away, leaving cunning, manipulative Martyn to seize his moment. It was always his way. Charlotte provided a few clues along the way, but I was so self-involved I was blind to them. Martyn was a coward, and a traitor to our lifelong friendship."

As Rohan moved further into the room both Prescott women stumbled back.

When exactly had Martyn turned bad? Lesley Prescott asked herself. How much of it was her fault? "Martyn is dead," she said, her face contorted with pain.

It took everything Rohan had to fall back on forgiveness. For the mother. Not the son. "Despite all the pain Martyn inflicted on us, Mrs Prescott, Charlotte and I *are* saddened by that. Come here to me, Charlotte." He held out an imperative hand.

Charlotte rushed to him, desperate for his comfort.

"The Valley will never accept you," Lesley Prescott told them heavily.

Rohan returned her a cool, confident look. "You're wrong about that, Mrs Prescott. I have big plans for the Valley. My enterprises will be creating a lot of jobs, and the von Luckners have come on board with their great expertise. Charlotte Vale will be producing ultra-premium wines. I have plans for the olive groves as well. Plans for a first-class restaurant. I think you'll find the Valley more than happy about it all after they absorb the initial shock that Christopher is my son. But then, I think a lot of people already know. We really should present some sort of a united front, Mrs Prescott. Charlotte and I want no enmity. The *one* person you should be angry at—the *one* person who betrayed us all—is Martyn. And your daughter definitely needs counselling. Jealousy is a cancer. She needs treatment. Neither of you should want to make an enemy of me," he warned, his hand tightening on Charlotte's. "Time to leave, Charlotte. It's over now."

"Are you okay to drive?" Rohan asked as they walked to her car. She was as pale as a lily.

"I'm fine, Rohan. Don't worry about me." She looked away to her father's Mercedes. "Dad lent it to you?"

"No problem. I took the chopper from Sydney. I was anxious about you. What time do you pick up Christopher?" He opened her car door, waiting for her to get behind the wheel.

"I'm always there ten minutes early, so two-fifty."

"I'll come with you. Follow me back to Riverbend."

She should have felt as if a great burden had been lifted from her shoulders. Instead she wondered what Rohan thought of her under his mask of gentleness and concern. However much he understood, his respect for her would have plummeted. She had never intended to tell him what Martyn had done. She had wanted to keep her self-respect.

It was well-documented the world over that innocent victims of abuse—physical and mental—can feel an irrational, yet powerful sense of guilt.

Charlotte had been one of them—much like an abused child. But the dark cloud that had hung over her for so long was about to be totally dispersed.

Mrs Burch opened the front door. She looked surprised to see them, noting with concern that both of them looked what she later described to her husband as "traumatised".

"Tea, thank you, Louise." Rohan kept a steadying hand on Charlotte. "We'll have it in the library."

Mrs Burch hurried away. All sorts of strange things were happening in the Valley. Beautiful Charlotte Prescott was clearly in shock. But if she was in any kind of trouble she had come to the right man.

Mrs Burch soon returned, wheeling a trolley set with tea things and a plate of home-baked cookies. She withdrew quietly, shutting the library door after her.

Rohan poured Charlotte a cup of tea. He added a little milk and two teaspoons of sugar, even though he knew she didn't take sugar in her tea. "Drink it down."

She responded with a quiet little smile.

Rohan took his tea black, but at the last moment added a teaspoon of sugar. "I need it," he said laconically, sinking into one of the burgundy leather armchairs that surrounded a reading table.

He allowed Charlotte to finish her tea in peace, then took the cup and saucer from her, leading her to the sofa.

"You're in no way to blame, Charlotte." He covered her hands with his own. "As I said to Mrs Prescott, we all failed you when you desperately needed help. I should accept the blame as I never considered for a moment that Martyn would force himself on you. My trust in him was woefully misplaced. Martyn always had his problems, but

I never believed he would hurt you. What a fool I've been!"
He sighed deeply. "The closest friends have been known to
turn into aggressors, even murderers. But Martyn! What a
catastrophe! You didn't think to let me know?"

She didn't lift her head, though relief was intensifying
in her.

"You didn't think to go to my mother?" he continued,
stroking her hand. "I know you couldn't go to *yours*!"

Charlotte spoke up. "I began to experience morning
sickness very early on, Rohan. I knew what was happening
to me. I believed I was pregnant by Martyn. How could I
let *you* of all people know? I had betrayed our love. How
could I go to your mother, tell her I was carrying Martyn
Prescott's baby? I could never put voice to the fact he had
forced me. I was suffering such shame. I *did* know Martyn
had always been in love with me. I felt I *should* have fore-
seen the danger. Afterwards he couldn't have been more
contrite. More sad and sorry."

"They *all* are!" Rohan said grimly.

"I suppose… Martyn broke down in tears, begging me
to forgive him. I tried hard, but I *did* keep some part of
myself remote."

"The sad and sorry bit doesn't jell with Nicole's damning
comments."

"No. But he *did* need my love, Rohan. He begged for it.
I tried to enter his world. It was a disaster. As time went
on his attitude changed. Became belligerent."

"He began to hit you." Rohan was barely holding down
his rage. "How low can a man sink? But then he wasn't a
man, was he?"

"In many ways he was like a greedy child who needed
instant gratification. But what he did weighed very heavily
on him I think."

Rohan couldn't conceal his disgust. "Stop making excuses for Martyn, Charlotte."

She looked into his blazing eyes. "Maybe it lessens *my* guilt."

"*No* guilt." Rohan gave his verdict.

"Any number of girls and women are brave enough to go it alone."

"And any number *aren't*. Not at eighteen, without support. I realise how frightened you must have been. How trapped. You had to endure years of being victimised by Martyn. You couldn't tell your father? Even Gordon Prescott? He would never have countenanced abuse. Nicole shouldn't have either. That woman needs a good psychiatrist."

"Maybe I do too."

"So does anyone who suffers abuse in silence." His voice was as gentle as any man's could be. "Forgive me for making moral judgements, my love. You were trying to tell me. I was too full of my own griefs. I love you, Charlotte. I've never stopped loving you. I gave you my heart. I don't want it back. We created our monster. His name was Martyn. Time now to lay poor Martyn to rest."

Rohan drew her to her feet. "Let's stroll down to the river. I feel like being out in the clean fresh air."

They walked hand in hand through the gardens, past the beds flushed with flowers, right down to the edge of the river. It sparkled in the sunshine, the glassy surface mantled with thousands of dancing sequins.

"If we could only go back in time," she said softly. "Mattie would be alive. You and I would be happily married. You would have asked Martyn to be your best man."

"A terrible irony in that!" He gathered her into his

embrace. "Don't let's speak of Martyn any more. Not in this place. We can never go back, however much we want to. What we *can* do is take control of our future. We're going to live it the way it would have been. Only better. We have one another. And we have our beautiful son. We're blessed. Do you love me, Charlotte?" He turned her face up to him, blue gaze intent.

"Heart and soul!" Her lovely smile was like a sunburst. "I've been so *alone* without you."

He held her to him. "We're together now. You have nothing and no one to fear. The sad years are over. A few hurdles won't go away like magic, but we'll contend with them. Believe me?" he asked.

"My belief in you has never wavered, Rohan," she answered without hesitation. "I can handle anything with you by my side." She paused, then added a little shakily, "I thought I would die of shame if you found out."

"Ah, *no*!" he groaned. "I love you, Charlotte. I'll always take care of you." He bent his head, touching his forehead to hers, then he kissed her so sweetly, so deeply, so passionately, the tormented element within her broke like a severed twine. "We have peace now, Charlotte," he murmured. "We have our whole lives. Ready to marry me?"

The world seemed bathed in a gorgeous brightness. It was as though the sun, moon and stars had come out together. *"I can't wait!"* she cried ecstatically.

Above them in the trees an invisible bird began to sing. The sound was so beautiful, so flute-like, so poignant, so far-carrying it seemed to travel the length and breadth of the river.

"Do you suppose that's Mattie?" Rohan asked, lifting his head.

Charlotte too was filled with such a sense of wonder she was nearly weeping. She stared above her into the green density of leaves. Hard to see a bird, but there was such a *glow*. It was spilling out of the trees. Pouring over them. "Why not?" she breathed.

Mattie wasn't really dead. He was an angel.

"Who knows what forces are at work in this universe?" Rohan mused, putting his arm around her slender shoulders. "We should be getting back, my love. It's almost time to pick up our son."

Its song completed, the invisible bird rose up into the sky on opalescent wings. It made a full circuit around Charlotte and Rohan before it disappeared.

Had it even been there?

THE SUMMER THEY
NEVER FORGOT

KANDY SHEPHERD

CHAPTER ONE

ON SANDY ADAMS'S thirtieth birthday—which was also the day the man she'd lived with for two years was getting married to another woman—she decided to run away.

No. Not run away. *Find a new perspective.*

Yes, that sounded good. Positive. Affirming. Challenging.

No way would she give even a second's thought to any more heartbreak.

She'd taken the first step by driving the heck out of Sydney and heading south—her ultimate destination: Melbourne, a thousand kilometres away. On a whim, she'd chosen to take the slower, scenic route to Melbourne on the old Princes Highway. There was time, and it went through areas she thought were among the most beautiful in the state of New South Wales.

Alone and loving it, she repeated to herself as she drove.

Say it enough times and she might even start to believe it.

Somewhere between the seaside town of Kiama and the quaint village of Berry, with home two hours behind her, she pulled her lime-green Beetle off onto a safe lay-by. But she only allowed herself a moment to stretch out her cramped muscles and admire the rolling green hills and breathtaking blue expanse of the Pacific Ocean before she got back in the car. The February heat made it too hot to stay outside for too long.

From her handbag she pulled out her new notebook, a birthday present from her five-year-old niece. There was a pink fairy on the cover and the glitter from its wings had already shed all through Sandy's bag. It came with a shocking-pink pen. She nibbled on the pen for a long moment.

Then, with a flourish, she headed up the page 'Thirtieth Birthday Resolutions' and started to scribble in pink ink.

1. Get as far away from Sydney as possible while remaining in realms of civilisation and within reach of a good latte.

2. Find new job where can be own boss.

She underscored the words 'own boss' three times, so hard she nearly tore the paper.

3. Find kind, interesting man with no hang-ups who loves me the way I am and who wants to get married and have lots of kids.

She crossed out 'lots of kids' and wrote instead '*three kids*'—then added, '*two girls and a boy*'. When it came to writing down goals there was no harm in being specific. So she also added, '*Man who in no way resembles That-Jerk-Jason*'.

She went over the word 'jerk' twice and finished with the date and an extravagant flourish. Done.

She liked making lists. She felt they gave her some degree of control over a life that had gone unexpectedly pear-shaped. But three goals were probably all she could cope with right now. The resolutions could be revisited once she'd got to her destination.

She put the notebook back into her bag and slid the car back onto the highway.

An hour or so later farmland had made way for bushland

and the sides of the road were lined with eucalypt forest. Her shoulders ached from driving and thoughts of a break for something to eat were at the front of her mind. When she saw the signpost to Dolphin Bay it took only a second for her to decide to throw the car into a left turn.

It was a purely reflex action. She'd planned to stop at one of the beachside towns along the way for lunch and a swim. But she hadn't given sleepy Dolphin Bay a thought for years. She'd adored the south coast when she was a kid—had spent two idyllic summer holidays at different resort towns with her family, revelling in the freedom of being let off the leash of the rigorous study schedule her father had set her during the school year. But one summer the family had stayed in Dolphin Bay for the first time and everything had changed.

At the age of eighteen, she'd fallen in love with Ben. Tall, blond, surfer dude Ben, with the lazy smile and the muscles to die for. He'd been exciting, forbidden and fun. At the same time he'd been a real friend: supportive, encouraging—all the things she'd never dreamed a boy could be.

Then there'd been the kisses. The passionate, exciting, first-love kisses that had surprised her for years afterwards by sneaking into her dreams.

Sandy took her foot off the accelerator pedal and prepared to brake and turn back. She'd closed the door on so many of the bittersweet memories of that summer. Was it wise to nudge it open again by even a fraction?

But how could it hurt to drop in to Dolphin Bay for lunch? It was her birthday, after all, and she couldn't remember the last proper meal she'd eaten. She might even book into Morgan's Guesthouse and stay the night.

She put her foot back to the accelerator, too excited at the thought of seeing Dolphin Bay again to delay any further.

As she cruised into the main street that ran between the rows of shops and the waterfront, excitement melted down in a cold rush of disappointment. She'd made a big mistake.

The classic mistake of expecting things to stay the same. She hadn't been to Dolphin Bay for twelve years. And now she scarcely recognised it.

Determined not to give in to any kind of let-down feelings, she parked not far from the wasn't-there-last-time information kiosk, got out, locked the car and walked around, trying to orientate herself.

The southern end of the bay was enclosed by old-fashioned rock sea walls to form a small, safe harbour. It seemed much the same, with a mix of pleasure boats and fishing vessels bobbing on the water. The typically Australian old pub, with its iron lace balconies was the same too.

But gone was the beaten-up old jetty. It had been replaced by a sleek new pier and a marina, a fishing charter business, and a whale-and dolphin-watching centre topped with a large fibreglass dolphin with an inane painted grin that, in spite of her shock, made her smile. Adjoining was a row of upmarket shops and galleries. The fish and chip shop, where she'd squabbled with her sister over the last chip eaten straight from the vinegar-soaked paper, had been pulled down to make way for a trendy café. The dusty general store was now a fashionable boutique.

And, even though it was February and the school holidays were over, there were people strolling, browsing, licking on ice cream cones—more people than she could remember ever seeing in Dolphin Bay.

For a moment disappointment almost won. But she laughed out loud when she noticed the rubbish bins that sat out on the footpath. Each was in the shape of a dolphin with its mouth wide open.

They were absolute kitsch, but she fell in love with them all over again. Surreptitiously, she patted one on its fibreglass snout. 'Delighted you're still here,' she whispered.

Then, when she looked more closely around her, she noticed that in spite of the new sophistication every business still sported a dolphin motif in some form or another, from a discreet sticker to a carved wooden awning.

And she'd bet Morgan's Guesthouse at the northern end of the bay wouldn't have changed. The rambling weatherboard building, dating from the 1920s, would certainly have some sort of a heritage preservation order on it. It was part of the history of the town.

In her mind's eye she could see the guesthouse the way it had been that magic summer. The shuttered windows, the banks of blue and purple hydrangeas her mother had loved, the old sand tennis court where she'd played hit-and-giggle games with Ben. She hoped it hadn't changed too much.

As she approached the tourist information kiosk to ask for directions on how to get there she hesitated. Why did she need the guesthouse to be the same?

Did it have something to do with those rapidly returning memories of Ben Morgan? Ben, nineteen to her eighteen, the surfer hunk all the girls had had wild crushes on.

Around from the bay, accessed via a boardwalk, was a magnificent surf beach. When Ben had ridden his board, harnessing the power of the waves like some suntanned young god, there had always been a giggling gaggle of admiring girls on the sand.

She'd never been one of them. No, she'd stood on the sidelines, never daring to dream he'd see her as anything but a guest staying for two weeks with her family at his parents' guesthouse.

But, to her amazement and joy, he'd chosen *her*. And then the sun had really started to shine that long-ago summer.

'Morgan's Guesthouse?' said the woman manning the information kiosk. 'Sorry, love, I've never heard of it.'

'The old wooden building at the northern end of the bay,' Sandy prompted.

'There's only the Hotel Harbourside there,' the woman said. 'It's a modern place—been there as long as I've been in town.'

Sandy thanked her and walked away, a little confused.

But she gasped when she saw the stark, modern structure of the luxury hotel that had replaced the charming old weatherboard guesthouse. Its roofline paid some kind of homage to the old-fashioned peaked roof that had stood there the last time she had visited Dolphin Bay, but the concrete and steel of its construction did not. The hotel took up the footprint of the original building and gardens, and rose several floors higher.

Hotel Harbourside? She'd call it Hotel Hideous.

She took a deep, calming breath. Then forced herself to think positive. The new hotel might lack the appeal of the old guesthouse but she'd bet it would be air conditioned and would almost certainly have a decent restaurant. Just the place for a solo thirtieth birthday lunch.

And as she stood on the steps that led from the beach to the hotel and closed her eyes, breathed in the salty air, felt the heat shimmering from the sand, listened to the sound of the water lapping at the edge of the breakwater, she could almost imagine everything was the same as it had been.

Almost.

The interior of the restaurant was all glass, steel and smart design. What a difference from the old guesthouse dining room, with its mismatched wooden chairs, well-worn old table and stacks of board games for ruthlessly played after-dinner tournaments. But the windows that looked out over the bay framed a view that was much the same as it had always been—although now a fleet of dolphin-watching boats plied its tourist trade across the horizon.

She found a table in the corner furthest from the bar and sat down. She took off her hat and squashed it in her bag but kept her sunglasses on. Behind them she felt safer. Protected. Less vulnerable, she had to admit to herself.

She refused to allow even a smidgeon of self-pity to intrude as she celebrated her thirtieth birthday all by herself whilst at the same time her ex Jason was preparing to walk down the aisle.

Casting her eye over the menu, Sandy was startled by a burst of masculine laughter over the chatter from the bar. As that sound soared back into her memory her heart gave an excited leap of recognition. No other man's laughter could sound like that.

Rich. Warm. Unforgettable.

Ben.

He hadn't been at the bar when she'd walked in. She'd swear to it. Unless he'd changed beyond all recognition.

She was afraid to look up. Afraid of being disappointed. Afraid of what she might say, do, to the first man to have broken her heart.

Would she go up and say hello? Or put her hat back on and try to slink out without him seeing her?

Despite her fears, she took off her sunglasses with fingers that weren't quite steady and slowly raised her head.

Her breath caught in her throat and she felt the blood drain from her face. He stood with his profile towards her, but it was definitely Ben Morgan: broad-shouldered, towering above the other men in the bar, talking animatedly with a group of people.

From what she could see from this distance he was as handsome as the day they'd said goodbye. His hair was shorter. He wore tailored shorts and a polo-style shirt instead of the Hawaiian print board shorts and singlet he'd favoured when he was nineteen. He was more muscular. Definitely more grown up.

But he was still Ben.

He said something to the guy standing near him, laughed again at his response. Now, as then, he held the attention of everyone around him.

Did he feel her gaze fixed on him?

Something must have made him turn. As their eyes connected, he froze mid-laugh. Nothing about his expression indicated that he recognised her.

For a long, long moment it seemed as if everyone and everything else in the room fell away. The sound of plates clattering, glasses clinking, and the hum of chatter seemed muted. She realised she was holding her breath.

Ben turned back to the man he'd been talking to, said something, then turned to face her again. This time he smiled, acknowledging her, and she let out her breath in a slow sigh.

He made his way to her table with assured, athletic strides. She watched, mesmerised, taking in the changes wrought by twelve years. The broad-shouldered, tightly muscled body, with not a trace of his teenage gangliness. The solid strength of him. The transformation from boy to man. Oh, yes, the teenage Ben was now very definitely a man.

And hotter than ever.

All her senses screamed that recognition.

He'd reached her before she had a chance to get up from her chair.

'Sandy?'

The voice she hadn't heard for so long was as deep and husky as she remembered. He'd had a man's voice even at nineteen. Though only a year older than her, he'd seemed light years ahead in maturity.

Words of greeting she knew she should utter were wedged in her throat. She coughed. Panicked that she couldn't even manage a hello.

His words filled the void. 'Or are you Alexandra these days?'

He remembered that. Her father had insisted she be called by her full name of Alexandra. But Alexandra was too much of a mouthful, Ben had decided. He'd called her by the name she preferred. From that summer on she'd been Sandy. Except, of course, to her father and mother.

'Who's Alexandra?' she said now, pretending to look around for someone else.

He laughed with what seemed like genuine pleasure to see her. Suddenly she felt her nervousness, her self-consciousness, drop down a notch or two.

She scrambled up from her chair. The small round table was a barrier between her and the man who'd been everything to her twelve years ago. The man she'd thought she'd never see again.

'It's good to see you, Ben,' she said, her voice still more choked than she would have liked it to be.

His face was the same—strong-jawed and handsome— and his eyes were still as blue as the summer sky at noon. Close-cropped dark blond hair replaced the sun-bleached surfer tangle that so long ago she'd thought was the ultimate in cool. There were creases around his eyes that hadn't been there when he was nineteen. And there was a tiny white crescent of a scar on his top lip she didn't remember. But she could still see the boy in the man.

'It's good to see you, too,' he said, in that so-deep-it-bordered-on-gruff voice. 'I recognised you straight away.'

'Me too. I mean, I recognised you too.'

What did he see as he looked at her? What outward signs had the last years of living life full steam ahead left on her?

'You've cut your hair,' he said.

'So have you,' she said, and he smiled.

Automatically her hand went up to touch her head. Of course he would notice. Her brown hair had swung below her waist when she'd last seen him, and she remembered how he'd made her swear never, *ever* to change it. Now it was cut in a chic, city-smart bob and tastefully highlighted.

'But otherwise you haven't changed,' he added in that husky voice. 'Just grown up.'

'It's kind of you to say that,' she said. But she knew how much she'd changed from that girl that summer.

'Mind if I join you?' he asked.

'Of course. Please. I was just having a drink…'

She sat back down and Ben sat in the chair opposite her. His strong, tanned legs were so close they nudged hers as he settled into place. She didn't draw her legs back. The slight pressure of his skin on her skin, although momentary, sent waves of awareness coursing through her. She swallowed hard.

She'd used to think Ben Morgan was the best-looking man she'd ever seen. The twelve intervening years had done nothing to change her opinion. No sophisticated city guy had ever matched up to him. Not even Jason.

She'd left the menu open on the table before her. 'I see you've decided on dessert before your main meal,' Ben said, with that lazy smile which hadn't changed at all.

'I was checking out the salads, actually,' she lied.

'Really?' he said, the smile still in his voice, and the one word said everything.

He'd caught her out. Was teasing her. Like he'd used to do. With no brothers, an all-girls school and zero dating experience, she hadn't been used to boys. Never hurtful or mean, his happy-go-lucky ways had helped get her over that oversensitivity. It was just one of the ways he'd helped her grow up.

'You're right,' she said, relaxing into a smile. 'Old habits die hard. The raspberry brownie with chocolate fudge sauce *does* appeal.' The birthday cake you had when you weren't having a birthday cake. But she wouldn't admit to that.

'That brownie is so good you'll want to order two servings,' he said.

Like you used to.

The unspoken words hung between them. Their eyes met for a moment too long to be comfortable. She was the first to look away.

Ben signalled the waiter. As he waved, Sandy had to suppress a gasp at the ugly raised scars that distorted the palms of his hands. What had happened? A fishing accident?

Quickly she averted her eyes so he wouldn't notice her shock. Or see the questions she didn't dare ask.

Not now. Not yet.

She rushed to fill the silence that had fallen over their table. 'It's been a—'

He finished the sentence for her. 'Long time?'

'Yes,' was all she was able to get out. 'I was only thinking about you a minute ago and wondering...'

She felt the colour rise up her throat to stain her cheeks. As she'd walked away from the information kiosk and towards the hotel hadn't she been remembering how Ben had kissed her all those years ago, as they'd lain entwined on the sand in the shadows at the back of the Morgan family's boat shed? Remembering the promises they'd made to each other between those breathless kisses? Promises she'd really, truly believed.

She felt again as gauche and awkward as she had the night she'd first danced with him, at a bushfire brigade fundraiser dance at the surf club a lifetime ago. Unable to believe that Ben Morgan had actually singled her out from the summer people who'd invaded the locals' dance.

After their second dance together he'd asked her if she had a boyfriend back home. When she'd shaken her head, he'd smiled.

'Good,' he'd said. 'Then I don't have to go up to Sydney and fight him for you.'

She'd been so thrilled she'd actually felt dizzy.

The waiter arrived at their table.

'Can I get you another drink?' Ben asked.

'Um, diet cola, please.'

What was wrong with her? Why was she so jittery and on edge?

As a teenager she'd always felt relaxed with Ben, able to be herself. She'd gone home to Sydney a different person from the one who had arrived for that two-week holiday in Dolphin Bay.

She had to stop being so uptight. This was the same Ben. Older, but still Ben. He seemed the same laid-back guy he'd been as her teenage heartthrob. Except—she suppressed a shudder—for the horrendous scarring on his hands.

'Would you believe this is the first time I've been back this way since that summer?' she said, looking straight into his eyes. She'd used to tell him that eyes so blue were wasted on a man and beg him to swap them for her ordinary hazel-brownish ones.

'It's certainly the first time I've seen you here,' he said easily.

Was he, too, remembering those laughing intimacies they'd once shared? Those long discussions of what they'd do with their lives, full of hopes and dreams and youthful optimism? Their resolve not to let the distance between Dolphin Bay and Sydney stop them from seeing each other again?

If he was, he certainly didn't show it. 'So what brings you back?' he asked.

It seemed a polite, uninterested question—the kind a long-ago acquaintance might ask a scarcely remembered stranger who'd blown unexpectedly into town.

'The sun, the surf and the dolphins?' she said, determined to match his tone.

He smiled. 'The surf's as good as it always was, and the dolphins are still here. But there must be something else to bring a city girl like you to this particular backwater.'

'B...backwater? I wouldn't call it that,' she stuttered. 'I'm sorry if you think I—' The gleam in his blue eyes told her he wasn't serious. She recovered herself. 'I'm on my way from Sydney through to Melbourne. I saw the turn to this wonderful non-backwater town and here I am. On impulse.'

'It's nice you decided to drop in.' His words were casual, just the right thing to say. Almost too casual. 'So, how do you find the place?'

She'd never had to lie with Ben. Still, she was in the habit of being tactful. And this *was* Ben's hometown.

'I can't tell you how overjoyed I was to see those dolphin rubbish bins still there.'

Ben laughed, his strong, even teeth very white against his tan.

That laugh. It still had the power to warm her. Her heart did a curious flipping over thing as she remembered all the laughter they'd shared that long-ago summer. No wonder she'd recognised it instantly.

'Those hellish things,' he said. 'There's always someone on the progress association who wants to rip them out, but they're always shouted down.'

'Thank heaven for that,' she said. 'It wouldn't be Dolphin Bay without them.'

'People have even started a rumour that if the dolphins are removed it will be the end of Dolphin Bay.'

She giggled. 'Seriously?'

'Seriously,' he said, straight-faced. 'The rubbish bins go and as punishment we'll be struck by a tsunami. Or some other calamity.'

He rolled his eyes. Just like he'd used to do. That hidden part of her heart marked 'first love' reacted with a painful lurch. She averted her gaze from his mouth and that intriguing, sexy little scar.

She remembered the hours of surfing with him, playing tennis on that old court out at the back of the guesthouse. The fun. The laughter. Those passionate, heartfelt kisses. Oh, those kisses—his mouth hard and warm and exciting on hers, his tongue exploring, teasing. Her body straining to his…

The memories gave her the courage to ask the question. It was now or never. 'Ben. It was a long time ago. But…but why didn't you write like you said you would?'

For a long moment he didn't answer and she tensed. Then

he shrugged. 'I never was much for letters. After you didn't answer the first two I didn't bother again.'

An edge to his voice hinted that his words weren't as carefree as they seemed. She shook her head in disbelief. 'You wrote me two letters?'

'The day after you went home. Then the week after that. Like I promised to.'

Her mouth went suddenly dry. 'I never got a letter. Never. Or a phone call. I always wondered why…'

No way would she admit how, day after day, she'd hung around the letterbox, hoping against hope that he'd write. Her strict upbringing had meant she was very short on dating experience and vulnerable to doubt.

'Don't chase after boys,' her mother had told her, over and over again. *'Men are hunters. If he's interested he'll come after you. If he doesn't you'll only make a fool of yourself by throwing yourself at him.'*

But in spite of her mother's advice she'd tried to phone Ben. Three times she'd braved a phone call to the guesthouse but had hung up without identifying herself when his father had answered. On the third time his father had told her not to ring again. Had he thought she was a nuisance caller? Or realised it was her and didn't want her bothering his son? Her eighteen-year-old self had assumed the latter.

It had been humiliating. Too humiliating to admit it even now to Ben.

'Your dad probably got to my letters before you could,' said Ben. 'He never approved of me.'

'That's not true,' Sandy stated half-heartedly, knowing she wouldn't put it past her controlling, righteous father to have intercepted any communication from Ben. In fact she and Ben had decided it was best he not phone her because of her father's disapproval of the relationship.

'He's just a small-town Lothario, Alexandra.' Her father's long-ago words echoed in her head. Hardly. Ben had treated

her with the utmost respect. Unlike the private school sons of his friends her father had tried to foist on her.

'Your dad wanted more for you than a small-town fisherman.' Ben's blue eyes were shrewd and piercing. 'And you probably came to agree with him.'

Sandy dropped her gaze and shifted uncomfortably in her seat. Over and over her father had told her to forget about Ben. He wasn't suitable. They came from different worlds. Where was the future for a girl who had academic talents like hers with a boy who'd finished high school but had no intention of going any further?

Underneath it all had been the unspoken message: *He's not good enough for you.*

She'd never believed that—not for a second. But she had come to believe there was no future for them.

Inconsolable after their summer together, she'd sobbed into her pillow at night when Ben hadn't written. Scribbled endless notes to him she'd never had the courage to send.

But he hadn't got in touch and she'd forced herself to forget him. To get over something that obviously hadn't meant anything to him.

'Men make promises they never intend to keep, Alexandra.' How many times had her mother told her that?

Then, once she'd started university in Sydney, Dolphin Bay and Ben Morgan had seemed far away and less and less important. Her father was right—a surfer boyfriend wouldn't have fitted in with her new crowd anyway, she'd told herself. Then there'd been other boys. Other kisses. And she'd been too grown up for family holidays at Dolphin Bay or anywhere else.

Still, there remained a place in her heart that had always stayed a little raw, that hurt if she pulled out her memories and prodded at them.

But Ben had written to her.

She swirled the ice cubes round and round in her glass, still unable to meet his eyes, not wanting him to guess how disconcerted she felt. How the knowledge he hadn't abandoned her teenage self took the sting from her memories.

'It was a long time ago…' she repeated, her voice tapering away. 'Things change.'

'Yep. Twelve years tends to do that.'

She wasn't sure if he was talking about her, him, or the town. She seized on the more neutral option.

'Yes.' She looked around her, waved a hand to encompass the stark fashionable furnishings. 'Like this hotel.'

'What about this hotel?'

'It's very smart, but not very sympathetic, is it?'

'I kinda like it myself,' he said, and took a drink from his beer.

'You're not upset at what the developers did on the site of your family's beautiful guesthouse?'

'Like you said. Things change. The guesthouse has… has gone forever.'

He paused and she got the impression he had to control his voice.

'But this hotel and all the new developments around it have brought jobs for a lot of people. Some say it's the best thing that's ever happened to the place.'

'Do you?'

Sandy willed him to say no, wanting Ben to be the same carefree boy who'd lived for the next good wave, the next catch from the fishing boats he'd shared with his father, but knew somehow from the expression on his face that he wouldn't.

But still his reply came as a surprise. 'I own this hotel, Sandy.'

'You…you do?'

'Yep. Unsympathetic design and all.'

She clapped her hand to her mouth but she couldn't take back the words. 'I'm…I'm so sorry I insulted it.'

'No offence taken on behalf of the award-winning architect.'

'Really? It's won awards?'

'A stack of 'em.'

She noted the convivial atmosphere at the bar, the rapidly filling tables. 'It's very smart, of course. And I'm sure it's very successful. It's just…the old place was so charming. Your mother was so proud of it.'

'My parents left the guesthouse long ago. Glad to say goodbye to the erratic plumbing and the creaking floorboards. They built themselves a comfortable new house up on the headland when I took over.'

Whoa. Surprise on surprise. She knew lots must have changed in twelve years, but this? 'You took over the running of the guesthouse?' Somehow, she couldn't see Ben in that role. She thought of him always as outdoors, an action man—not indoors, pandering to the whims of guests.

'My wife did.'

His wife.

The words stabbed into Sandy's heart.

His wife.

If she hadn't already been sitting down she would have had to. Stupidly, she hadn't considered—not for one minute—that Ben would be married.

She shot a quick glance at his left hand. He didn't wear a wedding ring, but then plenty of married men didn't. She'd learned that lesson since she'd been single again.

'Of course. Of course you would have married,' she babbled, forcing her mouth into the semblance of a smile.

She clutched her glass so tightly she feared it would shatter. Frantically she tried to mould her expression into something normal, show a polite interest in an old friend's new life.

'Did you…did you marry someone from around here?'

'Jodi Hart.'

Immediately Sandy remembered her. Jodi, with her quiet manner and gentle heart-shaped face. 'She was lovely,' she said, meaning every word while trying not to let an unwarranted jealousy flame into life.

'Yes,' Ben said, and a muscle pulled at the side of his mouth, giving it a weary twist.

His face seemed suddenly drawn under the bronze of his tan. She was aware of lines etched around his features. She hadn't noticed them in the first flush of surprise at their meeting. Maybe their marriage wasn't happy.

Ben drummed his fingers on the surface of the table. Again her eyes were drawn to the scars on his hands. Horrible, angry ridges that made her wince at the sight of them.

'What about you?' he asked. 'Did you marry?'

Sandy shook her head. 'Me? Marry? No. My partner… he…he didn't believe in marriage.'

Her voice sounded brittle to her own ears. How she'd always hated that ambiguous term *partner*.

'"Just a piece of paper," he used to say.' She forced a laugh and hoped it concealed any trace of heartbreak. 'Sure made it easy when we split up. No messy divorce or anything.'

No way would she admit how distraught she'd been. How angry and hurt and humiliated.

His jaw clenched. 'I'm sorry. Did—?'

She put her hand up to stop his words. 'Thank you. But there's no point in talking about it.' She made herself smile. 'Water under the bridge, you know.'

It was six months since she'd last seen Jason. And that had only been to pay him for his half of the sofa they'd bought together.

Ben looked at her as if he were searching her face for something. His gaze was so intense she began to feel uncomfortable. When—at last—he spoke, his words were slow and considered.

'Water under the bridge. You're right.'

'Yes,' she said, not sure what to say next.

After another long, awkward pause, he glanced at his

watch. 'It's been great to see you, Sandy. But I have a meeting to get to.' He pushed back his chair and got up.

'Of course.' She wanted to put out a hand to stop him. There was more she wanted to ask him. Memories she wanted to share. But there was no reason for him to stay. No reason for him to know it was her birthday and how much she would enjoy his company for lunch.

He was married.

Married men did not share intimate lunches alone with former girlfriends, even if their last kiss had been twelve years ago.

She got up, too, resisting the urge to sigh. 'It was wonderful to catch up after all these years. Please…please give my regards to Jodi.'

He nodded, not meeting her eyes. Then indicated the menu. 'Lunch is on the house. I'll tell the desk you're my guest.'

'You really don't have to, Ben.'

'Please. I insist. For…for old times' sake.'

She hesitated. Then smiled tentatively. 'Okay. Thank you. I'm being nostalgic but they were good old times, weren't they? I have only happy memories of Dolphin Bay.' *Of the time we spent together.*

She couldn't kiss him goodbye. Instead she offered her hand for him to shake.

He paused for a second, then took it in his warm grip, igniting memories of the feel of his hands on her body, the caresses that had never gone further than she'd wanted. But back then she hadn't felt the hard ridges of those awful scars. And now she had no right to recall such intimate memories.

Ben was married.

'I'm sorry I was rude about your hotel,' she said, very seriously. Then she injected a teasing tone into her voice. 'But I'll probably never stop wondering why you destroyed the guesthouse. And those magnificent gum trees—there's not one left. Remember the swing that—?'

Ben let go her hand. 'Sandy. It was just a building.'

Too late she realised it wasn't any of her business to go on about the guesthouse just because she was disappointed it had been demolished.

'Ben, I—'

He cut across her. 'It's fine. That was the past, and it's where it should be. But it really has been great seeing you again…enjoy your lunch. Goodbye, Sandy.'

'Good-goodbye, Ben,' she managed to stutter out, stunned by his abrupt farewell, by the feeling that he wasn't being completely honest with her.

Without another word he turned from her, strode to the exit, nodded towards the people at the bar, and closed the door behind him. She gripped the edge of the table, swept by a wave of disappointment so intense she felt she was drowning in it.

What had she said? Had she crossed a line without knowing it? And why did she feel emptier than when she'd first arrived back in Dolphin Bay? Because when she'd written her birthday resolutions hadn't she had Ben Morgan in mind? When she'd described a kind man, free of hang-ups and deadly ambition, hadn't she been remembering him? Remembering how his straightforward approach to life had helped her grow up that summer? Grow up enough to defy her father and set her own course.

She was forced to admit to herself it wasn't the pier or the guesthouse she'd wanted to be the same in Dolphin Bay. It was the man who represented the antithesis of the cruel, city-smart man who had hurt her so badly.

In her self-centred fantasy she hadn't given a thought to Ben being married—just to him always being here, stuck in a time warp.

A waitress appeared to clear her glass away, but then paused and looked at her. Sandy wished she'd put her sunglasses back on. Her hurt, her disappointment, her anger at herself, must be etched on her face.

The waitress was a woman of about her own age, with a pretty freckled face and curly auburn hair pulled back tightly. Her eyes narrowed. 'I know you,' she said suddenly. 'Sandy, right? Years ago you came down from Sydney to stay at Morgan's Guesthouse.'

'That's right,' Sandy said, taken aback at being recognised.

'I'm Kate Parker,' the woman said, 'but I don't suppose you remember me.'

Sandy dredged through her memories. 'Yes, I do.' She forced a smile. 'You were the best dancer I'd ever seen. My sister and I desperately tried to copy you, but we could never be as good.'

'Thanks,' Kate replied, looking pleased at the compliment. She looked towards the door Ben had exited through. 'You dated Ben, didn't you? Poor guy. He's had it tough.'

'Tough?'

'You don't know?' The other woman's voice was almost accusing.

How would she know what had gone on in Ben Morgan's life in the twelve years since she'd last seen him?

'Lost his wife and child when the old guesthouse burned down,' Kate continued. 'Jodi died trying to rescue their little boy. Ben was devastated. Went away for a long time—did very well for himself. When he came back he built this hotel as modern and as different from the old place as could be. Couldn't bear the memories…'

Kate Parker chattered on, but Sandy didn't wait to hear any more. She pushed her chair back so fast it fell over and clattered onto the ground. She didn't stop to pull it up.

She ran out of the bar, through the door and towards the steps to the shoreline, heart pumping, face flushed, praying frantically to the god of second chances.

Ben.

She just had to find Ben.

CHAPTER TWO

TAKING THE STEPS two at a time, nearly tripping over her feet in her haste, Sandy ran onto the whiter-than-white sand of Dolphin Bay.

Ben was way ahead of her. Tall and broad-shouldered, he strode along towards the rocks, defying the wind that had sprung up while she was in the hotel and was now whipping the water to a frosting of whitecaps.

She had to catch up with him. Explain. Apologise. Tell him how dreadfully sorry she was about Jodi and his son. Tell him… Oh, so much she wanted to tell him. Needed to tell him. But the deep, fine sand was heavy around her feet, slowing her so she felt she was making no progress at all.

'Ben!' she shouted, but the wind just snatched the words out of her mouth and he didn't turn around.

She fumbled with her sandals and yanked them off, the better to run after him.

'Ben!' she called again, her voice hoarse, the salt wind whipping her hair around her face and stinging her eyes.

At last he stopped. Slowly, warily, he turned to face her. It seemed an age until she'd struggled through the sand to reach him. He stood unmoving, his face rigid, his eyes guarded. How hadn't she seen it before?

'Ben,' she whispered, scarcely able to get the word out. 'I'm sorry… I can't tell you how sorry I am.'

His eyes searched her face. 'You know?'

She nodded. 'Kate told me. She thought I already knew. I don't know what to say.'

Ben looked down at Sandy's face, at her cheeks flushed pink, her brown hair all tangled and blown around her face. Her eyes were huge with distress, her mouth oddly stained bright pink in the centre. She didn't look much older than the girl he'd loved all those years ago.

The girl he'd recognised as soon as she'd come into the hotel restaurant. Recognised and—just for one wild, un-guarded second before he pummelled the thought back down to the depths of his wounded heart—let himself exult that she had come back. His first love. The girl he had never forgotten. Had never expected to see again.

For just those few minutes when they'd chatted he'd donned the mask of the carefree boy he'd been when they'd last met.

'I'm so sorry,' she said again, her voice barely audible through the wind.

'You couldn't have known,' he said.

Silence fell between them for a long moment and he found he could not stop himself from searching her face. Looking for change. He wanted there to be no sign of the passing years on her, though he was aware of how much he had changed himself.

Then she spoke. 'When did...?'

'Five years ago,' he said gruffly.

He didn't want to talk to Sandy about what the locals called 'his tragedy'. He didn't want to talk about it anymore full-stop—but particularly not to Sandy, who'd once been so special to him.

Sandy Adams belonged in his past. Firmly in his past. *Water under the bridge*, as she'd so aptly said.

She bit down on her lower lip. 'I can't imagine how you must feel—'

'No, you can't,' he said, more abruptly than he'd intended, and was ashamed at the flash of hurt that tightened her face. 'No one could. But I've put it behind me…'

Her eyes—warm, compassionate—told him she knew he was lying. How could he ever put that terrible day of helpless rage and despair behind him? The empty, guilt-ridden days that had followed it? The years of punishing himself, of not allowing himself to feel again?

'Your hands,' she said softly. 'Is that how you hurt them?'

He nodded, finding words with difficulty. 'The metal door handles were burning hot when I tried to open them.'

Fearsome images came back—the heat, the smoke, the door that would not give despite his weight behind it, his voice raw from screaming Jodi's and Liam's names.

He couldn't stop the shudder that racked his frame. 'I don't talk about it.'

Mutely, she nodded, and her eyes dropped from his face. But not before he read the sorrow for him there.

Once again he felt ashamed of his harshness towards her. But that was him these days. Ben Morgan: thirty-one going on ninety.

His carefree self of that long-ago summer had been forged into someone tougher, harder, colder. Someone who would not allow emotion or softness in his life. Even the memories of a holiday romance. For with love came the agony of loss, and he could never risk that again.

She looked up at him. 'If…if there's anything I can do to help, you'll let me know, won't you?'

Again he nodded, but knew in his heart it was an empty gesture. Sandy was just passing through, and he was grateful. He didn't want to revisit times past.

He'd only loved two women—his wife, Jodi, and, before her, Sandy. It was too dangerous to have his first love around, reminding him of what he'd vowed never to feel again. He'd resigned himself to a life alone.

'You've booked in to the hotel?' he asked.

'Not yet, but I will.'

'For how long?'

Visibly, her face relaxed. She was obviously relieved at the change of subject. He remembered she'd never been very good at hiding her emotions.

'Just tonight,' she said. 'I'm on my way to Melbourne for an interview about a franchise opportunity.'

'Why Melbourne?' That was a hell of a long way from Dolphin Bay—as he knew from his years at university there.

'Why not?' she countered.

He turned and started walking towards the rocks again. Automatically she fell into step behind him. He waited.

Yes. He wasn't imagining it. It was happening.

After every three of his long strides she had to skip for a bit to keep up with him. Just like she had twelve years ago. And she didn't even seem to be aware that she was doing it.

'You're happy to leave Sydney?'

'There's nothing for me in Sydney now,' she replied.

Her voice was light, matter-of-fact, but he didn't miss the underlying note of bitterness.

He stopped. Went to halt her with a hand on her arm and thought better of it. No matter. She automatically stopped with him, in tune with the rhythm of his pace.

'Nothing?' he asked.

Not meeting his gaze, swinging her sandals by her side, she shrugged. 'Well, my sister Lizzie and my niece Amy. But…no one else.'

'Your parents?'

Her mouth twisted in spite of her effort to smile. 'They're not together any more. Turns out Dad had been cheating on my mother for years. The first Mum heard about it was when his mistress contacted her, soon after we got home from Dolphin Bay that summer. He and Mum patched it up that time. And the next. Finally he left her for his reception-ist. She's two years older than I am.'

'I'm sorry to hear that.'

But he was not surprised. He'd never liked the self-righteous Dr Randall Adams. Had hated the way he'd tried to control every aspect of Sandy's life. He wasn't surprised the older man had intercepted his long-ago letters. He'd made it very clear he had considered a fisherman not good enough for a doctor's daughter.

'That must have been difficult for you,' he said.

Sandy pushed her windblown hair back from her face in a gesture he remembered. 'I'm okay about it. Now. And Mum's remarried to a very nice man and living in Queensland.'

During that summer he'd used to tease her about her optimism. 'You should be called Sunny, not Sandy,' he'd say as he kissed the tip of her sunburned nose. 'You never let anything get you down.'

It seemed she hadn't changed—in that regard anyway. But when he looked closely at her face he could see a tightness around her mouth, a wariness in her eyes he didn't recall.

Maybe things weren't always so sunny for her these days. Perhaps her cup-half-full mentality had been challenged by life's storm clouds in the twelve years since he'd last seen her.

Suddenly she glanced at her watch. She couldn't smother her gasp. The colour drained from her face.

'What's wrong?' he asked immediately.

'Nothing,' she said, tight lipped.

Nothing. Why did women always say that when something was clearly wrong?

'Then why did you stare at your watch like it was about to explode? Is it connected to a bomb somewhere?'

That brought a twitch to her lips. 'I wish.'

She lifted her eyes from the watch. Her gaze was steady. 'I don't know why I'm telling you this, but right at this very moment Jason—my...my former boyfriend, partner, live-in lover or whatever you like to call him—is getting married.'

Sandy with a live-in boyfriend? She'd said she'd had a partner but had it been that serious? The knowledge hit him in the gut. Painfully. Unexpectedly. Stupidly.

What he and Sandy had had together was a teen romance. Kid stuff. They'd both moved on. He'd married Jodi. Of course Sandy would have had another man in her life.

But he had to clear his throat to reply. 'And that's bad or good?'

She laughed. But the laugh didn't quite reach her eyes. 'Well, good for him. Good for her, I guess. I'm still not sure how I feel about coming home one day to find his possessions gone and a note telling me he'd moved in with her.'

'You're kidding me, right?' Ben growled. How could someone treat his Sandy like that. *His Sandy.* That was a slip. She hadn't been his for a long, long time.

'I'm afraid not. It was…humiliating to say the least.' Her tone sounded forced, light. 'But, hey, it makes for a great story.'

A great story? Yeah, right.

There went sunny Sandy again, laughing off something that must still cause her pain.

'Sounds to me like you're better off without him.'

'The further I get from him the more I can see that,' she said. But she didn't sound convinced.

'As far away as Melbourne?' he asked, finding the thought of her so far away unsettling.

'I'm not running away,' she said firmly. Too firmly. 'I need change. A new job, a new—'

'Your job? What is that?' he asked, realising how little he knew about her now. 'Did you study law like your father wanted?'

'No, I didn't. Don't look so surprised—it was because of you.'

'Me?' No wonder her father had hated him.

'You urged me to follow my dreams—like you were following yours. I thought about that a lot when I got back home. And my dream wasn't to be a solicitor.' She shuddered. 'I couldn't think of anything less me.'

He'd studied law as part of his degree and liked it. But he wasn't as creative as he remembered Sandy being. 'But you studied for years so you'd get a place in law.'

'Law at Sydney University.' She pronounced the words as though they were spelled in capital letters. 'That was my father's ambition for me. He'd given up his plans for me to be a doctor when I didn't cut it in chemistry.'

'You didn't get enough marks in the Higher School Certificate for law?'

'I got the marks, all right. Not long after we got back to Sydney the results came out. I was in the honour roll in the newspaper. You should have heard my father boasting to anyone who'd listen to him.'

'I'll bet he did.' Ben had no respect for the guy. He was a bully and a snob. But he had reason to be grateful to him. Not for ruining things with him and Sandy. But for putting the bomb under him he'd needed to get off his teenage butt and make himself worthy of a girl like Sandy.

'At the last minute I switched to a communications degree. At what my father considered a lesser university.'

'He must have hit the roof.'

Sandy's mouth tightened to a thin line. 'As he'd just been outed as an adulterer he didn't have a leg to stand on about doing the right thing for the family.'

Ben smiled. It sounded as if Sandy had got a whole lot feistier when it came to standing up to her father. 'So what career did you end up in?'

'I'm in advertising.' She quickly corrected herself. 'I *was* in advertising. An account executive.'

On occasion he dealt with an advertising agency to help promote his hotel. The account executives were slick, efficient, and tough as old boots. Not at all the way he thought of Sandy. 'Sounds impressive.'

'It was.'

'Was?'

'Long story,' she said, and started to walk towards the rocks again.

'I'm listening,' he said, falling into step beside her.

The wind had dropped and now the air around them seemed unnaturally still. Seagulls screeched raucously. He looked through narrowed eyes to the horizon, where grey clouds were banking up ominously.

Sandy followed his gaze. She wrinkled her cute up-tilted nose. 'Storm brewing,' she said. 'I wonder—'

'Don't change the subject by talking about the weather,' he said, stopping himself from adding, *I remember how you always did that.*

He shouldn't have let himself get reeled in to such a nostalgic conversation. There was no point in dredging up those old memories. Not when their lives were now set on such different paths. And his path was one he needed—wanted—to tread unencumbered. He could not survive more loss. And the best way to avoid loss was to avoid the kind of attachment that could tear a man apart.

He wanted to spend his life alone. Though the word 'alone' seemed today to have a desolate echo to it.

She shrugged. 'Okay. Back to my story. Jason and I were both working at the same agency when we met. The boss didn't think it was a good idea when we started dating…'

'So you had to go? Not him?'

She pulled a face. 'We…ell. I convinced myself I'd been there long enough.'

'So you went elsewhere? Another agency?'

She nodded. 'And then the economy hit a blip, advertising revenues suffered, and last one in was first one out.'

'That must have been tough.'

'Yeah. It was. But, hey, one door closes and another one opens, right? I got freelance work at different agencies and learned a whole lot of stuff I might never have known otherwise.'

Yep, that was the old Sandy all right—never one to allow adversity to cloud her spirit.

She took a deep breath. He noticed how her breasts rose under her tight-fitting top. She'd filled out—womanly curves softened the angles of her teenage body. Her face was subtly different too, her cheekbones more defined, her mouth fuller.

He wouldn't have thought it possible but she was even more beautiful than she'd been when she was eighteen.

He wrenched his gaze away, cleared his throat. 'So you're looking at a franchise?'

Her eyes sparkled and her voice rose with excitement. 'My chance to be my own boss, run my own show. It's this awesome candle store. A former client of mine started it.'

'You were in advertising and now you want to sell candles? Aren't there enough candle stores in this world?'

'These aren't ordinary candles, Ben. The store is a raging success in Sydney. Now they're looking to open up in other towns. They're interviewing for a Melbourne franchise and I put my hand up.'

She paused.

'I want to do something different. Something of my own. Something challenging.'

She looked so earnest, so determined, that he couldn't help a teasing note from entering his voice. 'So it's candles? I don't see the challenge there.'

'Don't you?' she asked. 'There's a scented candle for every mood, you know—to relax, to stimulate, to seduce—'

She stopped on the last word, and the colour deepened in her cheeks, flushed the creamy skin of her neck. Her eyelashes fluttered nervously and she couldn't meet his gaze.

'Well, you get the story. I wrote the copy for the client. There's not much I don't know about the merits of those candles.' She was almost gabbling now to cover her embarrassment.

To seduce.

When he'd been nineteen, seducing Sandy had been all he'd thought about. Until he'd fallen in love with her. Then respecting her innocence had become more important than his own desires. The number of cold showers he'd been forced to take...

Thunder rumbled ominously over the water. 'C'mon,' he said gruffly, 'we'd better turn back.'

'Yes,' she said. 'Though I suppose it's too late now for my birthday lunch...' She hesitated. 'Please—forget I just said that, will you?'

'It's your birthday today?'

She shrugged dismissively. 'Yes. It's nothing special.'

He thought back. 'It's your *thirtieth* birthday.'

And she was celebrating alone?

'Eek,' she said in an exaggerated tone. 'Please don't remind me of my advancing years.'

'February—of course. How could I forget?' he said slowly.

'You remember my birthday?'

'I'd be lying if I said I recalled the exact date. But I remember it was in February because you were always pointing out how compatible our star signs were. Remember you used to check our horoscopes in your father's newspaper every day and—?'

He checked himself. Mentally he slammed his hand against his forehead. He'd been so determined not to indulge in reminiscence about that summer and now he'd gone and started it himself.

She didn't seem to notice his sudden reticence. 'Yes, I remember. You're Leo and I'm Pisces,' she chattered on. 'And you always gave me a hard time about it. Said astrology was complete hokum and the people at the newspaper just made the horoscopes up.'

'I still think that and—' He stopped as a loud clap of thunder drowned out his voice. Big, cold drops of water started pelting his head.

Sandy laughed. 'The heavens are angry at you for mocking them.'

'Sure,' he said, but found himself unable to resist a smile at her whimsy. 'And if you don't want to get drenched we've got to make a run for it.'

'Race you!' she challenged, still laughing, and took off, her slim, tanned legs flashing ahead of him.

He caught up with her in just a few strides.

'Not fair,' she said, panting a little. 'Your legs are longer than mine.'

He slowed his pace just enough so she wouldn't think he was purposely letting her win.

She glanced up at him as they ran side by side, her eyes lively with laughter, fat drops of water dampening her hair and rolling down her flushed cheeks. The sight of her vivacity ignited something deep inside him—something long dormant, like a piece of machinery, seized and unwanted, suddenly grinding slowly to life.

'I gave you a head start,' he managed to choke out in reply to her complaint.

But he didn't get a chance to say anything else for, waiting at the top of the stairs to the hotel, wringing her hands anxiously together, stood Kate Parker.

'Oh, Ben, thank heaven. I didn't know where you were. Your aunt Ida has had a fall and hurt her pelvis, but she won't let the ambulance take her to hospital until she's spoken to you.'

CHAPTER THREE

SANDY WAS HALFWAY up the stairs, determined to beat Ben to the top. Slightly out of breath, she couldn't help smiling to herself over the fact that Ben had remembered her birthday. Hmm… Should she be reading something into that?

And then Kate was there, with her worried expression and urgent words, and the smile froze on Sandy's face.

She immediately looked to Ben. Her heart seemed to miss a beat as his face went rigid, every trace of laughter extinguished.

'What happened?' he demanded of the red-haired waitress.

'She fell—'

'Tap-dancing? Or playing tennis?'

Kate's face was pale under her freckles. 'Neither. Ida fell moving a pile of books. You know what she's like. Pretends she's thirty-five, not seventy-five—'

Ida? A seventy-five-year-old tap-dancing aunt? Sandy vaguely remembered Ben all those years ago talking about an aunt—a great-aunt?—he'd adored.

'Where is she?' Ben growled, oblivious to the rain falling down on him in slow, heavy drops, slicking his hair, dampening his shirt so it clung to his back and shoulders, defining his powerful muscles.

'In the ambulance in front of her bookshop,' said

Kate. 'Better hurry. I'll tell the staff where you are, then join you—'

Before Kate had finished speaking, Ben had turned on his heel and headed around to the side of the hotel with the long, athletic strides Sandy had always had trouble keeping up with.

'Ben!' Sandy called after him, then forced herself to stop. Wasn't this her cue to cut out? As in, *Goodbye, Ben, it was cool to catch up with you. Best of luck with everything. See ya.*

That would be the sensible option. And Sandy, the practical list-maker, might be advised to take it. Sandy, who was on her way to Melbourne and a new career. A new life.

But this was about Ben.

Ben, with his scarred hands and scarred heart.

Ben, who might need some support.

Whether he wanted it or not.

'I'm coming with you,' she called after him, all thoughts of her thirtieth birthday lunch put on hold.

Quickly she fastened the buckles on her sandals. Wished for a moment that she had an umbrella. But she didn't really care about getting wet. She just wanted to be with Ben.

She'd never met a more masculine man, but the tragedy he had suffered gave him a vulnerability she could not ignore. Was he in danger of losing someone else he loved? It was an unbearable thought.

'Ben! Wait for me!' she called.

He turned and glanced back at her, but made no comment as she caught up with him. Good, so he didn't mind her tagging along.

His hand brushed hers as they strode along together. She longed to take it and squeeze it reassuringly but didn't dare. Touching wasn't on the agenda. Not any more.

Within minutes they'd reached the row of new shops that ran down from the side of the hotel.

There was an ambulance parked on the footpath out of

the rain, under the awning in front of a shop named Bay Books. When she'd driven past she'd admired it because of its charming doorframe, carved with frolicking dolphins. Who'd have thought she'd next be looking at it under circumstances like this?

A slight, elderly lady with cropped silver hair lay propped up on a gurney in front of the open ambulance doors.

This was Great-Aunt Ida?

Sandy scoured her memories. Twelve years ago she'd been so in love with Ben she'd lapped up any detail about his family, anything that concerned him. Wasn't there a story connected to Ida? Something the family had had to live down?

Ben was instantly by his aunt's side. 'Idy, what have you done to yourself this time?' he scolded, in a stern but loving voice.

He gripped Ida's fragile gnarled hand with his much bigger, scarred one. Sandy caught her breath at the look of exasperated tenderness on his face. Remembered how caring he'd been to the people he loved. How protective he'd been of *her* when she was eighteen.

Back then she'd been so scared of the big waves. Every day Ben had coaxed her a little further from the shore, building her confidence with his reassuring presence. On the day she'd finally caught a wave and ridden her bodyboard all the way in to shore, squealing and laughing at the exhilaration of it, she'd looked back to see he had arranged an escort of his brother and his best mates—all riding the same break. What kind of guy would do that? She'd never met one since, that was for sure.

'Cracked my darn pelvis, they think. I tripped, that's all.' Ida's face was contorted with annoyance as much as with pain.

Ben whipped around to face the ambulance officer standing by his aunt. 'Then why isn't she in the hospital?'

'Point-blank refused to let me take her. Insisted on seeing you first,' the paramedic said with raised eyebrows and admirable restraint, considering the way Ben was glaring at him. 'Tried to get her to call you from hospital but she wasn't budging.'

'That's right,' said Ben's aunt in a surprisingly strong voice. 'I'm not going anywhere until my favourite great-nephew promises to look after my shop.'

'Absolutely,' said Ben, without a second's hesitation. 'I'll lock it up safely. Now, c'mon, let's get you in the ambulance and—'

His aunt Ida tried to rise from the gurney. 'That's not what I meant. That's not good enough—' she said, before her words were cut short by a little whimper of pain.

Sandy shifted from sodden sandal to sodden sandal. Looked away to the intricately carved awning. She felt like an interloper, an uninvited witness to Ben's intimate family drama. Why hadn't she stayed at the beach?

'Don't worry about the shop,' said Ben, his voice burred with worry. 'I'll sort something out for you. Let's just get you to the hospital.'

'It's not life or death,' said the paramedic, 'but, yes, she should be on her way.'

Ida closed her eyes briefly and Sandy's heart lurched at the weariness that crossed her face. *Please let her be all right—for Ben's sake.*

But then the older lady's eyes snapped into life again. They were the same blue as Ben's and remarkably unfaded. 'I can't leave my shop closed for all that time.'

The paramedic interrupted. 'She might have to lie still in bed for weeks.'

'That's not acceptable,' continued the formidable Ida. 'You'll have to find me a manager. Keep my business going.'

'Just get to the ER and I'll do something about that later,' said Ben.

'Not later. *Now*,' said Aunt Ida, sounding nothing like a

little old lady lying seriously injured on a gurney. Maybe she was pumped full of painkillers.

Sandy struggled to suppress a grin. For all his tough, grown-up ways she could still see the nineteen-year-old Ben. He was obviously aching to bundle his feisty aunt into the ambulance but was too respectful to try it.

Aunt Ida's eyes sought out Kate, who was now standing next to Sandy. 'Kate? Can you—?'

Kate shook her head regretfully. 'No can do, I'm afraid.'

'She's needed at the hotel. We're short-staffed,' said Ben, with an edge of impatience to his voice.

Ida's piercing blue gaze turned to Sandy. 'What about you?'

'Me?' Was the old lady serious? Or delirious?

Before Sandy could stutter out anything more, Kate had turned to face her.

Her eyes narrowed. 'Yes. What about you, Sandy? Are you on holiday? Could you help out?'

'What? No. Sorry. I'm on my way to Melbourne.' She was so aghast she was gabbling. 'I'm afraid I won't be able to—'

'Friend of Kate's, are you?' persisted the old lady, in a voice that in spite of her obvious efforts was beginning to tire.

Compelled by good manners, Sandy took a step forward. 'No. Yes. Kind of… I—'

She looked imploringly at Ben, uncertain of what to say, not wanting to make an already difficult situation worse.

'Sandy's an…an old friend of mine,' he said, stumbling on the word friend. 'Just passing through.'

'Oh,' said the older lady, 'so she can't help out. And I can't afford to lose even a day's business.'

Her face seemed to collapse and she looked every minute of her seventy-five years.

Suddenly she reminded Sandy of her grandmother—

her mother's mother. How would she feel if Grandma were stuck in a situation like this?

'I'm sorry,' she said reluctantly.

'Pity.' Ida sighed. 'You look nice. Intelligent. The kind of person I could trust with my shop.' Wearily she closed her eyes again. 'Find me someone like her, Ben.'

Her voice was beginning to waver. Sandy could barely hear it over the sound of the rain drumming on the awning overhead.

Ben looked from Sandy to his aunt and then back to Sandy again, his eyes unreadable. 'Maybe…maybe Sandy can be convinced to stay for a few days,' he said.

Huh? Sandy stared at him. 'But, Ben, I—'

Ben held her with his glance, his blue eyes intense. He leaned closer to her. 'Just play along with me and say yes so I can get her to go to the hospital,' he muttered from the side of his mouth.

'Oh.' She paused. Thought for a moment. Thought again. 'Okay. I'll look after the shop. Just for a few days. Until you get someone else.'

'You promise?' asked Ida.

Promise? Like a cross-your-heart-and-hope-to-die-type promise? The kind of promise she never went back on?

Disconcerted, Sandy nodded. 'I promise.'

What crazy impulse had made her come out with that? Wanting to please Ben?

Or maybe it was the thought of what she would have liked to happen if it was her grandmother, injured, in pain, and having to beg a stranger to help her.

Ida's eyes connected with hers. 'Thank you. Come and see me in the hospital,' she said, before relaxing with a sigh back onto the gurney.

'Right. That's settled.' Ben slapped the side of the ambulance, turned to the ambulance officer. 'I'll ride in the back with my aunt.'

A frail but imperious hand rose. 'You show your friend around Bay Books. Settle her in.'

Sandy had to fight a smile as she watched Ben do battle with his great-aunt to let him accompany her to the hospital.

Minutes later she stood by Ben's side, watching the tail-lights of the ambulance disappear into the rain. Kate was in the back with Ida.

'Your aunt Ida is quite a lady,' Sandy said, biting her lip to suppress her grin.

'You bet,' said Ben, with a wry smile of his own.

'Isn't she the aunt who…?' She held up her hand. 'Wait. Let me remember. I know!' she said triumphantly. 'The aunt who ran off with an around-the-world sailor?'

Ben's eyes widened. 'You remember that? From all that time ago?'

I remember because you—and the family I fantasised about marrying into—were so important to me. The words were on the tip of her tongue, but she didn't—couldn't—put her voice to them. 'Of course,' she said instead. 'Juicy scandals tend to stick in my mind.'

'It *was* a scandal. For these parts anyway. She was the town spinster, thirty-five and unmarried.'

'Spinster? Ouch! What an awful word.' She giggled. 'Hey, I'm thirty and unmarried. Does that make me—' she made quotation marks in the air with her fingers '—a spinster?'

'As if,' Ben said with a grin. 'Try *career woman about town*—isn't that more up to date?'

'Sounds better. But the message is the same.' She pulled a mock glum face.

Ben stilled, and suddenly he wasn't joking. He looked into her face for a long, intense minute. An emotion she didn't recognise flashed through his eyes and then was gone.

'That boyfriend of yours was an idiot,' he said gruffly.

He lifted a hand as if he was about to touch her, maybe run his finger down her cheek to her mouth like he'd used to.

She tensed, waiting, not sure if she wanted him to or not. Awareness hung between them like the shimmer off the sea on a thirty-eight-degree day.

He moved a step closer. So close she could clearly see that sexy scar on his mouth. She wondered how it would feel if he kissed her…if he took her in his arms…

Her heart began to hammer in her chest so violently surely he must hear it. Her mouth went suddenly dry.

But then, abruptly, he dropped his hand back by his side, stepped away. 'He didn't deserve you,' he said, in a huskier-than-ever voice.

She breathed out, not realising she had been holding her breath. Not knowing whether to feel disappointed or relieved that there was now a safe, non-kissing zone between her and the man she'd once loved.

She cleared her throat, disconcerted by the certain knowledge that if Ben had kissed her she wouldn't have pushed him away. No. She would have swayed closer and…

She took a steadying breath. 'Yeah. Well… I…I'm better off without him. And soon I'll be living so far away it won't matter one little bit that he chose his mega-wealthy boss's daughter over me.'

She wouldn't take cheating Jason back in a million years. But sometimes it was difficult to keep up the bravado, mask the pain of the way he'd treated her. It was a particular kind of heartbreak to be presented with a *fait accompli* and no opportunity to make things right. It made it very difficult for her to risk her heart again.

'Still hurts, huh?' Ben said, obviously not fooled by her words.

She remembered how he'd used to tease her about her feelings always showing on her face.

She shook her head. After a lacklustre love life she'd thought she'd got things right with Jason. But she wasn't going to admit to Ben that Jason had proved to be another disappointment.

'You talk the talk, Sandy,' Jason had said. *'But you always held back, were never really there for me.'*

She couldn't see the truth in that—would never have committed to living with Jason if she hadn't believed she loved him. If she hadn't believed he would change his mind about marriage.

'Only my pride was hurt,' she said now to Ben. 'Things between us weren't right for a long time. I wasn't happy, and he obviously wasn't either. It had to end somehow.…' She took a deep breath. 'And here I am, making a fresh start.' She nodded decisively. 'Now, that's enough about me. Tell me more about your aunt Ida.'

'Sure,' he said, glad for the change in subject. 'Ida got married to her wayfaring sailor on some exotic island somewhere and sailed around the world with him on his yacht until he died. Then she came back here and started the bookshop—first at the other end of town and now in the row of new shops I built.'

'So you're her landlord?'

'The other guy was ripping her off on her rent.'

And Ben always looked after his own.

Sandy remembered how fiercely protective he'd been of his family. How stubbornly loyal. He would have been just as protective of his wife and son.

No wonder he had gone away when he'd lost them. What had brought him back to Dolphin Bay, with its tragic memories?

He turned to face her, his face composed, no hint from his expression that he might have been about to kiss her just minutes ago.

'It was good of you to play along with me to make her happy. I just had to get her into that ambulance and on her way. Thank you.'

She shrugged. 'No problem. I'd like someone to do the same for my grandmother.'

He glanced down at his watch. 'Now you'd better go have your lunch before they close down the kitchen. Sorry I can't join you, but—'

'But what?' Sandy tilted her head to one side. She put up her hand in a halt sign. 'Am I missing something here? Aren't you meant to be showing me the bookshop?'

Ben swivelled back to face her. He frowned. 'Why would you want to see the bookshop?'

'Because I've volunteered to look after it for your aunt until you find someone else. I promised. Remember? Crossed my heart and—'

He cut across her words. 'But that wasn't serious. That was just you playing along with me so she'd go to the hospital. Just a tactic…'

Vehemently, she shook her head. 'A tactic? No it wasn't. I meant it, Ben. I said I'd help out for a few days and I keep my word.'

'But don't you have an interview in Melbourne?'

'Not until next Friday, and today's only Saturday. I was planning on meandering slowly down the coast…'

She thought regretfully of the health spa she'd hoped to check in to for a few days of much needed pampering. Then she thought of the concern in Ida's eyes.

'But it's okay. I'm happy to play bookshop for a while. Really.'

'There's no need to stay, Sandy. It won't be a problem to close the shop for a few days until I find a temporary manager.'

'That's not what your aunt thinks,' she said. 'Besides, it might be useful for my interview to say I've been managing a shop.' She did the quote thing again with her fingers. '"Recent retail experience"—yes, that would look good on my résumé.' An update on her university holiday jobs working in department stores.

Ben was so tight-lipped he was bordering on grim. 'Sandy, it's nice of you, but forget it. I'll find someone. There are agencies for emergency staff.'

Why was he so reluctant to accept such an easy solution to his aunt's dilemma? Especially when he'd been the one to suggest it?

It wasn't fair to blame her for not being aware of his 'tactic'. And she wasn't—repeat *wasn't*—going to let his lack of enthusiasm at the prospect of her working in the bookshop daunt her.

Slowly, she shook her head from side to side. 'Ben, I gave my word to your great-aunt and I intend to keep it.'

She looked to the doorway of Bay Books. Forced her voice to sound steady. 'C'mon, show me around. I'm dying to see inside.'

Ben hesitated. He took a step forward and then stopped. His face reminded her of those storm clouds that had banked up on the horizon.

Sandy sighed out loud. She made her voice mock scolding. 'Ben, I wouldn't like to be in your shoes if you have to tell your aunt I skipped out on her.'

His jaw clenched. He looked at her without speaking for a long second. 'Is that blackmail, Sandy?'

She couldn't help a smile. 'Not really. But, like I said, if I make a promise I keep it.'

'Do you?' he asked hoarsely.

The smile froze on her face.

Ben stood, his hands clenched by his sides. Was he remembering those passionately sworn promises to keep their love alive even though she was going back to Sydney at the end of her holiday?

Promises she hadn't kept because she'd never heard from him? And she'd been too young, too scared, to take the initiative herself.

She'd been wrong not to persist in trying to keep in touch

with him. Wrong not to have trusted him. Now she could see that. Twelve years too late she could see that.

'Yes,' she said abruptly and—unable to face him—turned on her heel. 'C'mon, I need to check out the displays and you need to show me how to work the register and what to do about special orders and all that kind of stuff.'

She knew she was chattering too quickly, but she had to cover the sudden awkwardness between them.

She braced herself and looked back over her shoulder. Was he just going to stay standing on the footpath, looking so forbidding?

No. With an exhaled sigh that she hoped was more exasperated than angry, he followed her through the door of Bay Books.

As Ben walked behind Sandy—forcing himself not to be distracted by the sway of her shapely behind—he cursed himself for being such an idiot. His impulsive ploy to placate Idy with a white lie about Sandy staying to help out had backfired badly.

How could he have forgotten just what a thoughtful, generous person Sandy could be? In that way she hadn't changed since she was eighteen, insisting on helping his mother wash the dishes at the guesthouse even though she'd been a paying guest.

Of course Sandy wouldn't lie to his great-aunt. He should have realised that. And now here she was, insisting on honouring her 'promise'.

The trouble was, the last thing he wanted was his old girlfriend in town, reminding him of what he'd once felt for her. What he didn't want to feel again. Not for her. Not for anyone.

Point-blank, he did *not* want Sandy helping out at Bay Books. Did not want to be faced by her positive get-up-and-go-for-it attitude, her infectious laugh and—he couldn't deny it—her lovely face and sexier-than-ever body.

He gritted his teeth and determined not to fall victim to her charm.

But as she moved through the store he couldn't help but be moved by her unfeigned delight in what some people called his great-aunt's latest folly.

He saw the familiar surrounds afresh through her eyes— the wooden bookcases with their frolicking dolphin borders, the magnificent carved wooden counter, the round tables covered in heavy fringed cloths and stacked with books both bestsellers and more off-beat choices, the lamps thought-fully positioned, the exotic carpets, the promotional posters artfully displayed, the popular children's corner.

'I love it—I just love it,' she breathed. 'This is how a bookshop should be. Small. Intimate. Connected to its customers.'

Reverently, she stroked the smooth wooden surface of the countertop, caressed with slender pink-tipped fingers the intricate carved dolphins that supported each corner.

'I've never seen anything like it.'

'It's different, all right. On her travels Aunt Ida became good friends with a family of Balinese woodcarvers. She commissioned them to fit out the shop. Had all this shipped over.'

Sandy looked around her, her eyes huge with wonder. 'It's unique. Awesome. No wonder your aunt wants it in safe hands.'

Some people might find the shop too quaint. Old-fashioned in a world of minimalist steel and glass. Re-dundant at a time of electronic everything. But obviously not Sandy. He might have expected she'd appreciate Aunt Ida's eccentric creation. Just as she'd loved his family's old guesthouse.

She twirled around in the space between the counter and a crammed display of travel paperbacks.

'It even smells wonderful in here. The wood, of course. And that special smell of books. I don't know what it is—the paper, the binding.' She closed her eyes and inhaled with a look of ecstasy. 'I could just breathe it in all day.'

No.

His fists clenched tight by his sides. That was not what he wanted to hear. He didn't want Sandy to fit back in here to Dolphin Bay as if she'd never left.

He wanted her gone, back on that highway and heading south. Not connecting so intuitively with the magic his great-aunt had tried to create here. Not being part of his life just by her very presence.

How could he bear to have her practically next door? Every day she'd be calling on him to ask advice on how to run the shop. Seeking his help. Needing him.

And he wouldn't be able to resist helping her. Might even find himself looking in on the off chance that she needed some assistance with Aunt Ida's oddball accounting methods. Maybe bringing her a coffee from the hotel café. Suggesting they chat about the business over lunch.

That couldn't happen. He wouldn't let it happen. He needed his life to stay just the way it was. He didn't want to invite love into his life again. And with Sandy there would be no second measures.

Sandy threw herself down on the low, overstuffed sofa his aunt provided for customers to sit on and browse through the books, then jumped up again almost straight away. She clasped her hands together, her eyes shining with enthusiasm. 'It's perfect. I am *so* going to enjoy myself here.'

'It's only for a few days,' he warned. 'I'll talk to the agency straight away.' Again his voice was harsher than he'd intended, edged with fear.

She frowned and he winced at the quick flash of hurt in her eyes. She paused. Her voice was several degrees cooler when she replied.

'I know that, Ben. I'm just helping out until you get a manager. And I'm glad I can, now that I see how much of her heart your aunt has put into her shop.'

Avoiding his eyes, she stepped behind the counter, placed her hands on the countertop and looked around her. Despite his lack of encouragement, there was an eagerness, an excitement about her that he found disconcerting. And way too appealing.

She pressed her lips firmly together. 'I'll try not to bother you too much,' she said. 'But I'll need your help with operating the register. Oh, and the computer, too. Is all her inventory in special files?'

He knew he should show some gratitude for her helping out. After all, he'd been the one to make the ill-conceived suggestion that she should stay. But he was finding it difficult when he knew how dangerous it might be to have Sandy around. Until now he'd been keeping everything together in his under-control life. Or so he'd thought.

'I can show you the register,' he said grudgingly. 'The computer—that's a mystery. But you won't be needing to operate that. And, besides, it's only temporary, right?'

'Yeah. *Very* temporary—as you keep reminding me.'

This time she met his gaze head-on.

'But what makes you think I won't want to do as good a job as I can for your aunt Ida while I'm here? You heard what she said about needing every day of business.'

'I would look after her if she got into trouble.'

The truth was he didn't need the rent his great-aunt insisted on paying him. Could easily settle her overheads.

'Maybe she doesn't want to be looked after? Maybe she wants to be totally independent. I hope I'll be the same when I'm her age.'

Sandy at seventy-five years old? A quick image came to him of her with white hair, all skewered up in a bun on top of her head, and every bit as feisty as his great-aunt.

'I'm sure you will be,' he said, and he forced himself

not to smile at the oddly endearing thought. Or, by way of comparison, look too appreciatively at the beautiful woman who was Sandy now, on her thirtieth birthday.

'What about paying the bills?' she asked.

'I'll take care of that.'

'In other words,' she said with a wry twist to her mouth, 'don't forget that I'm just a temporary caretaker?'

'Something like that,' he agreed, determined not to make it easy for her. Though somewhere, hidden deep behind the armour he wore around his feelings, he wished he didn't have to act so tough. But if he didn't protect himself he might fall apart—and he couldn't risk that.

She looked up at him, her expression both teasing and serious at the same time. But her voice wasn't as confident as it had been. There was a slight betraying quiver that wrenched at him.

'You know something, Ben? I'm beginning to think you don't want me in Dolphin Bay,' she said, her eyes huge, her luscious mouth trembling. She took a deep breath. 'Am I right?'

He stared at her, totally unable to say anything.

Images flashed through his mind like frames from a flickering cinema screen.

Sandy at that long-ago surf club dance, her long hair flying around her, laughing as she and her sister tried to mimic Kate's outrageously sexy dancing, smiling shyly when she noticed him watching her.

Sandy breathless and trembling in his arms as he kissed her for the first time.

Sandy in the tiniest of bikinis, overcoming her fear to bravely paddle out on her body-board to meet him where the big waves were breaking.

Sandy, her eyes red and her face blotchy and tear-stained, running to him again and again to hurl herself in his arms for just one more farewell kiss as her father impatiently honked the horn on the family car taking her back to Sydney.

Then nothing. *Nothing.*

Until now.

He fisted his hands so tightly it hurt the harsh edges of the scars. Scars that were constant reminders of the agony of his loss.

How in hell could he answer her question?

CHAPTER FOUR

HE SAID *SHE* showed her emotions on her face? She didn't need a PhD in psychology to read his, either. It was only too apparent he was just buying time before spilling the words he knew she wouldn't want to hear.

For an interminable moment he said nothing. Shifted his weight from foot to foot. Then he uttered just one drawn-out word. 'Well…'

He didn't need to say anything else.

Sandy swallowed hard against the sudden, unexpected shaft of hurt. Forced her voice to sound casual, light-hearted. 'Hey, I was joking, but…but you're serious. You really *don't* want me around, do you?'

She pushed the rain-damp hair away from her face with fingers that weren't quite steady. Gripped the edge of the countertop hard, willing the trembling to stop.

When he finally spoke his face was impassive, his voice schooled, his eyes shuttered. 'You're right. I don't think it's a great idea.'

She couldn't have felt worse if he'd slapped her. She fought the flush of humiliation that burned her cheeks. Forced herself to meet his gaze without flinching. 'Why? Because we dated when we were kids?'

'As soon as people make the connection that you're my old girlfriend there'll be gossip, speculation. I don't want that.'

She swallowed hard against a suddenly dry throat, forced the words out. 'Because of your…because of Jodi?'

'That too.'

The counter was a barrier between them but he was close. Touching distance close. So close she could smell the salty, clean scent of him—suddenly heart-achingly familiar. After their youthful making out sessions all those years ago she had relished the smell of him on her, his skin on her skin, his mouth on her mouth. Hadn't wanted ever to shower it away.

'But…mainly because of me.'

His words were so quiet she had to strain to hear them over the noise of the rain on the metal roof above.

Bewildered, she shook her head. 'Because of you? I don't get it.'

'Because things are different, Sandy. It isn't only the town that's changed.'

His voice was even. Too even. She sensed it was a struggle for him to keep it under control.

He turned his broad shoulders so he looked past her and through the shop window, into the distance towards the bay as he spoke. 'Did Kate tell you everything about the fire that killed Jodi and my son, Liam?'

'No.' Sandy shook her head, suddenly dreading what she might hear. Not sure she could cope with it. Her knees felt suddenly shaky, and she leaned against the countertop for support.

Ben turned back to her and she gasped at the anguish he made no effort to mask.

'He was only a baby, Sandy, not even a year old. I couldn't save them. I was in the volunteer fire service and I was off fighting a blaze somewhere else. Everything was tinder-dry from years of drought. We thought Dolphin Bay was safe, but the wind turned. Those big gum trees near the guesthouse caught alight. And then the building. The guests got out. But…but not…' His head dropped as his words faltered.

He'd said before that he didn't want to talk about his tragedy—now it was obvious he couldn't find any more words. With a sudden aching realisation she knew it would never get easier for him.

'Don't,' she murmured, feeling beyond terrible that she'd forced him to relive those unbearable moments. She put her hand up to halt him, maybe to touch him, then let it drop again. 'You don't have to tell me any more.'

Big raindrops sat on his eyelashes like tears. She ached to wipe them away. To do something, anything, to comfort him.

But he'd just said he didn't want her here in town.

He raised his head to face her again. 'I lost everything that day,' he said, his eyes bleak. 'I have nothing to give you.'

She swallowed hard, glanced again at the scars on his hands, imagined him desperately trying to reach his wife and child in the burning guesthouse before it was too late. She realised there were scars where she couldn't see them. Worse scars than the visible ones.

'I'm not asking anything of you, Ben. Just maybe to be… to be friends.'

She couldn't stop her voice from breaking—was glad the rain meant they had the bookshop all to themselves. That no one could overhear their conversation.

He turned his tortured gaze full on to her and she flinched before it.

The words were torn from him. 'Friends? Can you really be "just friends" with someone you once loved?'

She picked up a shiny hardback from the pile to the left of her on the counter, put it back without registering the title. Then she turned back to face him. Took a deep breath. 'Was it really love? We were just kids.'

'It was for me,' he said, his voice gruff and very serious, his hands clenched tightly by his sides. 'It hurt that you never answered my letters, never got in touch.'

'It hurt me that you never wrote like you said you would,' she breathed, remembering as if it were yesterday the anguish of his rejection. Oh, yes, it had been love for her too.

But a small voice deep inside whispered that perhaps she had got over him faster than he had got over her. She'd never forgotten him but she'd moved on, and the memories of her first serious crush had become fainter and fainter. Sometimes it had seemed as though Ben and the times she'd had with him at Dolphin Bay had been a kind of dream.

She hadn't fully appreciated then what was apparent now—Ben wasn't a player, like Jason or her father. When he loved, he loved for keeps. In the intervening years she'd been attracted to men who reminded her of him and been bitterly disappointed when they fell short. She could see now there was only one man like Ben.

They both spoke at the same time.

'Why—?'

'Why—?'

Then answered at the same time.

'My father—'

'Your father—'

Sandy gave a short nervous laugh. 'And my mother, too,' she added, turning away from him, looking down at a display of mini-books of inspirational thoughts, shuffling them backwards and forwards. 'She told me not to chase after you when you were so obviously not interested. Even my sister, Lizzie, got fed up with me crying over you and told me to get over it and move on.'

'My dad said the same thing about you. That you had your own life in the city. That you wouldn't give me a thought when you were back in the bright lights. That we were too young, anyway.' He snorted. '*Too young.* He and my mother got married when they were only a year older than I was then.'

She looked up to face him. 'I phoned the guesthouse, you know, but your father answered. I was too chicken to speak to him, though I suspect he knew it was me. He told me not to call again.'

'He never said.'

Sandy could hear the beating of her own heart over the sound of the rain on the roof. 'We were young. Maybe too young to doubt them—or defy them.'

An awkward silence—a silence choked by the echoes of words unspoken, of kisses unfulfilled—fell between them until finally she knew she had to be the one to break it.

'I wonder what would have happened if we had—'

'Don't go there, Sandy,' he said.

She took a step back from his sudden vehemence, banging her hip on the wooden fin of a carved dolphin. But she scarcely felt the pain.

'Never torture yourself with *what if?* and *if only*,' he continued. 'Remember what you said? Water under the bridge.'

'It…it was a long time ago.'

She didn't know what else she could say. Couldn't face thinking of the 'what ifs?' Ben must have struggled with after the fire.

While he was recalling anguish and irredeemable loss, she was desperately fighting off the memories of how much fun they'd had together all those years ago.

She'd been so serious, so strait-laced, so under her father's thumb. For heaven's sake, she'd been old enough to vote but had never stayed out after midnight. Ben had helped her lighten up, take risks—be reckless, even. All the time knowing he'd be there for her if she stumbled.

He hadn't been a bad boy by any means, but he'd been an exciting boy—an irreverent boy who'd thumbed his nose at her father's old-fashioned edicts and made her question the ways she'd taken for granted. So many times she'd snuck out to meet him after dark, her heart thundering with both fear of what would happen if she were caught and anticipation of being alone with him.

How good it had felt when he'd kissed her—kissed her

at any opportunity when they could be by themselves. How his kisses, his caresses, had stirred her body, awakening yearnings she hadn't known she was capable of.

Yearnings she'd never felt as strongly since. Not even for Jason.

Saying no to going all the way with Ben that summer was one of the real regrets of her life. Losing her virginity to him would have been an unforgettable experience. How could it not have been when their passion had been so strong?

She couldn't help remembering their last kiss—with her father about to drag her into the car—fired by unfulfilled passion and made more poignant in retrospect because she'd had no idea that it would be her last kiss from Ben.

Did he remember it too?

She searched his face, but he seemed immersed in his own dark thoughts.

Wearily, she wiped her hand over her forehead as if she could conjure up answers. Why had those kisses been printed so indelibly on her memory? Unleashed passion? Hormones? Pheromones? Was it the magic of first love? Or was it a unique power that came only from Ben?

Ben who had grown into this intense, unreadable, tormented man whom she could not even pretend to know any more.

The rain continued to fall. It muffled the sound of the cars swishing by outside the bookshop, made it seem as if they were in their own world, cocooned by their memories from the reality of everyday life in Dolphin Bay. From all that had happened in the twelve years since they'd last met.

Ben cleared his throat, leaned a little closer to her over the barrier of the counter.

'I'm glad you told me you never got my letters, that you tried to phone,' he said, his voice gruff. 'I never understood how you could just walk away from what we had.'

'Me too. I never understood how you didn't want to see me again, I mean.'

She thought of the tears she'd wept into her pillow all those years ago. How abandoned she'd felt. How achingly lonely. Even the agony of Jason's betrayal hadn't come near it.

Then she forced her thoughts to return to today. To Ben's insistence that he didn't want her hanging around Dolphin Bay, even to help his injured aunt at a time of real need for the old lady.

It was beyond hurtful.

Consciously, she straightened her shoulders. She forced a brave, unconcerned edge to her voice. 'But now we know the wrong my father did maybe we can forget old hurts and… and feel some kind of closure.'

'Closure?' Ben stared at her. 'What kind of psychobabble is *that*?'

Psychobabble? She felt rebuffed by his response. She'd actually thought 'closure' was a very well-chosen word. Under the circumstances.

'What I mean is…maybe we can try to be friends? Forgive the past. Forget there was anything else between us?'

She was lying. *Oh, how she was lying.*

While her mind dictated emotion-free words like 'closure' and 'friends' her body was shouting out that she found him every bit as desirable as she had twelve years ago. More so.

Just months ago—when she'd still had a job—she'd worked on a campaign for a hot teen surf clothing label. Ben at nineteen would have perfectly cast in the lead male role, surrounded by adoring bikini-clad girls.

Now, Ben at thirty-one could star as a hunky action man in any number of very grown-up commercials. His face was only improved by his cropped hair, the deep tan, the slight crinkles around his eyes and that intriguing scar on his mouth. His damp shirt moulded to a muscled chest and powerful shoulders and arms.

Now they were both adults. Experienced adults. She'd

been the world's most inexperienced eighteen-year-old. What would she feel if she kissed him now? A shudder ran deep inside her. There would be no stopping at kisses, that was for sure.

'You may be able to forget we were more than friends but I can't,' he said hoarsely. 'I still find you very attractive.'

So he felt it too.

Something so powerful that twelve years had done nothing to erode it.

Her heart did that flippy thing again, over and over, stealing her breath, her composure. Before she could stutter out something in response he continued.

'That's why I don't want you in Dolphin Bay.'

She gasped at his bluntness.

'I don't mean to sound rude,' he said. 'I…I just can't deal with having you around.'

What could she say in response? For all her skill as an award-winning copywriter, she couldn't find the right words in the face of such raw anguish. All she could do was nod.

That vein throbbed at his temple. 'I don't want to be reminded of what it was like to…to have feelings for someone when I can't…don't want to ever feel like that again.'

The pain behind his confession made her catch her breath in another gasp. It overwhelmed the brief flash of pleasure she'd felt that he still found her attractive. And it hurt that he was so pointedly rejecting her.

'Right,' she said.

Such an inadequate word. Woefully inadequate.

'Right,' she repeated. She cleared her throat. Looked anywhere but at him. 'I hear what you're saying. Loud and clear.'

'I'm sorry, I—'

She put up her hand in a halt sign. 'Don't be. I…I appreciate your honesty.'

Her heart went out to him. Not in pity but in empathy. She had known pain. Not the kind of agony he'd endured, but pain just the same. Her parents' divorce. Jason's callous dumping. Betrayal by the friends who'd chosen to be on Jason's side in the break-up and had accepted invitations to today's wedding of the year at St Mark's, Darling Point, the Sydney church famed for society weddings.

But the philosophy she'd evolved in those years when she'd been fighting her father's blockade on letting her lead a normal teenage life had been to refuse to let hurt and disappointment hold her back for long. She now firmly believed that good things were always around the corner. That light always followed darkness. But you had to take steps to invite that light into your life. As she had in planning to leave all the reminders of her life with Jason behind her.

Ben had suffered a tragedy she could not even begin to imagine. Would he ever be able to move out of the shadows?

'Honesty is best all round,' he said, the jagged edge to his voice giving a terrible sincerity to the cliché.

She gritted her teeth against the thought of all Ben had endured since they'd last met, the damage it had done to him. And yet…

From what she remembered of sweet-faced Jodi Hart, she couldn't imagine she would want to see the husband she'd loved wrapping himself in a shroud of grief and self-blame, not allowing himself ever again to feel happiness or love.

But it was not for her to make that judgement. She, too, belonged to Ben's yesterday, and that was where he seemed determined to keep her. He did not want to be part of her tomorrow in any way.

If only she could stop wondering if the magic would still be there for them…if they could both overcome past hurts enough to try.

She had to force herself not to sigh out loud. The attraction she felt for him was still there, would never go away. It was a longing so powerful it hurt.

'Now I know where I stand,' she said, summoning the strength to make her voice sound normal.

He was right. It was best to get it up-front. Ben was not for her. Not any more. The barriers he had up against her were so entrenched they were almost visible.

But in spite of it all she refused to regret her impulsive decision to return to Dolphin Bay. It was healing to meet up with Ben and discover that he hadn't, after all, heartlessly ditched her all those years ago. Coming after the Jason fiasco, that revelation was a great boost to her self-esteem.

She forced a smile. 'That's sorted, then. Let's get back on track. Tell me more about Bay Books. I'm going to be the best darn temporary manager you'll ever see.'

'So long as you know it's just that. Temporary.'

She nodded. She could do this. After all, she loved reading and she loved books—e-books, audiobooks, but especially the real thing. Added to that, the experience of looking after the bookshop might help her snag the candle store franchise. Maybe her reckless promise to Ida might turn out to benefit herself as much as Ben's great-aunt.

Yes, making that swift exit off the highway this morning had definitely been a good idea. But in five days she would get back into her green Beetle and put Dolphin Bay and Ben Morgan behind her again.

Five days of wanting Ben but knowing it could never be.

Five days to eradicate the yearning, once and for all.

But the cup-half-full part of her bobbed irrepressibly to the surface. There was one other way to look at it: five days to convince him they should be friends again. And after that who knew?

CHAPTER FIVE

BEN WATCHED THE emotions as they played across Sandy's face. Finally her expression settled at something between optimistic and cheerful.

He might have been fooled if he hadn't noticed the tight grip of her hands on the edge of the countertop. Even after all these years and a high-powered job in advertising she hadn't learned to mask her feelings.

He had hurt her. Hurt her with his blunt statements. Hurt her with his rejection of her friendship, his harsh determination to protect himself from her and the feelings she evoked.

He hated to cause her pain. He would fight with his fists anyone who dared to injure her in any way. But he had to be up-front. She had to know the score. The fire had changed him, snatched his life from him, forged a different person from the one Sandy remembered. *He had nothing left to give her.*

Her eyes were guarded, the shadows beneath them more deeply etched. She tilted her head to one side. A wispy lock of rain-damp hair fell across her face. He had to force himself not to reach out and tenderly push it aside, as he would have done twelve years ago.

She took a deep breath and again he couldn't help but appreciate the enticing swell of her breasts. She'd been sizzling at eighteen. As a woman of thirty she was sexual dynamite. Ignite it and he was done for.

Finally she spoke. 'Okay, so maybe promising to help your aunt wasn't such a great idea. But I crossed my heart. I'm here in Dolphin Bay. Whether you like it or not.'

Her lovely pink-stained mouth trembled and she bit down firmly on her lower lip. She blinked rapidly, as if fighting back tears, sending a wrenching shaft of pain straight to his heart.

She choked out her words. 'Don't be angry at me for insisting on staying. I couldn't bear that.'

'Like I'd do *that*, Sandy. Surely you know me better?'

She shook her head slowly from side to side. Her voice broke like static. 'Ben, I don't know you at all any more.'

A bruised silence fell between them. He was powerless to do anything to end it. Each breath felt like an effort.

Sandy's shoulders were hunched somewhere around her ears. He watched her make an effort to pull them down.

'If you don't want to be friends, where does that put us?'

'Seems to me we're old friends who've moved on but who have been thrown together by circumstance. Can't we leave it at that?'

Before she had a chance to mask it, disappointment clouded her eyes. She looked away. It was a long moment before she nodded and looked back up at him. Her voice was resolute, as if she were closing on a business deal, with only the slightest tremor to betray her. 'You're right. Of course you're right. We'll be grown-up about this. Passing polite for the next five days. Is that the deal?'

She offered him her hand to shake.

He looked at it for a long moment, at her narrow wrist and slender fingers. Touching Sandy wasn't a good idea. Not after all these years. Not when he remembered too well how good she'd felt in his arms. How much he wanted her—had always wanted her.

He hesitated a moment too long and she dropped her hand back by her side.

He'd hurt her again. He gritted his teeth. What kind of a man was he that he couldn't shake her hand?

'That's settled, then,' she said, her voice brisk and businesslike, her eyes not meeting his. 'By the way, I'll need somewhere to sleep. Any suggestions?'

Wham! What kind of sucker punch was that? His reaction was instant—raw, physical hunger for her. Hunger so powerful it knocked him for six.

He knew what he ached to say. *You can sleep in my bed. With me. Naked, with your legs twined around mine. On top of me. Beneath me. With your face flushed with desire and your heart racing with passion. Sleep with me so we can finish what we started so long ago.*

Instead he clenched his fists by his sides, looked somewhere over her head so he wouldn't have to see her face. He couldn't let her guess the thoughts that were taking over his mind and body.

'You'll be my guest at the hotel. I'll organise a room for you as soon as I get back.'

She put up her hand. 'But that won't be necessary. I—'

He cut short her protest. 'No buts. You're helping my family. You don't pay for accommodation. You'll go in a penthouse suite.'

She shook her head. 'I'm happy to pay, but if you insist—'

'I insist.' He realised, with some relief, that the rain had stopped pelting on the roof. 'The weather has let up. We'll get you checked in now.'

The twist to her mouth conceded defeat, although he suspected the argument was far from over. Like Idy, she was fiercely independent. Back then she'd always insisted on paying her way on their dates. Even if she only matched him ice cream for ice cream or soft drink for soft drink.

'Okay. Thanks. I'll just grab my handbag and—' She felt around on the counter, looked around her in panic. 'My bag!'

'It's at Reception. Kate picked it up.'

Kate, her eyes wide with interest and speculation, had whispered to him as they were helping Ida into the ambulance. She said Sandy had been in such a hurry to follow him out of the restaurant and onto the sand she'd left her bag behind.

Kate obviously saw that as significant. He wondered how many people now knew his old girlfriend was back in town.

The phone calls would start soon. His mother first up. She'd liked Sandy. She'd never pried into his and his brother Jesse's teenage love lives. But she'd be itching to know why Sandy was back in town.

And he'd wager that Sandy would have a stream of customers visiting Bay Books. Customers whose interest was anything but literary.

Sandy went to move from behind the counter.

'Sandy, before you go, there's something I've been meaning to tell you.'

She frowned. 'Yes?'

He'd been unforgivably ill-mannered not to shake her hand just to avoid physical contact. So what inexplicable force made him now lean towards her and lightly brush his thumb over her mouth where it was stained that impossibly bright pink? He could easily tell her what he had to without touching her.

His pulse accelerated a gear at the soft, yielding feel of her lips, the warm female scent of her. She quivered in awareness of his touch, then stood very still, her cheeks flushed and her eyes wide.

He didn't want her around. Didn't want her warmth, her laughter, falling on his heart like drops of water on a spiky-leaved plant so parched it was in danger of dying. A plant that needed the sun, the life-giving rain, but felt safe and comfortable existing in the shadows, living a half-life that until now had seemed enough.

'Sandy....' There was so much more he wanted to say. But couldn't.

She looked mutely back at him.

He drew a deep, ragged breath. Cleared his throat. Forced his voice into its usual tone, aware that it came out gruffer but unable to do anything about it.

'I don't know if this is the latest city girl look, but your mouth…it's kinda pink in the middle. You might want to fix it.'

She froze, then her hand shot to her mouth. 'What do you mean? I don't use pink lipstick.'

Without saying a word he walked around to her side of the counter and pulled out a drawer. He handed her the mirror his aunt always kept there.

Sandy looked at her image. She stared. She shrieked. 'That's the ink from my niece Amy's feather pen!'

It was difficult not to grin at her reaction.

Then she glared at him, her eyes sparking, though she looked about as ferocious as one of the stray puppies his mother fostered. '*You!* You let me go around all this time looking like this? Why didn't you tell me?'

He shrugged, finding it hard not show his amusement at her outraged expression. 'How was I to know it wasn't some fashion thing? I've seen girls wearing black nail polish that looks like bruises.'

'But this…' She wiped her hand ineffectively across her mouth. 'This! I look like a circus clown.'

He shrugged. 'I think it's kinda cute. In a…circusy kind of way.'

'You!' She scrutinised her image and scrubbed hard at her mouth.

Now her lips looked all pouty and swollen, like they'd used to after their marathon teen making out sessions. He had to look away. To force himself not to remember.

She glared again. 'Don't you ever, *ever* let me go out in public again looking weird, okay?'

'I said cute, not weird. But okay.' He couldn't help his mouth from lifting into a grin.

Her eyes narrowed into accusing slits. 'Are you laughing at me, Ben Morgan?'

'Never,' he said, totally negating his words by laughing.

She tried, but she couldn't sustain the glare. Her mouth quirked into a grin that spilled into laughter chiming alongside his.

After all the angst of the morning it felt good to laugh. Again he felt something shifting and stirring deep inside the seized and rusted engine of his emotions. He didn't want it to fire into life again. That way led to pain and anguish. But already Sandy's laughter, her scent, her unexpected presence again in his life, was like the slow drip-drip-drip of some powerful repair oil.

'C'mon,' he said. 'While the rain's stopped let's get you checked into the hotel. Then I have to get back to work.'

As he pulled the door of Bay Books closed behind him he found himself pursing his mouth to whistle. A few broken bars of sound escaped before he clamped down on them. He glanced to see if Sandy had noticed, but her eyes were focused on the street ahead.

He hadn't whistled for years.

CHAPTER SIX

SANDY SAT IN her guest room at Hotel Hideous, planning a new list. She shivered and hugged her arms to herself. The room was air conditioned to the hilt. There was no stinting on luxury in the modern, tasteful furnishings. She loved the dolphin motif that was woven into the bedcover and decorative pillows, and repeated discreetly on the borders of the curtains. And the view across the old harbour and the bay was beyond magnificent.

But it wasn't a patch on the charm of the old guesthouse. Who could have believed the lovely building would come to such a tragic end? She shuddered at the thought of what Ben had endured. Was she foolish to imagine that he could ever get over his terrible losses? Ever be able to let himself love again?

She forced herself to concentrate as she turned a new page of her fairy notebook. The pretty pink pen had been relegated to the depths of her handbag. She didn't have the heart to throw Amy's gift in the bin, even though she could never use it again.

She still burned at the thought of not just Ben but Kate, Ida and who-knew-who-else seeing her with the hot pink stain on her mouth. It was hardly the sophisticated image she'd thought she was putting across. Thankfully, several minutes of scrubbing with a toothbrush had eliminated the stain.

But maybe the ink stain had, in a roundabout way, served a purpose. Thoughtfully, she stroked her lip with her finger, where Ben's thumb had been. After all, hadn't the stain induced Ben to break out of his self-imposed cage and actually touch her?

She took a pen stamped with the Hotel Harbourside logo—which, of course, incorporated a dolphin—from the desk in front of her and started to write—this time in regulation blue ink.

1. *Reschedule birthday celebrations.*

No.

Postpone indefinitely.

Was turning thirty, with her life such a mess, actually cause for celebration anyway? Maybe it was best left unmarked. She could hope for better next year.

2. *Congratulate self for not thinking once about The Wedding.*

She scored through the T and the W to make them lower case. It was her friends who had dramatised the occasion with capital letters. Her so-called friends who'd gone over to the dark side and accepted their invitations.

She could thank Ben's aunt Ida for pushing all thoughts of That-Jerk-Jason and his lucrative trip down the aisle out of her mind.

Or—and she must be honest—was it really Ida who'd distracted her?

She realised she was gnawing the top of the pen.

3. *Quit chewing on pens for once and for all. Especially pens that belong to first love.*

First love now determined not even to be friends.
Which brought her to the real issue.

4. *Forget Ben Morgan.*

She stabbed it into the paper.

Forget the shivery delight that had coursed through her when his finger had traced the outline of her mouth. Forget how he'd looked when he had laughed—laughed at her crazy pink ink stain—forget the light in his eyes, the warmth of his smile. Forget the stupid, illogical hope that sprang into her heart when they joked together like in old times.

She slammed the notebook shut, sending glitter shimmering over the desk. Opened it again. She underscored the last words.

Then got on to the next item.

5. *Visit Ida and get info on running bookshop.*

She had to open Bay Books tomorrow and she didn't have a clue what she should be doing. This was scary stuff.

She leaned back in her chair to think about the questions she should ask the older lady when the buzzer to her room sounded.

'Who is it?' she called out, slamming her notebook shut again in a flurry of glitter.

'Ben.'

In spite of her resolutions her heart leaped at the sound of his voice. 'Just give me a second,' she called.

Her hands flew to her face, then smoothed her still-damp-from-the-shower hair. She tightened the belt on the white towelling hotel bathrobe. She ran her tongue around suddenly dry lips before she fumbled with the latch and opened the door.

Ben filled the doorway with his broad shoulders and impressive height. Her heart tripped into double time at the sight of him. He had changed into jeans and a blue striped shirt that brought out the colour of his eyes. Could any man be more handsome?

She stuttered out a greeting, noticed he held a large brown paper grocery bag in one hand.

He thrust the bag at her. 'For you. I'm not good at gift wrapping.'

She looked from the bag up to him. 'Gift wrapping?'

'I feel bad your birthday turned out like this.'

'This is a birthday gift?'

He shrugged. 'A token.'

She flushed, pleased beyond measure at his thoughtfulness. 'I like surprises. Thank you.'

Not sure what to expect, she delved into the bag. It was jam-packed with Snickers bars. 'Ohmigod!' she exclaimed in delighted disbelief.

He shifted from foot to foot. 'You used to like them.'

She smiled at him. 'I still do. They're my favourite.'

She didn't have the heart to add that when she was eighteen she'd been able to devour the chocolate bars by the dozen without gaining weight, but that at thirty they were an occasional indulgence.

'Thank you,' she said. 'You couldn't have given me anything I'd like more.'

She wasn't lying.

Ben's thoughtfully chosen gift in a brown paper bag was way more valuable than any of the impersonal 'must-have' trinkets Jason had used to choose and have gift wrapped by the shop. Her last present from him had been an accessory for her electronic tablet that he had used more than she ever had.

Her heart swelled with affection for Ben. For wounded, difficult, vulnerable Ben.

She looked up at him, aching to throw her arms around him and kiss him. Kiss him for remembering her sweet tooth. Kiss him for the simple honesty of his brown-bagged gift. Kiss him for showing her that, deep down somewhere beneath his scars and defences, her Sir Galahad on a surfboard was still there.

But she felt too wary to do so. She wasn't sure she could handle any more rejection in one day. His words echoed in her head and in her heart: *'I don't want you in Dolphin Bay.'*

'Thank you,' she said again, feeling the words were totally inadequate to express her pleasure at his gesture.

He looked pleased with himself in a very male, tell-me-again-how-clever-I-was way she found endearing.

'I bought all the shop had—which just happened to be thirty.'

She smiled up at him. 'The shopkeeper must have thought you were a greedy pig with a desperate addiction to chocolate.'

'Nah. They know chilli corn chips are more to my taste.'

She hugged the bag of chocolate bars to her chest. 'So I won't have to share? Because you might have to fight me for them.'

'That makes *you* the greedy pig,' he said. 'They're all yours.' He stood still, looking deep into her eyes. 'Happy birthday, Sandy.'

She saw warmth mixed with wariness—which might well be a reflection of what showed in her own eyes.

Silence fell between them. She was aware of her own quickened breathing over the faint hum of the air-conditioning. Felt intoxicated by the salty, so familiar scent of him.

Now.

Surely now was the moment to kiss him? Suddenly she desperately wanted to feel his mouth—that sexy, sexy mouth—on hers. To taste again the memory that had lingered through twelve years away from him.

She felt herself start to sway towards him, her lips parting, her gaze focusing on the blue eyes that seemed to go a deeper shade of blue as he returned her gaze. Her heart was thudding so loudly surely he could hear it.

But as she moved he tensed and took an abrupt step backwards.

She froze. *Rejection again.* When would she learn?

She stepped back too, so hastily she was in danger of tripping backwards into the room. She wrapped her robe tighter around her, focused on the list of hotel safety instructions posted by the door rather than on him. A flush rose up her neck to sting her cheeks.

She couldn't think of a word to say.

After an excruciatingly uncomfortable moment Ben cleared his throat. 'I've been sent on a mission from Aunt Ida to find and retrieve you and take you to the hospital to meet with her.'

Sandy swallowed hard, struggled to make her voice sound light-hearted. 'Sounds serious stuff. Presumably an urgent briefing on the Bay Books project?'

He snapped his fingers. 'Right first guess.'

She smiled, knowing it probably looked forced but determined to appear natural—not as if just seconds ago she'd been longing for his kiss.

'Let me guess again. She's getting anxious about filling me in on how it all works?'

'Correct again,' he said. 'I promised to return with you ASAP to complete the mission.'

'Funnily enough I have no other pressing social engagements in Dolphin Bay.' She turned and started to walk back into the room, then stopped and looked back over her shoulder at him. 'Do you want to come in while I get dressed?'

His glance went briefly to her open neckline. He cleared his throat. 'Not a good idea.'

She blushed even redder and clutched the robe tighter. 'I mean… I didn't mean…' she stuttered.

'How about I come back to get you in half an hour?'

Her voice came out an octave higher. 'Twenty minutes max will be fine. Where will you be if I'm ready earlier?'

'Downstairs in my office.'

'Pick me up in twenty, then.'

He turned to go.

She swallowed against the sudden tension in her throat. 'Ben?' she said.

He swung back to face her, a question on his face.

'Thank you for the Snickers. I won't say I'll treasure them for ever, because they'll be devoured in double quick time. But...thank you.'

'You're welcome,' he said. 'It was—'

Afterwards she wondered at the impulse that had made her forget all caution, all fear of rejection. Before she could think about whether it was a good thing or not to do, propelled by pure instinct, she leaned up on her bare toes and kissed him lightly on his cheek.

Then she staggered at the impact of his closeness, at the memories that came rushing back in a flood of heat and hormones. The feel of his beard-roughened cheek beneath her lips, the strength of his tightly muscled body, the out-and-out maleness of him. She clung to him, overwhelmed by nostalgia for the past, for when she'd had the right to hold him close. *How could she ever have let go of that right?*

His hands grasped her shoulders to steady her. She could feel their warmth on her skin through the thick cloth of her robe. Swiftly, he released her. He muttered something inarticulate.

Reeling, she lifted her head in response, saw the shutters come down over his eyes—but not before she'd glimpsed something she couldn't read. It could have been passion but was more likely panic.

Bad, bad idea, Sandy, she berated herself. *Even a chaste peck is too much for him to handle.*

Too much for you to handle.

But no way was she was going to let herself feel ashamed

of a friendly thank-you kiss. She was used to spontaneous expressions of affection between friends.

She forced her breath to steady, tilted her chin upwards. 'See you in twenty,' she said, praying he didn't notice the tremor in her voice.

Ben stood back and watched as Sandy talked with his great-aunt in her room at the brand new Dolphin Bay Memorial Hospital. He might have known they would hit it off.

On doctor's orders, Ida was lying flat on her back in her hospital bed. She'd been told she had to hold that position for six weeks to heal her cracked pelvis.

Sandy had pulled up a chair beside her and was chatting away as if she and Ida were old friends.

Why, although they were talking about authors and titles of favourite books, did he sense this instant alliance could mean trouble for him? Trouble not of the business kind—hell, there was nothing he couldn't handle *there*— but a feminine kind of trouble he was not as well equipped to deal with.

Sandy was laughing and gesticulating with her hands as she spoke. His aunt was laughing too. It pleased him to see a warm flush vanquishing the grey tinge of pain from her face.

'What do you think, Ben?' Sandy asked.

'Me?'

'Yes. Who is the primary customer for Bay Books?'

He shrugged. 'People off the boats looking for something to read? Retirees?'

His aunt nodded. 'They're important, yes. But I sell more books to the telecommuters than to anyone else. They're crazy for book clubs. A book club gives them human contact as an antidote to the hours they spend working away on their computers, reporting to an office somewhere miles and miles away.'

Ben rubbed his hands together in simulated glee. 'All

those people fleeing the cities, making a sea-change to live on the coast—the lifeblood of commerce in Dolphin Bay. They're buying land, building houses, and spending their socks off.'

Sandy wrinkled up her nose in the way he remembered so well. It was just as cute on her at thirty as it had been at eighteen.

'That seems very calculating,' she said.

'What do you expect from the President of the Dolphin Bay Chamber of Commerce?' said Aunt Ida, her voice dripping with the pride all his family felt at his achievement. 'The town has really come on under his leadership.'

Sandy's eyes widened. 'You're full of surprises, Ben.'

On that so expressive face of hers he could see her wondering how he'd come from fisherman's son to successful businessman. Her father had judged him not good enough, not wealthy enough. He'd had no idea of how much land Ben's family owned. And Sandy didn't know how spurred on to succeed Ben had been by the snobby older man's low opinion of him.

'We have a lot to catch up on,' she said.

No.

More than ever he did *not* want to spend more time than was necessary with Sandy, reviving old feelings that were best left buried.

She was modestly dressed now, in a neat-fitting T-shirt and a skirt of some floaty material that covered her knees. But she'd answered the door to him at the hotel wrapped in nothing more than a Hotel Harbourside bathrobe.

As she'd spoken to him the robe had slid open to reveal the tantalising shadow between her breasts. Her face had been flushed and her hair damp. It was obvious she'd just stepped out of the shower and the thought of her naked had been almost more than his libido could take.

Naked in one of his hotel bathrooms. Naked under one of his hotel's bathrobes. It hadn't taken much to take the thought a step further to her naked on one of his hotel's beds. With the hotel's owner taking passionate possession.

He'd had to grit his teeth and force his gaze to somewhere above her head.

When she'd kissed him it had taken every ounce of his iron-clad self-control not to take her in his arms and kiss her properly. Not on the cheek but claiming her mouth, tasting her with his tongue, exploring her sexy body with hungry hands. Backing her into the room and onto the bed.

No.

There'd be no catching up on old times. Or letting his libido lead him where he had vowed not to go.

He cleared his throat. 'Isn't this conversation irrelevant to you running the bookstore for Aunt Ida?'

Sandy met his gaze in a way that let him know she knew only too well he was steering the conversation away from anything personal.

'Of course. You're absolutely right.'

She turned to face the hospital bed.

'Ida, tell me about any special orders.' Then she looked back at him, her head at a provocative angle. Her eyes gleamed with challenge. 'Is that better, Mr President?'

He looked to Ida for support, but her eyes narrowed as she looked from him to Sandy and back again.

It was starting. The speculation about him and Sandy. The gossip. And it looked as if he couldn't count on his aunt for support in his battle to protect his heart.

In fact she looked mighty pleased at the prospect of uncovering something personal between him and her temporary manager.

'You can tell me more about your past friendship with Sandy some other time, nephew of mine,' she said.

Sandy looked as uncomfortable as he felt, and had trouble meeting his gaze. 'Can we get back to talking about Bay Books, Ida?' she asked.

His aunt laughed. 'Back to the not nearly so interesting

topic of the bookshop? Okay, my dear, have you got something you can take some notes in? The special orders can get complicated.'

Looking relieved, Sandy dived into her handbag. She pulled out a luminous pink notebook and with it came a flurry of glitter that sparkled in the shafts of late-afternoon sun falling on his aunt's hospital bed.

'Sorry about the mess,' she said, biting down on her bottom lip as the particles settled across the bedcovers.

Ida seemed mesmerised by the glitter. 'It's not mess, it's fairy dust!' she exclaimed, clapping her hands with delight. Her still youthful blue eyes gleamed. 'Oh, this is wonderful, isn't it, Ben? Sandy will bring magic to Dolphin Bay. I just know it!'

Ben watched the tiny metallic particles as they glistened on the white hospital sheets. Saw the pleasure in his aunt's shrewd gaze, the gleam of reluctant laughter in Sandy's eyes.

'Magic? Well, it *did* come from my fairy notebook,' she said.

Something called him to join in their complicity, to believe in their fantasy.

Hope he'd thought long extinguished struggled to revive itself. Magic? *Was* it magic that Sandy had brought with her? Magic from the past? Magic for the future? He desperately wanted to believe that.

But there was no such thing as magic. He'd learnt that on a violently blazing day five years ago, when he had been powerless to save the lives of his family.

He would need a hell of a lot more than some so-called fairy dust to change his mind.

CHAPTER SEVEN

THE FIRST THING Sandy noticed on the beach early the next morning was the dog. A big, shaggy golden retriever, it lay near a towel on the sand near the edge of the water with its head resting on its paws. Its gaze was directed out to the surf of Big Ray Beach, the beach she'd reached via the boardwalk from the bay.

Twelve years ago she'd thought 'Big Ray' must refer to a person. No. Ben had informed her the beach had another name on the maps. But the locals had named it after the two enormous manta rays that lived on the northern end of the beach and every so often undulated their way to the other end. He had laughed at her squeals and hugged her close, telling her they were harmless and that he would keep her safe from anything that dared hurt her.

This morning there were only a few people in the water; she guessed one of them must be the dog's owner. At six-thirty, with strips of cloud still tinged pink from sunrise, it was already warm, the weather gearing up for sultry heat after the previous day's storm. Cicadas were already tuning up their chorus for the day.

Sandy smiled at the picture of doggy devotion. *Get dog of own once settled in Melbourne,* she added in a mental memo for her 'to do' list. That-Jerk-Jason had allergies and wouldn't tolerate a dog in the house. How had she been so in love with him when they'd had so little in common apart from their jobs?

She walked up to the dog and dropped to her knees in the sand. She offered it her hand to sniff, then ruffled the fur behind its neck. 'Aren't you a handsome boy?' she murmured.

The dog looked up momentarily, with friendly, intelligent eyes, thumped his plumed tail on the sand, then resumed his vigil.

She followed the animal's gaze, curious to see the object of such devotion. The dog's eyes were fixed on a man who was body-surfing. His broad, powerful shoulders and athletic physique were in perfect sync with the wave, harnessing its energy as it curled behind him and he shot towards shore.

The man was Ben.

She knew that even before he lifted his head from the water, a look of intense exhilaration on his face as he powered down the face of the wave. He was as at home on a wave as he had been when he was nineteen, and for a moment it was as if she were thrown back into the past. So much of her time with him that summer had been spent on this beach.

She was transported back to a morning like this when she'd run from the guesthouse to the sand and found him riding a wave, accompanied by a pod of dolphins, their grey shapes distinct on the underside of the wave. Joy and wonder had shone from his face. She'd splashed in to meet him and shared a moment of pure magic before the pod took off. Afterwards they'd lain on their backs on the beach, holding hands, marvelling over the experience. Did he remember?

Now he had seen her watching, and he lifted off the wave as it carried him into shore. She wanted to call out to him not to break off his ride on her account, but knew he wouldn't hear her over the sound of the surf.

He waved a greeting and swam, then strode towards her through the small breaking waves that foamed around his legs. Her breath caught in her throat at his near-naked magnificence. He was so tall and powerfully built that he seemed to dominate the vastness of the ocean and the horizon behind him.

His hair was dark and plastered to his head. The water was streaming off his broad shoulders and honed muscles. Sunlight glistened off the drops of water on his body so he seemed for one fanciful moment like some kind of mythical hero, emerging from the sea.

Desire, sudden and overwhelming, surged through her. Her nipples tensed and she seemed to melt inside. She wanted him. Longed for him. How could she ever have left him? She should have defied her parents and got back to Dolphin Bay. Somehow. Anyhow. Just to be with him.

That was back then. Now they were very different people who just happened to have found themselves on the same beach. But the attraction was as compelling as ever, undiluted by the years that had passed.

Why couldn't she forget that special time they had shared? What kept alive that fraction of hope that they could share it again? It wasn't just that she found him good-looking. This irrational compulsion was more than that. Something so powerful it overrode his rejection of her overtures. He didn't want her here. He had made that clear from the word go. She should just return his acquaintance-type wave and walk on.

But she ran in to the knee-deep waves to meet him. The dog splashed alongside her, giving a few joyous barks of welcome. She squealed at the sudden chill of the water as it sprayed her.

Remember, just friends, she reminded herself as she and Ben neared each other. Give him even a hint of the desire that had her so shaky and confused and he might turn back to that ocean and swim all the way to New Zealand.

'Good morning, Mr President,' she said. Ben as leader of the business community? It took some getting used to.

And yet the air of authority was there when he dealt with his staff at the hotel—and they certainly gave him the deference due to a well-respected boss.

'Just Ben will do,' he said as he walked beside her onto the dry sand. As always, she had trouble keeping up with his stride.

She was finding it almost impossible not to look at his body, impressive in red board shorts. Kept casting sideways glances at him.

'So you've met Hobo,' he said, with an affectionate glance at the dog.

'No formal introductions were made, but we said hello,' she said, still breathless at her physical reaction to him. 'Is he yours?'

She felt self-conscious at Ben's nearness, aware that she was wearing only a bikini covered by the skimpiest of tank tops.

'My mother helps out at a dog shelter. Sometimes she brings dogs home to foster until they find permanent homes. This one clapped eyes on me, followed me to my house and has been with me ever since.' He leaned down to pat the dog vigorously. 'Can't get rid of you, can I, mate?' He spoke with ill-concealed affection.

So he had something to love.

She was glad.

'He's adorable. And he guarded your towel like a well-trained soldier.'

Ben picked up the towel from the sand and flung it around his neck. *How many times had she seen him do that in just the same way? How many times had he tucked his towel solicitously around her if her own towel was damp?*

'What brings you to the beach so early?' he asked.

She pulled a face. 'Had to walk those Snickers bars off.'

'How many gone?'

'Only two.'

'One for dinner and one for breakfast?'

'Chocolate for breakfast? I've got a sweet tooth, but I'm not a total sugar freak.' She scuffed her foot in the sand. 'I couldn't sleep. Kept thinking of all I don't know about managing a bookstore.' *Kept thinking about you.*

He picked up a piece of driftwood and threw it for Hobo. The dog bounded into the water to retrieve it.

'You took a lot of notes from Aunt Ida yesterday.'

'It's just nerves. Bay Books is so important for Ida and I want to get it right.'

'You'll be fine. It's only for a few days.'

No doubt he meant to sound reassuring. But it seemed as if he was reminding her yet again that he wanted her out of Dolphin Bay.

'Yes. Just a few days,' she echoed. 'I guess I won't bankrupt the place in that time.'

Hobo splashed out of the shallows with the driftwood in his mouth, grinning a doggy grin and looking very pleased with himself. He dropped it between their feet.

Sandy reached down to pick it up at the same time as Ben did. She collided with his warm, solid shoulders, felt her head connect with his. 'Ouch!' She rubbed the side of her temple.

'Are you okay?' Ben pulled her to her feet and turned her to face him.

They stood very close, her hands on his shoulders where she'd braced herself for balance. He was damp and salty and smelled as fresh and clean as the morning. It would be so easy to slide her hands down, to tangle her fingers in his chest hair, test the strength of his muscles. Every cell in her body seemed to tingle with awareness where his bare skin touched hers.

She nodded, scarcely able to speak. 'That's one tough skull you've got there. But I'm fine. Really.'

He gently probed her head, his fingers sending currents of sensation coursing through her. 'There's no bump.'

'I think I'll live,' she managed to choke out, desperately attempting to sound flippant.

His big scarred hands moved from her scalp to cradle her face. He tilted her head so she was forced to look up into his eyes. For a long moment he searched her face.

'I don't want to hurt you, Sandy,' he said, his voice hoarse.

She knew he wasn't talking about the collision. 'I realise that, Ben,' she whispered.

Then, with her eyes drowning in his, he kissed her.

She was so surprised she stood stock-still for a moment. Then she relaxed into the sensation of Ben's mouth on hers. It felt like coming home.

When Ben had lifted his head from the wave and had seen Sandy standing on the beach, it had been as if the past and the present had coalesced into one shining moment. A joy so unexpected it was painful had flooded his heart.

And here he was, against all resolutions, kissing her.

Her lips were warm and pliant beneath his. Her breasts were pressed to his chest. Her eyes, startled at first, were filled with an expression of bliss.

He shouldn't be kissing her. Starting things he could not finish. Risking pain for both of them. But those thoughts were lost in the wonder of having her close to him again.

It was as if the twelve years between kisses had never happened.

He twined his hands in her shiny vanilla-scented hair, tilted her head back as he deepened the kiss, pushed against her lips with his tongue. Her mouth parted to welcome him, to meet the tip of his tongue with hers.

She made a small murmur of appreciation and wound her arms around his neck. His arms slid to her waist, to the smooth, warm skin where her top stopped, drawing her close. He could feel her heart thudding against his chest.

He wanted her. She could surely feel his arousal. But

this wasn't just about sex. It had always been so much more than that with Sandy.

The world shrank to just him and her, and the surf was a muted pounding that echoed the pulsing of their hearts, the blood running hot through his veins.

He could feel her nipples hard against him. Sensed the shiver of pleasure that vibrated through her. He pulled her tighter, wanting her as close to him as she could be.

But then something landed near his foot, accompanied by a piteous whining. Hobo. The driftwood. *Damn!*

He ignored it. Sand was dug in a flurry around them, stinging his legs. The whining turned to sharp, demanding barks.

Inwardly he cursed. Willed Hobo to go away. But the dog just kept on digging and barking. Ben broke away from the first time he'd kissed Sandy in twelve years for long enough to mutter, 'Get lost, boy.'

But when he quickly reclaimed Sandy's lips she was trembling. Not with passion but repressed laughter. 'He's not going to go away, you know,' she murmured against his mouth.

Ben groaned. He swore. He leaned down, grabbed the driftwood and threw it as far away as he could—so hard he nearly wrenched his shoulder.

Now Sandy was bent over with laughter. 'He wasn't going to let up, was he?'

Ben cursed his dog again.

'I know you don't really mean that,' she said, with a mischievous tilt to her mouth. 'Poor Hobo.'

'Back to the shelter for him,' Ben growled.

'As if,' said Sandy.

She looked up to him, her eyes still dancing with laughter. She looked as though she'd been thoroughly kissed. He didn't shave until after his morning surf and her chin was all pink from his beard. He felt a surge of possessiveness so fierce it was primal.

'That…that was nice, Ben.'

Nice? He struggled for a word to sum up what it had meant to him. When he didn't reply straight away, the soft, satisfied light of a woman who knew she was desired seemed to dim in her eyes.

'More than nice,' he said, and her eyes lit up again.

He reached out to smooth that wayward lock of hair from her eyes. She caught his hand with hers and dropped a quick kiss on it before she let it go.

'Why did you kiss me, Ben, when with every second breath you're telling me go away?'

Did he know the answer himself? 'Because I—'

He couldn't find the words to say, *Because you're Sandy, and you're beautiful, and I still can't believe you've come back to me, but I'm afraid to let you in because I don't want to love you and then lose you again.*

Her eyes were huge in her flushed face. She'd got damp from hugging him while he was still wet from the surf. Her tank top clung to her curves, her nipples standing erect through the layers of fabric.

She ran the edge of her pink pointy tongue along her lips to moisten her mouth. He watched, fascinated, aching to kiss her again.

A tremor edged her voice. 'It's still there, isn't it, Ben? That attraction. That feeling there isn't anyone else in this world at this moment but you and me. It was like that from the start and it hasn't changed.' She took a deep gulp of air. 'If only…'

He clenched his fists so hard his scars ached. 'I told you—no if-onlys. That—the kiss—it shouldn't have happened.'

'Why not?' Her eyes were still huge. 'We're both free. Grown-up now and able to choose what we want from our lives, choose who we want to be with.'

Choose to leave when we want to.

Even after that one brief kiss he could feel what it would

be like, having found her, to lose her again. He'd managed fine these past years on his own. He couldn't endure the pain of loss again.

She looked very serious, her brow creased. 'That time we had together all those years ago was so special. I don't know about you, but I was too young to appreciate just how special. I never again felt that certainty, that rightness. Maybe this unexpected time together is a gift. For us to get to know each other again. Or…or…maybe we have to try it again so that we can let it go. Have you thought of that?'

He shook his head. 'It's not that easy, Sandy.'

'Of course it isn't easy. It isn't easy for me either. I'm not in a rush to get my heart broken again.'

He noticed again the shadows under her eyes. Remembered her ex had got married yesterday. Typically, she wasn't letting on about her pain. But it was there.

'I can see that,' he said.

He was glad the beach was practically deserted, with just a few people walking along the hard, damp sand at the edge of the waves, others still in the surf. Hobo romped with another dog in the shallows.

Her voice was low and intense. 'Maybe if we gave it a go we'd…we'd burn it out.'

'You think so?' He couldn't keep the cynicism from his voice.

She threw up her hands. 'Who knows? After all this time we don't really know what the other is like now. Grown-up Sandy. Grown-up Ben. We might hate each other.'

'I can't see that happening.' Hate Sandy? No way. Never.

She scuffed the sand with her bare toes, not meeting his eyes. 'How do you know? I like to put a positive spin on things when I can. But, fact is, I haven't had a lot of luck with men. When I started dating—after I gave up on us seeing each other again—it seemed to me there were two types of men: nice ones, like you, who would ultimately betray me—'

He growled his protest.

She looked back up at him. 'I know now it was a mis-understanding between us, but I didn't know that then. If anyone betrayed me it was my father. By lying to me about you. By cheating on our family.'

He didn't disagree. 'And the second type of man?'

'Forceful, controlling guys—'

'Like your father?'

She nodded. 'They'd convince me they knew what was best for me. I'd be in too deep before I realised they had anything but my interests at heart. But obviously I must have been at fault, too, when things went wrong.'

'You're too hard on yourself.' He hated to see the tight expression on her face.

Her mouth twisted into an excuse of a smile. 'Am I? Even little things about a person can get annoying. Jason used to hate that I never replaced the empty toilet roll. It was only because the fancy holder he installed ruined my nails when I tried, but—'

Ben couldn't believe what he was hearing. 'What kind of a loser *was* this guy?'

'He wasn't a loser. He was smart. Clever. It seemed I could be myself with him. I thought at last I'd found Mr Perfect. But that was one of the reasons he gave for falling out of love with me.' She bit down hard on her lower lip. 'And he said I was noisy and a show-off.'

Ben was so astounded he couldn't find an appropriate response.

Her eyes flickered to his face and then away. 'When I first knew him he said I lit up a room just by coming into it. *Effervescent* was the word he used. By the end he said I embarrassed him with my loud behaviour.'

Her voice was forcedly cheerful but there was a catch to it that tore at Ben.

'But you don't want to hear about that.'

Anger against this unknown man who had hurt Sandy

fuelled him. 'You're damn right I don't. It's crap. That jerk was just saying that to make himself feel better about betraying you.'

She pulled a self-deprecating face. 'I tell myself that too. It made me self-conscious around people for a while—you know…the noisy show-off thing. I couldn't help wondering if people were willing me to shut up but were too polite to say so. But…but I've put it behind me.'

With his index finger he tilted her face upwards. 'Sandy. Look at me. I would never, ever think you were an embarrassing show-off. I never have and I never will. Okay? You're friendly and warm and you put people at ease. That's a gift.'

'Nice of you to say so. Kind words are always welcome.' Her voice made light of what she said.

'And I would never give a damn about a toilet roll.'

Her mouth twitched. 'It sounds so dumb when you say it out loud. A toilet roll.' The twitch led to a smile and then to full-blown giggles. 'What a stupid thing for a relationship to founder over.'

'And what a moron he was to let it.'

Ben found himself laughing with her. It felt good. Again, like oil on those rusty, seized emotions he had thought would never be kick-started into life again.

'I was just using the toilet roll as an example of how little things about a person can get annoying to someone else,' she said. Her laughter died away. 'After a few days of my company you might be glad to see the end of me.'

'And vice-versa?' The way he'd cut himself off from relationships, she was more likely to get the worst end of the bargain. He was out of the habit of being a boyfriend.

She nodded. 'Then we could both move on, free of… free of this thing that won't let go of us. With…with the past washed clean.'

'Maybe,' he conceded.

She wanted to rekindle old embers to see if they burned

again or fizzled away into lifeless ash. But what if they raged away like a bush fire out of control and he was the one left scorched and lifeless? *Again.*

She took hold of his arm. Her voice was underscored with urgency. 'Ben, we should grab this second chance. Otherwise we might regret it for the rest of our lives. Like I regret that I didn't trust in what we had. I should have come back to you to Dolphin Bay. I was eighteen years old, for heaven's sake, not eight. What could my parents have done about it?'

'I came looking for you in Sydney.' He hadn't meant to let that out. Had never intended to tell her.

Her brows rose. 'When?'

'A few months after you left.'

'I didn't know.'

'You wouldn't. My mates were playing football at Chatswood, on the north shore. I had my dad's car to drive down with them.' He'd been up from university for the Easter break. 'After the game I found your place.'

'The house in Killara?'

He nodded. It had been a big house in a posh northern suburb, designed to show off her father's social status. 'I parked outside, hoping I'd see you. Not sure what I'd do if I did.'

'Why didn't you come in?'

'I was nineteen. You hadn't written. Or phoned. For all I knew you'd forgotten all about me. And I knew your father wouldn't welcome me.'

'Was I there? I can't believe while you were outside I might have been in my room. Probably sobbing into my diary about how much I was missing you.'

'Your hat was hanging on the veranda. I could see it from outside. That funny, stripy bucket hat you used to wear.'

She screwed up her face. 'I remember... I lost that hat.'

'No, you didn't. I took it. I jumped over the fence and snatched it.'

Her eyes widened. 'You're kidding me? My old hat? Do…
do you still have it?'

'Once I was back in the car my mates grabbed it from me.
When we crossed the Sydney Harbour Bridge they threw
it out of the window.'

'Hey! That hat cost a whole lot of hard-earned babysit-
ting money.'

She pretended outrage, but he could tell she was shaken
by his story.

'I didn't steal it to see it squashed by a truck. I wanted to
punch my mates out. But they told me to stop bothering with
a girl who didn't want me when there were plenty who did.'

Sandy didn't say anything for a moment. Then she
sighed. 'Oh, Ben, if only…' She shook her head. 'I won't
say it. You're right. No point.'

'That's when I gave up on you.'

He'd said enough. He could never admit that for years
afterwards when he'd driven over that spot on the bridge
he'd looked out for her hat.

'And there *were* other girls?' She put her hand up in her
halt sign. 'No. Don't tell me about them. I couldn't bear
it.' Her eyes narrowed. 'I used to imagine all those blonde
surfer chicks. Glad the city interloper was gone. Able to
have their surf god all to themselves again.'

He stared at her incredulously. 'Did you just call me a
surf god?'

Colour stained her cheeks. 'Hey, I'm in advertising. I
get creative with copy.' But when she looked up at him her
eyes were huge and sincere. 'I adored you, Ben. You must
know that.' Her voice caught in her throat.

Ben shifted from foot to foot in the sand. 'I… Uh… Same
here.' *He'd planned his life around her.*

'Let's spend these four days together,' she urged. 'Forget all that's happened to us since we last saw each other.
Just go back to how we were. Sandy and Ben. Teenagers

again. Carefree. Enjoying each other's company. Recapturing what we had.'

'You mean a fling?'

'A four-day fling? No strings? Why not? I'm prepared to risk it if you are.'

Risk. Was he ready to risk the safe life he'd so carefully constructed around himself in Dolphin Bay? He'd done so well in business by taking risks. But taking this risk—even for four days—could have far greater complications than monetary loss.

'Sandy. I hear what you're saying. But I need time.'

'Ben, we don't have time. We—'

Hobo skidded at their feet, the driftwood in his mouth, wet and eager and demanding attention.

Sandy glared at the animal. 'You have a great sense of timing, dog.'

'Yeah, he's known for it.' Ben reached down for the driftwood and tossed it just a short distance away. 'I've got to get him back. Dogs are only allowed unleashed on the beach before seven a.m.'

'And you can't be seen to be breaking the rules, can you?'

Was she taunting him?

No. The expression in her eyes was wistful, and he realised how she'd put herself on the line for him. For them. Or the possibility of them.

He turned to her. 'I'll consider what you said, Sandy.'

Her tone was again forcedly cheerful. 'Okay, Mr President.'

He grinned. 'I prefer surf god.'

'I'm going to regret telling you I called you that, aren't I? Okay, surf god. But don't take too long. These four days will be gone before we know it and then I'm out of here. Let's not waste them.' She turned to face the water. 'Are the mantas still in residence?'

'Yes. More likely their descendants, still scaring the hell out of tourists.'

He remembered how she'd started off being terrified of the big black rays. But by the end of that summer she'd been snorkelling around them. She had overcome her fears. Could he be as brave?

She reached up and hugged him. Briefly, he held her bare warmth to him before she pushed him away.

'Go,' she said, her voice not quite steady. 'Me? I'm having my first swim at Big Ray Beach for twelve years. I can't wait to get into the surf.'

With unconscious grace she pulled off her skimpy tank top, giving him the full impact of her body in a brief yellow bikini. *Her breasts were definitely bigger than they'd been when she was eighteen.*

Was he insane not to pull her back into his arms? To kiss her again? To laugh with her again? To have her as part of his life again?

For four days.

She headed for the water, treating him to a tantalising view of her sexy, shapely bottom. 'Come see me when you've done your thinking,' she called over her shoulder, before running into the surf.

She squealed as the cold hit her. Water sprayed up over her slim brown legs and the early sunlight shattered into a million glistening crystals. *More fairy dust.*

He looked at the tracks her feet had made in the sand. After the fire he had felt as if he'd been broken down to nothing—like rock into sand. Slowly, painfully, he had put himself back together. But there were cracks, places deep inside him, that still crumbled at the slightest touch.

If he let it, could Sandy's magic help give him the strength to become not the man he had been but someone better, finer, forged by the tragedy he had endured? Or would she break him right back down to nothing?

CHAPTER EIGHT

EVERY TIME THE old-fashioned bell on the top of the entrance door to Bay Books jangled Sandy looked up, heart racing, body tensed in anticipation. And every time it wasn't Ben she felt so let down she had to force herself to smile and cheerfully greet the customers, hoping they wouldn't detect the false note to her voice.

When would he come? Surely he wanted to be with her as much as she ached to be with him?

Or was he staying away because she had driven him away, by coming on too strong before he was ready? His reaction had both surprised and hurt her. Why had he been so uncertain about taking this second, unexpected chance with her? It was only for four days. Surely they could handle that?

She knew she should stop reliving every moment on the beach this morning over and over again, as if she were still eighteen. But she couldn't stop thinking about the kiss. That wonderful, wonderful kiss. After all those years it could have been a let-down. But kissing Ben again had been everything she had ever fantasised about. In his arms, his mouth claiming hers, she'd still felt the same heady mix of comfort, pleasure and bone-melting desire. It was as if their twelve-year separation had never happened.

Although there was a difference. Now she wanted him with an adult's hunger—an adult's sensual knowledge of the pleasures that could follow a kiss.

She remembered how on fire with first-time desire she'd felt all that time ago, when they'd been making out behind the boat shed. Or in the back seat of his father's car, parked on the bluff overlooking the ocean. They hadn't even noticed the view. Not that they could have seen it through the fogged-up windows.

And yet she hadn't let him go all the way. Hadn't felt ready for that final step. Even though she had been head-over-heels in love with him.

Her virginal young self hadn't appreciated the effort it must have taken for Ben to hold back. 'When you're ready,' he'd always said. Not like her experiences with boys in Sydney—'suitable' sons of her fathers' friends—all grabby hands and then sulks when she'd slapped them away. No. Ben truly had been her Sir Galahad on a surfboard.

Would a four-day fling include making love with Ben? That might be more than she—or Ben—could handle. They should keep it to kissing. And talking. And lots of laughing. Like it had been back then. Carefree. Uncomplicated.

She refused to listen to that nagging internal voice. *Could anything be uncomplicated with the grown-up Ben?*

She forced her thoughts back to the present and got on with her work. She had to finish the job Ida had been in the middle of when she'd fallen—unpacking a delivery and slotting the books artfully onto the 'new releases' table.

Just minutes later, with a sigh of satisfaction, she stepped back to survey her work. She loved working in the book-shop. Even after just a few hours she felt right at home. The individuality and quirkiness of Ida's set-up connected with her, though she could immediately see things she'd like to change to bring the business model of this bricks-and-mortar bookstore more in step to compete with the e-bookstores. That said, if she could inject just a fraction of Bay Books' charm into her candle shop she'd be very happy. She must write in her fairy notebook: *Ask Ida about Balinese woodcarvers.*

But it wasn't just about the wooden dolphins with their enchanting carved smiles. The idyllic setting was a vital part of Bay Books. Not, she suspected, to be matched by the high-volume-retail-traffic Melbourne mall the candle people would insist on for their shop. It might be hard to get as excited about that.

Here, she only had to walk over to the window to view the quaint harbour, with the old-fashioned stone walls that sheltered it from the turquoise-blue waters of the open sea—only had to push the door open to hear the squawk of seagulls, breathe in the salt-tangy air.

This morning, in her hotel room, she had been awoken by a chorus of kookaburras. When she'd opened the sliding doors to her balcony it had been to find a row of lorikeets, the small, multi-coloured parrots like living gems adorning the balcony railing. On her way to the beach she'd surprised two small kangaroos, feeding in the grass in the bushland between the boardwalk and the sand dunes of Big Ray. It was good for the soul.

What a difference from fashionable, revitalised inner-city Surry Hills, where she lived in Sydney. It had more restaurants, bars and boutiques than she would ever have time to try. But it was densely populated and in summer could be stiflingly hot and humid. Driving round and round the narrow streets, trying to find somewhere to park her car, she'd sometimes dreamed of living in a place closer to nature.

And here she was back in Dolphin Bay, working in a stranger's bookshop, reconnecting with her first love.

It seemed surreal.

She paused, a paperback thriller in her hand. Remembered her pink-inked resolution. *Get as far away from Sydney as possible.*

That didn't necessarily have to mean moving to Melbourne.

But she had only ever been a city girl. Could she settle for small-town life and the restrictions that entailed?

The bell sounded again. She looked up, heart thudding, mouth suddenly dry. But again it wasn't Ben. It was red-haired Kate, the waitress from the hotel.

'Hey, nice to see you, Kate,' she said, masking her disappointment that the woman wasn't her tall blond surf god.

'You too,' said Kate. 'We all love this shop and the personal service Ida gives us. It's great you're able to help her out.'

'Isn't it? I'm getting the hang of things. Can I help you with a book?' she asked.

Kate smiled and Sandy wondered if she could tell how inexperienced a shopkeeper she was.

'Ida ordered some titles for me, but in all the drama yesterday I didn't get a chance to see if they were in.'

'Sure,' said Sandy, heading behind the counter to access Ida's computer. She had the special orders file open when Kate leaned towards her over the carved wooden counter.

'So, I heard you and Ben were kissing on the beach this morning.'

Sandy was so flabbergasted she choked. She coughed and spluttered, unable to utter a word in response.

Kate rushed around the counter and patted Sandy's back until her breath came more easily.

'Thanks,' Sandy finally managed to choke out.

'Don't be so surprised. News travels fast in Dolphin Bay.'

Sandy took another ragged breath. 'I'm beginning to see that.'

Kate's green eyes gleamed. 'So you *were* kissing Ben?'

Again Sandy was too aghast to reply. 'Well, I…' she started.

'She who hesitates is thinking of how to tell me to mind my own business,' said Kate with a grin.

Sandy laughed at her audacity. 'Well, now that you mention it…'

'Feel free to tell me to keep my big mouth shut, but… well, I love Ben to pieces and I don't want—'

Ben and Kate?

Sandy felt dizzy—not from lack of air but from the feeling that her heart had plummeted to the level of her ballet flats. 'I'm sorry, Kate, I didn't know… He didn't say…'

Kate's auburn eyebrows rose. 'I don't mean *that* kind of love. My mum and Ben's mum are friends. I grew up with Ben. It's his brother, Jesse, I have a thing for. Unrequited, unfortunately.'

'Oh,' said Sandy, beyond relieved that Kate hadn't marched into the bookshop to stake a claim on Ben.

Kate leaned closer. 'You *do* realise that for Ben to be kissing a woman in public is a big, big deal?'

Sandy took a step back. 'It was six-thirty in the morning on a practically deserted beach.'

'That might be private in Sydney, but not in a place like Dolphin Bay. Here, it takes one person to see for everyone to know.'

'I had no idea.' Sandy felt suddenly dry in the mouth. What kind of pressure did this put on Ben? On her?

'You and Ben together is big news.'

'Then next time—if there is a next time—I'll make sure we're completely alone.'

She spoke with such vehemence that Kate frowned and took a step back from her. 'I'm sorry, Sandy. But this is a small town. We all look out for each other. If you're not serious about Ben don't start something you're not prepared to see through.'

Sandy gripped the edge of the counter. She knew Ben had been to hell and wasn't yet all the way back. She didn't need anyone to tell her.

Pointedly, she scrolled through the special orders file on Ida's computer, looked up again at Kate. 'I don't see your order here, but your contact number is. How about I call you when it comes in?'

Kate shifted from foot to foot. 'You must think I'm the nosiest busybody you've ever met.'

Sandy didn't disagree.

'But I've only got Ben's interests at heart,' Kate continued, sounding hurt.

Sandy gentled her tone of voice. 'I appreciate that.'

She was gratified at Kate's smile as she said goodbye. Despite the redhead's total lack of tact, she thought she could get to like her.

But Kate's visit, with her revelation about the undercurrents of small-town life, had left her reeling. She'd had no idea that any reunion would be conducted under such watchful eyes. What had seemed so simple on the beach at dawn suddenly seemed very complicated.

It made her self-conscious when dealing with the customers who came in dribs and drabs through the doors. Were they genuinely interested in browsing through the books—or in perusing her? Her doubts were realised when two older ladies, hidden from full view behind a display of travel books, spoke in too-loud whispers they obviously thought she couldn't hear.

'She seems nice, and Ida likes her,' said the first one. 'That's a point in her favour.'

Sandy held her breath when she realised they were talking about her.

'It might be a good thing. Ben's been in mourning for too long. His mother's worried about him,' said the other.

'I wonder what Jodi's parents will think.' The first lady sighed. 'Such a sweet girl. What a loss. No wonder Ben's stayed on his own all this time.'

Sandy slammed her hand over her mouth so the ladies wouldn't hear her gasp. *Jodi.* Ben's late wife. The gentle woman Ben had loved enough to marry and have a child with.

She stared ahead without seeing. Noticed a poster promoting a bestselling new celebrity biography had come adrift at one corner. But she felt too shaken to do anything about it. Would there always be the memory of another woman coming between her and Ben? *Could she cope with coming second? With being just a disposable fling while his wife always held first place in his heart?*

She couldn't meet the ladies' eyes when they scurried out through the door without buying a book.

An old familiar panic had started to overwhelm her—the same panic she'd used to feel when she'd been faced with those big waves rearing up so aggressively as she'd stood dry-mouthed with terror on the beach. Ben had helped her conquer that fear and discover the joy of riding the waves— and she'd used the memory to help her deal with any number of challenges she'd faced in her career. But now what she'd thought would be smooth water ahead might be filled with swirling undercurrents. Did she have the strength to battle through the rough water?

Was it worth it for a four-day fling?

The bell on the top of the door jangled again. She jumped. More ladies to check her out and assess her suitability?

Ben shouldered his way through the door, carrying two large take-away coffee containers. The smile he gave her made her heart do the flippy thing—backwards, forwards and tumbling over itself. Her breath seemed to accelerate, making her feel light-headed, giddy.

Her surf god. In the flesh and hotter than ever.

He was back in shorts, and a blue polo shirt that hugged the breadth of his shoulders and brought out the blue of his eyes. She preferred the semi-naked beach look, but in true surf god manner he looked wonderful in anything he wore.

She smiled back in her joy at seeing him again. It was four hours and thirty-five minutes since she'd said goodbye to him on the beach.

She prayed no customers would intrude. More than ever she needed to be alone with Ben. To be reassured that the thing between them was worth taking the risks of which she'd been so blithely ignorant.

Kate's words had hit home. Made her all too aware of

the power she had to wound Ben. After all, she was the one who had left him all those years ago. Then he'd been young and untroubled, and still she had hurt him. Now he was anything but untroubled.

Could he deal with a walk-away-from-it fling?

Could *she*?

The expectations of her were frightening. But what if the reality of Ben didn't match up to her memories? What if they didn't have a thing in common and she wanted to run after the first twenty-four hours? What if he wanted her to stay and she hurt him all over again? Or if she fell hard for him again but couldn't match up to his wife? Then it would be her with her heart broken again.

She caught her breath in what felt dangerously like a sob.

Could she do this?

'You okay?'

His marvellous blue eyes were warm with concern for her. That sexy, sexy mouth was set in a serious line that just made her want to kiss it into a smile. Wordlessly, she nodded.

Could she not do it?

'Apparently we were seen on the beach this morning,' she said.

'Seen and duly noted. Makes you wonder what else people have to do with their time.'

'You're big news in Dolphin Bay.'

He put the coffee down on the counter. 'You're bigger news.'

'Tell me about it. The predatory city slicker hunting down the town's favourite son.'

She'd meant that to sound like a joke. But as soon as it came out she knew it was anything but funny.

Ben frowned. 'Did someone say that?'

'Yes. Well, not in so many words. Kate dropped in.' She couldn't help the wobble in her voice.

Why had Kate and those women come in and ruined

everything? Made her feel suddenly so self-conscious with Ben?

She just wanted to fall back into his arms and continue where they'd left off this morning. But the exchange she'd overheard had unsettled her.

She bit down on her lower lip and looked up at Ben, not certain what to do next. How could she tell him she was having cold feet because she was so terrified of hurting him? Could she find the courage to ask him about Jodi?

CHAPTER NINE

To Ben, Sandy looked as if she'd always stood behind the counter of Bay Books. The short hair he was still getting used to was tucked behind her ears. Just below her left shoulder she had pinned a round metal badge that urged people to get involved with a local literacy campaign. She looked smart, efficient—every inch the professional sales-person. Yet her yellow dress seemed to bring the sunlight right into the corners of the dark wooden carvings so fa-voured by Aunt Ida, and her vanilla scent brought a sweet new warmth.

She fitted right in.

Ida would be delighted.

But Sandy looked anything but happy—she was wary, guarded, with a shadow behind her eyes. She was chewing her lip so hard she was in danger of drawing blood.

Fear gripped him deep in his gut. What gave here?

'Hey,' he said, and went around the counter to pull her into his arms, expecting her warm curves to relax against him. Instead she stiffened and resisted his embrace.

Why the sudden cold change? Hell, he'd worked damn hard to pull down a chink in those barriers he'd built up. Had she now decided to put up a few of her own?

It didn't figure.

'What's going on?' he asked.

Sandy took a step back, her struggle to decide what to tell

him etched on her face. She picked up a waxed paper coffee cup, took a sip. Her hand wasn't quite steady and the froth on the top wobbled dangerously. She put it down and the foam slid over the lid of the cup and dribbled down its side.

'Leave it,' he said as she reached for a cloth to wipe it up.

'No. It might damage the wood,' she said.

She cleaned the spill too thoroughly. A delaying tactic if ever he'd seen one.

She put the cloth away, started to speak way too rapidly. 'Why don't we take our coffee over to the round table?' She was gabbling, her eyes blinking rapidly as she looked everywhere but at him. 'It's a cosier place to have coffee. Y'know, I'm thinking it would be great for Ida to have a café here. Maybe knock through to the vacant shop next door so that customers—'

She went to pick up the coffee cup again, but he closed his hand around her wrist to stop her. He wouldn't give her an excuse to evade him. Her hand stilled under his. 'Tell me. Now.'

Her eyes flickered up to meet his and then back down. When she spoke, her words came out in a rush. 'Kate told me the whole town is watching to see if I hurt you.'

In his relief, he cursed. 'Is that all?' He let go her wrist.

'What do you mean, *is that all*?' Hands on hips, she glared at him with the ferocity of a fluffed-up kitten. 'Don't you patronise me, Ben Morgan. Kate really freaked me out.'

He used both hands to push down in a gesture of calm. 'Kate exaggerates. Kate and the old-school people who were here before Dolphin Bay became a hotspot for escapees from the city. They all mind each other's business.'

Sandy's chin tilted upwards. 'And your business in particular, if Kate's to be believed.'

He shook his head. 'It's no big deal.'

'Are you telling me that's part and parcel of living in a small town?'

He picked up his coffee. Drank a few mouthfuls to give

him time to think. It was just as he had predicted. *Ben's old girlfriend is back.* He could practically hear the hot news humming through cyberspace. 'Yeah. Better get used to it.'

'I don't know if I can.' Her voice rose to a higher pitch. 'I'm used to the don't-give-a-damn attitude of the city.'

Ben thought back to how the town had pulled together for him after the fire. How it had become so stifling he'd had to get away. He'd thrown himself into high-risk money-making ventures because he'd had nothing to lose when he'd already lost everything. They'd paid off in spades. And he'd come back. Dolphin Bay would always be home. No matter that sad memories haunted him at every turn.

But why should that hothouse concern for him bother Sandy?

Her arms were crossed defensively against her chest. Was she using her fear of the townfolk's gossip to mask some deeper reluctance? Some concern she had about him?

He chose his words carefully. 'I can see that. But you're only here for four more days. We're not thinking beyond that, right? Why worry about what they think?'

'I just do,' she said, in a very small voice.

He put down his coffee, put his finger under her chin and tilted it upwards so she was forced to meet his gaze. 'What else did Kate say?'

'It wasn't Kate. There were some other women. Customers. They…they were talking about…about Jodi.'

Pain knifed through him at the sound of Jodi's name. People tended to avoid saying it in front of him.

His feelings must have shown on his face, because Sandy looked stricken.

'Ben, I'm so sorry…'

She went to twist away from him, but he stopped her.

'I should tell you about Jodi.'

The words would be wrenched from him, but he had to tell Sandy about his wife. There should be no secrets between them. Not if they were to enjoy the four days they had together.

'Ben. No. You don't have to—'

He gently put his hand over her mouth to silence her and she nodded.

He dropped his hand. 'I loved Jodi. Don't ever think otherwise. She was a good wife and a wonderful mother.'

'Of course.' Sandy's eyes were warm with compassion—and a touch of wariness.

'I'd known her all my life. But I didn't date her until I'd finished university and was working in Melbourne.'

Sandy's brows rose. 'University? You said—'

'You wouldn't catch me in a classroom again?'

'That's right. You said it more than once. I remember because I was looking forward to going to uni.'

'You can thank your father for my business degree.'

She frowned. 'My father? I—'

'He used to look at me as if I were something scraped off the bottom of his shoe. Left me in no doubt that I wasn't worthy of his daughter.' Ben would have liked to apply some apt swear words to his memories of Dr Randall Adams, but Sandy might not appreciate that.

Sandy protested. 'Surely he didn't say that to you? I can't believe he—'

'He didn't have to say it. I saw his sneer.'

Her mouth twisted. 'No wonder I never got your letters.'

Teen testosterone had made him want to flatten the guy. 'But he had a point. To be worthy of his daughter I needed to get off my surfboard and make something of myself. I had deferred places at universities in both Sydney and Melbourne to choose from.'

'You never said…'

'At the time I had no intention of taking either. I just wanted to surf every good break at Big Ray Beach and work for my dad when I needed money to travel to other surf beaches. That summer… I guess it made me grow up.'

He'd been determined to prove Dr Adams wrong. And broadening his horizons had been the right choice, even if made for the wrong reasons. And now fate had brought Sandy back to him. Now they met as equals in every way.

'You could have been studying at the same uni as me,' Sandy said slowly. She pulled a face that looked sad rather than funny. 'I won't say *if only* again.'

They both fell silent. But Ben refused to give in to musing about what might have been. He had tortured himself enough.

Sandy cleared her throat. 'What happened after you finished uni?'

'I was offered a job in a big stockbroking firm in Melbourne. Got an apartment and stayed down there.'

'But you came home for holidays? And…and met up with Jodi again?'

He could tell Sandy was finding the conversation awkward. She twisted the fabric of her skirt between the fingers of her right hand without seeming to be aware she was doing it.

'I had an accident in the surf. Got hit in the face with the fin of my board.' His hand went to the scar on his lip. 'Jodi was the nurse who looked after me at the hospital.'

And it had started from there. A relaxed, no-strings relationship with a sweet, kind-hearted girl that had resulted in an unplanned pregnancy.

He'd said there were to be no secrets from Sandy, but Liam's unexpected conception was something he didn't want to share with her. Not yet. Maybe never.

'Jodi moved down to Melbourne with me after we got married.'

'What…what brought you both back to Dolphin Bay?'

'I'm not a city guy. I'd had it with Melbourne. The insane work hours, the crowds, the traffic. Mum and Dad were tired of running the guesthouse. Jodi wanted to be with family when she had the baby.'

He gritted his teeth, trying not to let himself be over-whelmed by emotion when he thought of his baby son. The son he'd loved so fiercely from the moment he'd been placed in his arms as a newborn and yet hadn't been able to protect.

'I could trade shares from here. Start business projects here.'

There was another pause. Sandy twisted the edge of her skirt even tighter. 'Those ladies… They…they said Jodi's parents wouldn't be happy with me coming onto the scene.'

Ben clenched his hands into fists. Who *were* these busy-body troublemakers? If he found out he'd tell them to damn well butt out of his business.

He shook his head. 'Not true. Jodi's mum and dad are good people. They want me to…to have someone in my life again.'

Sandy's eyes widened. 'You know that for sure?'

'Yes. They've told me not to let the…the tragedy ruin my life. That…that it's not what Jodi would have wanted.'

'And you believe that? About Jodi?'

He nodded. His words were constricted in his throat. 'The night Liam was born she told me that if anything hap-pened to her—she was a nurse and knew there could be complications in childbirth—she didn't want me to be on my own. She…she made me promise I would find some-one else…'

'Oh, Ben.'

Sandy laid her hand on his arm. He realised she was close to tears. When she spoke again her voice was so choked he had to strain to hear her.

'How can I live up to such a wonderful woman?'

In a few shaky steps she made her way around the coun-ter and stood with her back to him. She picked up a book from the display and put it back in exactly the same place.

'Sandy, it isn't a competition.'

Her voice was scarcely a murmur. 'There would always

be a third person in our relationship. I don't know that I could deal with that...'

'Sandy, didn't you hear what I said? Jodi would *want* me to take this chance to spend time with you.'

She turned to face him, the counter now a barrier between them. Her eyes, shadowed again, searched his face. 'Jodi sounds like...like an angel.'

Ben forced himself to smile through the pain. 'She'd laugh to hear you say that. Jodi *was* special, and I loved her. But she was just a human being, like the rest of us, with her own strengths and weaknesses.'

'Ben, I'm no angel either. Don't expect me to be. I'm quick to make judgements, grumpy when I'm hungry or tired—and don't dare to cross me at my time of the month. Oh, and there's the toilet roll thing.'

Despite the angst of talking about Jodi, Sandy made him smile. Just as she'd done when she was eighteen. 'You can let me deal with that.'

She pushed the hair away from her forehead in a gesture of weariness. 'I...I don't know that I've thought this through very well.'

'What do you mean?' he asked.

Fear knifed him again.

He'd had five major turning points in his life. One when he'd decided to go to university. The second when he'd married Jodi. The third when Liam was born. Fourth, the fire. And the fifth when he'd looked up from that wave this morning and seen Sandy standing on the shore next to his dog, as if she were waiting for him to come home to her.

Since he'd kissed her he'd thought of nothing but Sandy. Of the impact she'd made in less than twenty-four hours on his safe, guarded, ultimately sterile life.

He hadn't wanted her here. But her arrival in town had forced him to take stock. And what he saw was a bleak, lonely future—a half-life—if he continued to walk the solitary path he had mapped for himself. He had grieved. A part of him would always grieve. But grief that didn't heal could twist and turn and fester into something near madness—if he let it.

He would *not* allow Sandy to back away from him now. She'd offered four days and he was going to take them.

She took a deep breath. 'The you-and-me thing. What if it doesn't work out and I…and I hurt you again? You've endured so much. I couldn't bear it if I caused you more pain.'

'Leave that to me. It's a gamble I'll take.'

Sandy was his best bet for change. The ongoing power of his attraction to her improved the odds. Her warmth, her vivacity, made him feel as though the seized-up machinery that was his heart was slowly grinding back to life.

She gave him hope.

Maybe that was her real magic—a magic that had nothing to do with shop-bought fairy glitter.

There were four more days until she had to leave for Melbourne. He didn't know what he brought to the table for *her* in terms of a relationship. But he'd be a fool not to grab the second chance she'd offered him. No matter the cost if he lost her again.

'Are you still worried about the townsfolk? They're nothing to be scared of.'

She set her shoulders, tossed back her head. 'Scared? Who said I'm scared?' Her mouth quirked into the beginnings of a smile. 'Maybe…maybe I *am* a little scared.'

Scared of him? Was that the real problem? Was she frightened he would rush her into something before she was ready?

He ached to make love to Sandy. Four days might not be enough to get to that stage. But he could wait if that was what she needed. Even though the want, the sheer physical ache to possess her, was killing him.

'No need to be. I'm here to fight battles for you. Never forget that.'

At last her smile reached her eyes. 'You're sure about that?'

She looked so cute he wanted to kiss the tip of her nose.

He stepped around the counter towards her at the same time she moved towards him. He took both her hands in his and pulled her to him. This time she didn't resist. Her face was very close. That warm vanilla scent of hers was already so familiar.

'As sure as I am about taking that second chance we've been offered. Let's give it everything we've got in the next four days. Turn back the clock.'

She stared at him. He couldn't blame her for being surprised at his turnaround. The shadow behind her eyes was not completely gone. Had she told him everything that was worrying her?

'Are you serious?' she choked out.

'Very.'

She reached up her hand to stroke the side of his cheek. As if checking he was real. When it came, her smile was tender and her eyes were warm. 'I'm so happy to hear you say that. It's just that...' She paused

'What?' he asked.

'All these expectations on us. It...it's daunting. And what will we tell people?'

'Nothing. Let them figure it out for themselves.' He gripped her hands. 'This is just about you and me. It's always just been you and me.'

'And we—'

'Enough with the talking,' he growled, and he silenced her with a kiss.

A kiss to seal their bargain. A kiss to tell her what words could not.

But the kiss rapidly escalated to something hot and hungry and urgent. She matched his urgency with lips, teeth, tongue. He let go her hands so he could pull her tight. Her curves shaped to him as though they were made to fit and she wound her arms around his neck to pull him closer. The strap of her yellow dress slid off her shoulder. He wanted to slide the dress right off her.

He broke away from the kiss, his breath hard and ragged. 'We're out of here. To get some privacy.'

'Wh…what about the shop?' Her own ragged breathing made her barely coherent.

'How many books have you sold today?'

'Just…just a few.'

'Yeah. Not many customers. Too many gossips.' He stroked the bare warm skin on her shoulder, exalted in her shiver of response.

'They did seem to spend more time lurking around corners and looking at me than browsing,' she admitted.

Her hands slid through his hair with an unconscious sensuality that made him shudder with want.

'You shut down the computer. I'll set the alarm.'

'But Ida…'

'Don't worry about Ida.' He could easily make up to his aunt for any drop in sales figures.

Sandy started to say something. He silenced her with another kiss. She moaned a throaty little sound that made him all the more determined to get her out of here and to somewhere private, where he could kiss her without an audience.

The old-fashioned doorbell on the top of the shop door jangled loudly.

Sandy froze in his arms. Then she pulled away from him, cheeks flushed, eyes unfocused. Her quiet groan of frustration echoed his. She pressed a quick, hard kiss on his mouth and looked up wordlessly at him.

To anyone coming into the store they would look as guilty as the pair of teenagers they'd once been. He rolled his eyes. Sandy started to shake with repressed giggles.

He kept his arm firmly around her as they turned to face the two middle-aged women who had entered the shop. Both friends of his mother.

Two sets of eyebrows had risen practically to their hairlines.

News of kiss number two for the day would be rapidly telegraphed through the town.

And he didn't give a damn.

'Sorry, ladies,' he said, in a voice that put paid to any argument. 'This shop is closed.'

CHAPTER TEN

DESTINATION? SOMEWHERE THEY could have privacy. Purpose? To talk more freely about what had happened to each other in the twelve years since she'd left Dolphin Bay. And Sandy didn't give a flying fig that the two bemused ladies Ben had ousted from Bay Books stood hands on hips and watched as she and Ben hastened away from the shop.

Even just metres down the street she fell out of step with Ben and had to skip to catch up. He turned to wait for her, suppressed laughter still dancing around his mouth, and extended his hand for her to take.

Sandy hesitated for only a second before she slid her fingers through his. Linked hands would make quite a statement to the good folk of Dolphin Bay. Anticipation and excitement throbbed through her as he tightened his warm, strong grip and pulled her closer. She smiled up at him, her breath catching in her throat at his answering smile.

When she'd very first held hands with Ben the simple act had been a big deal for her. Most of her schoolfriends had already had sex with their boyfriends by the age of eighteen. Not her. She'd never met a boy she'd wanted to do more with than kiss. When she'd met Ben she'd still been debating the significance of hands held with just palms locked or, way sexier, with fingers entwined.

And Ben?

Back then he'd had no scars.

'Where are we going?' she asked, surprised when her voice came out edged with nervousness.

'My place,' he said. His voice didn't sound nervous in the slightest.

Did he live at the hotel? That would make sense. Maybe in an apartment as luxurious as the room where she was staying.

'Do you remember my family's old boathouse?' he asked as he led her down the steps in front of the hotel.

'Of course I do,' she said, and she felt herself colour. Thirty years old and blushing at the memory of that ramshackle old boathouse. Dear heaven, she hoped he didn't notice.

On the sand outside the boathouse, in the shelter of Ben's father's beached dinghies, she and Ben had progressed from first base to not-ready-to-progress-further-than-third.

She glanced quickly up at Ben. Oh, yes, he remembered too. The expression in those deep blue eyes made that loud and clear.

She blushed a shade pinker and shivered at the memory of all that thwarted teen sexuality—and at the thought of how it might feel to finally do something about it if she and Ben got to that stage this time around.

'I live in the boathouse,' he said.

'You *live* there?' She didn't know what else to say that would not come out sounding ill-mannered.

Instead, she followed Ben across the sand in silence, wondering why a successful businessman would choose to live in something that was no more than a shack.

But the structure that sat a short distance to the right of the hotel bore little resemblance to the down-at-heel structure of her memory. Like so much of Dolphin Bay, it had changed beyond recognition.

'Wow! I'm impressed,' she said.

Ben's remodelled boathouse home looked like something that could star on a postcard. Supported by piers on the edge of the bay, its dock led out into the water. Timber-panelled walls were weathered to a silvery grey in perfect harmony with the corrugated iron of the peaked roof. Window trim and carriage lamps had been picked out in a deep dusky blue. Big tubs of purple hydrangeas in glazed blue pots sat either side of the door.

Ben leaned down to pluck a dead leaf from one of the plants without even seeming to realise he did it. She wouldn't have taken him for a gardener—but then she knew so very little of what interests he might have developed in the years since they'd last been together at this rich-in-memories part of the beach.

'The boathouse was the only part of the guesthouse to survive the fire,' Ben said. He pushed open the glossy blue door. 'Jesse lived here before he went away. I had it remodelled as guest accommodation, but liked it so much I kept it for myself.'

'I can see why,' she said. 'I envy you.'

A large ceramic dog bowl filled with water, hand-painted with the words 'Hobo Drinks Here', sat just outside the door. She remembered the look of devotion in the dog's big eyes and Ben's obvious love for him.

'Where's your adorable dog?' she asked, stepping through the door he held open for her, fully expecting the retriever to give Ben a boisterous greeting.

'Mum dog-sits him the days I can't take him to work with me,' he said. 'Seems she always has a houseful of strays. He fits right in.'

Sandy was about to say something about his mother, but the words were stopped by her second, 'Wow!' as Ben stepped aside and she got her first glimpse of the interior of the boathouse.

She only had a moment to take in a large open-plan space, bleached timber and shades of white, floor-to-ceiling windows facing the water at the living room end and a vast wooden bed at the other.

The thought that it would be a fabulous location for an advertising shoot barely had time to register in her mind, because the door slammed shut behind them and she was in Ben's arms.

Ben didn't want to give a tour of the boathouse. He didn't want to talk about the architectural work Jesse had done on the old building. He just wanted, at last, to have Sandy to himself.

For a long, still moment he held her close, his arms wrapped tightly around her. He closed his eyes, breathed in the vanilla scent of her hair, scarcely able to believe it was real and she was here with him. He could feel the warm sigh of her breath on his neck, hear the thud-thud-thud of her heartbeat. Then he kissed her. He kissed the curve of her throat. He kissed the delicate hollow beneath her ear. He pressed small, hungry kisses along the line of her jaw. Then he kissed her on the mouth.

Without hesitation Sandy kissed him right back. She tasted of coffee and chocolate and her own familiar sweetness. As she wound her arms around his neck, met his tongue with hers, she made that sexy little murmur deep in her throat that he remembered from a long time ago. It drove him nearly crazy with want.

Secure in the privacy of the boathouse, he kissed her long enough for them to catch right up on the way they'd explored kissing each other all those years ago. Until kissing no longer seemed enough.

The straps of her yellow dress gave little resistance as he slid them down her smooth shoulders. She shrugged to make it easier for him. Without the support of the straps, the top of her dress fell open. He could see the edge of her bra, the swell of her breasts, the tightness of her nipples. He kissed down her neck and across the roundness of her breasts, until she gasped and her hands curled tightly into his shoulders.

He couldn't get enough of her.

But with an intense effort he forced himself to pull back. 'Do you want me to stop?'

'No,' she said immediately. 'Not yet. I couldn't bear it if you stopped.'

In reply, he scooped her up into his arms. Her eyes widened with surprise and excitement. Her arms tightened around his neck and she snuggled her cheek against his shoulder.

She laughed as he marched her towards the bedroom end of the boathouse. 'Even more muscles than when you were nineteen,' she murmured in exaggerated admiration, her voice husky with desire.

She was still laughing as he laid her on the bed—his big, lonely bed. Her dress was rucked up around her slender tanned thighs, giving him a tantalising glimpse of red panties. She kicked off her shoes into the air, laughed again as they fell to the wooden floor with two soft thuds. Then she held out her arms to urge him to join her. Warm, vibrant Sandy, just as he remembered her. Only more womanly, more confident, more seductive.

He kicked off his own shoes and lay down next to her. He leaned over her as she lay back against the pillows, her face flushed, her eyes wide.

'I never thought I'd see you back here.' His voice was hoarse with need for her.

She kissed him. 'Do you remember the sand outside this place? How scratchy it was?' she asked. 'How we'd sneak off there whenever we could get away from everyone.'

'How could I forget?' he replied. Ever since she'd walked into the hotel and back into his life he'd thought of little else.

'This is so much more comfortable,' she said, with on-purpose seduction in her smile. She pulled him down to her to kiss him again. 'And private,' she murmured against his mouth.

Her kiss was urgent, hungry, and he responded in kind.

Outside on that sand as teenagers they'd fooled around as though they had all the time in the world. Now they had a clock ticking on their reunion. And they were playing grown-up games.

Within minutes he'd rid her of her dress and her bra. He explored the lush new fullness of her breasts. Kissed and teased her nipples.

He lifted his head and she made a murmur of protest. His voice was ragged. 'You sure you're ready for this?'

Sandy's eyes were huge. 'I should say no. I should say we need to spend more time together first, that we can't rush into anything we might regret.' Her voice broke. 'But I can't say no. I want you too much. Have always wanted you… Don't stop, Ben. Please don't stop.'

What she'd said about not rushing made sense. This was going faster than he could have anticipated. He should be the sensible one. Should stop it. But he was beyond thinking sensibly when it came to Sandy. *He only had four days with her.*

She kissed him. He kissed her back and was done for. The last restraints gone. He stroked down the curve of her belly, felt her tremble at his touch. Then her panties were gone and he explored there too.

'Not fair. I want to get you naked as well,' she murmured as she started to divest him of his clothes.

She kissed a hot trail across his chest as she slid off his shirt, stroked right down his arms. Her fingers weren't quite steady as she fumbled with the zipper on his shorts. It made the act of pulling them over his hips a series of tantalising caresses along his butt and thighs that made his body harden so much it ached.

Then they were naked together.

Sandy's heart was doing the flipping over thing so rapidly she felt dizzy. Or maybe the dizziness was from the desire that throbbed through her, that made her press her body close to Ben. Close. Closer. *Not close enough.*

Did that urgent whimper come from her as Ben teased her taut nipples with his tongue? As he stroked her belly and below until she bucked against his hand with need? She gasped for breath as ripples of pleasure pulsed everywhere he touched. Revelled in the intensity of the intimacy they were sharing.

This was further than they'd gone the last time they'd been on this beach together. Now she wanted more. Much more. He was as ready for her as she was for him. She shifted her hips to accommodate him, to welcome him— at last.

Then she stilled at the same time as he did. Spoke at the same time as he did.

'Protection.'

'Birth control.'

He groaned, pressed a hard, urgent kiss against her mouth, then swung himself off the bed.

Sandy felt bereft of his warmth and presence. The bed seemed very big and empty without him. *Hurry, hurry, hurry back!* She wriggled on the quilt in an ecstasy of anticipation, pressed her thighs together hard. Twelve years she'd waited, and she didn't want to wait a second longer.

But she contained her impatience enough to watch in sensual appreciation as Ben, buck naked, strode without a trace of self-consciousness towards the tall dresser at the other side of the bed. He was magnificent, her surf god, in just his skin. Broad shoulders tapering to the tight defined muscles of his back; firm, strong buttocks, pale against the tan of the rest of him; long, muscular legs. A wave of pure longing for him swept through her and she gripped her hands tight by her sides.

He reached the dresser, pulled out the top drawer.

Yes! Get the protection and get back here. Pronto!

But he hesitated—that taut, magnificent body was sud-

denly very still. Then he reached for a small framed photo
that stood on the top of the dresser. It was too far away for
Sandy to make out the details, just that there was a woman.
Ben picked it up and slid it into the drawer, face downwards.

Sandy caught her breath.

Jodi. The photo must be of Jodi.

Ben didn't want her to see it. Didn't want Jodi seeing
her naked on his bed.

And that was okay. Of course it was.

She had absolutely no reason to be upset by his action.
He'd told her his late wife had loved him so unselfishly
that she didn't want him to be alone. Sandy couldn't allow
herself even a twinge of jealousy that Jodi had been the
perfect wife.

But the desire that had been simmering though her suddenly went right off the boil. Despite the warmth of the day,
she shivered. She pulled herself up on her elbows, looked
around for something to cover her nakedness. She found
his shirt, clutched it against her. It was still warm from his
body heat.

Ben's gaze caught hers in a long, silent connection.
Sandy's throat tightened. He knew she'd seen. But he didn't
say anything. She knew he wouldn't. Knew she couldn't
ask—in spite of his earlier frankness.

She realised with a painful stab of recognition that Ben
had gone so far away, in such a different direction from the
youth they'd shared, that she didn't know him at all any
more. For all they'd shared over the last twenty-four hours,
today's Ben had been forged by loss and grief beyond her
comprehension.

She'd loved Ben back then, with the fierce intensity of
first love. But now? How could she love him when she didn't
know him any more? Wasn't this just physical attraction she
was feeling? She had never had sex without love. The fact
was, though, she was the one who had encouraged this encounter. How could she back down now?

And yet his look of excited yet respectful anticipation made her swell with emotion. Did she love him again already? Was that what the heart-flipping thing was all about? Had her heart just taken up where it had left off twelve years ago? What if these four days were all she would ever have of him?

Desire warmed her again. She wanted him. She would take the chance.

She smiled as Ben impatiently pulled open the drawer. But the smile froze as he continued to dig through the contents. He swore. Slammed the door shut. Looked through another drawer. Then another. He threw out his hands in a gesture to indicate emptiness.

'None. No protection. You got any?' His voice was a burr of frustration and anger and something that could have been despair.

'No. I...uh...don't carry it with me.'

She'd had no use for protection for a long time. Seemed as if Ben was in the same boat.

He strode back and sat on the bed next to her. He smoothed back a lock of hair that had drifted across her cheek in a caress that was both gentle and sensual.

'I want you so much. But I won't risk getting you pregnant.'

An unplanned pregnancy wasn't on her agenda either. No way would she suggest taking that risk, much as she yearned for him. 'I'm not on the pill. S...sorry.'

'Why should you apologise?' He groaned. 'I should have—'

'Could we...could we go buy some?' As soon as the words were out of her mouth she knew that was a ridiculous idea. Ben acknowledged it with a grim smile. No doubt some busybody citizen of Dolphin Bay would be behind the counter at the pharmacy and only too eager to broadcast the news that Ben and his old girlfriend were in need of contraceptives.

'Okay…bad idea.' She didn't know what else she could say.

Ben's handsome face was contorted with frustration, his voice underscored with anguish. 'Sandy. You have to know I won't be a father again. Won't have another child. Not after what happened to my little boy. Can't risk that loss…that pain.'

Oh, Ben. Her heart felt as if it was tearing in sorrow for him, for the losses she couldn't even begin to imagine.

'I…I understand,' she stuttered. But did she? Could she ever comprehend the agony he felt at losing his child? 'D… do you want to talk about it?'

He shifted his body further from her. But more than a physical distance loomed between them. He took a deep, shuddering breath.

'You have a right to know why I feel this way.'

'Of course,' she murmured.

'When my mother knew Liam was on the way she told me that I wouldn't know what love was until I held my first child in my arms. I scoffed at her. I thought I knew what it was to love.'

'Lizzie said something similar after Amy was born.'

Ben swallowed hard. It must be agony for him to relive his memories.

'A father's love—it was so unexpected. So overwhelming. My mother was right. I would have done anything for my son.'

'Of course you would have,' she murmured, feeling helpless. She didn't know what to say—a thirty-year-old single whose only experience of loving a child was her niece.

'Changing nappies. Getting up at all hours of the night the minute I heard a whimper. Rocking him in my arms for hours to soothe him when he was teething. I did all that. But…but I couldn't save his life.'

Survivor's guilt. Post-traumatic stress. Labels she thought might apply—but what did she know about how to help him?

'Ben, you're carrying a big burden. Did you have counselling to help you come to terms with your loss?'

As soon as the question left her mouth she knew it was a mistake. Ben so obviously *hadn't* come to terms with it.

His eyes were as bleak as a storm-tossed sea. 'I had counselling. But nothing can change the fact I couldn't save my baby son. End of story. On the day I buried him I vowed I would never have another child.'

'Because…because you think you don't deserve another child?'

'That too. But I couldn't bear the agony of loss again.'

She knew it wasn't the time to say that new life could bring new hope. That there was the possibility of loss any time you put your heart on the line. But how could she possibly understand what he'd gone through? Could she blame him for never wanting to risk finding himself in that unimaginably dark place again?

'Ben, I'm so sad for you.' She took his scarred, damaged hand in hers and squeezed it, wanting him to know how much she felt for him but was unable to express. He put his arms around her and pulled her tight. She nestled her face just below his shoulder, against the warm, solid muscle of his chest.

But she was sad for herself, too.

She thought back to her birthday goals. *Get married and have lots of kids. Three kids—two girls and a boy.*

It was as if Ben had read her mind. 'Remember how we used to talk about having kids? When were barely more than kids ourselves?'

'Yes,' she said. She swallowed hard against the lump of disappointment that threatened to choke her. She'd always seen being a mother in her future. Had never contemplated any other option.

He pulled back from her and she was forced to meet his gaze.

'So me not wanting kids could be a deal-breaker?'

She had to clear her throat before she answered, trying not to let him guess how shaken she was. 'Perhaps. For something long-term. But we're only talking four days, aren't we? It doesn't matter for...for a fling.'

'I guess not. But I wanted to make sure you knew where I stood.'

At the age of thirty she couldn't afford to waste time on any relationship—no matter how brief—that didn't have the possibility of children. Knowing that parenthood wasn't an option for Ben should make her pack up and leave Dolphin Bay right now. But she didn't have to think further than four days—and nothing could stop her from having this time with Ben. Come what may.

'I'm sorry, Sandy,' said Ben. 'This wasn't the way I thought things would pan out today.'

'It doesn't matter. I...I've lost the mood,' she confessed.

Suddenly she felt self-conscious being naked. With a murmur about being cold she disengaged herself from his arms. Fumbled around on the bed and found her dress. Pulled it over her head without bothering about wasting minutes with her bra. Wiggled into her panties. Found his clothes and handed them to him.

She felt very alone when he turned his back to her and dressed in awkward silence.

She sat on the edge of the bed and wondered how everything could have gone so wrong. 'Sunny Sandy', Ben had used to call her. But it was hard to see the glass-half-full side of finding out that he didn't ever want to have another child. And then there was that photo. How ready was he *really* to move on to another woman?

Ben wanted to pound the wall with his fists to vent his frustration and anger. He wanted to swear and curse. To fight his way through raging surf might help, too.

But he could do none of that. Sandy looked so woebegone sitting there, biting on her lip, her arms crossed defensively across her beautiful breasts. He had to control himself. Do anything in his power to reignite her smile.

His revelation that he didn't want more children had knocked the sunshine out of her. He appreciated how kind she'd been, how understanding, but dismay had shown on her face. But he'd had to put his cards on the table about a future with no children. He couldn't mislead her on such an important issue. Not that they were talking beyond these four days.

He reached out, took both her hands and pulled her to her feet.

'Sandy, I'm sorry—' he started.

'Don't say it again,' she said with a tremulous smile, and put her finger to his mouth. 'I'm sure we'll laugh about it one day.'

He snorted his disbelief. He would never see the humour in what had happened. Or had not happened.

'So what now?' she asked. 'Do I go back to the book-shop?'

He tightened his grip on her hands. 'No way. It's shut for the day. You're staying with me. We'll have lunch, then tonight I want to take you to a dinner dance.'

Her eyebrows rose. 'A dinner dance? In Dolphin Bay?'

She was such a city girl. She had no idea of how much the town had grown. How big his role as a business leader had become.

'The Chamber of Commerce annual awards night is being held at the hotel. As president, I'm presenting the awards. I'd like you to come.'

'As...as your date?'

'As my date.'

Her smile lit the golden sparks in her eyes in the way he remembered. 'I'd like that. This could be fun.'

'The speeches? Not so much. But there'll be a band and dancing afterwards.'

'Do you remember—?' she started.

'The dance?'

'I couldn't believe it when you asked me to dance with you.'

'I wasn't sure you'd say yes. You were the most beautiful girl there.'

She leaned up and kissed him on the mouth. 'Thank you for saying that.'

'You'll be the most beautiful girl there tonight.'

That earned him another kiss.

'Will I know anyone?'

'My parents. My brother, Jesse—he's back home for a couple days. Kate...'

Sandy's face tightened at the sound of Kate's name.

'Kate has a big mouth, but she also has a big heart,' he said.

'She can be confrontational.'

'Don't judge her too harshly. She means well.' He didn't want Sandy to feel alienated during her time in Dolphin Bay. That was one of the reasons he'd asked her to be his date for tonight, to go public with him. Encouraging a friendship with Kate was another.

'I'm sure she does. It's just that...'

'Yes?'

'Nothing,' she said, with an impish twist to her mouth.

He wasn't in the mood to argue with a female 'nothing'. 'C'mon. I'll make us some lunch.'

He kept her hand in his as he led her towards the kitchen.

'I didn't know you could cook,' she said.

She didn't know a lot about him. Some things she might never know. But his cooking prowess—or lack of it—was no secret.

'Basic guy-type stuff. Mostly I eat at the hotel. We could order room service if you want.'

'No. I like the idea of you cooking for me.'

She started to say something else but stopped herself.

He wondered if her ex had ever cooked for her. He sounded like a selfish creep, so that was probably a no.

'What's on the menu, chef?' she asked.

'Take your pick. Toasted cheese sandwich or...' he paused for dramatic emphasis '...toasted cheese sandwich.'

'With ketchup? And Snickers for dessert? I have some in my handbag.'

'Done,' he said as he headed towards the fridge.

Without realising it, he started to whistle. He stopped himself. Why would he want to whistle when he was furious at himself for the disaster in the bedroom and fresh with the memories of his loss?

'That's a sound I haven't heard for a long time,' Sandy said as she settled herself on one of the bar stools that lined the kitchen counter.

'It's rusty from disuse,' he said.

'No, it isn't. I like it. Don't stop. Please.'

Her eyes were warm with concern and understanding. Her yellow dress flashed bright in the cool, neutral tones of the kitchen. Her brown hair glinted golden in the sunshine that filtered through the porthole windows. Sandy. Here in his home. The only woman he had brought here apart from his mother and the maids from the hotel who kept it clean.

He picked up the tune from where he had left off and started to whistle again.

CHAPTER ELEVEN

SANDY WAS ONLY too aware that every detail of her appearance would be scrutinised by the other guests at the Chamber of Commerce dinner dance. Every nuance of her interaction with Ben would be fuel for the gossipmongers of Dolphin Bay.

In one way it amused her. In another it scared her witless.

In spite of Ben's reassurances Kate's warning still disconcerted her. All the people who would be there tonight knew Ben. Had known Jodi. Had even—and her heart twisted painfully at the thought—known his baby son. She wouldn't be human if that didn't worry her.

She wished she and Ben could spend the entire time they had together alone in his boathouse home. Just him and her, and no one else to poke their noses into the one step forward and two steps back of their reunion. But it seemed it would be played out on the open stage of Ben's tight-knit community.

Thank heaven she'd packed a take-her-anywhere outfit for Melbourne. She checked her image in the mirror of her hotel room with a mega-critical eye. Dress? Red, strapless, short but not too short. Jewellery? A simple yet striking gold pendant and a blatantly fake ruby-studded gold cuff from one of her fashion accessory clients. Shoes? Red, sparkling, towering heels. She thought she would pass muster.

The look in Ben's eyes when he came to her room to pick her up told her she'd got it right.

For a moment he stood speechless—a fact that pleased her inordinately. He cleared his throat. 'You look amazing,' he said.

Amazing was too inadequate a word to describe how Ben looked in a tuxedo. The immaculately tailored black suit emphasised his height and the breadth of his shoulders, and set off the brilliant blue of his eyes. There was little trace of the teen surfer in the urbane adult who stood before her in the doorway to her room, but she didn't mourn that. The crinkles around his eyes when he smiled, the cropped darker hair, only added to his appeal. It struck her that if she met the grown-up Ben now, for the first time, as a total stranger, she'd be wildly attracted to him.

For a moment she was tempted to wind her arms around his neck and lure him into her room with whispered words of seduction. She thought of the birth control she had discovered tucked into a corner of her suitcase, accompanied by a saucy note from her sister, Lizzie: *In case you get lucky in Melbourne.*

But Ben had official duties to perform. She couldn't make him late.

'You look amazing yourself,' she said. She narrowed her eyes in a mock-appraising way. 'Kinda like a surf god crossed with a tycoon god.'

He rolled his eyes at her words but smiled. 'If you say so.'

Her stratospheric heels brought her to kissing distance from his face. She kissed him lightly on the cheek, but he moved his face so her lips connected with his mouth. She nearly swooned at the rush of desire that hit her. As she felt his tongue slip familiarly into her mouth she calculated how much time they had before they were due at the dinner dance. Ten minutes. Not enough time for what she needed from Ben if things were going to get physical again.

Besides, she wasn't so sure that was the way to go when

their time together was so short. She didn't want to leave Dolphin Bay with a pulverised heart.

With a deep sigh of regret, she pulled away.

'C'mon, haven't you got awards to present?' she said.

She slipped her arm through his and they headed towards the elevator.

The first person Sandy saw when she walked with Ben into the hotel conference room where the dinner dance was being held was his mother. She clutched Ben's arm, shocked at the feeling of being cast back in time.

Maura Morgan had been wearing jeans and a T-shirt the last time she'd seen her; now she was wearing an elegant brocade dress. She was handsome, rather than beautiful, and she'd hardly changed in the intervening years. Her hair held a few more strands of grey, her figure was a tad more generous, but her smile was the same warm, welcoming smile that had made Sandy's stay at the guesthouse all those years ago so happy. And her voice still held that hint of a lyrical Irish accent that was a legacy of her girlhood in Dublin.

'Eh, Sandy, it's grand to see you. Who would have thought we'd see you here after all these years?' The older woman swept her into a warm hug.

'It's wonderful to see you again.' It was all Sandy could think of to say. But she meant every word. That summer, so long ago, there had been a wire of tension between her parents that at times had come close to snapping. Maura had been kind to her, and covered for her with her father when she'd snuck out to meet Ben.

Maura stepped back, with her hands still on Sandy's shoulders. 'Look at you, all grown up and even lovelier than when you were a girl—and friends with Ben again.' Her face stilled. 'Fate works in amazing ways.'

'It sure does,' Sandy agreed, reluctant to talk more deeply with Ben's mother. Not wanting to bring up the tragedies that had occurred since her last visit. She didn't know what

Ben had told Maura about her reasons for staying in Dolphin Bay. The reignited feelings between her and Ben were so fragile—still just little sparks—she wanted to hug them close.

Maura released her. 'Your mum and dad…?'

Sandy shrugged. 'Divorced.'

Maura shook her head slowly. 'Why does that not surprise me? And your sister?'

'Lizzie's still my best friend. She has a little girl, Amy, who's five years old and a real cutie.'

As soon as she mentioned Amy, Sandy wished she hadn't. Ben's son Liam had been Maura's only grandchild. But Maura's smile didn't dim. 'It's lovely to hear that,' she said. 'And do you—?'

Ben interrupted. 'Mum, I've sat you and Dad at my table so you'll get a chance to talk to Sandy during the evening.

Maura laughed. 'So quit the interrogation? I hadn't yet asked Sandy if she has room in her heart for a homeless puppy.'

Ben groaned, but Sandy could hear the smile in his protest.

'A puppy? I'd love one,' she said without hesitation. 'That is if…' Her voice trailed away. *Get dog of own once settled in Melbourne.* Could she really commit to a dog when her future had become so uncertain? Until she knew exactly how she felt about Ben at the end of the four days?

Maura patted her hand. 'I won't hold you to the puppy until we've talked some more.'

The genuine warmth in her voice did a lot to reassure Sandy that Maura did not appear to have any objection to her reunion with Ben.

She felt she could face the rest of the evening with a degree less dread.

Sandy outshone any other woman in the room, Ben thought as he watched her charm the bank manager and his wife.

It wasn't just the red dress, or the way the light caught her glittery shoes just like that darn fairy dust. It had more to do with the vivacity of her smile, the way her eyes gleamed with genuine interest at the details of the couple's daughter's high school results. He knew she was nervous, but no one would guess it.

It was a big, public step to bring her tonight—and he was glad he'd made it. It felt good to have her by his side. Instead of ill-disguised sorrow or embarrassed pity, he saw approval in the eyes of his family and friends. It was a big step forward.

But for the first time since he'd been elected president of the chamber Ben resented his duties. He didn't want to make polite chit-chat with the guests. He didn't want to get up there on stage and make a speech about the business community's achievements. Or announce the awards. He wanted to spend every second of the time he had left with Sandy—alone with her. They had less than four days—three days now—of catching up to do. If that included being behind closed doors, slowly divesting Sandy of that red dress and making love to her all night long, that was good too.

'We must catch up for coffee some time,' the banker's wife gushed in farewell to Sandy as Ben took Sandy's elbow to steer her away towards his table. He wanted her seated and introduced to everyone else at the table before he had to take his place on stage for the awards presentation.

'I'd like that,' Sandy called over her shoulder to the banker's wife as Ben led her away.

'Would you?' he asked in an undertone.

'Of course. She seems like a nice lady. But not any time soon.' She edged closer so she could murmur into his ear. 'We've only got a few days together. I want to spend every second of my spare time with you.'

'I'll hold you to that,' he said.

It felt unexpectedly good, being part of a couple again— even if only temporarily. He'd been on his own for so long.

Maybe too long. But his guilt and regret still gnawed at him, punishing him, stopping him from getting close to anyone.

And now Sandy was back with him in Dolphin Bay.

The president's table was at the front of the room. His parents were already seated around it, along with Kate, his brother, Jesse, and two of the awards finalists—both women.

If his father remembered how disparaging he had been all those years ago about the sincerity of a city girl's feelings towards his son, he didn't show it. In his gruff way he made Sandy welcome.

Jesse couldn't hide the admiration in his eyes as he rose from his seat to greet Sandy. 'I would have recognised you straight away,' his brother said as he kissed her on the cheek.

Ben introduced Sandy to the awards finalists, then settled her into the seat between him and Kate. 'I have to finalise the order of proceedings. I'll be back in five minutes—in time for the appetiser,' he said.

He wanted to kiss Sandy. Claim her as more than a friend in front of all eyes. But it wasn't the right time. Instead, he brushed his hand over her bare shoulder in parting before he headed backstage. Only Kate's big grin made him realise the simple gesture was more a sign of possession than a friendly kiss on Sandy's cheek would ever have been.

Sandy heaved a quiet sigh of relief as she sank into her chair. The worst of the ordeal was behind her. From the moment she'd entered the room she'd been aware of the undercurrent of interest in her presence beside Ben. Her mouth ached from smiling. From formulating answers in reply to questions about how long she intended to be in town. Even though Ben had smoothed the way, she felt she was being judged on every word she spoke. She reached gratefully for her glass of white wine.

Ben's empty seat was to her left, between her and Kate. Tall, dark-haired Jesse—every bit as handsome as in her memories of him—sat on the other side of her, engaged in conversation with his mother.

Kate sidled close enough to whisper to Sandy. 'Note that Ben didn't sit me next to Jesse. Probably worried I'd fling myself on his brother, wrestle him to the ground and have my way with him under the table.'

Sandy nearly choked on her drink. 'Really?'

'Nah. Just kidding. I actually asked him not to put me near Jesse.' Kate's green eyes clouded. 'It's hard to make small-talk with the guy I've wanted all my life when he sees me as more sister than woman.'

'Can't he see how gorgeous you are?' Sandy asked. In an emerald silk dress that clung to her curves and flattered the auburn of her hair, Kate looked anything but the girl next door.

Kate pulled a self-deprecating face. 'Thanks. But it doesn't matter what I wear. To Jesse I'll always just be good old Kate, his childhood pal.'

'You never dated him?'

'We kissed when I was thirteen and he was fourteen. I never stopped wanting him after that.'

'And Jesse?'

Kate shrugged. 'He was a shy kid, and I guess I was a convenient experiment. It never happened again. Though I must have relived it a million times.'

'He certainly doesn't look shy now.'

Jesse's full attention was beamed on the attractive blonde award finalist.

'Yep. He's quite the man of the world these days, and quite the flirt.' Kate kept her gaze on Jesse for a moment too long before returning it to Sandy.

Sandy's heart went out to Kate. 'That must be so tough for you. Ben told me Jesse's only visiting for a few days.'

'Yes. Jesse leads a construction team that builds low-cost housing in areas that have been destroyed by natural disasters. Think India, Africa, New Orleans. He only ever comes here between assignments.'

Sandy glanced again at Jesse. 'Good looks *and* a kind heart. No wonder you're hooked on him.'

'Kind hearts run in the Morgan family—as I think you well know.'

Was Kate about to give her another lecture about Ben? If so, she wasn't in the mood to hear it. 'Kate, I—'

Kate laughed and threw her hands up in a gesture of self-defence. 'I'm staying right out of the you-and-Ben thing. I've been warned.'

'Warned? By Ben?'

'Of course by Ben. You're important to him. Ben protects the people he cares about.'

Sandy loved the feeling Kate's words gave her. But, again, she sensed she might be getting out of her depth. Three more days in Dolphin Bay. That was all she was talking about after this evening. Deep in her heart, though, she knew there was a chance it could end up as so much more than that. She didn't know whether to be excited or terrified at the prospect.

After the starter course Ben took his place on stage. To Sandy, he looked imposing and every inch the powerful executive as he took the microphone to give a brief review of the year's past business activities. From the applause and occasional catcall from the audience it was apparent Ben was still very much the town's favourite son.

As he made a particularly pertinent point about the growth in revenue tourism had brought to Dolphin Bay Sandy thought she would burst with pride at his achievements, and at the way he had overcome such tragedy to get to this place. She wanted to get up from her seat and cheer. She caught his mother Maura's eye and saw the same pride and joy reflected in her face.

Maura acknowledged the thread of emotion that united

them with a smile and a brief nod, before turning back to face the stage and applaud the end of Ben's speech.

Sandy smiled back—a wobbly, not very successful smile. *Maura knew.* She bit her lip and shredded the edge of her dolphin-printed serviette without really realising she was doing so.

Could she kid herself any further that all she wanted from Ben was a fling? Could she deny that if she didn't protect her heart she might fall right back in love? And then where would she be, if Ben decided four days of her was enough?

CHAPTER TWELVE

BUT SANDY'S HEART was singing as she danced with Ben. He danced as he'd danced with her that first time twelve years ago, and it seemed as if the years in between had never happened. Although they kept a respectable distance apart their bodies were in tune, hips swaying in unison with each other, feet moving to the same beat.

Most of the people in the room had also got up to dance once the formalities of the evening were done, but Sandy was scarcely aware of them. She couldn't keep her eyes off Ben or stop herself from 'accidentally' touching him at any opportunity—shoulders brushing, hips bumping, her hand skimming his as they moved their bodies in time to the music of a surprisingly good local band. And, in spite of the other guests' ill-concealed interest in the fact they were dancing together, Ben did nothing to move away.

She longed to be alone with him. He had rhythm, he had energy, he had power in that big, well-built body—and she ached to have it all directed to *her*. Upstairs in her bedroom.

When the band changed to slow dancing music, she was done for. As Ben pulled her into his arms and fitted his body close to her she wound her arms around her neck and sighed. 'How much longer do we have to endure this torture? If I have to explain to one more person than I'm just here for a few more days, I'll scream.'

'Same. The strain of all this focus on us is too much.'

'How much longer do we have to stay?'

He nuzzled into her neck, murmured low and husky. 'See those doors that open up to the balcony?'

She looked across the room. 'Yes.'

'We're going to dance our way over there and out on to the balcony, as if we're going for some fresh air—'

'Won't everyone think we've gone to make out?'

'Who cares?' He pulled her tighter. 'That way we don't have to announce our escape by exiting through the main doors.'

'What about your duties?'

'I'm done with duty.'

'So now you're all mine for the rest of the evening?' she murmured, with a provocative tilt of her head.

His eyes darkened to a deeper shade of blue and his grip tightened on her back. 'From the balcony we'll take the door to the empty conference room next door and then to the foyer.'

'And then?' Her voice caught in her throat.

'That's up to you.'

Her heart started doing the flippy thing so fast she felt dizzy. She pulled his head even closer to hers, brushed her lips across his cheek. 'Let's go,' she murmured.

He steered her through the crowd, exchanging quick greetings with the people they brushed past, but not halting for a moment longer than necessary. Sandy nodded, smiled, made polite responses, held on to his hand and followed his lead.

They sidled along the balcony, then burst into the empty conference room next door, laughing like truant schoolkids. Ben shut the door behind him and braced it in mock defence with an exultant whoop of triumph.

Sandy felt high on the same exhilaration she'd felt as a teenager, when Ben and she had successfully snuck away from their parents. She opened her mouth to share that thought with him, but before she could form the words to congratulate him on their clever escape he kissed her.

His kiss was hard and hungry, free of doubt or second thoughts. She kissed him back, matching his ardour. Then broke the kiss.

She took a few deep breaths to steady her thoughts. 'Ben, I'm concerned we're moving too fast. What do you think?'

Ben glanced at his watch. 'This day is nearly over. That leaves us three days. I want you, Sandy. I've always wanted you.'

'But what if we regret it? What if you—?' She was so aware of how big a deal it was for him to be with her. And the heartbreak she risked by falling for him again. She feared once she made love with him she would never want to leave him.

'I'll regret it more if we don't take this chance to be together. On our terms. No one else's.'

'Me too,' she said. No matter what happened after these three remaining days, she never wanted to feel again the regret that had haunted her all those years ago.

Please, let this be our time at last.

'My room or yours?' she said, putting up her face to be kissed again.

Ben couldn't bear to let go of Sandy even for a second. Still kissing her, he walked her through the door, out of the conference room and into the corridor. Still kissing her, he punched the elevator's 'up' button.

As soon as the doors closed behind them he nudged her up against the wall and captured her wrists above her head with one of his so much bigger hands. The walls were mirrored and everywhere he looked he saw Sandy in that sexy red dress, her hair tousled, her face flushed, her lips swollen from his kisses. Beautiful Sandy, who had brought hope back into his life.

The raising of her arms brought her breasts high out

of her strapless dress to tease him. In the confines of the elevator the warm vanilla female scent of her acted like a mainline hit of aphrodisiac. He could make love to her there and then.

But, as it always had been with Sandy, this was about so much more than sex. This step they were about to take was as much about intimacy and trust and a possible move towards a future beyond the next three days. The responsibility was awesome.

It was up to him to make it memorable. He'd waited so long for her and he wanted their first time to be slow and thorough, not a heated rush that might leave her behind.

He trailed kisses down her throat to the swell of her breasts. She gasped and he tightened his grip on her hands. She started to say something but he kissed her silent. Then the elevator reached her floor.

Still kissing her, he guided Sandy out of the elevator and towards her room. He fished his master keycard out of his pocket, used it, then shouldered the door open. They stumbled into the room and he kicked the door shut behind them.

Sandy had imagined a sensual, take-their-time progression through the bases for her first-time lovemaking with Ben. But she couldn't wait for all that. It felt as if the entire day had been one long foreplay session. Every sense was clamouring for Ben. *Now.* Her legs were so shaky she could hardly stand.

She pulled away from the kiss, reached up and cradled his chin in her hands, thrilled at the passion and want in his eyes that echoed hers. Her breathing was so hard she had to gulp in air so her voice would make sense.

'Ben. Stop.'

Immediately, gentleman that he was, he made to pull away from her. Urgently she stilled him.

'Not stop. I mean go. Heck, that's not what I mean. I mean stop delaying. I swear, Ben, I can't wait any longer.'

She whimpered. Yes, she whimpered—something she'd never thought she'd do for a man. 'Please.'

His eyes gleamed at the green light she'd given him. 'If you knew how difficult it's been to hold back…' he groaned.

'Oh, I have a good idea what it's been like,' she said, her heart pounding, her spirit exulting. 'I feel like I've been waiting for this—for you—all my life.'

She kicked off her shiny shoes, not caring where they landed. Ben yanked down the zipper of her dress. She tugged at his tuxedo jacket and fumbled with the buttons on his shirt. Before she knew it she stood in just the scantiest red lace thong and Ben was in nothing at all—his body strong and powerful and aroused, his eyes ablaze with need for her.

Beautiful wasn't a word she'd usually use to describe a man. But all her copywriting skills deserted her as she sought to find another word.

He was her once-in-a-lifetime love and she knew, no matter what happened tomorrow or the day after or the day after that, that tonight she would be irrevocably changed. As she took a step towards him she froze, overwhelmed—even a little frightened—of what this night might unleash. Then desire for this man took over again. Desire first ignited twelve long years ago. Desire thwarted. Desire reignited. Desire aching to be fulfilled.

Ben swept her into his arms and walked her towards the bed. Soon she could think of nothing but him and the urgent rhythm of the intimate dance they shared.

Ben didn't know what time it was when he woke up. There was just enough moonlight filtering through the gaps in the curtains for him to watch Sandy as she slept. He leaned on his elbow and took in her beauty.

She lay sprawled on her back, her right arm crooked above her head, the sheet tucked around her waist. Her hair was all mussed on the pillow. He was getting used to seeing it short, though he wished it was still long. In repose, her face had lost the tension that haunted her eyes. A smile danced at the corners of her mouth. She didn't look much older than the girl he'd thought he'd never see again.

It didn't seem real that she was here beside him. Magic? Coincidence? Fate? Whatever—being with Sandy made him realise he had been living a stunted half-life that might ultimately have destroyed him.

How could he let her go in three days' time?

But if he asked Sandy to stay he had to be sure it would be to stay for ever.

With just one finger he traced the line of her cheekbones, her nose, her mouth.

She stirred, as he'd hoped she would. Her eyelids fluttered open and her gaze focused on him. His heart leapt as recognition dawned in her eyes. She smiled the slow, contented smile of a satisfied woman and stretched languorously.

'Fancy waking up to you in my bed,' she murmured. She took his hand and kissed first each finger in turn and then his palm with featherlight touches over the scars he hated so much. She placed his hand on her breast and covered it with her own.

'You were *so* worth waiting twelve years for,' she whispered.

'Yes.' He couldn't find any more words. Just kissed her on her forehead, on her nose, finally on her mouth.

Want for her stirred again. He circled her nipple with his thumb and felt it harden. She moaned that sweet moan of pleasure. She returned his kiss. Softly. Tenderly. Then she turned her body to his.

Afterwards she lay snuggled into him, her head nestled on his chest, their legs entwined. The sweet vanilla scent of her filled his senses. He held her to him as tightly as he could without hurting her. He didn't want to let her go.

Did she feel the same way about what had just happened—a connection that had been so much more than physical?

Did she know she had ripped down a huge part of the barricade that had protected him against feeling anything for anyone?

Hoarsely, he whispered her name.

The tenor of her breathing changed and he realised she was falling back to sleep. Had she heard him?

'Ben…' she murmured as her voice trailed away.

As Sandy drifted back into sleep, satiated not just with sexual satisfaction but with joy, she realised a profound truth: she'd never got it right with anyone but Ben. Not just the physical—which had been indescribably wonderful—but the whole deal.

Right back when she was eighteen she'd thought she'd found the man for her—but those close to her, those who had thought they knew what was best for her, had dissuaded her.

She tightened her grip on his hand and smiled.

Her heart had got it right the first time.

CHAPTER THIRTEEN

'So, IS THE sex with my nephew good?'

Sandy nearly fell off the chair near Aunt Ida's hospital bed, too flummoxed even to think about a reply.

Ida laughed. 'Not a question you expect a little old lady to ask?'

'Uh…not really,' Sandy managed to splutter as hot colour flooded her cheeks. She'd come to talk about the Bay Books business, not her private life with Ben.

Ida shifted her shoulders and resettled herself on the pillows, a flash of pain tightening her face. Sandy ached to help her, but Ben's great-aunt was fiercely independent.

'You don't actually have to answer me,' said Ida. 'But great sex is so important to a healthy relationship. If you don't have those fireworks now, forget having a happy future together.'

Sandy realised she had blushed more times since she'd been back in Dolphin Bay than she had in her entire life.

'I… Uh… We…' How the heck did Ida know what had happened with Ben last night? How did she know there'd been fireworks aplenty?

Ida chuckled. 'I'll take that as a yes, then. Any fool can see the chemistry between you two. Good. No matter what the world dishes up to you, you'll always have that wonderful intimacy to keep your love strong. It was like that for me and Mike.'

'Oh?' Sandy literally did not know where to look. To talk about sex with someone of her grandmother's age was a new and unnerving experience.

'I suppose you know about my scandalous past?'

'I heard that you—'

'But I guess you don't want to hear about that.'

The expression in Ida's eyes made it clear that Ida wanted very much to tell her story. And Sandy was curious to hear it. There hadn't been much talking about relationships in her family's strait-laced household. No wonder she'd been so naïve at the age of eighteen, when she'd met Ben.

Sandy settled herself back in her chair. 'Did you really run away with a sailor, like Ben says?'

'Indeed I did. Mike was sailing up the coast. We clicked instantly. I went back to his boat with him and—'

Sandy found herself gripping the fabric of her skirt where it bunched over her knees. She wanted to hear the story but she didn't—she *really* didn't—want to hear the intimate details.

'I never left. I quit my job. Threw my hat in with Mike. We got married on an island in Fiji.'

One part of Sandy thought it romantic, another thought it foolhardy.

'Even though you hardly knew him?' *But how well did she actually know Ben? Enough to risk her heart the way she'd done last night?*

'I knew enough that I wanted to spend every waking and sleeping moment with him. I was thirty-five; he was five years older. We didn't have time to waste.'

Was that message aimed at her and Ben? The way she felt right now Sandy hated being parted from him even for a minute. But there were issues still unresolved.

'What about…what about children? Did you regret not having kids?'

'Not for a moment. We couldn't have had the life we had with kids. Mike was enough for me.'

Could Ben be enough for her? Right now her heart sang with the message that he was all she wanted. But what about in years to come? If things worked out with Ben, could she give up her dreams of a family?

Ida continued. 'And I don't have time to waste now. Once I'm over this injury I want to go back to the places I visited with Mike. It might be my last chance.'

Sandy put up a hand in protest. 'Surely not. You—'

'Still have years ahead of me? Who knows? But what I *do* know is I need to sell Bay Books—and I want you to buy it from me.'

Again, Sandy was too flabbergasted to reply to the old lady. Just made an incoherent gasp.

'You told me you want to run your own business,' said Ida. 'And I'm talking a good price for stock, fittings and goodwill.'

'Yes… But…'

But why not?

Candles came a poor second to books. And she already had so many ideas for improving Bay Books. Hadn't she thought, in the back of her mind, that if there were a chance she might stay in Dolphin Bay she would need to earn her living?

'Why the "but"?' Ida asked.

'The "but" is Ben,' said Sandy. 'We're not looking beyond these next few days right now. I have to take it slowly with him. I'm interested in your proposition. But I can't commit to anything until I know if there might be anything more with Ben.'

Ida's eyes were warm with understanding. 'I know what Ben's been through. I also know he needs to look to the future. I'm hoping it's with you.'

'Thank you,' said Sandy, touched by the older lady's faith in her.

'I'll keep my offer on the table. But I'll be selling—if not to you, to someone else.'

'Can we keep this between us?' Sandy asked. 'I'd rather not mention it to Ben just yet. I don't want him to think I'm putting any pressure on him.'

'Of course,' said Ida.

Sandy felt guilty, putting a 'Back in One Hour' sign on the door of Bay Books—but meeting Ben for lunch was more important.

Ida's words echoed through her head. *She didn't have time to waste.*

She made her way to the boathouse to find the door open and Ben unpacking gourmet sandwiches from the hotel café and loading cold drinks into the refrigerator.

Again, he was whistling, and she smiled at the carefree sound. He hadn't realised she was there and she was struck by the domesticity of the moment. Did she want this with Ben? Everyday routine as well as heart-stopping passion? Much, much more than a few days together?

The answer was in his eyes when he looked up and saw she was there. *Yes. Yes. Yes.*

Yes to sharing everything.

Everything but the rearing of kids.

He put down the bottle he was holding, she dropped her handbag, and they met in the middle of the room. Ben held her close. She stood in his arms, exulting in the warm strength of him, the thudding of his heart, the way he smelled of the sea.

'I'm glad you're here,' he said.

'Me too,' was the only reply she could manage.

Her heart started a series of pirouettes—demanding its message be heard.

She loved him.

Emotion, overwhelming and powerful, surged through her. So did gratitude for whatever power had steered her back to him.

But could wounded, wary Ben love her back in the way she needed?

He kissed her—a brief, tender kiss of welcome—then pulled away.

'How did it go with Ida at the hospital?'

When she told him about Ida's questioning about their love-life he laughed, loud and uproariously.

'The old girl is outrageous,' he said, with more than a hint of pride. 'So what did you say to her?'

'I was so embarrassed I didn't know where to look.'

He pulled her close again. His voice was deep and husky and suggestive. 'What *would* you have told her?'

She twined her arms around his neck. 'I think you know last night was the most amazing experience of my life.' She had trouble keeping her voice steady. 'Why didn't I say yes all those years ago? Why, why, *why* didn't I fight harder for you?'

'Water under the bridge, remember?'

'Yes, but—'

'It mightn't have been such an amazing experience when I was nineteen.'

'Not true. You were the best kisser. Still are.'

'Always happy to oblige,' he said.

She smiled. 'Last night…the dinner dance…it was fun, wasn't it?'

'You were a big hit.'

'Was I? I'm still not quite sure how to handle the town-folk. In particular the way they compare me to Jodi.' *And I'm not sure how, if we have a future, I'll handle being second in your life.*

'You're still worrying about that?' He took her hand and led her to the bedroom. 'There's something I want to show you.'

'And I'm quite happy to see it,' she quipped. 'We can eat lunch afterwards.'

He laughed. 'That's not what I meant. But we can do that too.'

He went to the dresser. He opened the top drawer and pulled out the framed photo he had put there yesterday—the yesterday that seemed a hundred years ago. She braced herself, not at all sure she could cope with seeing Jodi and Ben together in happy times. She prayed the baby wouldn't be in the photo. One day she would have to go there. But not now. Not when this was all too raw and new.

Ben held the photo so she couldn't see what it was. 'It concerned me when you said you were worried about coming second with me. About being in the shadow of the memory of another woman. It's ironic that Jodi felt the same way about you.'

Sandy frowned. 'What do you mean?'

He handed her the photo. Astounded, she looked from it to him and back again. 'But it's of me. Of you. Of *us*.'

The simple wooden frame held a faded snap of her very young self and Ben with their arms around each other. She—super-slim—was wearing a tiny pink floral-patterned bikini; her hair was wet and tangled with salt and fell almost to her waist. She was looking straight at the camera with a confident, happy smile. Ben's surfer hair was long and sun-streaked and he was wearing blue Hawaiian print board shorts. He wasn't looking at the camera but rather down at her, with an expression of pride and possession heartrendingly poignant on a teenager.

She had to clear her throat before she spoke. 'Where did you get this from?'

'From you. Don't you remember?'

Slowly the memory returned to her. 'Lizzie took this photo. We had to get the film developed at the chemist in those days. I bought the frame from the old general store. And I gave it to you to…to remember me by.' She'd had a copy, too. Had shoved it in the back of an old photo album that was heaven knew where now.

'Jodi found it at the bottom of a drawer in my room just before we got married. She brought it to me and said we needed to talk.'

'I…I thought you would have thrown it out.'

'She thought so too. She asked me was I still carrying a torch for you.'

'Wh…what did you say?'

'I said I'd cared for you once but was now totally committed to her.'

Sandy swallowed hard against a kick of that unwarranted jealousy. 'You…you were getting married. Wouldn't she *know* that?'

'We were getting married because she was pregnant with Liam.'

Sandy let out a gasp of surprise. 'I…I didn't know that.'

'Of course you didn't. But she was sensitive about it. Wanted me to reassure her that I wasn't marrying her just because I "had to".'

'Poor Jodi.' Her heart went out to the lovely girl who had cared so much for Ben, and she wished she had more than vague memories of her.

'So, you see, as far as Jodi was concerned you were the "third person", as you put it, in our marriage.'

'I…I don't really know what to say. If…if you were married I wouldn't come anywhere near you.'

'I know that. You know that. And I'm sure Jodi knew that. But no matter how much I reassured her that we would have got married anyway, just maybe not so soon, she had that little nagging doubt that she was my second choice.'

'And yet you…you didn't throw out the photo.' She was still holding the frame in her hands, her fingers tightly curled around the edge.

'No. I went to put it in the bin, to prove my point, but Jodi stopped me. Said it was unrealistic to expect we wouldn't each come into the marriage with a past. She just wanted to make sure you stayed in the past.'

'And here I am...in...in the future.'

'I hadn't thought about this photo in years. Then, after that morning on the beach with you and Hobo, I dug it out from a box in the storeroom at the hotel.'

'And put it on display?'

Ben took the photo frame from her hands and placed it back on top of the dresser. 'Where it will stay,' he said.

'So...so why did you hide it from me yesterday?'

'I thought you'd think it was strange that I'd kept it. It was too soon.'

'But it's not too soon now?'

'We've come a long way since yesterday.'

'Yes,' she said. She made a self-conscious effort to laugh. But it came out as something more strangled. 'Who knows where we'll get to in the next three days?'

It was a rhetorical question she wished she hadn't uttered as soon as she'd said it. But Ben just nodded.

He picked up the photo frame and then put it back down again. 'If you're okay with it, I'll keep it here.'

'Of course,' she said, speaking through a lump of emotion in her throat. 'And I don't expect you to keep photos of Jodi buried in a drawer while I'm around.'

But, please, no photos of Liam on display. No way could she deal with that while she was dealing with the thought that if it worked out with Ben she would see the demise of her dream of having her own kids.

'She was a big part of my life. I'm glad you don't want to deny that.'

'Of course I recognise that. Like...like she did about me.'

She looked again at the long-ago photo and wondered how Jodi had felt when she'd seen it. How sensible Jodi had been not to deny Ben his past. She had to do the same. But there was still that nagging doubt.

'I still can't help but wonder if I can compete with the memory of someone so important to you.'

He cupped her chin with his big scarred hands. 'As I said

before, it's not a competition. You're so different. She was the safe harbour, calm waters. You're the breaking waves, the white-water excitement.'

'Both calm waters and breaking waves can be good,' she said, understanding what he meant and feeling a release from her fears. She hoped she, too, could at times become a safe harbour for him.

If she were to carry the wave analogy to its conclusion, Jason had been the dumper wave that had started off fast and exciting and then crashed her, choking and half drowning, onto the hard, gritty sand.

But what she felt for Ben defied all categorisation. He was both safe harbour and wild wave, and everything else she wanted, in one extraordinary man. And she longed to be everything to him.

But she couldn't tell him that. Not yet. Not until the three days were over.

'How long until you have to be back at the shop?' Ben asked.

'How long do we need?' she murmured as she slid her arms around his waist and kissed him.

CHAPTER FOURTEEN

SANDY TURNED THE 'Back in One Hour' sign—it had stretched to one and a half hours—so it read 'Open' and dashed into the shop. She spent a few minutes fixing her hair and make-up so the next contingent of too-interested ladies who came in wouldn't immediately guess how she'd spent her lunch hour. Wouldn't *that* make the Dolphin Bay grapevine hum…?

But customers were few—maybe she wasn't such a novelty any more. Or maybe, because it was such a hot day, people would rather be on the beach. She lifted her hair from her neck to cool it. It was warm in here today, despite her fiddling with the air-conditioning controls.

In the lull, after a lady had been seeking the latest celebrity chef cookbook and a man had wanted a history of the Dolphin Bay fishing fleet, she pulled out her fairy notebook. The glitter shimmered onto the countertop. It was time to revisit her thirtieth birthday resolutions.

She read them through again, with her Hotel Harbourside pen poised to make amendments.

1. Get as far away from Sydney as possible while remaining in realms of civilisation and within reach of a good latte.

Tick.

Dolphin Bay was four hours away from Sydney, and Ben's hotel café did excellent coffee. But her stay depended on a rekindled relationship of uncertain duration.

2. Find new job where can be own boss.

Tick.

The possibility of owning Bay Books exceeded the 'new job' expectations. She scribbled, *Add gift section to bookshop—enquire if can be sub-franchisee for candles.*

But, again, the possible job depended entirely on her relationship with Ben. She wouldn't hang around in Dolphin Bay if they kissed goodbye for good on Wednesday.

She hesitated when she came to resolution number three. As opposed to the flippy thing, her heart gave a painful lurch.

3. Find kind, interesting man with no hang-ups who loves me the way I am and who wants to get married and have three kids, two girls and a boy.

She'd found the guy—though he came with hang-ups aplenty—and maybe he was the guy on whom she'd subconsciously modelled the brief. But as for the rest of it....

Could she be happy with just two out of three resolutions fulfilled? How big a compromise was she prepared to make?

Now her heart actually ached, and she had to swallow down hard on a sigh. Children had always been on the agenda for her—in fact she'd never imagined a life that didn't include having babies. Then her mother's oft-repeated words came to mind: '*You can't have everything you want in life, Alexandra.*'

She put down her pen, then picked it up again. Channelled 'Sunny Sandy'. Two out of three was definitely a cup more than half full. Slowly, with a wavering line of ink, she scored through the words relating to kids, then wrote: *If stay in DB, ask Maura about puppy.* She crossed out the word 'puppy' and wrote *puppies.*

Unable to bear any further thoughts about shelving her dreams of children, she slammed the fairy notebook shut.

As she did so the doorbell jangled. She looked up to see a very small person manfully pushing the door open.

'Amy! *Sweetpea!*'

Sandy flew around the counter and rushed to meet her niece, then looked up to see her sister, Lizzie, behind her. 'And Lizzie! I can't believe it.'

Sandy greeted Lizzie with a kiss, then swept Amy up into her arms and hugged her tight. Eyes closed at the bliss of having her precious niece so close, she inhaled her sweet little-girl scent of strawberry shampoo and fresh apple.

'I miss you, bub,' she said, kissing Amy's smooth, perfect cheek.

'Miss you too, Auntie Ex.'

Her niece was the only person who called her that— when she was tiny Amy hadn't been able to manage 'Alexandra' and it had morphed into 'Ex', a nickname that had stayed.

'But you're squashing me.'

'Oh, sorry—of course I am.' Sandy carefully put her niece down and smoothed the fabric of Amy's dress.

Amy looked around her with wide eyes. 'Where are the books for children?' she asked.

'They're right over here, sweetpea. Are your hands clean?'

Amy displayed a pair of perfectly clean little hands. 'Yes.'

'Then you can take books and look at them. There's a comfy purple beanbag in the corner.'

Amy settled herself with a picture book about a crocodile. Sandy had trouble keeping her eyes off her little niece. Had she grown in just the few days since they'd said goodbye in Sydney? Amy had been a special part of her life since she'd been born and she loved being an aunt. She'd looked forward to having a little girl just like her one day.

Her breath caught in her throat. *If she stayed with Ben no one would ever call her Mummy.*

'Nice place,' said Lizzie, looking around her. 'But what the heck are you doing here? You're meant to be on your way to Melbourne.'

'I could ask the same about you. Though it's such a nice surprise to see you.'

'Amy had a pupil-free day at school. I decided to shoot down here and see what my big sis was up to!'

'I texted you.'

'Just a few words to say you were spending some time in Dolphin Bay. Dolphin Bay! Why *this* end-of-nowhere dump? Though I have to say the place has smartened itself up. And Amy loves the dolphin rubbish bins.'

'I took the scenic route down the coast. It was lunchtime when I saw the turn-off, and—'

Lizzie put up her hand to halt her. 'I suspected it, but now I get it. This is about Ben Morgan, isn't it? What else would the attraction be here? And don't even *think* about lying, because you're blushing.'

'I have caught up with Ben. Yes.'

Lizzie took a step closer. 'You've done a lot more than "caught up" with Ben, haven't you?'

Sandy rolled her eyes skyward and laughed. Then she filled her sister in on what had happened since she'd driven her Beetle down the main street of Dolphin Bay. Including Ida's offer to sell her Bay Books, but excluding Ben's decision not to have any more children.

'So, are you going to stay here with Ben?' Lizzie asked.

Sandy shrugged. 'We're testing the waters of what it might be like. But I feel the same way about him as I did back then.'

Lizzie stayed silent for a long moment before she spoke

again. 'You're not just getting all sentimental about the past because of what happened with Jason?'

Sandy shook her head. 'Absolutely not. It's nothing to do with that. Just about me and Ben.'

Just mentioning their names together made her heart flip.

'I remember what it was like between you. Man, you were crazy about each other.'

Sandy clutched her sister's arm. Lizzie had to believe that what she'd rediscovered with Ben was the real deal. 'It's still there, Lizzie, that feeling between us. We took up where we left off. I'm so happy to have found him again. Even if these few days are all we have. And I don't give a toss about Jason.'

'I'm thrilled for you—truly I am. I always liked Ben. And I love this shop. It would be cool to own it. Way better than candles.' Lizzie shifted from foot to foot. 'But now I've brought up the J word I have to tell you something. You're going to hear it sooner or later, and I'd rather you heard it from me.'

Sandy frowned. 'Is it about the wedding?' She hadn't given it another thought.

'More about the bump under What's-Her-Name's wedding gown.'

Sandy had to hold on to the edge of the closest bookshelf. 'You mean—?'

'They're not admitting to it. But the wedding guests are betting there'll be a J-Junior coming along in about five months' time.'

Sandy felt the blood drain from her face. Not that she gave a flying fig for That-Jerk-Jason. But envy of his new bride shook her. Not envy of her having Jason's baby. The thought of anyone other than Ben touching her repulsed her. But envy because *she* would never be the one with a proudly displayed bump, would never bear Ben's child.

'Are you okay, Sandy?'

Sandy took a deep breath, felt the colour rush back into her face. 'Of course I'm okay. It's a bit of a shock, that's all.'

Lizzie hugged her. 'Maybe you'll be next, if you end up with Ben. You're thirty now—you won't want to leave it too long.'

'Of course not,' said Sandy, her voice trailing away.

Lizzie was just the first to say it. If, in some hypothetical future, she and Ben decided to stay together it would start. First it would be, *So when are you two tying the knot?* followed by, *Are you putting on weight or have you got something to tell us?*

Would she would be able to endure her friends' pregnancy excitement, birth stories, christenings, first-day-at-school sob-stories? All the while knowing she could never share them?

She understood Ben's stance against having another child. Was aware of the terrible place it came from. But she couldn't help but wonder if to start a relationship with Ben predicated on it being a relationship without children would mean a doomed relationship. It might be okay to start with, but as the years went by might she come to blame him? To resent him?

'You sure you're okay?' asked Lizzie. 'You look flushed.'

'Really, I'm fine.' Sandy fanned her face with both hands. 'It's hot. I suspect this rattly old air-conditioner is on its last legs.'

'You could put in a new one if you bought the business.'

'I guess…' she said, filled with sudden new doubt.

Holding Amy in her arms, hearing about Jason's bride's bump, had shaken her confidence in a long-term relationship with Ben that didn't include starting a family.

She changed the subject. 'What are you guys planning on doing? Can you stay tonight?'

'That depends on you. I promised Amy I'd take her to see the white lions at Mogo Zoo. Then we could come back here, have dinner with you and Ben, stay the night and go home tomorrow.'

'That would be amazing. Let's book you into Ben's gorgeous hotel.'

When had her thoughts changed from Hotel Hideous to 'Ben's gorgeous hotel'?

She didn't feel guilty about putting the 'Back in Ten Minutes' sign up on the bookshop door—Ida had quite a collection of signs, covering all contingencies. It was hot and stuffy inside Bay Books and she was beginning to feel claustrophobic.

And she wanted to see Ben again, to be reassured that loving him would be enough.

Ben was stunned to see Sandy coming towards Reception with a little girl. The child was clutching one of Bay Books' brown paper bags with one hand and holding on tight to Sandy's hand with the other. All the while she kept up a steady stream of childish chatter and Sandy looked down to reply, her face tender and her eyes warm with love.

That newly tuned engine of his heart spluttered and stalled at the sight. It looked natural and right to see Sandy hand in hand with a child. The little girl might be her daughter.

Anguish tore through him. Liam would have been around the same age if he'd lived. *He could not go there.* Getting past what would have been Liam's first birthday had seen him alone in his room with a bottle of bourbon. The other anniversaries had been only marginally better.

Sandy caught sight of him and greeted him with a big smile. Was he imagining that it didn't reach her eyes? He forced himself to smile back, to act as though the sight of her with a child had not affected him.

He pulled her into a big hug. His need to keep their relationship private from the gossiping eyes of Dolphin Bay was in the past. He'd been warmed and gratified by the good wishes he'd been given since the night of the Chamber of Commerce dance. He hadn't realised just how concerned his family and friends had been about him.

'This is my niece, Amy,' Sandy said. 'Amy, this is my friend Ben.'

Ben hunkered down to Amy's height. 'Hi, Amy. Welcome to Dolphin Bay.'

'I like dolphins,' Amy said. 'They smile. I like crocodiles too. I've got a new crocodile book.' She thrust the brown paper bag towards him.

'That's good,' Ben said awkwardly. He was out of practice with children. Hadn't been able to deal with them since he'd lost Liam.

Sandy rescued him from further stilted conversation. 'Do you remember my sister, Lizzie?' she asked, indicating the tall blonde woman who had joined them.

'Of course I remember you, Lizzie,' he said as he shook hands. Though, truth be told, back then he'd been so caught up with Sandy he'd scarcely noticed Lizzie, attractive though she was.

'Who would have thought I'd see you two together again after all these years?' said Lizzie.

'Yes,' he said.

He looked down at Sandy and she smiled up at him.

'Can we book Lizzie and Amy into a room with a water view?' she asked.

We. She'd said 'we'. And he wasn't freaked out by it as much as he'd thought he would be. In fact he kind of liked it.

He put his arm around her and held her close. She clutched onto him with a ferocity that both pleased and worried him. There was that shadow again around her eyes. *What gave?*

He booked Lizzie and Amy into the room adjoining Sandy's, talking over their protests when he told them that the room was on the house.

'Dinner tonight at the hotel?' he asked, including Lizzie and Amy in the invitation.

Sandy nodded. 'Yes, please—for all of us. Though it will have to be early because of Amy's bedtime.'

'I'm good with that.'

The sooner Lizzie and Amy were settled in their room, the sooner he could be alone with Sandy. Their time together was ticking down.

Lizzie glanced at her watch. 'We have to get to the zoo.' She took Amy's book and packed it in her bag. 'C'mon, Amy, quick-sticks.'

Amy indicated for Sandy to pick her up and Sandy obliged. She embraced Sandy in a fierce hug.

'I'll bring you a white lion, Auntie Ex,' she said.

Auntie Ex? Ben was about to ask for an explanation of the name when Amy leaned over from her position in Sandy's arms and put her arms up to be hugged by him.

'Bye-bye, Ben,' she said. 'Do you want a white lion, too?'

Ben froze. He hadn't held a child since he'd last held Liam. But Amy's little hands were resting on his shoulders, her face close to his. For a moment it was the three of them. A man. A woman. A child.

He panicked. Had to force himself not to shake. He looked to Sandy over the little girl's blonde head. Connected with her eyes, both sad and compassionate.

He cleared his throat and managed to pat the little girl gently on the back. 'A white lion would be great—thanks, Amy.'

'A girl one or a boy one?' Amy asked.

Ben choked out the words. 'A…a boy one, please.'

'Okay,' she said, and wiggled for Sandy to put her down. Amy ran over to her mother.

'How are you going to get the white lions back here, Amy?' asked Sandy.

'In the back of the car, of course, silly,' Amy replied.

The adults laughed, which broke the tension. But Ben was still shaken by the emotion that had overtaken him when he'd stood, frozen, in that group hug with Sandy and Amy. And he couldn't help but notice how Sandy's eyes never left her delightful little niece. There was more than being a doting aunt in her gaze.

'Okay, guys, I have to get back to the bookshop,' Sandy said. She hugged Amy and Lizzie. Then turned to him and hugged him. 'I'm going to stay back for a little while after I shut up shop and flick through Ida's files. I'll see you for dinner.'

He tightened his arms around her. Something was bothering her—and that bothered him. 'Don't be too long,' he said, wanting to urge her to stay.

Lizzie and Amy headed for their car. Ben watched Sandy as she walked through the door. Her steps were too slow, her head bowed. She seemed suddenly alone, her orange dress a flash of colour in the monochrome decor of the reception area.

Was she thinking about how much she'd miss Lizzie and Amy if she settled in Dolphin Bay?

He suspected it was more than that.

Sandy had accepted his reasons for not wanting to risk having another child. But he'd seen raw longing in her eyes when she'd been with Amy.

When she was eighteen she'd chattered on that she wanted three kids. He'd thought two was enough—but he hadn't argued about wanting to be a parent. Fatherhood had been on his future agenda, too.

The ever-present pain knifed deeper. Being father to Liam had been everything he'd wanted and more. He'd loved every minute of his son's babyhood.

He took in a deep, shuddering breath. By denying Sandy her chance to be a mother he could lose her. If not now, then later.

It might make her wave goodbye and leave for Melbourne

on Wednesday, never to return to Dolphin Bay. Or, if she decided to stay with him, she might come to resent him. Blame him for the ache in her heart that only a baby could soothe.

Could he let that happen?

CHAPTER FIFTEEN

THE NEXT AFTERNOON Sandy trudged towards the hospital entrance. Fed up with the muggy atmosphere in Bay Books, and the rattling, useless air-conditioner, she'd shut up shop on the dot of five o'clock. To heck with going through more of Ida's files. She'd talk to Ida in person.

Whether or not she'd be able to have a sensible business conversation was debatable. She was too churned up with anxiety about the reality that a long-term relationship with Ben meant giving up her dream of having children. She tried summoning the techniques Ben had taught her to overcome her fear of monster waves but without any luck.

Her anxiety was like a dark shadow, diminishing the brilliance of her rediscovered love for Ben. Even memories of their heavenly lovemaking the night before, the joy of waking again in his arms, was not enough.

It felt like that long-ago summer day when she had been snorkelling with Ben at Big Ray Beach, out in the calm waters of the headland. It had been a perfect day, the sun shimmering through the water to the white sand beneath them, illuminating shoals of brightly coloured little fish darting in and out of the rocks. She and Ben had dived to follow some particularly cute orange and white clown fish.

Then suddenly everything had gone dark. Terrified, she'd gripped Ben's arm. He'd pointed upwards and she'd seen one of the big black manta rays that had given its name to the beach swim directly above them. She'd panicked, thinking she didn't have enough air to swim around it and up to the surface. But the ray had cruised along surprisingly quickly and she and Ben had been in sunshine again. They'd burst through to the top, spluttering and laughing and hugging each other.

Right now she felt the way she had when the light had been suddenly cut off.

She couldn't ignore Ben's stricken reaction when Amy had reached out to him yesterday. Her niece was discerning when it came to the adults she liked. She'd obviously picked Ben as a good guy and homed in like a heat-seeking missile. But all it had done was bring back painful memories for Ben.

If Sandy had held on to any remnant of hope that Ben might change his mind about having a child she'd lost it when she'd seen the fear and panic in his eyes.

And it hadn't got any better during dinner. She'd seen what an enormous effort it had been for Ben to take part in Amy's childish conversation. Amy, bless her, hadn't noticed. Her little niece had been too pleased she'd managed to get a toy girl white lion for her Auntie Ex and a boy one for Ben.

It must be so painful for Ben to endure—every child he encountered a reminder to him of what he had lost.

But it was painful for her, too, to know that Amy would be the only child she would ever have to love if she and Ben became a long-term couple.

Could she really do this? Put all her hopes of a family aside?

Would she be doomed to spend the next ten years or so hoping Ben might change his mind? Counting down the fertile years she had left? Becoming embittered and resentful?

She loved Ben; she didn't want to grow to hate him.

If she had any thought that her relationship with Ben might founder over the children issue should she think seriously of breaking it off now, to save them both future pain?

Her heart shrivelled to a hard, painful knot at the thought of leaving him.

She couldn't mention her fears to Lizzie—now back home in Sydney. Lizzie would tell her to run, not walk, away from Dolphin Bay. Her sister had often said giving birth to Amy was the best thing that had ever happened to her. She wouldn't want Sandy to miss out on motherhood.

Ben's decision not to have more children really could be a deal-breaker. Tomorrow was Wednesday and their future beyond tonight had become the elephant in the room. No. Not just an elephant but a giant-sized woolly mammoth.

As she neared the big glass doors of the hospital entrance she knew she had to tell Ida to take her out of the Bay Books equation. She couldn't consider her offer while she had any doubt at all about staying in Dolphin Bay.

But almost as soon as she was inside the hospital doors she was waylaid by the bank manager's wife, a hospital administrator, who wanted to chat.

By the time she got to Ida's bedside it was to find Ben's aunt in a highly agitated state.

'Why haven't you answered your mobile? There's smoke pouring out of Bay Books. Ben's there, investigating.'

It was nothing Ben could put his finger on, but he could swear Sandy had distanced herself from him last night. Especially through that awkward dinner. At any time he'd expected outspoken Lizzie to demand to know what his intentions were towards Sandy. And Sandy's obvious deep love for Amy had made him question again the fairness of depriving her of her own children.

But tomorrow was Wednesday. He *had* to talk with Sandy about her expectations—and his—if they were to go beyond these four awesome days.

She wasn't picking up her mobile. Seeing her would be better. He headed to Bay Books.

Ben smelled the smoke before he saw it—pungent, acrid,

burning the back of his throat. Sweat broke out on his forehead, dampened his shirt to his back. His legs felt like lead weights. Terror seized his gut.

Sandy. Was she in there?

He was plunged back into the nightmare of the guesthouse fire. The flames. The doorknob searing the flesh of his hands. His voice raw from screaming Jodi's name.

His heart thudded so hard it made him breathless. He forced his paralysed legs to run down the laneway at the side of the shop, around to the back entrance. Dark grey smoke billowed out through a broken pane in the back window.

The wooden carvings. The books. So much fuel for the fire. A potential inferno.

Sandy could be sprawled on the floor. Injured. Asphyxiated. He had to go in. Find her.

Save her.

He shrugged off his jacket, used it to cover his face, leaving only a slit for his eyes. He pushed in his key to the back door and shoved. The door gave. He plunged into the smoke.

'Sandy!' he screamed until his voice was hoarse.

No response.

Straight away he saw the source of the smoke. The old air-conditioning unit on the wall that Ida had refused to let him replace. Smouldering, distorted by heat, but as yet with no visible flames.

The smoke appeared to be contained in the small back area.

But no Sandy.

Heart in his mouth, he shouldered open the door that led through into the shop. No smoke or flames.

No Sandy there either.

All the old pain he'd thought he'd got under control gripped him so hard he doubled over. What if it had been a different story and Sandy had died? By opening up to Sandy he'd exposed himself again to the agony of loss.

He fought against the thought that made him wish Sandy had never driven so blithely back into Dolphin Bay. Making him question the safe half-life that had protected him for so long.

Like prison gates clanging shut, the old barriers against pain and loss and anguish slammed back into place. He felt numb, drained.

How could he have thought he could deal with loving another woman?

A high-pitched pop song ringtone rang out, startling him. It was so out of place in this place of near disaster. He grabbed Sandy's mobile phone from next to the register and shoved it in his pocket without answering it. Why the *hell* didn't she have it with her?

He headed back to the smouldering air-conditioning unit, grabbed the fire extinguisher canister from the nearby wall bracket and sprayed fire retardant all over it.

Then he staggered out into the car park behind the shop.

He coughed and spluttered and gulped in huge breaths of fresh air.

And then Sandy was there, her face anguished and wet with tears.

'Ben. Thank heaven. *Ben.*'

Sandy never wanted to experience again the torment of the last ten minutes. All sorts of hideous scenarios had played over and over in her head.

She scarcely remembered how she'd got from the hospital to Bay Books, her heart pounding with terror, to find horrible black smoke and Ben inside the shop.

But Ben was safe.

His face was drawn and stark and smeared with soot. His clothes were filthy and he stank of acrid smoke. But she didn't care. She flung herself into his arms. Pressed herself to his big, solid, blessedly alive body. Rejoiced in the pounding of his heart, the reassuring rise and fall of his chest as he gulped in clean air.

'You're okay…' That was all she could choke out.

He held her so tightly she thought he would bruise her ribs.

'It wasn't as bad as it looked. There's just smoke damage out the back. It didn't reach the books.'

He coughed. Dear heaven, had the smoke burned his throat?

Relief that he was alive morphed into anger that he'd put himself in such danger. She pulled back and pounded on his chest with her fists. 'Why did you go in there? Why take the risk? Ida must have insurance. All that wood, all that paper… If it had ignited you could have been killed.' Her voice hiccupped and she dissolved into tears again.

He caught her wrists with his damaged hands. 'Because I thought you were in there.'

She stilled. 'Me?'

'You weren't answering your phone. I was worried.'

The implication of his words slammed into her like the kind of fast, hard wave that knocked you down, leaving you to tumble over and over in the surf. His wife and son had been trapped inside a fire-ravaged building. What cruel fate had forced him to face such a scenario again? Suffer the fear that someone he cared for was inside?

She sniffed back her tears so she was able to speak. 'I'd gone to visit Ida. To talk…to talk business with her.' *And to mull over what a future without kids might mean.* 'I'm so sorry. It was my fault you—'

'It was my choice to go in there. I had to.'

His grip on her hands was so tight it hurt.

'All I could think about was how it would be if I lost you.'

He let go her hands and stepped back.

Something was wrong with this scenario. His eyes, bluer than ever in the dark, smoke-dirtied frame of his face, were tense and unreadable. He fisted his hands by his sides.

She felt her stomach sink low with trepidation. 'But you didn't lose me, Ben. I'm here. I'm fine.'

'But what if you hadn't been? What if—?'

She fought to control the tremor in her voice. 'I thought we'd decided not to play the "what-if?" game.'

Beads of sweat stood out on his forehead. 'It was a shock.'

She heard the distant wail of a fire engine and was aware of people gathering at a distance from the shop.

Ben waved and called over to them. 'Nothing to worry about. Just smoke—no fire.'

He wiped his hand over his face in a gesture of weariness and resignation that tore at her. A dark smear of soot swept right across his cheek.

'Sandy, I need to let the fire department know they're not needed. Then go get cleaned up.'

'I'll come with you,' she said immediately.

This could be their last evening together.

He hesitated for just a second too long. 'Why don't you go back to the hotel and I'll meet you there?' he said.

One step forward and two steps back? Try ten steps forward and a hundred steps back.

'Sure,' she said, forcing the fear out of her voice.

He went to drop a kiss on her cheek but she averted it so the kiss landed on her mouth. She wound her arms around his neck, clung to him, willing him with her kiss to know how much she cared for him. How much she wanted it to work out.

'Woo-hoo! Why don't you guys get a room?'

The call—friendly, well-meant—came from one of the onlookers. She laughed, but Ben glared. She dropped her arms; he turned away.

So she *wasn't* imagining the change in him.

She forced her voice to sound Sunny-Sandy-positive. 'Okay. So I'll see you back at the hotel.'

She headed back towards Hotel Harbourside, disorientated by a haunting sense of dread.

Ben hated the confusion and hurt on Sandy's face. Hated that he was the cause of it. But he felt paralysed by the fear of losing her. He needed time to think without her distracting presence.

Thanks to this special woman he'd come a long way in the last few days. But what came next? Sandy deserved commitment. Certainty. But there were big issues to consider. Most of all the make-or-break question of children. He'd been used to managing only his own life. Now Sandy was here. And she'd want answers.

Answers he wasn't sure he could give right now.

CHAPTER SIXTEEN

SANDY WAS JUST about to turn in to the hotel entrance when she stopped. It wasn't exactly anger towards Ben that made her pause. More annoyance that she was letting herself tiptoe around vital issues she and Ben needed to sort out if they were to have any hope of a future together.

Ben needed to be treated with care and consideration for what he'd been through. But she had to consider her own needs, too. Decision time was looming. If she was to go to Melbourne and interview for the candle shop franchise she had to leave here by the latest tomorrow morning.

She turned right back around and headed down the steps to the beach.

The heat was still oppressive, the sand still warm. At this time of year it wouldn't get dark until nearly nine.

Before the sun set she needed answers.

She found Ben sitting on the wooden dock that led out from the boathouse into the waters of the bay. His broad shoulders were hunched as he looked out towards the breakwater.

Without a word she sat down beside him. Took his hand in hers. In response, he squeezed it tight. They sat in silence. Her. Ben. And that darn woolly mammoth neither of them seemed capable of addressing.

Beyond the breakwater a large cargo ship traversed the horizon. Inside the harbour walls people were rowing dinghies to shore from where their boats were anchored. A large seagull landed on the end pier and water slapped against the supporting posts of the dock.

She took a deep breath. 'Ida wants to sell me Bay Books.'

'Is that what you want?' His gaze was intent, the set of his mouth serious.

She met his gaze with equal intensity. 'I want to run my own business. I think I could make the bookshop work even better than it already does. But you're the only reason for me to stay in Dolphin Bay.'

'An important decision like that should be made on its own merits.'

'The bookshop proposition's main merit is that it allows me to stay here with you.' *Time to vanquish that mammoth.* 'We have to talk about where we go from here.'

His voice matched the bleakness of his face. 'I don't know that I can give you what you want.'

'I want you, Ben. Surely you know that.'

'I want you too. More than you can imagine. If it wasn't for…for other considerations I'd ask you to stay. Tell you to phone that candle guy and cancel your interview in Melbourne. But…but it's not that straightforward.'

'What other considerations?' she asked, though she was pretty sure she knew the answer.

He cleared his throat. 'I saw how you were with Amy.'

'You mean how I dote on her?'

He nodded. 'You were meant to be a mother, Sandy. Even when you were eighteen you wanted to have kids.'

'Two girls and a boy,' she whispered, the phrase now a desolate echo.

'I can't endure loss like that again. Today brought it all back.'

She wanted to shake him. Ben was smart, educated, an astute businessman. Why did he continue to run away from life? From love.

'I appreciate your loss. The pain you've gone through. But haven't you punished yourself enough for what happened?'

He made an inarticulate response and she knew she had hurt him. But this had been bottled up for too long.'

'Can't you see that any pleasure involves possible pain? Any gain possible risk. Are you *never* going to risk having your heart broken again?'

His face was ashen under his tan. 'It's too soon.'

'Do you think you'll ever change your mind about children?'

She held her breath in anticipation of his answer.

'Since you've been back I've thought about it. But four days isn't long enough for me to backtrack on something so important.'

Deep down she knew he was only giving voice to what she already knew. She wanted Ben. She wanted children. But she couldn't have both.

Slowly she exhaled her breath in a huge sigh. 'I can take that as a no then. But, Ben, you're only thirty-one. Too young to be shutting down your life.'

His jaw set in a stubborn line. 'It wouldn't be fair for me to promise something I can't deliver.'

'I…I understand.' But she didn't. Not really.

She shifted. The hard boards of the dock were getting uncomfortable.

'And I appreciate your honesty.'

His gaze was shrewd. 'But it's not good enough for you?'

She shook her head. 'No. It's not.'

Now she felt the floodgates were open. 'It was compromise all the way with Jason. I wanted marriage and kids. He said he had to get used to the idea. I moved in with him when I didn't want to live together without being married. Fine for other people. Too insecure for me. But I went along with him, put my own needs on hold.' Her attempt at laughter came out sharp-edged and brittle. 'Now I hear he's not only married, but his wife is pregnant.'

'That…that must have been a shock.'

'I can't go there again, Ben. Can't stay here waiting for heaven knows how long for you to get the courage to put the past behind you and commit to a future with me.'

Ben looked down at where the water slapped against the posts. She followed his gaze to see a translucent jellyfish floating by to disappear under the dock, its ethereal form as insubstantial as her dreams of a life with Ben.

'I'm sorry,' he said.

She didn't know whether he was apologising for Jason or because he couldn't give her the reassurances she wanted.

'I…I won't make all the compromises again, Ben,' she said brokenly. 'No matter how much I love you.'

She slapped her hand to her mouth.

The 'L' word.

She hadn't meant to say it. It had just slipped out.

Say it, Ben. Tell me you love me. Let me at least take that away with me.

But he didn't.

Maybe he couldn't.

And that told her everything.

'I'm sorry,' he said again, his voice as husky as she'd ever heard it. 'I can't be what you want me to be.'

If he told her she could do better than him she'd scream so loud they'd hear it all the way to New Zealand.

Instead he pulled her to him, held her tight against his powerful chest. It was the place she most wanted to be in the world. But she'd learned that compromise which was all one way wouldn't make either of them happy.

'I'm sorry too,' she murmured, fighting tears. 'But I'm not sorry I took that turn-off to Dolphin Bay. Not sorry we had our four-day fling.'

He pulled her to her feet. 'It's not over. We still have this evening. Tonight.'

She shook her head. 'It's perfect the way it is. I don't want to ruin the memories. I…I couldn't deal with counting down the hours to the last time we'll see each other.'

With fingers that trembled she traced down his cheek to the line of his jaw, trying to memorise every detail of his face. She realised she didn't have any photos to remember him by. Recalled there'd been a photographer at the dinner dance. She would check the website and download one. But not until she could look at his image and smile rather than weep.

'Sandy—' he started.

But she silenced him with a kiss—short, sweet, final.

'If you say you're sorry one more time I'll burst into tears and make a spectacle of myself. I'm going back to my room now. I've got phone calls to make. E-mails to send. Packing to do.'

A nerve flickered near the corner of his mouth. 'I'll call by later to…to say goodbye.'

'Sure,' she said, fighting to keep her voice under control. 'But I'm saying my goodbye now. No regrets. No what-ifs. Just gratitude for what we had together.'

She kissed him again. And wondered why he didn't hear the sound of her heart breaking.

Ben couldn't bear to watch Sandy walk away. He turned and made his way to the boathouse. Every step was an effort, as if he were fighting his way through a rip.

His house seemed empty and desolate—the home of a solitary widower. There was a glass next to the sink with Sandy's lipstick on the rim, but no other trace of her. He stripped off his smoke-stained clothes, pulled on his board shorts and headed for Big Ray Beach.

He battled the surf as if it were a foe, not the friend it had always been to him. He let the waves pound him, pummel him, punish him for not being able to break away from his self-imposed exile. The waves reared up over him, as if harnessing his anger at the cruel twist of fate that had brought Sandy back into his life but hadn't given him the strength to take the second chance she had offered him.

Finally, exhausted, he made his way back to the boat-house.

For one wild moment he let himself imagine what it would be like to come back to the house to find Sandy there. Her bright smile, her welcoming arms, her loving presence.

But the house was bare and sterile, his footsteps loud and lonely on the floorboards. That empty glass on the draining board seemed to mock him. He picked up the photo of him and Sandy on the beach that long-ago summer. All their dreams and hopes had stretched out ahead of them—untainted by betrayal and pain and loss.

He put down the photo with its faded image of first love. He'd lost her then. And he'd been so damned frightened of losing her at some undefined time in the future he'd lost her now.

He slammed his fist down so hard on the dresser that the framed photo flew off the top. He rescued it from shattering on the floor only just in time.

What a damn fool he was.

He'd allowed the fears of the past to choke all hope for the future.

Sandy had offered him a second chance. And he'd blown it.

Sandy. Warm, vibrant, generous Sandy. With her don't-let-anything-get-you-down attitude.

That special magic she'd brought into his life had nothing to do with the glitter she trailed around with her. Sandy's magic was hope, it was joy, but most of all it was love.

Love he'd thought he didn't deserve. With bitterness and self-loathing he'd punished himself too harshly. And by not forgiving himself he'd punished Sandy, too.

The final rusted-over part of him shifted like the seismic movement of tectonic plates deep below the floor of the ocean. It hurt. But not as much as it would hurt to lose Sandy for good.

He had to claim that love—tell her how much she meant to him. Show her he'd found the courage and the purpose to move forward instead of tripping himself up by looking back.

He showered and changed and headed for the hotel.

Practising in his head what he'd say to her, he rode the elevator to Sandy's room. Knocked on the door. Once. Twice. But no reply.

'Sandy?' he called.

He fished out the master key from his wallet and opened the door.

She was gone.

The suitcase with all her stuff spilling out of it was missing. Her bedlinen had been pulled down to the end of the bed. There was just a trace of her vanilla scent lingering in the air. And on the desk a trail of that darn glitter, glinting in the coppery light of the setting sun.

In the midst of the glitter was a page torn out from the fairy notebook she always carried in her bag. It was folded in two and had his name scrawled on the outside.

His gut tightened to an agonising knot. With unsteady hands he unfolded the note.

Ben—thank you for the best four days of my life. I'm so glad I took a chance with you. No regrets. No 'what ifs'. Sandy xx.'

He fumbled for his mobile. To beg her to come back. But her number went straight to voicemail. Of course it did. She wouldn't want to talk to him.

He stood rooted to the ground as the implications of it all hit him.

He'd lost her.

Then he gave himself a mental shaking.

He could find her again.

It would take at least ten hours for her to drive to Melbourne. More if she took the coastal road. It wasn't worth pursuing her by car.

In the morning he'd drive to Sydney, then catch a plane to Melbourne.

He'd seek her out.

And hope like hell that she'd listen to what he had to say.

Sandy had abandoned her plan to mosey down the coastal road to Melbourne. Instead she cut across the Clyde Mountain and drove to Canberra, where she could connect to the more straightforward route of the Hume Highway.

She didn't trust herself to drive safely in the dark after the emotional ups and downs of the day. A motel stop in Canberra, then a full day's driving on Thursday would get her to Melbourne in time to check in to her favourite hotel and be ready to wow the candle people on Friday morning.

She would need to seriously psyche herself up to sound enthusiastic about a retail mall candle shop when she'd fallen in love with a quaint bookshop on a beautiful harbour.

Her hands gripped tight on the steering wheel.

Who was she kidding?

It was her misery at leaving Ben that she'd have to overcome if she was going to impress the franchise owners.

She'd cried all the way from Dolphin Bay. Likely she'd cry all the way from Canberra to Melbourne. Surely she would have run out of tears by the time she faced the interview panel?

She pulled into the motel.

Ben would have read her note by now. Maybe it had been cowardly to leave it. But she could not have endured facing him again, knowing she couldn't have him.

No regrets. No regrets. No regrets.

Ben was her once-in-a-lifetime love. But love couldn't thrive in a state of inertia.

She'd got over Ben before. She'd get over him again.

Soon her sojourn in Dolphin Bay would fade into the realm of happy memories. She had to keep on telling herself that.

And pray she'd begin to believe it.

CHAPTER SEVENTEEN

BEN REMEMBERED SANDY telling him about her favourite hotel in the inner-city Southbank district of Melbourne—all marble, chandeliers and antiques. He'd teased her that it sounded too girly for words. She'd countered that she liked it so much better than his preferred stark shades of grey.

He'd taken a punt that that was where she would be staying. A call to Reception had confirmed it. He walked from his ultra-contemporary hotel at the other end of the promenade that ran along the banks of the Yarra River. He'd wait all day at her hotel to see her if he had to.

It was a grey, rainy morning in Melbourne, mitigated by the brilliant colours of a myriad umbrellas. Ben watched a hapless duck struggling to swim across the wide, fast-flowing brown waters of the Yarra.

Was his mission doomed to such a struggle?

He found the hotel and settled in one of the comfortable velvet chairs in the reception area. He didn't have to wait for long. He sensed Sandy was there before he glanced up.

He was shocked at how different she looked. She wore a sleek black suit with a tight skirt that finished above her knees and high-heeled black shoes. A laptop in a designer bag was slung across her shoulder. Her hair was sleek, her mouth glossy with red lipstick.

She looked sexy as hell and every inch the successful businesswoman.

Sandy the city girl.

It jolted him to realise how much he'd be asking her to give up. Now she was back in her own world would she want to settle for running a small-town bookshop in Dolphin Bay?

She must have felt his gaze on her, and stopped mid-stride as he rose from the chair. He was gratified that her first reaction was a joyous smile. But then she schooled her face into something more neutral.

For a moment that seemed to stretch out for ever they stood facing each other in the elegant surrounds of the hotel. He had to get it right this time. There wouldn't be another chance.

Sandy's breath caught.

Ben.

Unbelievably handsome and boldly confident in a superbly cut charcoal-grey suit. Her surf god in the city. She had trouble finding her voice.

'What are you doing here?' she finally managed to choke out.

He stepped closer. 'I've come to tell you how much I love you. How I always loved the memory of you.'

Ben. This troubled, scarred man she adored. He had come all the way to Melbourne to tell her he loved her, smack in the middle of a hotel lobby.

She kept her voice low. 'I love you too. But it doesn't change the reasons why I left Dolphin Bay.'

'You gave me the kick in the butt I needed. I'm done with living with past scars. I want a future. With you.'

He looked around. Became aware they were attracting discreet interest.

'Can we talk?'

'My room,' she said.

They had the elevator to themselves and she ached to kiss him, to hold him. That would only complicate things, but for the first time she allowed herself a glimmer of hope for a future with Ben.

Ben was grateful for the privacy of Sandy's hotel room. He took both her hands in his. Pulled her close. Looked deep into her eyes. 'More than anything I want a life with you.'

'Me too, Ben.'

'That life would be empty without a child. *Our* child.'

He watched her face as the emotions flashed over it. She looked more troubled than triumphant.

'Oh, Ben, you don't have to say that. I don't want you to force yourself to do something so important as having children because you think it's what *I* want. That…that won't work.'

The fear he'd been living with for five years had been conquered by her brave action in walking away from him.

'It's for your sake, yes. But it's also for my own.' He took a deep breath. 'I want to be a dad again some day.'

The loss of Liam had been tragic. All potential for that little life gone in a terrible, pointless fire. But no matter how much he blamed himself, he knew deep in his gut he had not been responsible for those out-of-control flames. No one could have predicted how the wind had changed. No one could have saved Jodi and his son.

'I know you were a brilliant father in the little time you were granted with Liam. Everyone told me that.'

'I did my best.'

The four words echoed with sudden truth.

He deserved a second chance. Another son. A daughter. A baby who would grow into a child, like Amy, and then a teenager like he and Sandy had been when they met. It would not diminish the love he'd felt for Jodi and Liam.

'I want a family again, Sandy, and I want it with you. We'll be good parents.'

Exulting, he kissed her—a long, deep kiss. But there was more he needed to talk about before he could take her back home with him. He broke the kiss, but couldn't bear to release her hands from his.

'How did your interview go?' he asked.

'The Melbourne store is mine if I want it.' She was notably lacking in enthusiasm.

'*Do* you want it? Because if your answer is yes I'll move to Melbourne.'

Her eyes widened. 'You'd do that?'

'If it's what it takes to keep you,' he said.

She shook her head. 'Of course I don't want it. I want to buy Bay Books from Ida and knock through into the space next door to make a bookshop/café. I want to have author talks. Cooking demonstrations. A children's storyteller.'

The words bubbled out of her—and they were everything he wanted to hear.

'I want to ask Ida to order matching carvings for the café from her Balinese woodcarver.'

'That can be arranged. I own the café. The lease is yours.' He ran his finger down her cheek to the corner of her mouth. 'Will you come back to Dolphin Bay with me?'

Sandy was reeling from Ben's revelations. But he hadn't mentioned marriage—and she wanted to be married before she had children.

She'd feared he was too damaged to love again—and look what had happened. What was to stop her proposing?

'Yes,' she said. 'I want to come back to Dolphin Bay. Be with you. But I—'

He silenced her with a finger over her mouth. 'One more thing.'

'Yes?' she said.

'Life is short. There's no time to waste. We could date some more. Live together. But I'd rather we made it permanent. Marry me?'

In spite of all his pain and angst and loss he'd come through it strong enough to love again. To commit.

But she didn't kid herself that Ben's demons were completely vanquished. He'd still need a whole lot of love, support and understanding. As his wife, she could give it to him by the bucketload. Ben still had scars—and she'd help him to heal.

'Yes, I'll marry you. Yes, yes and *yes*.'

He picked her up and whirled her around until she was dizzy.

They were laughing and trying to talk at the same time, interspersing words with quick, urgent kisses.

'I don't want a big white wedding,' she said.

'I thought on the beach?'

'Oh, yes! In bare feet. With Amy as a flower girl. And Hobo with a big bow around his neck.'

Her fairy notebook would be filling up rapidly with lists.

'We can live in the boathouse.'

'I'd love that.'

'Build a big, new house for when we have kids.'

Maybe it was because her emotions had been pulled every which way, but tears welled in her eyes again. Ben had come so far. And they had so far to go together.

She blinked them away, but her voice was wobbly when she got the words out. 'That sounds like everything I've ever dreamed of...'

She thought back to her goals, written in pink.

Tick. Tick. Tick.

* * * * *